BOOK ONE
of the
Mandolin

Ørma

The Song of the Lark

Jac Forsyth

T

Troubador Publishing Ltd
Unit E2 Airfield Business Park,
Harrison Road, Market Harborough,
Leicestershire LE16 7UL
Tel: 0116 279 2299
Email: books@troubador.co.uk
Web: www.troubador.co.uk

ISBN 978-1-80514-421-2

British Library Cataloguing in Publication Data.
A catalogue record for this book is available from the British Library.

Printed and bound by CPI Group (UK) Ltd, Croydon, CR0 4YY
Typeset in 11pt Minion Pro by Troubador Publishing Ltd, Leicester, UK

In association with Silver Crow Books

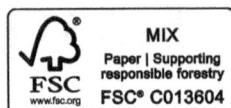

FSC
www.fsc.org

MIX
Paper | Supporting
responsible forestry
FSC® C013604

Mike, Adam, Rachael and Lucas
You kept the faith even when I forgot where I put it
This is for you

I am forever indebted to Daniel, whose bravery and sassy spirit inspired me to write this story, and in whose splendid company *Ørma* came to be. My dear friend Dom, who bought me countless cups of tea and listened to rough draft ideas without even yawning. And Frome Writers' Collective for their unwavering wisdom, support and camaraderie. Thanks, guys.

I'd also like to say a huge thanks to the wonderful Gill and Brenda at Silver Crow Books. *Ørma* would never have made it out alive without you.

THE START

It didn't seem like the start; it seemed like just another reality TV series. And we invited it in. Into our homes. Into our chat. Into our minds. Day after day, something so foul and so unthinkable. Day after day, until it became something ordinary. Something thinkable.

WØLF was our hope, I suppose. And we burned with it. Not like flames, but like leaves and dry tinder. A whole nation army, ignited and consumed in the fire of hope.

1

Trouble at sea

———————

Mac Eden was a side character in a game no one knew about. Her skills included stamina, dexterity and all seven deadly forms of domestic service. As a no-frills archetype, she cut her fringe with the kitchen scissors. She left plaque to harden on her teeth. She didn't pluck or wax or shave. She remained in the background roles, and embraced the nefarious joys of being overlooked in all the right stereotypes.

Today, the game was a beach at midnight. The tide was out. The moon was edgy. Mac moved unsteadily over the last of the intertidal rocks, clutching a striped beach towel tight to her chest, slipping and sliding through shallow pools of starfish and starlight. The cave was close now; congealed in a clot of primordial darkness. Mac stepped down onto the beach, unwrapping herself from the towel, and enough rehearsed drama about it to shame a preschool nativity play. 'Oh dear,' she said, 'this isn't the campsite.'

'Oi, that's my line.'

'Goodness, a strange stranger seems to be talking to me from inside that suspicious looking cave.' Mac adjusted the gusset of her floral swimming costume. 'Cos I ain't noticing anyone on the beach, Effie Cox.'

'I got bored waiting around.' Effie was three decades older than Mac, three stone dumpier, and three times more intent on swirling a ribbon of black seaweed around the cave entrance like a gymnast. 'Trouble?'

'Those bloody rocks are lethal in a flip-flop.' Mac frowned, marching across the secluded beach as Effie pirouetted through a tubular spiral. 'I thought you was wearing the lilac tabard camouflage tonight?'

'Aye.'

'Except, you ain't wearing it,' Mac said, pushing Effie aside. 'I went and colour matched us and everything.'

'Product recall.' Effie gathered the seaweed into a ball and stuffed it down the neck of her fleece hoodie. 'It was all in the update link.'

'What update link?'

'From yesterday,' Effie said. 'The Operating System piggybacked it into that scam email about a direct debit being declined on your TV licence.'

'Seems I forwarded it to the BBC then.' Mac dumped her towel on a limpet-heavy stump, bracing her hands against the cave wall to stretch out her Achilles tendon. 'How come the tabards got recalled?'

'Too many fictional assassins pretending to be cleaners so they can go about their business unnoticed.' Effie was breathing deeply, patting her ribcage to distribute the eggy fragrance of rotting seaweed. 'Thriller writers have ruined the tabard camouflage for everyone.'

'What, like doing the bins and toilets?'

'Just pushing the trolley around, usually.'

'Editorially speaking,' Mac puffed through several squats and an arm stretch, 'that ain't authentic at all.'

'These new hoodie camos are made from recycled plastic,' Effie said, stroking the fleece monstrosity. 'The tech lab adapted a polyester recipe from 1963. They pop out of the wash already dry.'

Mac stopped mid-squat. 'This update link mention anything about Afghanistan?'

4

'Await further instructions.'

'That's it?'

'There was quite a big mention about this new *WØLF* reality TV show that's been filming out there,' Effie said. 'The series premiere is on Friday, if you're interested.'

'*Await further instructions.*' Mac reached for a pebble, standing slowly, testing the weight of it in her hand. 'Thirty thousand years the Mandolin have kept themselves secret. A secret we've been forced into defending at our own cost.'

'Afghanistan is a tactical gameplay, that's all,' Effie said. 'They show their existence, but they conceal their identity. No one wants the true name of the Mandolin spoken, least of all the Mandolin. The secret is safe.'

'Safe!' Mac threw the pebble at the cave wall, ricocheting it past Effie's ear and taking out a seagull.

'And always will be,' Effie said. 'Meanwhile, if the genius science boffins of the world have identified the Mandolin as a superspecies spontaneous evolution event, who are we to argue?'

'A superspecies spontaneous evolution event what used a dirty bomb on a military base in Afghanistan.' Mac strode a crunchy circle. 'Afghanistan, of all fucking places. Every country's on high alert. Every news network has their press out there. Thirty thousand years Effie, and suddenly the Mandolin decide to take the game public in the one place guaranteed to draw everyone's attention.'

'You ask me, it's down to some newcomer chasing the big scores,' Effie said. 'They're trying to dethrone the high-rank players.'

'No, that bomb delivered a message.' Mac had stopped pacing, but her annoyance bounced around the cave like a rumour about residential parking permits. 'A literal send-to-all message: *We grow tired of waiting for you to go extinct.*'

'We all had a wobble about the message,' Effie said, holding her phone up to scan a pair of squabbling gulls and a dropped chip packet that currently occupied a corner of the beach. 'There's change coming, but nothing changes. Not for the likes of us.'

'Bloody birds should be asleep.' Mac leant in to look at Effie's phone. 'What you got?'

'*Larus argentatus*,' Effie said. 'European herring gull.'

Mac took a muggy lungful of night air. 'I could eat those chips, mind.'

'Talking of,' Effie said, prancing an acrobatic diagonal across the cave, 'a few of us are getting together to watch the *WØLF* series premiere on Friday. Why don't you come along?'

'Fuck off.' Mac flexed her arms, in danger of exposing more than her frustration. 'Plug Productions, they were pushing for exclusive filming rights the moment that bomb went off. Bastards have no respect for anything except making money.'

'Ack, we've known for years this might happen.' Effie dragged a battered plastic bottle out of the sand, shaking its contents over her hair. 'All that media technology poking around and posting things for marketing purposes. It stands to reason we'd eventually have to deal with this kind of situation.'

'Reason?' Mac hissed through her teeth. 'Plug Productions would make a reality TV show about making a reality TV show if they could snag enough sponsorship revenue out of it.'

'Exactly,' Effie said. 'No one takes their shows seriously.'

'Except *WØLF* isn't just a reality TV show, is it?' Mac said. '*WØLF* is a full budget, cross network, industry standard, live event, social experiment featuring something that no everyday person has a right to know about.' Mac picked up another pebble, turning it in her hand. 'Meantime, we just carry on doing what we've always done.'

'What we've always done,' Effie said, 'is engineer things to our advantage.'

'Have you seen how big this show is trending, Effie?'

'A flouncy squad of flouncy wannabees bickering over how

to turn the hair straightener on?' Effie shook her head. 'They're only interested in being famous, lass. And that sort of nonsense won't fit well with the British army.'

'There's a bloody fandom already, artwork and shipping and all sorts.' Mac shuffled uncomfortably. 'The news networks are calling *WØLF* state-of-the-art reality entertainment. A new kind of filmmaking for a new kind of war.'

'They're calling it a war?'

'God love them.'

'Well then, that's something we can engineer to our advantage.' Effie flashed a toothy grin. 'Let the Ministry of Defence call it a war. Let them think they've discovered some fancy new enemy to fight. Let the whole country clap for the armed forces on a Thursday evening if it comes down to it. No one ever wins a war in Afghanistan.'

'War would be better than this.' Mac dropped the pebble. 'War has an expiry date. Even the worst of them eventually comes to an end. But a game, a game can run forever.'

'Why don't you come along on Friday?' Effie said, skipping the gap between them. 'We're making a wee night of it. Paula's had a curry in the slow cooker since last Wednesday, and Sue's getting some pear cider in. Dolly's coming, and Shelly. A good laugh puts everything into perspective.'

'Pass,' Mac said. 'You mark my words, Effie Cox, this bloody TV series will go dragging the whole world into the game. All the non-player characters sat on their non-player sofas, eating their non-player suppers, dragged into a game we've shielded them from all these years.'

'I'm not belittling your concerns,' Effie said, 'but we both know it's deception that fuels the Mandolin. These new players will soon realise that tormenting the townsfolk isn't half as much fun when it's out in the open. Once the novelty's worn off, they'll crawl back into hiding. The armed forces claim their victory. Bring on the homecoming parade, hand out the medals and it's

7

three cheers for the triumphant Homo sapiens.' Effie picked up a jumble of green fishing net, draping it around Mac's neck like a scarf. 'A bit of tactical refraction and everyone's happy.'

'*We grow tired of waiting for you to go extinct.*' Mac untangled herself, shoving the net back at Effie. 'The sheer nerve of it, when all we've ever done is...'

'Play the game.'

'Play the bloody...' Mac finally succumbed to a smile '... game.'

'Too close to see. Too simple to understand. Too familiar to remember,' Effie said, dodging back into the shadows as a large bird landed heavily on a rocky outcrop. 'If you wanted main character autonomy, you shouldn't have taken the oath.'

'It's the swimming costume,' Mac said, staring down at the floral landscape of lumps and bumps. 'Swimming costumes ain't built to contain a wobble.'

'They're built to allow a wobble, lass, and that's the important thing to remember.' Effie was on her phone again. '*Phalacrocorax carbo.*'

Mac leant in. 'Cormorant?'

'Three of them, on the stack.' Effie dragged an oversized barcode scanner out of her joggers, leaning back into the cold damp of the cave wall. 'Time to finish what we came here for.'

Mac gave a brief nod. 'I'd best get myself into trouble at sea then.'

'Don't go out too far. The riptide here is lethal.'

'That's what I'm counting on,' Mac said, winking in the manner of unhinged individuals everywhere.

Mac gripped the beach towel to her chest, a soft silhouette on a nightscape of hard edges. She was looking around, almost fragile with her movements as she negotiated the tidal pools in a pair of pink flip-flops. Clambering from plateau to plateau until she reached the skyline of jagged rocks that formed a natural breakwater. The intertidal zone was full of potholes, and greasy with blue-green algae. By the time Mac reached the apex of narrow rocks she was shaking down to her bones. Every step she took was silently overlooked by the three reptilian birds. Shaking was all part of the show, but Mac was sickly aware that her heart was beating more for fear than oxygen. Mandolin wore death like a slogan. Success or failure made no difference to them. They didn't care about numbers. Territory meant nothing to them. Time meant nothing to them. Damn sure Mac Eden meant nothing to them. But the game did. The game was all that mattered.

Mac unfurled the beach towel and sat unsteadily. There was moonlight to spare on the restless sea. A butchered, troublesome light that threaded the surf and stitched an upholstered tapestry on the sand and rotting debris of the beach below. Nothing decent ever came out of a sea like this, and Mac Eden held her arms wide to welcome it home.

2

Strong enough to give us nightmares

The crew camera circled slowly, encasing a wound that looked gnarly enough for Gemma Quinn to grip her daughter's arm. 'She's hurt, Holl.'

'It's mostly iron powder,' Hollow said. 'A stray bullet must have hit her or something.'

'No, no, there's blood, look.' Gemma leant forward, close to touching the TV screen that dominated their lounge. 'See, by her elbow. There's white showing, that's bone.'

'That's not bone.'

'It's bone.'

'They wouldn't show it if it was bone.'

Gemma squared herself on the sofa, rearranging the gold tasselled cushion that leaked feathers. 'They showed that American soldier run into an incendiary last week. There was enough bone on show that night to make you wish you hadn't seen it, is all I'm saying.'

'Look.' Hollow pointed as the camera pulled back. 'It's a bit of ozone strip. It's torn away from her uniform.'

'It's white, though. All her strips are showing green.'

'It's probably malfunctioning,' Hollow said. 'The whole camp would be dead if it was white for real.'

'It's that Sylvie Stevens, she takes too many chances. Bloody scares the life out of me to watch her sometimes. You saw me when she wouldn't let them kill that Afghan baby.' Gemma

10

grabbed a bottle of wine off the coffee table and poured herself another glass. 'I nearly had a panic attack.'

'You nearly had a panic attack when they announced the earth was speeding up and now we have to have a leap second.'

'As if you'd understand.' Gemma downed her wine, turning back to the screen as *WØLF* company medic Captain Lancaster Dupont took hold of Sylvie Stevens' bloodied arm. She held the glass to her lip for a while. 'Everyone up the farm shop has a crush on Caster Dupont.'

'The French accent, right?'

'Virtue signalling, more like.' Gemma fluttered her eyelashes melodramatically. 'Oh, me? Don't look at me. I'm only an implausibly decent, naturally kind, naturally chiselled, naturally Mediterranean Adonis doing his best to heal others in a cruel and unfair world.' Gemma tapped her nails on the empty wine glass. 'He's not really my type.'

Hollow threw a cursory glance towards her phone. 'Caster Dupont is fulfilling the fantasy prince trope. He's everyone's type.'

'I could have been an environmental influencer.' Gemma's voice came softer than usual, brushing the air like a whisper. 'I could have done something with my life.'

ITM SCENE
COMMENTARY
CASTER DUPONT:
Temperatures regularly top fifty degrees in Helmand Province. Meanwhile, our cardiovascular system is at full stretch, trying to maintain an internal temperature of thirty-seven degrees. Any kind of added stress can overwhelm the body's ability to cope with the heat.

Add on increased blood loss and rapid dehydration, and even a minor scrape has the potential to be a life-threatening injury out here.

PRODUCER:
How does your role here compare to back home?

CASTER DUPONT:
As doctors, we hear the confessions, we bear the terrible truth and we look at the things no one else wants to see. This is the same battlefront no matter where you practise medicine.

The *WØLF* company medic was frowning. 'Are you hit?'

'The GPM gun slipped its housing.' Sylvie Stevens tucked a sun-bleached curl back under the battered moulding of her helmet. 'The impact split an ammo clip. There was iron powder everywhere.'

'Iron powder doesn't explain the blood.'

'The gun clipped me,' Sylvie said. 'It was my own stupid fault for not getting out of the way.'

'I can take an educated guess as to what level of blunt velocity trauma a general-purpose machine gun generates, but that's all it would be.' Caster gently turned Sylvie's arm. 'A magnetic wash should clear the powder, enough for a scan at least. We'll also need to check you for iron inhalation. Any chills, aches?'

'Hospital?'

'I'm afraid so.'

'There's no time, Caster.' Sylvie looked up into his dark eyes, and enough delicate shadow between them to enhance the symmetry of their youth. 'I have to go back for the others.'

'I?'

'We.' Sylvie stumbled through a laugh. 'A few months out in the field, and your unit becomes a part of you.'

'Hospital,' Caster said. 'I'll let your commanding officer know.'

'It's a low-grade impact injury. I wouldn't have bothered you at all, but you know what this place is like for infection.' Sylvie

12

took a step away from Caster, shy with her smile. '*Aide-moi, s'il te plaît.*'

'I'm not your friend, not like this,' Caster said. 'No one is indispensable in the army, Sylvie, not even you.'

'We're all dispensable, that's the problem.' Sylvie tilted her head, a paradox of doubt and the untamed wild of old bones. 'I'm Medivac, Caster, I know what a wound dressing and a shot of antibiotics will buy me.'

ITM SCENE
COMMENTARY
SYLVIE STEVENS:
It's nothing. A scratch. The iron powder makes it look a lot worse than it is.

PRODUCER:
A doctor can override any unit orders or personal desire. Why did you challenge Caster's decision?

SYLVIE STEVENS:
If Captain Dupont had ordered me to go to the hospital, I would have gone. I didn't challenge his decision, not really.

I know how it sounds, Elspeth, but Mika and Mattoo are heading back into a Mandolin-controlled zone. I won't abandon my unit for something as superficial as a bruised arm.

PRODUCER:
Abandon them?

SYLVIE STEVENS:
Mika or Mattoo would say the same thing.

Gemma picked a white feather from her sleeve. 'That's more than a bruised arm. If it was me, I'd have come in on a stretcher.'

'They probably needed the stretcher,' Hollow said. 'For all the makeup.'

'She's my twin flame.'

'Sylvie Stevens is your twin flame?'

'Legit, not just me saying it.' Gemma blew gently on the feather, straightening it out with her finger. 'Gran Lizeth did the tea leaves. We had to break a teabag open, but it still counts.'

'Gran Lizeth?' Hollow looked sideways at Gemma. 'The old woman who lives in the shoe?'

'It's not a shoe, actually,' Gemma said. 'It only looks like a shoe since the extension collapsed.'

'She talks to herself on the bus.'

'Not to herself.' Gemma paused for dramatic effect. 'To those who have passed. She said there's a few of them who ride the bus, mostly for the company, but some are trying to get to the office.'

'She should watch out saying stuff like that. Any supernatural work is under licence from the intelligence services.'

'It's just a bit of fun,' Gemma said. 'No one believes it.'

'Except you, apparently.' Hollow pulled her hair into a makeshift bun, grabbing her phone from the table. 'See you tomorrow, Gemma.'

'You're going to bed?'

'I wanted to do some gaming tonight. This second semester is intense, and they said we needed to schedule our downtime.'

'*WØLF* has a half hour left,' Gemma said. 'You'll get a ping from the Homeland App.'

'I won't get pinged.'

'Maddie next door left her phone by the TV and the TV on while she went for a bath. She still had to prove it was medically unavoidable before they put her civic rating back to Outstanding.'

'Come on,' Hollow said, 'how would the app even know Maddie wasn't watching TV?'

'She reckons the bath told the immersion and the immersion told the smart meter,' Gemma said. 'And we all know smart meters can't keep a secret.'

'Switches get stitches, right?'

'It's not a joke, Holl. It'll register on your data history. Took me ages to get you back up to Excellent after you went and got reported for inciting public discomfort.'

'I lit a cigarette.'

'You shouldn't even be bloody smoking. I've never been so embarrassed. Everyone talking about you behind my back, saying what happens if you let your civic rating drop too low. Drifters and ne'er-do-wells, that's who get an automatic transfer to the military service programme.' Gemma straightened the feather again. 'Drifters and ne'er-do-wells. Imagine me explaining that up the farm shop.'

Hollow shrugged, scrolling her phone. 'It's pretty self-explanatory.'

'I don't understand you,' Gemma said. 'We literally just watched that documentary on how they came to make *WØLF*. It was a genuine shock when those kids heard they were being posted to Afghanistan. I didn't see any of them whinging to the studio about how intense Afghanistan was. They just got on with it. They went where they were needed, protecting us from all kinds of dreadful atrocities.'

'Jar complained about everything,' Hollow said. 'And he threw up when they told him he was going back to Afghanistan.'

'Jar's got PTSD, but he's still turning up to fight for his country.' Gemma brushed the feather on her cheek. 'Maybe you should think about that when you're shooting people on your computer.'

'Do you know anything about gaming?' Hollow said.

Gemma didn't answer; she just carried on looking at Hollow, longer than was comfortable for either of them.

'What?'

'Nothing.'

'Tell me.'

'Tess Medley's daughter signed up six months ago,' Gemma said, 'and she's not seventeen till December. Tess rounded on me in Asda. All over the out-of-date vegetables, showing me pictures of Luka in her full-dress uniform, asking me what my daughter was doing. What am I supposed to say to that?'

'Duh, the truth.'

'What sort of friend would I be if I went jabbering on about a sports psychology degree when her daughter is away at war?'

'You want me to enlist, is that what you want?' Hollow laughed, but she was gripping her phone like it could teleport her to another place. 'Give you something to brag about up the farm shop.'

'I just want you to be respectful,' Gemma said. 'These young people, they've given up every choice they had in their life so you still get a choice. And all you have to do in return is sit down for an hour and witness what they go through.' She stared down at the feather; delicate, white as a wedding gown against her skin. 'Seems like you can't even manage to do that.'

'In what universe is WØLF what they go through?' Hollow said. 'WØLF is a manufactured entertainment system designed to recruit more volunteers. A bunch of pseudo-celebrities drive an armoured ambulance around and talk about their feelings. How is that remotely like fighting in a war?'

'Go play your computer games.' Gemma folded her arms into her lap and turned away, sending the little white feather tumbling in the air between them. 'I don't suppose your bastard father would have paid them much respect either.'

'Mum…' Hollow choked, backing away '…why would you say that?'

'So it's Mum now?'

In the countless milliseconds of the unbearable moment, Hollow gathered up everything that mattered. She even managed a laugh of sorts. 'Jeez, what are we like, eh?'

'Ourselves,' Gemma said, as the second-hand light of a dozen contact tracers flickered across her face. 'We're just like ourselves.'

On the screen, a network of fixed rig cameras skimmed the bustling compound, each shot bringing something new to the portrait of Camp Bastian until filming reached the iconic Unit One Ridgeback and Mattoo Bolte. The newly promoted lieutenant was a man in his early twenties, but everything about him was carved and windswept like he was made of driftwood. The media called him striking, but striking wasn't right; it wasn't enough. Mattoo Bolte was honourable, courageous, breathtakingly unique in a world of standardised beauty. And there wasn't much room for all of that in a fixed word count.

Mattoo grabbed his companion's sleeve, pulling him around to the front of the Ridgeback field ambulance. 'Over the horizon targeting. That rescue site is lit up for the whole damn world to see. We need to leave right now Mika, or we'll lose our chance.'

Mika Kamari wandered a lazy look over to where Sylvie Stevens talked with the WØLF company medic. 'Looks like our Sylvie needs more time with Captain Dupont.'

'I told her to keep it short.'

'Code of companions notwithstanding,' Mika said, waving an acknowledgement to a swathe of deployment arrivals, 'Sylvie was up in the cage when the GPM gun slipped its housing. We were joking about her being crushed to death. By the time I realised she'd been hurt, we were back at camp.'

'Sylvie's injured?'

'The ammo clip took the worst of it,' Mika said, 'but her arm's a bit of a mess.'

'How much of a mess?'

'Enough to hide it.' Mika shrugged. 'My guess, she's trying to charm the dear doctor into patching her up.'

'You should have called this in, Mika.'

'Called what in?' Mika said, climbing into the Ridgeback cab. 'The clip literally exploded. There was iron powder everywhere, and we had a P2 bleeder rapidly dropping to P1. I had more pressing things to worry about.'

Mattoo flicked his radio to the Unit One channel. 'You fit for duty, Stevens?'

'On my way, Lieutenant.'

'Such fleeting moments,' Mika said, altering the steering wheel alignment to suit his slight frame. 'What it is to be lovers in a time of war.'

'You're the senior medic on this pickup.' Mattoo shooed Mika over. 'Keep your mind on the job.'

'Imagine their children. They'd be veritable gods.' Mika grabbed a pair of protective goggles from the dashboard, shielding his eyes like he was driving into the sun. 'To look upon them would be as to look upon an atomic sunrise.'

Mattoo adjusted the steering wheel, too raw with it for it to be impatience. 'We need to reach this site before artillery wipes it from the map.'

Mika leant towards Mattoo. 'I heard that Caster and Syl—'

'Enough,' Mattoo growled. 'Keep your mind on the job, Private Kamari.'

Mika shrugged and turned away, but there was a smile reflected in the window of the Ridgeback for the audience at home to see. Where Mattoo embodied the noble knight, Mika Kamari was a sky hunter. Quick to act, quicker to strike, he moved through the reality show like a hawk. There was grace, strength, and a lineage of exquisite mystery to be found in him, but not if you were a mouse or a vole. 'Just keeping you acquainted with events, Lieutenant,' he said.

Mattoo clicked his radio again. 'Stevens, if you're not here in two minutes, we leave without you.'

'Understood, Lieutenant.'

The orchestration of cameras returned to Sylvie Stevens as

Captain Lancaster Dupont sprayed the last of the liquid dressing around her wound. 'This isn't healthy, Sylvie,' he said. 'You're treating your body like it's the enemy, and that's a war you really don't want to win.'

ITM SCENE
COMMENTARY
CASTER DUPONT:
It's not that any of us thrive here, if we're lucky we find a way to survive. But Sylvie cuts this war from her own flesh. All I can do is watch over her, and if I can't bear to watch, I walk away. That's how it is.

PRODUCER:
You worry about her?

CASTER DUPONT:
I worry about everyone.

PRODUCER:
And who's watching over you, Caster?

CASTER DUPONT:
Really? Because that's not how it works out here.

Caster tucked Sylvie's sleeve back in place. 'You have a malfunctioning ozone strip. It's reset at toxic white. Make sure you get that fixed.'

'I will.'

'And keep an eye on the other strips. Don't just assume it's wrong.'

'Caster...' Sylvie hesitated. 'I can't—'

Mattoo punched the Ridgeback horn, running the armoured truck in a tight circle, heading back towards the main gate.

'Time's up.' Sylvie smiled, but there was enough sadness in it to fill a graveyard.

Caster stopped her as she turned away. 'Come and find me.'

'I have to go.' Sylvie was already sprinting towards the Ridgeback. 'Sorry, Caster, I have to go.'

'Iron inhalation sickness,' Caster called after her. 'Your whole unit reports to the hospital as soon as you get back, and that's an order.'

Gemma flopped back into the sofa. 'It was the ozone strip then.'

'It looked like bone, though.'

'I suppose it did.'

'I might stay down here for a bit.' Hollow picked up the feather and tucked it into her back pocket. 'See if they get those other soldiers out okay.'

'It'll be the sponsor announcements now.'

'Good timing. I'll make us some cheese on toast. Hopefully, I won't get pinged for that.' Hollow edged towards the kitchen, looking to Gemma for something to catch hold of. 'Not unless I use the vegan cheese, right?'

'There's decent cheddar behind the bowl of olives.'

'Extra strong?'

Gemma turned the wine glass against her lip. 'Strong enough to give us nightmares.'

'Crap, I hope not,' Hollow shouted from the kitchen. 'I've got biomechanics tomorrow.'

'Go play your computer game.'

'Say again, the grill's running a safety scan.'

'I said, go and play on your computer game.'

'I'm not bailing, Mum,' Hollow said, leaning against the door. 'I'm just waiting on the grill.'

'You're too much like him, Holl,' Gemma said. 'All this time, and you're eighteen years too much like him.'

And of all the things that could've been said, there was

nothing more brutal in the whole world. Although you wouldn't have known it from the way Hollow crossed her arms and went back to waiting on the grill.

ITM SCENE
COMMENTARY
MIKA KAMARI:
Sylvie thinks she's protecting us by not saying anything, and I'm not just talking about physical injury. I'm talking about the things you can't see. Underneath all that wholesome beauty, she's patched up with her own skin.

PRODUCER:
It sounds like you feel bad for her?

MIKA KAMARI:
Of course I feel bad for her. Because nothing stays secret for long at Camp Bastion. Not the visible stuff. Not the invisible stuff. We're all too starved for gossip to worry about respecting personal information. The more you think you can keep things hidden by not talking about them, the more they explode.

PRODUCER:
Things like love?

MIKA KAMARI:
Hey now, I didn't say she was in love with Caster. Frankly, I'm not sure Sylvie Stevens is bothered by such emotional trinkets as love.

PRODUCER:
I wasn't talking about Sylvie.

MIKA KAMARI:

Such a cruel and leading question. I'm unsure how to respond.

PRODUCER:

Try.

MIKA KAMARI:

Mattoo is consumed with denying his feelings for Captain Dupont. There's nothing left for anyone else.

PRODUCER:

Are you afraid to tell Mattoo how you feel?

MIKA KAMARI:

Afraid? You have no idea how much I wish it was fear. You can push through fear. What you can't push through is love. And it breaks my heart to love him. Every day, it breaks my heart.

Strange, that a heart can break so many times, and yet still love.

Tell me, Elspeth, how do you explain all that heartbreak to someone without sounding like a bloody nonce?

3

You brought coleslaw?

Even though they'd known each other since preschool, Hollow Quinn and Ezra Blake weren't friends. In many ways, they were so jarringly incompatible it was a wonder they knew each other at all. But sixteen years ago their hands had collided over the cuddle rights to a stuffed elephant, and sixteen years later they were still holding hands. Skipping afternoon lectures had been Hollow's idea. The road outside the university was lost to rain, bubbling at the gutters and nothing much else to show where the boundaries were. A Perspex bus shelter had braced the worst of the storm across one corner, but there was too much wind to call it dry. Hollow ducked an overspill and watched the shuttle bus come and go.

'Did we miss it?' Ezra scrabbled to the back of the shelter.

'Yep.'

'Balls, sorry.'

'It's fine,' Hollow said, like it wasn't.

'When's the next one?'

Hollow glanced up at the LED display. 'Half hour.'

'We could always wait in the library.' Ezra shook off the rain and tucked up close to Hollow. 'There's a stack section on experimental cinematography that no one ever goes to.'

'Classic experimental cinematography.'

'Or we could go back to mine, if you want.'

Hollow shrugged. 'Will your mums be there?'

'Not till after six.' Ezra pulled out a transparent phone, flicking away a dozen notifications. 'I'll just confirm on the family chat.'

'The family chat?' Hollow scuffed her boot through the odds and ends of gravel and leaves. 'You're such a dork.'

'I'm not a dork,' Ezra said. 'I'm a communicator.'

'A communicator of dork.' Hollow angled her body to the driest corner of the shelter, dragging a grubby sandwich bag out of her pocket. 'I got some flavoured tobacco off a postgrad in the chem lab. You want some?'

'Um, no.'

'Tastes like mercury.'

Ezra glanced up as lightning turned the sky above the university electric blue. 'Why is that even a selling point?'

Hollow handed over a packet of cigarette paper. 'Roll us a smoke, though.'

Ezra opened the slim box and took out a single sheet, carefully laying it straight before adding a line of tobacco. Rolling it was easier with a filter, but Hollow never had any filters, so Ezra bit the end and hoped for the best. 'You know you shouldn't inhale this rubbish, right?'

Hollow took the cigarette, pulling a strand of loose tobacco from Ezra's lip. 'Like any of us will make it to lung cancer.'

'Don't even say that, H.'

Hollow shrugged, popping the lid on a battered Zippo lighter as a couple of students huddled at the edge of the bus stop. They were flapping with a purple umbrella, but smoking on campus was prohibited and they wouldn't commit to the shelter. Ezra leant next to Hollow, watching her negotiate the elements of fire, wind and rain. Sometimes, the paper didn't catch. Sometimes, it caught fire. Most of the time, lighting a roll-up was as risky as smoking it. When the first thread of brimstone smoke snaked over Hollow's fingers, it felt almost heroic.

'Look at you, blatantly skipping lectures,' Hollow said. 'Next thing, you'll be asking to bum a cigarette.'

Ezra glanced over to the university. 'So, I might have told my lecturer I wasn't feeling well.'

'Right.'

'I also might have foreshadowed it in study skills this morning.' Ezra grimaced. 'If anyone sees us...'

'I'll tell them you fainted and I had to prop you up with a traffic cone.' Hollow tugged Ezra's sunshine-yellow coat. 'You could have worn a less conspicuous colour.'

'I always wear bright colours,' Ezra said. 'If I'd worn black and floated the history corridors like a formless wraith, they'd have thought it was you.'

'Rude.' Hollow coughed with the next drag, tapping her heel on the back of the bus shelter, turning the cigarette between her fingers like she was looking for something to do. She threw a nod towards the armed forces drop-in centre opposite. 'That place was a convenience store six months ago. Now I have to walk further to buy crisps than I do to enlist.'

'They're popping up everywhere,' Ezra said. 'There's even one in the old church building at the end of my road.'

'War comes to the middle-class exclusion zone?' Hollow coughed again. 'We must really be in trouble.'

'It's the fascination of popular culture.' Ezra flinched through a grumble of thunder. 'Did you even see all that gore on Sylvie's arm last night? It looked like she'd got a compound fracture, but it was just the white of the—'

'Makeup?'

'Stop it,' Ezra said, laughing for the company.

Hollow took a long drag. 'Gemma thought it was bone.'

'Everyone thought it was bone.' Ezra lay back against the Perspex and sighed. 'And what about Mika? You must admit, that was epic TV.'

'*Strange, that a heart can break so many times, and yet still love.*' Hollow was a sneer short of malice. 'Tragic.'

'Yeah, but we all love a flawed hero,' Ezra said. 'That smile when he knew he'd hurt Mattoo, it's all over the fandom.'

'You went on the fandom?'

'I get it, though,' Ezra said, glancing up as another flicker of lightning illuminated the bus shelter. '*WØLF* gave us something we thought we'd lost.'

'The TV remote?'

'No.' Ezra tapped a reprimand on Hollow's arm. '*WØLF* is like…the story of us at our best. And maybe this is what hope feels like. I don't know. We've never lived in a time when there was much of anything to hope for.'

'Us at our best? Grow up, Ez, the Coen Brothers laid this shit down years ago.' Hollow let the smoke fall from her mouth, talking enough sedition through the clouds of it to be reported. 'Telling your audience it's a true story is all part of the story.'

Ezra leant in, nonchalant as fuck. 'It's not safe to talk like this.'

'Have you noticed how no one mentions the Mandolin directly any more. Not on *WØLF*, not on the news, not anywhere. Eight months ago, we were obsessed with them. Now it's like they don't even matter.' Hollow flicked another look at the drop-in centre, caging her fingers to keep the cigarette from fading out. 'I suppose a TV reality show is the only part of reality that matters in the end.'

Even the smoke-choked air felt altogether too treasonous for a thunderstorm in October. Ezra leant closer. 'You're kidding, right?'

Hollow winked. 'Pitfall.'

'God, H.' Ezra waited on the thunder to growl another mile closer to the lightning. 'You had me believing you.'

'Dumb arse.'

'Eight months.' Ezra drew a sad emoji on the Perspex where their breath still clung to it. 'I was in London with Dobs the day it started. Wayne got us tickets to the premier of *Methuselah*. We were talking through the trailers, excited about the photo we just got with Zara Seraphim, even more excited to see her cinematic genius in I-3D. Then the Emergency Alert Notification went off. The trailers kept on playing, but no one was watching the big screen.'

'*We grow tired of waiting for you to go extinct.*' Hollow almost laughed. 'Freakiest hack of all time. Gemma went to bed for five days.'

'Not just Gemma. Mum Tulip said there would've been all sorts of riots back in the day. Now we all just go to bed.' Things could have turned to silence then, but the rain had already cried too many tears for the sad emoji. Ezra turned back to Hollow. 'Say what you like about *WØLF*, at least it made the end of the world into something we can actually get out of bed for.'

'I miss the masks, though.'

'We all miss the masks.'

'I'm not dissing *WØLF*.' Hollow kicked her boot against a crack in the Perspex. 'It's just all this waiting around, it does my head in. I was out running when the Emergency Alert hack happened. I didn't even have my phone with me. This random family flagged me down and said we had to get to a shelter. We stayed inside the cathedral until the army cleared us to leave. Everyone was saying that nothing would be the same again. Except it is the same; it's all the fucking same.' Hollow tilted her head so it almost rested on Ezra's shoulder. 'Our first paraspecies war is a lot duller than I thought.'

'It's the word paraspecies,' Ezra said, ignoring a perfectly timed complement of thunder. 'They could've picked something that at least sounds like we're in a fantasy trilogy. By all that is holy, the first quisling war is upon us. Pass me my brother's sword and my book of magic skills.'

'The King rolls a twelve-sided dice to decide what happens next.'

Ezra laughed. 'And everyone gets to create their own character.'

'Meh, we already do that.' Hollow kicked at the crack again. 'Did you speak to your mums about the GiFT year?'

'Yeah,' Ezra said. 'You?'

'No chance.'

'Gemma might come through, you never know.'

Hollow shook her head, and nothing more to add to it. 'So what did Team Ezra Blake decide?'

'Ideally, something connected to my history degree,' Ezra said. 'Something I could shine in. We looked at getting a placement with the university, but apparently the Department of Wartime Employment is quite strict about what qualifies as an essential service industry. Mum Sheila said museums sometimes get listed, but it's always a one-place, last-minute thing. Basically, you wait and you take your chances. And, yeah, a museum would be great, but it's also such a big risk. Decide by the deadline or you're on a military GiFT. I would not shine on a military GiFT. I would do the opposite of shine. I would un-shine things. I thought a hospital would be okay, or a care home.'

'You'd shine in a care home?'

'Why not?' Ezra said.

'Um, the heavy lifting.' Hollow looked Ezra up and down. 'You'd have to bulk up a bit.'

'I can go to the gym.' Ezra tried a smile for size. 'Is this what you needed to talk to me about?'

'Fuck, no. I just wanted to duck out of biomechanics.'

Ezra choked, rounding a stare on her. 'I carried coleslaw in my backpack for five hours.'

'You brought coleslaw?'

'I'm fake ill, H.' Ezra sighed. 'I mean, it's probably a life form by now.'

Hollow nudged Ezra, enough alliance in it to brighten the storm. 'We can leave some on the bus if it makes you feel better.'

'Hopefully, it's not a new superspecies. I don't think even *WØLF* could bring normality to a war with sentient cabbage.'

'An NHS care home, though? That's like, serious hard work.' Hollow puffed. 'You moan if we have to go up any stairs.'

'I also get the contextual gravity of a GiFT year,' Ezra said. 'We could do it, H. We could gift our time to the same place. Spend a year helping people. It might even be fun. What do you reckon?'

'Maybe war is always like this for the people who stay home.' Hollow let smoke pool around her. 'Soldiers fighting a faraway enemy that you only know about through propaganda, and everything in your own life staying the same.'

'Not as much as you'd think,' Ezra said. 'In fact, medieval societies had no concept of the—'

'We should enlist,' Hollow said.

'I can't even deal with you today.' Ezra went to share a smirk. 'What are the odds they put actual mercury in that tobacco?'

But there was nothing coming back. Just Hollow, framed in lightning, looking over at the armed forces drop-in centre. 'Yeah, let's do it.'

'Are you serious?'

'Come on, it'll be a laugh.'

'A laugh!'

'Yeah,' Hollow said, 'let's do it.'

'No!' Ezra yelped, loud enough to warrant a wide arc from a rain-soaked runner. 'Absolutely NO.'

'Come on. Let's do it.'

'You actually want a military GiFT?'

'Hey, it's a plan.'

'We don't need a plan, Hollow.' Ezra spoke carefully, taking time with each word like it had its own swimming pool. Trying to slow it down. Trying to stop it. 'We already have a plan.'

'It can't hurt to take a look.'

'What's going on, H?'

'Nothing.' Hollow looked up at the sky, her face chopped into blocks of light by the bus shelter. 'It'll be dry at least.'

'Did Gemma say something?'

'Since when do I give a shit what Gemma says.'

Ezra's touch was delicate against Hollow's hand. 'The whole care home thing, it was only an idea. We can find something else.'

It didn't feel like a significant personal moment; it felt like when the storm came together overhead and the rain fell and the bus shelter rattled, and everyone forgot to remember that thunder and lightning are never a separate thing.

'Whatever.' Hollow took one last drag, dropped the cigarette and screwed it out with her boot. 'You coming or what?'

4

Because of the feathers

Enough pain and a dentist appointment could feel like redress. The armed forces drop-in centre shone out strong, contemporary and superstar-bright. As Hollow and Ezra ran across the road, they were action anticipated, logged in, preference checked and ad amended. Even the doors adapted to their pace, swooshing open with such perfect timing they didn't even break their stride. If they'd hoped to find something old and familiar inside, they were disappointed. The only thing remaining of the convenience store was the convenient space it had occupied.

A preppy soldier, dressed in the same cookie-dough camo they wore on *WØLF*, met Hollow and Ezra two steps in. 'What a stinker of a day, eh?'

'We're just having a quick look,' Ezra said.

'All levels of looking are welcome on a day like today. Let's see if we can dry you off at least. My name is Ash. Excuse the funky smell.' The soldier grinned. 'Unauthorised overnight floodwater. You should have smelled it before we took the tiles up.'

'We were thinking about enlisting,' Hollow said.

'For a GiFT,' Ezra gave Hollow a look, 'but probably not.'

'I can certainly help with that,' Ash said. 'And just to let you know, a GiFT donation year is welcomed within any of our armed services. They're all slightly different. Did you have any preference today?'

Hollow answered; no thinking it over or discussing it. 'Army.'

'Then the absolute best person to speak to is Henri.' Ash leant in for a chummy whisper. 'Henri is the person I spoke to when I first came here. I can personally vouch for her.'

'Sounds good,' Hollow said.

Ash pulled a couple of square brochures from an army display unit, guiding Hollow and Ezra towards a plush seating area. 'There's a load of information online, but this gives you a quick-start overview of the various options available within our Gifted Free Time programme. Grab yourself a seat, guys. I'll see if Henri's around for a chat. Can I get your names?'

'I'm Hollow.'

Ash waited on Ezra, all cute and daringly hopeful. But it was obvious from the way Ezra stared back that it'd take several hours and a waterboard approach to get anything usable. 'No worries,' Ash said. 'I'll go and find Henri.'

Ezra flumped down onto the sofa, watching Ash as he trotted off to a glass-partitioned workspace at the back of the building. The sofa was over-proportioned, super reassuring, and the slate grey upholstery went great with any shade of clothing you cared to arrive in. On the wall behind them an image of Lieutenant Mattoo Bolte bloomed and faded into another. The air smelled like shoe polish and fish sauce. At the base of the wall, all the carpet tiles were ripped up, exposing grey concrete and old glue. For a place of such organised conscription, the armed forces drop-in centre was caught out trying to be two different things. It was hard to look away from Mattoo Bolte.

'What the actual are we doing here, H?'

Hollow was flicking through the brochure. 'It's something to do, that's all.'

'Enlisting is something to do?'

'Stand down, panic stations.' Hollow carried on flicking through the brochure. 'They'd have chucked us out already if they didn't think we were serious.'

'And are we serious? Because I lost the plot back at the bus shelter.'

Hollow shrugged. 'What do you think.'

'I think you can't throw a word like enlist around and not expect people to panic.' Ezra snatched the brochure from Hollow and threw it on a glass-top coffee table. 'I'm jamming the brakes on H, but you keep jumping gears. And right now it's hard to tell which one we're crashing in.'

'We're just keeping dry,' Hollow said.

'Are we, though?'

Hollow might have answered, but instead she stood up. 'Hi, Henri?'

'Ah, you must be Hollow,' Henri said, all friendly smile and altogether trustworthy haircut. Not for one single minute looking like the Internet of Things had already provided her with a pre-entry data check: names, basic character profiles and a list of recommended approach scenarios. 'Ash tells me you're interested in donating some time to our GiFT programme.'

'Henri,' Ezra said, 'you're late to this discussion and we're going to be honest with you. There's a massive thunderstorm outside and we missed the bus. Strictly speaking, I missed the bus. But Hollow waited. And there wasn't much else to do, no offence. And even if we did consider thinking about a military GiFT year, it won't be until after we finish university. Which is three years away. Four years, depending on industry placements. And they're saying the war will be over by next year. So everything's likely to change again. As you can appreciate, this isn't a time for making decisions. Except for deciding that we're not deciding anything.'

'The army—'

'In summing up,' Ezra blocked Henri's attempt to reverse into the conversation parking space, 'we are exploring GiFT options. We are not exploring GiFT decisions. Any questions?'

'This is Ezra,' Hollow said.

'It's good to get some context, Ezra,' Henri said. 'And the army certainly appreciates a long-term plan. Have you guys set up a user profile with us yet?'

'We'll come back when we have more time.' Ezra was looking towards the front window, searching the road like an undeniable excuse would appear at any minute. 'We ought to get going, H. We don't want to miss the bus again.'

'Should we have set up a profile?' Hollow said, moving along the sofa, closer now to Henri than she was to Ezra.

'Not at all,' Henri said, 'but we'll need to set one up before we can go any further.'

'No, you're fine,' Ezra said. 'We should head back to the bus stop now anyway. Sometimes, it's early.'

'Is fifteen minutes enough time?' Hollow said.

'The army call it a profile.' Henri pulled a glass screen out of the arm of the sofa. 'But it's more of a basic user account. It lets the army know you've shown an interest, and in return gives you access to all the online material. The required fields are innocuous and appallingly dull. It only takes a couple of minutes. And don't worry, Ezra, this is the army. We'll have you on your bus.'

'They run every half hour,' Hollow said.

'Well, if you're willing to give me half an hour, I can chat through some of the GiFT options available to you. You might even get a coffee thrown in if I can persuade this new software that the smell is down to floodwater.'

'No,' Ezra said. 'Thank you.'

'I wouldn't mind hearing the options,' Hollow said.

'Good man,' Henri said. And for all the world it sounded like she meant it.

Hollow knew it was far too easy. She guessed Henri was using pheromone augmentation. It didn't matter. She wasn't fighting coercion; she was looking for it. There were pages of GiFT options to choose from. Everything felt slick and expensive,

34

full of tag lines and encouraging imagery. 'This ambulance one looks pretty good,' she said.

'Ambulance crew?' Henri sounded impressed even though WØLF must have elevated the GiFT to everyone's first choice. 'It's certainly our most challenging year, but it's also the most rewarding.'

'It looks lovely,' Ezra said, not looking at it. 'We're actually thinking of a nonmilitary-based GiFT, possibly in an NHS care home.'

Henri was serious with her reply. 'My grandmother passed away waiting for a place in a state-funded care home. Donating a year to the NHS is a worthwhile use of your GiFT. But that's a decision for the future, and today is a chance to explore alternative ideas. Different footpaths on the map, if you like. What most people don't realise is that, first and foremost, we are your army. And that means we're fighting for you, whatever path you decide.'

'I've never thought of it that way,' Hollow said, looking over at Ezra.

But Ezra was still watching the road outside. Two students were inside the bus shelter, chatting to a woman dressed in a full-length ballgown. A rain-soaked runner was stretching, one foot propped against a lamppost. A cyclist lost the cycle lane, narrowly missing an oncoming car. A poodle rode pillion on a motorbike, chewing at the strap of its helmet. If the everyday absurdity of the scene had made a sound, it was lost in thunder. The lights inside the drop-in centre flickered and went out, pulsing back with the artistic grace of a motorway speed camera.

Henri's smile came soft then, more comfort than the situation was prepared for. 'A user profile is just a user profile. No one is going to turn up at your door with a uniform for you to put on.'

'Right,' Hollow said, 'actually, I—'

Ezra stood up, sudden and surprising everyone. 'We need to go.'

'Of course.' Henri sat back, easing the situation down. 'Before

35

you leave, I should let you know that our Gifted Free Time programme is designed to mimic the gap year commission. Donators spend a year attached to a unit, shadowing a troop officer in the field and learning how to lead under pressure. Adventure and education are built in to everything we do in the army, and our GiFT programme is no different. If you're looking for something else from your donation, then a nonmilitary GiFT might suit you better.'

'We like adventure and education,' Hollow said, looking up at Ezra, sweeter than usual.

'Unlike a nonmilitary GiFT,' Henri said, 'the moment you enlist, any university tuition fees you might have incurred are automatically dropped to zero. A lot of students see a military-based donation as an investment in their future. And, as a mandatory year out of your life, it's also a lot more interesting than scrubbing floors.'

'Uni fees drop to zero?' Ezra shrugged. 'So, financially, we'd be better off waiting until our final year.'

'If you have to prioritise money over personal growth, then yes,' Henri said. 'And, unfortunately, that is the situation for some of our GiFT donators. For my part, I was a nothing kind of kid before the army. I spent most of my time sat in front of a computer screen. Everyone told me I was lost, but I wasn't lost, I was waiting for something. I just didn't know what.' She nodded towards the front of the building. 'I enlisted on a day like this. Full of doubt. Asking all the same questions, wondering if I had the guts to be more than I was. Fifteen years later, and I'm still here. All I can tell you is that the army takes all the jumbled-up pieces and puts them together in a way that makes sense.'

Ezra spoke straight to Hollow then. 'You said we were just keeping dry.'

'Can you stay, Ez?' Hollow said, pulling at Ezra to sit down. 'Just so I'm not here on my own.'

'Fine.' Ezra perched on the edge of the sofa. 'But I'm only here for you.'

'Sometimes, all we have is each other,' Henri said, like Ezra had magically pulled a crème brûlée of loyalty and friendship out of the oven of awkwardness.

Ezra didn't even look up. 'Right.'

'Despite what people might tell you,' Henri said, 'this choice you're facing is never easy. It can seem like avoiding it is the absolute best thing to do. But we didn't choose this war; this war came looking for us. It's a faraway thing right now, but it might be that one day the Mandolin will find us here, in our own streets and in our own homes. That's what our armed services are fighting to stop, every single day. You can ignore it for a while, but there's no avoiding this war. As much as we might want things to be different, this isn't a choice any of us can dip out of.'

'I'm only here for my friend,' Ezra said.

Henri sat forward. 'The Covid outbreaks taught us that you can only win a war when you fight for every single human life. Ambulance crew does that. It's a good choice, Hollow.'

'Would I have to be able to drive?' Hollow said.

'Now that's the first straight-thinking question I've heard all day.' Henri flicked through a series of tick boxes on the glass screen. 'Being able to drive is fine, but we prefer it if you have no previous driving experience. Military driving isn't the same as civilian driving, and it's better for us to teach you from scratch. Bad habits can be hard to break.'

'Is it tough, though?'

'A smart kid like you, you'll be driving within a week.'

'No, I don't mean...' Hollow looked at Ezra again. 'I mean the war. Is the war tough?'

'God help us if war ever stops being tough.' Henri took a moment. 'But this war is different. The International War Agency was created so that every country knows it has a part in this victory. That's every country. We're not fighting against each other this time, we're fighting *for* each other. To be involved in something like that, it's new. It's shaping who we become as a species.'

'What are they like?' Hollow said. 'The Mandolin.'

'That's a great question,' Henri said. 'Direct, honest, courageous. You'll do well on the psychology profile tests, Hollow.'

Ezra frowned. 'Did you just deflect her?'

'The Mandolin are a complex life form to explain,' Henri said. 'How about you two tell me what you know?'

Hollow nudged over towards Ezra. 'We've heard a few things, not much really.'

'Good man, tell me what you've heard.'

Hollow looked around the drop-in centre like she was thinking her way around an obstacle course. Despite months of war and a starring role in a major-league reality TV series, the Mandolin remained an unknown quantity. There'd been video footage when it all started, shit-scary scenes that felt uncomfortable even when they were still being trolled as fake. The truth, when it came, was blunt and unequivocal from a podium outside 10 Downing Street, and nothing much more than a Keep Calm to be going on with. *WØLF* focused everything on why the soldiers were fighting, where they were fighting, when they were fighting, what they were fighting for. Nothing much was ever said about who they were fighting. Hollow took a breath. 'That video footage from Afghanistan was pretty weird.'

'Will we get pinged for talking about this?' Ezra said.

'This is a secure zone. All you'll get is credits for being here,' Henri said. 'And yes, Hollow, I must admit, it freaked me out the first time I saw the footage. Fear is generally our first response when we come across an unidentified experience. And just like everyone else, I looked for the disinformation watermark. When

I couldn't find it, I went scrolling through the comments to find the logical explanation. It took me a while to realise that I'd rather find a comfortable answer than an uncomfortable truth.'

Hollow glanced at Ezra. 'So they actually can switch states?'

Henri tugged her sleeve straight, holding the reply like it was worth their visit. 'At zero degrees, water can be a liquid, a solid or a gas. We live with water, so we take for granted that certain conditions allow it to shift between states. Imagine the intensity of your reaction if you'd never come across anything like water before. Research is advancing our knowledge every day. We know that the Mandolin are a superspecies of some kind, and the product of a spontaneous evolution event. We know that they can de-nature their biological state, appearing invisible to our eyes. We also know that they strip oxygen as fuel for this process, helpfully creating ozone as a by-product so we can easily detect them. And despite iron making up thirty-five per cent of the earth, we know the Mandolin cannot survive direct contact with it.' Henri paused for a moment, straightening her sleeve again. 'Admittedly, we've got a way to go before we fully understand their physiology, but when you bring it back to basics, they're as natural as rain or ice or steam.'

'We're not at war with water,' Ezra said, categorically not wanting to be engaging with the conversation, and super-size pissed off that now it was a bastard hundred times more interesting than anything.

'And yet water can kill us in all sorts of states and all sorts of ways. We respect that without worrying too much about it.' Henri nodded to Hollow. 'Anything else?'

'Psych scams?'

'Ah, interesting, isn't it, how quickly we develop new language.' If Henri was caught on the back foot, she didn't give anything away. 'Imagine you get woken up close to midnight in an isolated house with someone freaking out about seeing a clown face at the window, you're probably going to freak out too.'

'Depends,' Ezra said, ignoring Hollow's irritated eyebrows, 'it could just be someone messing around.'

'But it would be freaky, right?' Hollow said.

'Fear is contagious.' Henri nodded towards an image of Mattoo Bolte standing courageously between an Afghan family and a curiously large explosion in their fireplace. 'Just like bravery is contagious. We don't call these things psych scams. Advertisements exploit human psychology to persuade us to buy things, and we don't call advertisements psych scams. The words sound more sinister than the reality. Yes, the Mandolin use neural manipulation to get what they want, but scroll through any social media and you're scammed into seeing things that aren't there.'

'They're evolved from birds?' Ezra said.

'Birds?'

'Because of the feathers.'

'I'll be honest with you, guys.' Henri sat back like she'd said it a thousand times. 'While it's a great life experience, the military GiFT programme is UK soil only. There is absolutely no chance of being exposed to the Mandolin.'

'What if I want to enlist for real?' Hollow said. 'In the army.'

Ezra choked. 'Hollow!'

But Henri just answered the question in an everyday kind of way. 'Our non-commission entries are three years as standard, with an evaluation point built into the end of every six months. Entry automatically furloughs your university place and any module grades you already have.' She leant in, looking around the room like she was telling them a secret. 'And if you're still set on the ambulance career route, three years' experience in Rescue and Medical Evacuation counts for a whole lot more respect than a GiFT year when you go looking for work.'

'Medivac?'

Thanks to many years of intensive army training, Henri didn't flinch at the Americanised noun. 'Medivac.'

'You think I should do it?'

'We all have to make that choice for ourselves, Hollow,' Henri said, 'but from a personal perspective, there really is only one way to find out.'

'Okay, yeah, I think I'll do it.'

'Wait!' Ezra spluttered. 'I'll do the GiFT with you, H. After uni, we can do it together, ambulance if you want, whatever you want.'

Time was running at a hundred miles an hour, and everything was in slow motion, even Hollow's smile. 'It's too late for that now, Ez.'

'You're sure about this?' Henri said.

'I'm sure.'

Henri didn't smile. She just nodded. 'We can fill in the initial application here. I'll give you some information links to look at. Have a good read through them tonight. If you have any questions or any second thoughts, just come back here tomorrow and ask for me, okay?'

'Okay.'

'It's standard procedure to run a data trail back through your social media accounts and assess any unsympathetic or political tendencies. Is this likely to be a problem?'

'I...' Hollow looked down at her hands '...got an inciting public discomfort notice last April.'

'Smoking?'

Hollow nodded.

'That's nothing to worry about.' Henri turned the glass screen towards Hollow. 'In a few days, you'll get a message inviting you back here for a briefing and some health and fitness tests. You can have a longer chat with one of our career advisors about Medivac then. It takes around four weeks for the application to be processed. This can be a good time to teach yourself to run. You might think you're in good shape already, but army fit isn't the same as civilian fit. There's an app specifically designed for the period before boot camp. It was created by a couple of soldiers who've been right where you are now. It's not new, but it is effective. It sets you up with a daily routine, baseline and progression targets. I'm not saying it's mandatory, but it'll give you a good head start if you're looking for one.'

'Sounds good.'

Henri nodded again. 'You've just taken a huge step, Hollow. That takes a lot of guts. You should be very proud of yourself.'

'Thanks, yeah.' Hollow shrugged her way through a bland acknowledgement, but in truth it was a moment of respect and approval like nothing she'd ever felt before. 'Thanks, Henri.'

They made it back to the bus stop in time to catch the next bus. Hollow had nothing to say. Ezra had so much to say, it could fill a Siberian borehole. 'Do you have any idea what you just did?'

'Joined the army?'

Ezra slammed into an empty seat. 'Care to explain?'

'Done is done, Ez.' Hollow shoved Ezra towards the window. 'Shut up talking about it now.'

'Three years,' Ezra jolted with the bus, one hand on the steamed-up window, 'in a paraspecies war. Are you insane?'

'Pass me my brother's sword and my book of magic skills.'

'No, you don't get to turn this back on itself.'

Hollow shrugged. 'Did you get to watch the Zara Seraphim film in the end?'

'What?'

'*Methuselah*. I heard it was pretty good.'

'We had a plan.' Ezra took several steadying breaths. 'We made a pact, H.'

'Big deal,' Hollow said. 'So we made a pact. Things change.'

'I was happy with red ink. But you insisted it had to be blood.'

'Blood fades quicker than ink.'

'No,' Ezra hissed. 'Blood fixes it. You said blood fixes it.'

'Hey, Gemma went to see that Gran Lizeth in the shoe house,' Hollow said. 'She reckons there are loads of dead people riding the bus around. Imagine if we were sat in one right now.'

'We cut ourselves open, H.'

'And we were twelve years old.' Hollow curled her fingers to hide the scar that cut her lifeline in two. 'We knew squat about the world.'

'We still know squat about the world.'

'Sure.'

Ezra nodded, calming everything down, working it all through. 'Henri said you could go back tomorrow, if you were having second thoughts. That means you're allowed to change your mind, right? She wouldn't have said it if you couldn't change your mind. We should make a pros and cons list.'

'No, you're good.'

'I'm not good, H. Neither are you. Neither are any of us any more.' Ezra watched a couple of dogs face each other off, all tangled leads and teeth. 'We had to ask someone to leave our D&D group last night.'

'You kicked someone out?'

'So, D&D is a cooperative, and you don't kick people out of a cooperative,' Ezra said. 'You respectfully ask them to leave.'

'What the fuck did they do?' Hollow pulled her hair out of its makeshift bun. 'Please tell me they admitted that fantasy role playing is lame.'

'They were killing people.'

'I thought that was the point?'

'No, it's not,' Ezra said, 'and I was serious about doing the GiFT with you.'

'Yeah, thanks.'

'Right. Because the actual last thing on earth I want to be doing for my GiFT is joining the army. But I'd do it for you,

H.' Ezra filtered through a dozen emotions. 'You could at least pretend to appreciate the magnitude of my generosity.'

'No, I do. I do appreciate it.'

'Will you at least talk to Gemma about this?'

'Shit, Ez, Gemma thinks she's Sylvie Stevens' twin flame.' Hollow looked around the bus. 'I'm not sure she's the right person to consult on matters of reality.'

'Gemma is Sylvie Stevens' twin flame?'

'Gran Lizeth did the leaves,' Hollow said. 'The evidence is there.'

'Under licence from the intelligence services.' They shared a smile, but Ezra couldn't hold it for long. 'Aren't you even a little bit terrified of what'll happen to you if you go to Afghanistan?'

'Course.' Hollow was picking at a thread on the worn seat of the shuttle bus. 'But I think I'm more scared about what'll happen to me if I stay here.'

Hollow didn't say anything to her mum until she'd been to the briefing. Until she'd had a chat with one of the army career advisors. Until she'd aced the fitness trials. Until she could run ten kilometres every morning before lectures. Until the day the message came through confirming her application had been approved.

Gemma carried on stacking plates into the dishwasher. 'I suppose it had to be the bloody army, didn't it.'

The Oath of Allegiance took place the following Tuesday. There might have been drums and camaraderie and blood once, but now it was just a fifteen-minute slot with Henri and Gemma. Standing in the same slick drop-in centre, with the same slick mechanisms of recruitment, and the same smell of shoe polish and fish sauce. Hollow wore the military-buttoned jacket she'd saved for her graduation, repeating words after Henri like they were getting married. Still, it was an oath to king and country that bound her. Not only in law, but in the place inside of her that resonated. Instead of a ring, Henri handed her a rail warrant, a travel schedule and an appointment to get her temporary QRID tattoos done. Change trains at London. Use the tube. A coach will be waiting at Woking. Welcome to the army.

It should have been harder than missing a bus.

5

I'm not a vampire

Ezra had buffered on furious for weeks. Not a ranting, boiling kind of furious that led to restraining orders, more a low-volume, unacknowledged kind of furious that led to health problems in later life. Everyone knew Hollow was a bite of the poisoned apple, just like everyone knew Ezra was a unicorn. They didn't belong together, not even in a fairy tale. That's why they'd made the pact, so they were bound together even if they had a massive argument and never spoke again. And they hadn't spoken, not since the bus stop day when rain had flooded out the road and Hollow had enlisted in the British army. Without much knowing it, they'd faced down the same choice, and they'd come out on different sides. And even though Ezra absolutely stood by the decision not to enlist along with Hollow, everything in life suddenly felt empty and stupidly pointless. When a shortfall GiFT flagged up at Fabian Evirate House, Ezra applied. As a social sciences GiFT, it generated a lot of chatter. As did the interview process and the outbreak of disappointed announcements on social media. Even with several glowing recommendations and a photograph with Zara Seraphim, no one was more surprised than Ezra when the call came through, and the answer didn't even need thinking about.

The GiFT package had been itemised as low-risk admin, live chat and social media, but Emporia Precipice Mantlepiece had been a public liaison officer for over thirty-five years, and she could smell untapped potential when she saw it.

'Welcome back to Fabian Evirate House,' Emporia said, embellishing her greeting with a floral handkerchief. 'I trust your journey was a pleasant one.'

'Thank you for the opportunity,' Ezra said.

'It is you who should be thanked, my dear.' Emporia tucked a wayward silver hair back into its lacquered and somewhat Queen Elizabeth II orderliness. 'Without our young GiFT donators, I'll wager we would be a far gloomier establishment. As to your induction day, there is a veritable mountain of paperwork awaiting you. But I rather favour showing our young volunteers around the facility before they commit to signing anything. I understand that you have a gold loyalty card?'

Fabian Evirate House was a sprawling stronghold of Gothic Revival architecture. It resembled a cathedral insofar as it had stained glass windows, flying buttresses and pointed arches. The tilted cruciform of its hematite foundations was often considered cathedral-like, as was the thrusting iron sword that towered above the visitor entrance. And, as home to the Fabian Evirate Collection and enduring host to the fully immersive Great Exhibition of Enchantment, every echoing hall, eerie passageway and ribbed vault stood in testament to an unchanged, cathedral-like world. Every echoing hall, eerie passageway and ribbed vault was also filled with paratechnology and cutting-edge innovation. The combination of such opposing elements should have been a mismatched confusion, but there was a counterpoint melody to each component that enhanced the whole without diminishing itself. As a city landmark, the nine great towers of Fabian Evirate House split the skyline like blades of grass through a crack in the pavement, and even in the depths of winter the jewelled windows shone like a lighthouse to those lost at sea. On a sunny day, an array of holographic lightforms cast by the paratech matrix of stained glass windows stalked the stone pavements outside the building like phantastic billboards. On a rainy day, the lightforms entertained the cafés and restaurants of the paved square below. And once you'd seen Fabian Evirate House by moonlight, it was hard not to believe in magic. 'They've upgraded me to a platinum wristband,' Ezra said.

'Most admirable.' Emporia tried to catch the attention of a young security guard by raising her hand slightly higher than her waist. 'It saves time, you know, if a GiFT donator has already encountered the various lightforms, gargoyles and...clock. We have smelling salts, of course, but these things can eat away at an induction day.'

'No smelling salts necessary,' Ezra said.

'Being a platinum wristband holder, you will of course be aware...' Emporia subtly signalled to the security guard again '...that Fabian Evirate House does not align with a traditional approach to curatorship, although there are certainly ancient and thought-provoking things on display in our various rooms and corridors. Still, there are those who arrive with expectations and personal intricacies regarding the nature and subsequent contradiction of this vast nine-towered labyrinth we dare to call a house. Which brings me to a rather delicate matter.' Emporia attempted to catch the attention of the guard for a third time. 'While no one here would deny that a word like crypt must attract a certain gothic appreciation, our last GiFT donator had rather an interest in vampire lore. A most fascinating young person, and our induction tour proceeded splendidly until we reached the crypt. As the sun blazed upon us, there arose a cacophony of flinching, writhing, howling, several fruit bats and a rather startling amount of cheesecloth. My dear, the day was saved only by the distraction of a spilled paperclip container. From there, only candlelight and a mutual agreement to part ways could save either of us. Thankfully, a GiFT shortfall in the social sciences is easily remedied. I do apologise, Ezra, but I must discreetly enquire. Contrary to expectation, the office crypts are not located beneath the building, but at the tallest point of the western walkway. And is something of a natural suntrap.'

'I'm not a vampire,' Ezra said.

'I had dared to surmise from such bright attire.' Emporia waved her handkerchief towards the security guard with such increasing speed and intensity she resembled a Morris dancer banishing the dark days of winter. 'But times change and one must never jump to conclusions. Where did you meet our dear filmmaker Zara Seraphim, if I am permitted to ask?'

'At the premier of *Methuselah*,' Ezra said.

'Ah, but of course.' Emporia nodded respectfully. 'Many of us here at Fabian Evirate House follow her on social media. She has a particular skill for giving an audience what they want in a way they would never expect. There are many things to be learnt from watching a Zara Seraphim film. Mostly about oneself, I have found. Ha ha ha.'

'Thank you again, for the opportunity,' Ezra said, skipping deftly to one side as a lightform shoal of assorted tropical fish darted a path between them.

'One imagines it would be a simple thing, to know oneself,' Emporia trailed her fingers through the spines of a lionfish, 'but instead, one finds oneself constantly bewildered, don't you think?'

Ezra nodded along, formulating an answer that would at once sound enlightening and yet also charmingly sweet and uncertain. 'Yep.'

'We of course discussed the windows at your interview. At length, as I recall.'

'I said too much.'

'And yet I sense you had more to say.' Emporia chortled, discreetly tucking another silver hair behind a hairgrip. 'Never hesitate to share your thoughts, my dear.'

'It's more of a working metaphor.' Ezra sidestepped a pufferfish that had detached from the shoal. 'The paratechnology works with light, just like stonemasons work with stone. Except, instead of carving stone, the windows use a multiple-source light combination based on temporal spectrum variables.'

'An interesting comparison. Although, perhaps we could—'

But Ezra was already searching through the comprehensive collection of guidebooks available on the reception desk. 'Variables that also include weather conditions, solar activity, lunar alignment and planetary positions. Then there's traffic pollution, new buildings, pigeon poop on the glass. All that ordinary, everyday information, collected up and carved into lightforms.'

'Indeed.' Emporia glanced towards the security guard again, casually brushing the corner of her handkerchief against a large DO NOT TOUCH sign.

'And stonemasons empowered grotesques and gargoyles with the power of fear. Even evil spirits were scared of them.' Ezra held up the photograph that Tulip Blake had framed and presented, along with a year pass to Fabian Evirate House, on Ezra's seventh birthday. The photograph was grainy, monotone, and taken with a pinhole camera in 1900. It was the only photograph ever taken of the lightforms, not through lack of trying, but through lack of success. Cameras and window paratechnology both harvested light to capture an image, and it was this necessity of fundamental requirements that had never seemed to overlap again. Ezra ran a finger over the image. 'A carving that scares evil spirits has to change because what we're afraid of is change. And the Fabian Evirate House lightforms aren't the same from one hour to the next because...' Ezra put the guidebook down carefully '...that's exactly how we all feel right now.'

'Despite our advancements, we remain such orphaned creatures. And yet, our dear founder still dared to hope that the exhibition might one day go out of style.'

'Fabian Evirate?'

'Ahem.' The figure that loomed over them resembled a large, slightly dishevelled question mark. 'I'll trouble you to observe the DO NOT TOUCH sign to your left.'

'Samuel Shakespeare, splendid.' Emporia bustled an etiquette distance away. 'Samuel, may I introduce you to our latest GiFT donator, Ezra Blake.'

'Welcome,' Samuel said, gripping hold of his torch.

'A platinum wristband holder, I might add.' Emporia dabbed her cheek with the floral handkerchief. 'Seventy visits. And from one so young.'

'Platinum wristband, eh?' Samuel said, with what might have been a wink had it not been derailed by several beads of sweat. 'I thought they were just a myth.'

'There was a ceremony,' Ezra said. It was hard not to dwell on the strained buttons of Samuel's uniform, and even harder not to notice the glistening tentacles of a surf-and-turf lightform that lapped suggestively around his leg. 'The crown was a bit unexpected, but the trumpets were nice.'

'Samuel has been on security duty with us for five years,' Emporia said. 'Not consecutively, of course. Ha ha ha.'

'I beg to differ.' Samuel grinned invitingly. 'A security guard is never off duty. Ezra Blake, I am obliged to inform you that I will forcibly remove you from the building if necessary.'

'Thank you for the…opportunity,' Ezra said.

'Now, I know what you're thinking.' Samuel shook off a wayward tentacle. 'You're thinking, why hasn't this person enlisted along with every other eligible hench?'

'I don—'

'When the war started, I considered a career with the navy,' Samuel continued, 'but submarines are cramped for space, and I'm not comfortable walking any corridor that doesn't allow you to spin a full circle.' Samuel added a flamboyant arc. 'Meet me here after work and I'll give you the unofficial tour. Show you where all the best passageways are. I might even let you hold my torch.'

'I'll probably go straight home,' Ezra said.

'Ah, the bold, unconquerable spirit of youth.' Emporia sighed into her handkerchief. 'When I was a young girl, we would spend our leisure hours colouring in maps of the British Empire. One must suppose there has been a great deal of free colouring-in time since decolonisation.'

'They made this torch out of old bus tyres,' Samuel said.

Across the city square, the cathedral bell struck nine. Each echoing ring upholding a sense of place in a time of such great uncertainty.

'Cometh the hour,' Emporia said. 'Samuel, we must return you to your post and resume our introductory adventure.'

'Ya'll have a nice time, now,' Samuel said, attempting to sound cool, and missing the boat by half a century.

'Who is this Yawl?' Emporia said. 'Am I acquainted with them?'

'No...' Samuel sighed a flock of lightform goldfinches into flight '...it's a saying, Emporia. It means, make sure you have a very nice time, all of you. Or one of you, depending on the circumstance.'

'What might be such circumstance?' Emporia said.

'If there was one of you.'

Emporia puzzled the idea for a while. 'Ezra, Mr Ipswich awaits us in the orangery, and there was more rain last night. Heaven knows what state the snails will be in.'

'A meeting with the big boss already, eh?' Samuel pitched a fist bump but changed it to a handshake halfway. 'Good for you, Ezra Blake. Good for you.'

'Thank you for the...'

'And don't forget my offer,' Samuel said, holding his torch suggestively.

Their strange little folk dance meeting had only lasted for a few minutes, but as with all folk dances, it had felt like an eternity. As Ezra's induction tour progressed on to the lounge travelator, the morning sun burst through the visitor entrance, catching rainbows on the glass doors and obliterating the security guard's reflection as if it had never been there. It wasn't magic. Well, not the sort of magic anyone was interested in anyway.

Ezra didn't look back; nothing good ever came from looking back.

'You must of course ignore the thrupenny bit,' Emporia said, linking arms with Ezra as if they were two chums off on a jolly to Fuerteventura.

Samuel watched Ezra and Emporia leave, imagining their laughter as it bubbled and bobbed along without him. Their departure was also unfairly accompanied by the flock of lightform goldfinches, cheeping and twittering and click-clacking against the stained glass windows in a desperate attempt to break free.

'You know where to find me,' Samuel called, wandering over to the visitor entrance. 'I'm not going anywhere.'

'Excuse me.' A boldly striped woman tapped Samuel's shoulder like he was a door or something. 'Which level is the semi-mortal clock on?'

Samuel straightened up. 'DO NOT TOUCH!'

'I'm looking for the semi-mortal clock.'

'Second-floor balcony.'

'Second-floor balcony.' The woman went to hurry away.

'Wait.' Samuel shoved his torch in front of the woman like a barrier. 'We are currently experiencing some technical difficulties. Too many visitors are wearing stripes. You'll have to remove any striped clothing or wait here until I get clearance.'

'Oh.' The woman weighed up the pros and more obvious cons. 'Will it take very long?'

'Depends,' Samuel said.

They leant against the reception desk and watched the goldfinches for a while. Each sweet little bird taking its turn to try for window freedom, each sweet little bird dying on the threshold of its own creation. Samuel had meant to do better. A year ago, the morning would have played out very differently, but the Sebastian Incident had changed them all.

6

Ah, the inevitable question

Ezra squinted through the intricate ironwork of the Victorian greenhouse construction like a zoo visitor trying to spot a rare breed of stick insect in a stick-based habitat. In truth, there wasn't much to see beyond snail slime and runner bean plants. 'What am I looking for, Mr Ipswich?'

'Ah, I am reminded of my late father,' the curator said, flashing a brief smile. Anyone blessed with a gap between their front teeth was supposedly in possession of a lucky life. Some were even blessed with a gap that could accommodate a thrupenny bit, and Richard Ipswich had the thrupenny bit stuck there to prove it. He rarely smiled, but when he did, it was like arriving at a parking meter to find a coin jammed in the slot.

'Did he grow runner beans, Mr Ipswich?' Ezra said.

'I may share his name, but my father was an altogether less agreeable Richard Ipswich,' the curator said, twirling what would have been an integrated musketeer moustache had he not witnessed the Sebastian Incident first-hand. 'A man whom, as many recall, despised the name Dicky as much as he despised the *persona non grata* I have become.'

'A dreadful injustice.' Emporia added a sympathetic flurry. 'No man should be incarcerated for standing true to his heart.'

'Incarcerated, Mr Ipswich?' Ezra said.

Emporia nodded reverently. 'Military confinement.'

The curator looked at his reflection in the greenhouse glass. 'Returning from the Falkland Islands conflict, I laid my weapon at the feet of Princess Anne and vowed I would never pick up another. I refused to cooperate with the army because I no longer had the reason or the capacity. I spent many weeks in military confinement, and many hours defending my stand. Had I known I could claim a Right to Discharge due to conscientious objection, I would have left earlier.'

'Conscientious objection is really brave, Mr Ipswich,' Ezra said.

'And refusal is not always a choice.' The curator sighed. 'Upon my release, I chose to introduce myself as Dicky while in my father's company. A habit that seems to have stuck. Please, call me Dicky.'

'I will, Mr Ipswich.'

'I'm informed that we have you on live chat and social media duty. You'll be stationed up in the crypt offices. One of the quieter work environments, I think you'll find. The lightforms tend towards domestic felines, and there's a decent view over the teashop.' Dicky pulled a pen out of his top pocket. 'Although, judging by your CV, Emporia may have other plans for you.'

'Not just the CV.' Emporia chuckled into her handkerchief. 'If our arrival encounter is to be trusted, this newest edition to our team does seem to have rather a high tolerance for bravado.'

'Ah, a role with the public, perhaps?'

'My thoughts exactly,' Emporia said.

'But we are not here to discuss such minor things.' Dicky tapped his pen against the glass. 'What do you see, Ezra?'

Ezra peered into the greenhouse again. 'Runner beans?'

'Look beyond the runner beans.'

Ezra tried to look beyond the runner beans, beyond the long stalks of scarlet flowers, beyond the thrusting boldness of leaves and delicate curling tendrils. 'There's a snail under the shelf?'

'Darnation,' Dicky said. 'Pass me the bucket, Emporia.'

'If I might elucidate?' Emporia said, fanning forward with the sophisticated grace of a bumblebee. 'Ezra Blake, as a newly appointed GiFT donator for the upcoming year, you are in the esteemed company of the Three Unbreakable Clauses.'

'Am I?'

'*Upon the foundation stone this shall be written.*' Emporia drifted her hand over a slime trail. 'Our founder, Maudie Clump, included three unbreakable clauses in the deeds. Clause three: The building must always be free to visitors. Clause two: The building must forever be named after the most Noble and Devious Fabian Evirate. Clause one: There must always be runner beans.'

'I thought Fabian Evirate was your founder?'

'As do all but those who ask,' Dicky said.

'Interesting.' Ezra was still scrutinising the greenhouse glass. 'Why must there always be runner beans?'

'Oh, no, my dear.' Emporia gathered her hands to her chest. 'We cannot challenge the existence of runner beans.'

'Because?'

'Because they remind us that the clauses can never be broken.'

'That actually makes sense.' Ezra wandered around the integrated arches of the west wing orangery. 'Permission to ask about the founder.'

'Permission granted,' Dicky said, jovially.

'Who was Fabian Evirate, then?'

'Ah, the inevitable question.' Dicky searched through an embroidered pocket and pulled out a battered click counter. 'A question I have been asked forty-two thousand, seven hundred and eighty-nine times before.'

'Because they're so mysterious,' Ezra said. 'The only thing anyone knows about Fabian Evirate is that they founded Fabian Evirate House, and now that's not even true either.'

Dicky clicked the counter and popped it back into his pocket. 'Maudie Clump didn't expand on the Noble and Devious.'

'But you do know who they were?'

'We are the seeker, Ezra, and we are all the gaps. And the unsolved puzzle, at least a little hopeful to our bones, perhaps.' Dicky cleared his throat. 'We do not know whose name we represent, nor shall we ever know. It is a closed mystery, yet many thousands of visitors continue to enquire as to the identity of Fabian Evirate. To my knowledge, none have bothered to ask about Maudie Clump.'

'Oh...' Ezra said.

'The Fabian Evirate House website has much of her history,' Emporia said. 'However, data analysis shows a disappointing flatline of page visits. Admittedly, it pays to know these things, but the immutable lack of public interest in our founder demoralises a soul.'

'Did you include Fabian Evirate on the page metta tags?'

'Page metta tags?' Dicky stared into the vast technology space between three generations. 'Is that some sort of universal goodwill message?'

'I mean...' Ezra said.

'I fear our young companion is referring to another, more electronic, metta.' Emporia shooed a ladybird from Dicky's shoulder. 'I myself only know of such things having built a blog relating to my recent interaction with the post office on being informed that even though it has been out of circulation since 1988, the one-pound note can still be deposited into a bank account.'

'Metta tags are identity labels,' Ezra said. 'With bits of text on them, so the search engines can find the appropriate page.'

'Good heavens,' Dicky said.

Emporia chuckled. 'Technology stretches far beyond rational understanding and yet requires a simple label to keep it working. In my many blogging hours, I have found myself appreciative of the simplicity, somehow.'

'I'd assumed the search engines just knew where to go.' Dicky tapped his heels together. 'I shall draw back the ignorance curtain and speak to the website management team this very day. A metta tag mentioning Fabian Evirate just might enlighten the world to the story of a most remarkable woman.'

'You'll have to get a separate clicker,' Ezra said, deftly stepping around a lightform fox and her three cubs, 'for all the Maudie Clump questions.'

'Perhaps,' Emporia said. 'And what rich and varied questions they would be. For our dear founder was born in Whitechapel, in 1851. A commonplace child, notable only for the fact that she survived several cholera outbreaks and a nasty fall from the church roof. Following in the footsteps of her mother, she walked the streets for almost two decades.' Emporia leant in. 'As a community midwife, there were no bicycles available for the streets of Whitechapel. Then, one foggy September night, as she was returning home from delivering a baby, she met Jack the Ripper.'

'No way!'

'Yes way.' Emporia indulged Ezra's enthusiasm. 'In fact, it would have been more fitting to say that Jack the Ripper met Maudie Clump. This building was built upon the outcome of that meeting.'

'It's a great story...' Ezra said, looking down at the red-tiled floor.

'Speak your mind, my dear.'

'The story denies the fact that no one survived meeting Jack the Ripper.'

'A prudent observation.' Emporia shooed another ladybird from Dicky's shoulder. 'The answer to which is, no one ever asks about Maudie Clump.'

Ezra looked up. 'What if Jack the Ripper was Fabian Evirate?'

'Or perhaps not.' Dicky smiled at Emporia. 'An ordinary midwife from Whitechapel creates something unfathomable, and still it's the serial killer who gets the attention.'

'Gaaagh,' Ezra said, 'why is it so hard to notice her?'

Emporia picked up a grass-lined bucket and handed it to Dicky. 'When Fabian Evirate House was opened to the public, many refused to believe a woman capable of such an endeavour. Instead, a rumour circulated that the building was not built at all, but magically appeared overnight, having always been there.'

'A rumour, I might add,' Dicky said, his fingers lingering on Emporia's, 'that was compounded by the recent invention of electric light.'

Emporia fumbled her handkerchief to hide a blush. 'In her diary, Maudie Clump explained that creating something that looked as if it were of supernatural origin was exactly what was needed in a time of approaching darkness. Nonetheless, it took ten years and an emergency baby delivery before the city planners were willing to approve the application. And so the Great Exhibition of Enchantment was born.'

'And just like the Great Exhibition at Crystal Palace,' Dicky said, hauling the door of the greenhouse open, 'the building itself was the greatest exhibit.'

'Beyond all other,' Emporia said, with a shy glance. 'Myself, I took up employment here over forty years ago. None know the building as well as I, and yet, to see the towers from within, to sit upon the mercury steps of the catacombs as light finds you in such colours as only the company of fey could bring...' Emporia stared down at her handkerchief as though it belonged to a memory, before stuffing it hastily into her pocket. 'My dear, you compared our window paratechnology to stonemasons working with stone. I would add to that a dash of rice. Wine or boiled. The choice was never ours to make.'

'Is this a lunch question?'

'Rice can be cooked or made into wine,' Dicky said, stooping into the greenhouse. 'As with all things, it is a matter of process. Most windows process light so it remains light. Our windows distil light into something that isn't light any more.

The lightforms might be a product of light, but the experience is where they truly exist.'

'I knew loads about this place yesterday,' Ezra said, rubbing at the greenhouse glass to get a better look at Dicky trying to dislodge a snail from a low potting shelf. 'Today, I don't know anything.'

'Welcome to Fabian Evirate House.' Dicky eased the snail free, gently placing it in the bucket. 'The more you learn about it, the less you know.'

'We must take our leave, Mr Ipswich,' Emporia called. 'Ezra has yet to encounter the associated paperwork, and I thought I might take a slight detour via the phylactery.'

'OMG.' Ezra clapped excitedly. 'Can we go inside?'

'I wonder,' Emporia said, 'am I alone in finding such abbreviations bewildering beyond the confines of messaging?'

Dicky pulled another snail free. 'Language is our identity and we hum with the bones of the hive. It is a lost and rebuilt thing, the change that no generation can hold.'

'Will we see the semi-mortal clock?' Ezra said.

'Of that you can be assured,' Emporia said. 'For none may enter the phylactery without first gaining permission from the semi-mortal clock.'

'I say, Ezra.' Dicky popped his head out of the greenhouse. 'Jolly good thinking on the metta tags.'

'Thank you, Mr Ipswich.'

'I might have an intriguing project for you. We'll speak again once the mandatory induction period has expired.'

'Amazing.'

'For you, Emporia.' Dicky produced a stem of runner bean flowers from behind his back. 'The usual arrangements for coffee?'

'The usual arrangements.' Emporia took the flowers, waving a bashful farewell to Dicky and turning away like an actor auditioning for a hotly contested part in a BBC romcom.

'The flowers are nice,' Ezra said.

'They are not flowers, my dear. They are the thing that happens before runner beans.' Emporia inhaled a scent that only insects could appreciate. 'Petals of defiant scarlet and everything focused on metamorphosis like such orchid tenderness could be the caterpillar. A small beauty lost in a larger reckoning. Not even flowers when they fade and fall the way that roses do.'

'Are you and Mr Ipswich an item?'

'An item of what?'

'Of interest?'

'Certainly, we share many interests.' Emporia tucked the flowers into her hair, bustling through a narrow passageway, ducking under a low ceiling and neatly avoiding a swarm of honey bees that had settled on a double-helix of supporting pillars. 'I also believe there is such a thing as sexual infatuation. Perhaps this is the item of interest you refer to?'

'No,' Ezra said. 'Not in any way imaginable.'

'Ah, you refer to love? I must admit, I have never found myself swept away in such emotions as love would bring. But I rather think that affection can come in a quieter form, gentle and enduring. It's all a silly nonsense, of course.' Emporia waited out a melodic reminder notification on her phone. 'Heavens, my dear, the caffeine hour is almost upon us. We must make haste with our induction tour. The semi-mortal clock can deny us entry, of course, but it is a Monday morning, and Monday mornings seem to be a favourable component as far as entry permissions go.'

'I heard that it accepted bribes,' Ezra said.

'Poppycock, my dear, the clock would never stoop to such political depths.' Emporia shooed a bee out of the flowers in her hair. 'Unless, that is, you happen to have a compact of ant powder about your person?'

'I…don't.'

'No matter. We shall use mine, should the situation require.' Emporia broke into a skip as she approached a giant crystal wheel that rotated gracefully between floor levels as if gravity wasn't a thing. 'The Ferris wheel is the most direct route and offers a wonderful view of the building, providing you don't look down. Or up.' Emporia stepped over the NO ENTRY sign and into the waiting zone. 'Or indeed, in any direction beyond the safety rail video link until you are more accustomed to the experience.'

Ezra stopped. 'We're taking the Ferris wheel?'

'You are staff now, my dear.'

'I thought...' Ezra watched as the vast hanging weights of the Fabian Evirate House Ferris wheel changed their balance ratio and the sparkling structure rotated through ninety degrees. 'Is it safe?'

'No one has plunged to their death yet,' Emporia said. 'Of course, privacy regulations forbid me from asking if you suffer from an inner ear infection, vertigo or low blood pressure. But we shall return to the stairs if you happen to suggest it.' Emporia smiled kindly. 'While I myself adore the Ferris wheel mode of transportation, I appreciate that it can be rather a startling experience.'

'Oh, go on then,' Ezra said, half tripping over the sign and inches from being the first Ferris wheel casualty.

'All hearts that love must have an end,' Dicky said, scanning the potting shelf for more snails. 'In the moments I find you, I lose my friend.'

7

Bello te Prepares

It was Monday evening. Hollow stood in her bedroom, lights out and holding a framed photograph taken with Ezra at Goodwood Revival. The one where they'd spent the whole brilliant, infinite day pretending to be American jazz musicians. Young enough to prompt smiles and old enough to notice. She stayed for a bit, her finger resting next to Ezra.

'You done, then?' Gemma said, flicking on the light.

'Yeah, nearly.'

'Is that all you're keeping?'

'I thought you could use this as a guest bedroom.'

Gemma puffed and huffed. 'For goodness' sake, Holl, way to act like you're not coming back.'

'It's just, I'll be different. And I'd rather come home to a guest bedroom than a shrine to a person I used to be.' Hollow dropped the photograph into a black bin bag. 'Besides, most of the stuff in here is from when I was a kid. It's overdue a good clear-out.'

'Not that picture with Ez?'

'It's a long time since we've been American jazz musicians.'

Gemma walked around the room, stopping in front of Hollow's computer desk. 'I might have guessed you wouldn't be throwing this bloody thing out.'

'I need to terminate some games and passwords and stuff,' Hollow said. 'I'll pack it all into boxes before I head off tomorrow.'

'And leave it cluttering up the landing, I suppose.'

'Yeah…' Hollow spoke slowly, careful with her words. 'Sorry, I should've taken it down the tip already. I ran out of time.'

'The tip?'

'They have a data-secure collection point,' Hollow said. 'It's down by the goodwill container.'

'You can't just throw your computer away. It cost a bloody fortune.'

'I've enlisted for three years, Gemma. The processor will be next to useless by the time I get out.'

'You'll take your laptop, though?'

'It's the army, not fucking boarding school.'

'I best hang onto all of it,' Gemma said, more jovial than she intended, 'for when they kick you out of boot camp.'

'Do what you want.' Hollow tied the bin bag and put it with the rest. 'I'm not bothered about keeping anything.'

It was more than just a clear-out. Hollow was demolishing her life. Gemma understood what was behind it, but there wasn't much she could put into words her daughter could hear. Later that night, they ordered a takeout and watched *WØLF* with the rest of the country. Almanac Johansson made out with Jar; the gossip boosted squad morale. Consolidation work to the Minuet of Jam was put on hold after a friendly suicide attack. Aerial shots caught a golden eagle in flight. Sylvie Stevens was quieter than usual. Mattoo Bolte had dysentery and wrote a poem to Captain Lancaster Dupont.

"Yesterday,
I wrote a poem
that wasn't there

in all the silent places
the bombs and barbed wire places
the burning, dying, unseen places

65

my words like a dead bird
no weight to the bones
and feathers

there were moments when
I thought I longed for you
in all the squandered verses

and I looked for you
like you were there,
yesterday."

Neither Hollow nor Gemma had much to say outside the comings and goings of the TV screen. When the programme ended, Hollow said she should get an early night and went to her room, sitting in the dark until she heard Gemma climbing the stairs. She'd set her alarm for three-thirty in the morning, but it didn't seem worth trying to sleep. In the end, she fired up her computer and logged into the virtual town she'd built when she was thirteen. She drove one last tour around the lives of its ninety-nine inhabitants before she terminated the programme and dismantled her computer. Each version of the basic character was the same: their appearance; their intellect; their hopes; their fears; their deepest, darkest secrets. And to each of these meticulously engineered clones, Hollow had gifted an individual life. A life unique. Some of the characters had flourished where others had turned to violence. Some had grown without changing, while some had fallen into a black depression. Some had even found a way to be happy beyond all circumstantial expectations. Regardless of their respective successes and failures, these beings of code were as close to family as Hollow could get. For one last night she stayed with them, watching over the inhabitants until the last of them had gone to bed. Her finger resting next to the delete button.

A few hours later, it was Tuesday. Hollow sat on the low brick wall outside her house. The taxi was late, not enough to miss the train but enough for her to feel anxious. The coach to army training camp would be waiting at Woking station and no one had said what would happen if she missed it. She stood up, hugging a black travel bag close to her body. New underwear and a spare set of civvies. Everything else was army issue from now on. Her choice of urban sportswear didn't do much to keep out the curling damp of an autumn morning, but it felt right and covered the army QRID temp-tattooed on her wrist. Hollow checked the time twice in the same minute. Her house was pitch dark. She'd said all her goodbyes last night. All there was to do was to sit on the wall and try not to worry about using the tube. Traffic on the motorway sounded like the sea. There was a scuttle of fallen leaves on tarmac. A muted siren. The taxi as it turned into the street. Everything else was silence; four-thirty in the morning was already too late for burglars or regrets.

A coach was parked outside Woking station. Hollow knew it was the right one because it came with a sergeant in number two dress uniform.

She didn't bother to look at Hollow. 'QRID.'

Hollow fumbled her bag, dragging at her jacket sleeve. It was tight on her wrist and her hand was stupidly clammy. 'Sorry, I have it, I have it.'

The sergeant looked down at her clipboard like every second was a second wasted. 'Name?'

'Quinn, Hollow Quinn.'

'On the coach, recruit.'

'Do you still need the QRID?'

Everyone at the drop-in centre – the recruitment officers, the careers officers, the soldiers she'd met at the briefing, at the fitness trials, all of them, every single one – had spoken to Hollow like they'd seen something in her no one else could see.

The sergeant looked through her like she was made of glass. 'Just get on the coach.'

The coach was almost full, and no one was talking much. Hollow picked the nearest available seat, keeping her movements contained, unbreachable. There was a young woman in the window seat, a curtain of blue-black hair and closed in on herself to hide her phone screen. She didn't look up.

The sergeant was last on, staring straight down the centre aisle. 'Every journey starts with a single step.' It was the sort of tag-line motivation that might have meant something if you'd read it in a brochure.

First impressions had a habit of rearranging the boundaries of normality. Everything about the military base was grey. Not the strong, reassuring grey of the drop-in centre, a greyer kind of grey, metal windows and concrete everything else. But as the coach pulled through the first checkpoint, it was the guns that rearranged Hollow's normality. People carrying guns around like it was something everyone did. She hadn't thought about carrying a gun.

The other recruits were restless, looking out of the windows as the sergeant stood up and walked the length of the coach, leaching silence like radiation. 'You do not speak. You do not stand. You do not move. You do not do anything unless I tell you to. Understood?'

A few of them mumbled an answer, limp with uncertainty.

'Recruits, I asked you a question.'

Voices from the back of the coach came in stronger this time, older and more used to the formalities of authority. 'Yes, Sergeant!'

'When I give you the order to disembark, you will leave the coach. You will form a line. You will march when you are told to march. You will stop when you are told to stop. Understood?'

This time, it was all of them. 'Yes, Sergeant!'

As soon as the sergeant turned away, the woman sat next to Hollow was back on her phone. With no apparent requirement to engage in light conversation, Hollow put her headphones in and closed her eyes. She'd found solace in the army programme for distance running and, as a sports psychology student, she knew why. But Henri hadn't said anything about learning how to march. When the sergeant gave the order, Hollow watched the others. Standing up with them. Hesitant with them. Holding her nerve with them. Waiting to get off the coach with them like they'd just reached their destination on a field trip to Auschwitz. The older recruits were pushing forward, already gravitating together, first off and first to decide where the line would be. The younger ones hung back, trying not to be the one who messed up. Hollow fitted herself in the middle of the line, on both teams but not right with either. She moved in time with the sergeant, quickly into the rhythm as they marched single file, away from the coach and across the parade ground to the square brick-built administration block. From there, they were checked in, passed on, sorted and regimented in the efficient, military sort of way that made a mass vaccination centre look badly organised. The government had only sanctioned a partial mobilisation of troops, and offered nothing but reassuring denial at the mention of conscription. For the general population, military service remained a voluntary choice, yet coach after coach arrived. Decanted. Left. In less than half an hour, five hundred new recruits had picked up their kitbags, received their welcome packs and been delivered to their respective accommodation blocks.

Hollow unzipped the black military-issue bag which contained her new kit. Full Dress. Service Dress. Utility. PT. Everything that wasn't military green was black. Folded and ironed like it came into the world that way. 'It's a bit more colour than I'm used to,' she said.

Fifteen minutes later, they were told to change into service dress and report to HB station. For Hollow and the rest of the new recruits, Hair & Beauty meant a standardised close crop, basic body hygiene and a talk on the perils of sexually transmitted diseases. At the admin station, they had their ID pictures taken and surrendered any potential contraband into the amnesty bins. Hollow dumped what was left of the tobacco and told the quartermaster she wanted to quit. From admin, they were directed to the medical station for eye tests, blood tests and vaccinations: hepatitis, polio, tetanus, multivirals. Day one in the army was station queues. When they were finally dismissed to the mess hall, Hollow was pulled out of line and told to report back to HB.

'What did we do wrong?' The young woman from the window seat slid up next to Hollow, dragging a guy with her. 'Did they tell you what we did wrong?'

'No,' Hollow said, walking a straight line, keeping a rhythm to the march she'd just learnt.

'Sake, I thought you'd know.' Without her waist-length hair, the woman's dark features had been exaggerated into the wide-eyed look of an anime illustration. 'We must have missed something, Joan.'

The guy leant in. He was shorter, stockier than his friend, fair skin and top heavy features like his nose was trying to beat his chin across the finish line of a four hundred-metre sprint. 'Did you get sent outside for chatting at the enrolment briefing?'

'No,' Hollow said.

'The Oath of Allegiance?'

'No,' Hollow said.

'Is it just us three?'

'I don't know anything.'

'So I'm Fish,' the young woman said, running to keep up with Hollow. 'And this is Joanie. It's his real name and everything.'

'After my grandma,' the guy said.

'Hollow.'

'That's a great name, mind,' Fish said, waiting on a story and getting nothing but a crick in her neck from trying to march and look at Hollow at the same time.

The fourth member of their group was already waiting at HB station. Gracelessly self-assured and wearing his uniform like he'd never grown out of pretending to be a soldier. Even in a group of teenagers, Hubert Frank looked painfully young. 'The Hubert got the look,' he said, nodding a leisurely circle around the strange disquiet of an emptied-out building.

From HB, they were marched to a small meeting room. There was a buffet laid out on a table by the wall and a smaller table with tea, coffee and cold drinks. The windows were closed and all the blinds down. Fish was tight with Joanie, whispering about hoping for nothing worse than a dressing-down about chatting at an enrolment briefing. Hubert Frank helped himself to a slice of pizza. And Hollow prepared herself to see the look of triumph not even hidden on Gemma's face when her daughter didn't make it past the first day. Five minutes later, they were joined by a stern-as-fuck army major and a tall middle-aged man carrying a bundle of electronic clipboards. Both were formidable characters in their own right, and both were entirely overshadowed by the unforgettable, unforgiving presence of *WØLF* field producer, Elspeth Hart.

Even on a normal day, it was a lot to process. Hollow kept her eyes fixed on the major, not looking at Elspeth Hart, hardly listening to the congratulations, holding the non-disclosure agreement, the terms and conditions, the fingerprint signature machine, like any minute now it would turn out to be an induction test or something.

'You must have a million questions.' Elspeth took off her glasses, sitting back into the relative comfort of a standard-issue folding metal chair. 'Fire away.'

'Is this shit for real?'

'Yes.' Elspeth shared a smile with the major but didn't get a return on her investment. 'Yes, Zaafirah, this shit is for real.'

'It's Fish,' Fish said, automatically. 'So are people leaving WØLF?'

The middle-aged man leant forward. 'As the Plug Productions legal representative, I will remind you that anything you hear in this room is completely confidential. The non-disclosure agreement you have just signed prevents you from discussing anything beyond this room, regardless of whether you decide to proceed or not. Any breach of the NDA, no matter how trivial you might consider it to be, will result in a criminal prosecution. Don't think this won't apply to you.'

'Thank you, Kier,' Elspeth said, tapping the arm of her glasses on a deep scar that ran the length of her cheek and burrowed into her lip. The unconscious gesture might have been an admission to lost vanity, but nothing Elspeth Hart did was unconscious. She sat forward, her moon-dark eyes taking them in, each one in turn, each one like there was no one else in the room. Finally, she sat back. 'To answer your question, Fish, we're filming army personnel in an active war zone. If a soldier is critically injured, or even killed, the way the squad is currently set up, it can't operate to full capacity. That puts all of us in danger. We have subsequently decided to increase the size of the squad to twelve, with one unit continually cycling in reserve. That way, we always have three people resting.' Elspeth flicked a look to the major. 'Do you have anything you'd like to add at this point, Major Hyde?'

'Not at this stage.'

'Contrary to popular opinion, the existing WØLF cast weren't chosen because they had a particular kind of look,' Elspeth said. 'As a production team, we wait for new recruits to go through the usual army procedures. Buzz cut. Identical uniforms. No makeup. No money-generated style. No cross-platform commentary. The army dismantles all culture concepts the day you arrive at boot camp, and we have a look at what's left. Each one of you has a natural uniqueness. Something that separates you from the standardised product.'

Major Hyde had spent many years waiting to be told that he'd been promoted to major, and subsequently sat in any chair like he was about to receive the news. He straightened the banded service cap tucked under his arm. 'Congratulations.'

'It's normal to feel a bit overwhelmed,' Elspeth said. 'You might experience some anxiety or emotional shutdown. You might even be exploding with excitement. These are unreliable emotions and until this initial reaction has settled down you can't make an informed decision. We also have a duty to make sure you understand exactly what you're signing up for.' Elspeth turned to the production company's legal representative. 'Over to you, Kier.'

'Moving forward from today,' Kier said, 'by signing the Plug Productions indenture, you'll be agreeing to hand over ownership of your image, your voice and your actions for the duration of your contract. All material, seen and unseen, remains the property of Plug Productions. This includes all forms of intellectual property. Plug Productions retain all rights to creative editing and stylistic composition for filming purposes. Electronic film production technology may be upgraded at any time without prior notification. We reserve the right to use fixed rig and concealed equipment without mapping its location. We reserve the right to use wireless mic packs that you can't switch off. Some scenes may be uncomfortable. Some in-the-moment commentaries will involve questions created to evoke a response. Plug Productions may broadcast material pertaining to your personal and private life, including, but not limited to, material which could be perceived as sensitive or detrimental to your life beyond WØLF. This is a non-negotiable agreement as stated on your contract.'

'And that's the hardest part,' Elspeth said. 'For all of us, crew included. But it's also the nature of reality television. If you're likely to struggle with legal bindings and personal freedom, it's best to walk away now.'

'Non-negotiable.' The Plug Productions legal representative had the unwavering look of someone who could never be taken seriously enough. 'Speak to the legal department before you speak to anyone else.'

'You have been warned,' Elspeth Hart said. 'Which brings us to the point in today's selection process where we give you some time to yourselves. Grab something to eat, read through the terms and conditions and get to know each other. If you choose to proceed to the next stage, your life will change in unimaginable ways. It's important that you talk about what this will mean for you, your families and your life beyond the war. Be unapologetically honest, with each other and with yourselves. This business will tear you apart if you can't stand in the truth of who you are.'

'Not to the degree of an IED,' the major said.

'No,' Elspeth said. 'So that's something to remember.'

'On a practical note,' Kier said, 'we'll have to ask you not to leave this room other than for an emergency. If you need a bathroom break, there's a studio runner outside the door who can escort you. Do not discuss WØLF with this runner. Do not discuss WØLF with anyone outside of this room. If you encounter any enquiries relating to your whereabouts today, refer those enquiries straight to Major Hyde.'

'Any questions at this point?' Elspeth said.

Hubert Frank flicked a nod towards Elspeth. 'You ever think of getting plastic surgery?'

'I was rather hoping for questions relating to this introductory meeting,' Elspeth said. 'But seeing as you ask, Hubert, the answer is no. A closed answer to a closed question. For future reference, investigate the art of asking open questions.' Elspeth Hart looked at each of them again, longer this time, and seriously enough to feel like she was genuinely invested in holding their interests above her own. 'Don't worry about getting this wrong or making a mess of things. Speaking as someone who's worked on the show since the beginning, there's a heart-warming honesty that only comes from people who think they're making a mess of everything. I know you're all more than capable of doing this, but what I don't know is whether you have the capacity to handle the pressure. Only you know the answer to that. There's no shame if you decide WØLF isn't for you. In your favour, you'll be second-generation WØLF, so you'll have the advantage of knowing the format. You'll also be working within an established team, which has its pros and cons, as you can imagine.'

Major Hyde stood up. 'As the allocated representative of the military services, I would like to add that when you took your Oath of Allegiance, you signed a contract with the army. You are recruits in Phase One of your military training. That contract has not changed. Do not imagine that you can escape your duty to the army just because you are appearing on television.'

'Major Hyde is right,' Elspeth said. 'You may have wireless mic packs and a couple of camera crews following you around, but the army won't be treating you any differently. The reason you're sat in this room is because you enlisted to serve your country, and *only* because you enlisted to serve your country. As much as WØLF is breaking new ground, in many ways it's just like any other reality show. That means the more you can forget you're on camera, the better it is across the board. Who you are right now is who we want. Don't play to the gallery. Don't try to be more interesting, or instigate drama just for the sake of it. Above all, don't aspire to be some perfect version of yourself. It's no slur on your character if you can't show your real face to the world. And remember, this room is a safe environment protected by legal enforcement, so don't hold back.' Elspeth stood up, close to the major but not companions. 'Excellent, well, we'll give you guys some space. This introduction might feel a little negative heavy, but Plug Productions insist we highlight the most challenging parts of this role from the start. Mostly, it's a whole lot of fun. And as a life experience, there's nothing quite like it. See you in two hours.'

Major Hyde put his service cap back on, tapping the doorframe as he left. '*Bello te Prepares*,' he said, without any explanation or indeed context, if it was needed.

It was surreal. Four random people, not altogether up to speed with what was happening, half feeling like they were on camera already.

'So, first things first.' Fish dumped a pile of pasta on her plate and handed the spoon to Hollow. 'You all need to forget you heard Zaafirah. My name is Fish. Everyone calls me Fish. Except the government and the old guy who lives next door, but he's got type three diabetes, so everyone is his daughter Peg, except his actual daughter Peg. Fingers crossed I can convince the army.' Fish nudged Joanie. 'Joanie's my stand-in brother. We're beyond relief that we both got picked for *WØLF* because we'd have broken the non-disclosure agreement already. Can you believe this pumpkin ravioli?'

'Belief,' Hubert Frank said, striking a pose with his hands.

'It's like my brain can't catch up,' Fish said, peering into a bowl of dipping sauce. 'This morning, we're staring at our bedroom ceilings, wondering if we should eat breakfast before we get the train. Next minute, we have no hair and we're getting picked out for *WØLF*. Did I mention I'm obsessed with this pumpkin ravioli?'

'We the soldier,' Hubert Frank said, to his own applause. 'Enemy of the enemy, ain't no screen mission no more, this is war.'

'It's probably a test,' Joanie said. 'The whole intake has been split into groups of four and think they're on *WØLF*.'

'Could be, could be,' Fish said. 'That's a lot of recruits for Elspeth Hart to get around, mind.'

'Not for CGI reality.'

'Makes sense why I feel a bit sick,' Fish said, eating mustard straight from the spoon. 'We're still on the bus with tubes keeping us alive.'

'Where are you from then, Hollow?' Joanie said.

'London.'

'Which part of London?'

'Chelsea.'

'Posh, though,' Joanie said. 'I'd have thought you'd be heading straight to officer camp.'

Hollow shrugged, not sure why she'd lied to him and already in too deep to back out. 'The academy route might be easier, but this way feels more authentic.'

'That's pretty decent,' Joanie said.

Fish shot a laugh like she knew it was a lie, but she didn't say anything.

'I've actually been to Chelsea,' Joanie said. 'To the Flower Show at least. My dad won tickets in a Christmas raffle. We got there four hours early, and it was a bit awkward when we accidentally went into the press area. Dad said I could choose a garden and he'd try to reproduce it in knotted embroidery.'

'How's your dad doing?' Fish said.

'Oh, he's good. He got the Traffic Interceptor promotion.'

'Sweet,' Fish said. 'What about your mum, how's she holding up?'

'Variable,' Joanie said. 'On the positive, she's talking a lot more with Dad lately. And you saw them at the station this morning. They even held hands for a bit.'

'Wait.' Fish gripped a look on him. 'Please tell me that's not why you enlisted.'

'Not all of it.'

Fish shoved her plate onto the buffet table. 'Sake, Joan.'

Joanie nodded to an army training schedule stuck on the wall above the buffet. 'Clear, defiant and in exact alignment with the light switch – Major Hyde probably slipped that in to remind us of what we're back to once Elspeth Hart has gone.'

Hollow waited on the others, but she was the only reply provider available. 'Probably.'

'Why do you think everything is still hard copy in the army?' Joanie said. 'I figure it's to do with an IOT failure. Even if we lose all our internet-based technology in an attack, at least we still know what's happening tomorrow.'

'An attack?' Hollow said. 'On the IOT?'

'The world would literally crash without the Internet of Things.' Joanie shooed a fly away. 'They'd have to wheel out all the old people who still know how to do things without a phone.'

'Shit, if we lost the IOT, we'd be washing our hair in the river and reading each other books for entertainment.' Hollow shook her head. 'It'd never happen. There's too many safeguards.'

Joanie leant in, all casually casual. 'I can't tell you something.'

'About WØLF?'

'No.'

'What then?'

'I told you.'

Hollow rubbed her shaved head. 'I don't think you did.'

'I told you I can't tell you something.'

'What the fiddly-fuck are you talking about?'

Fish shoved her plate again. 'You said you wanted to enlist because of the war, Joan.'

'It was because of the war.' Joanie pushed Fish's plate back in front of her. 'Mostly because of the war.'

'Mostly!'

Joanie just shrugged. 'So, Hollow, how do you think your family will deal with all this?'

'Yeah, good. They're okay if I'm okay.'

Hubert Frank barged a space next to Fish. 'You Afghan, then?'

'I'm from Bristol,' Fish snapped, trying to tuck her hair behind her ears and finding nothing but buzzcut stubble. 'Where are you from, Nazi Germany?'

'Chill, bru. It's all blood under the skin.'

Joanie drew an arc around the room with a fork. 'Personally, I'm not that bothered about being a TV star. But the moment we got on the coach at Woking, it felt like we belonged to someone else. Like we went from being people to being a commodity. If it's a choice between belonging to WØLF or belonging to the army, I say it might as well be WØLF. Not even mentioning the fact that we get to work with Sylvie Stevens. I mean, Sylvie Stevens. I'll probably pass out, but that's good TV, right?'

Hubert Frank nodded along. 'We always a commodity, bru.'

'And they'll at least try to keep us safe,' Joanie said. 'What with us having the natural uniqueness and everything.'

'I can't believe you, Joan.' Fish crossed her arms. 'You lied to me. For the first time in your bloody life, you lied to me.'

'I'd never lie to you.'

'Too late.'

'It *was* because of the war.' Joanie waited on the noise of an armoured tractor to trundle past the window. 'All the stuff with fixing my parents, it was just a stupid side quest, that's all. I didn't think it was important.'

'Sorry, you'll have to speak up. I can't hear you above the military vehicle,' Fish said, and sassy with it. 'Because we fucking enlisted in the fucking army.'

'Yes, we enlisted,' Joanie said, 'but you can't tell me there's not one little part of you that relishes the opportunity to work through some refugee guilt.'

'Refugee guilt!' Fish kicked the leg of the table, glaring switchblades at Joanie. 'You think I'm here for outsource therapy?'

Joanie went back to looking at the schedule. 'Attestation, what the hell is an attestation?'

'It's a formal ceremony to join the British army,' Hollow said.

'I thought we did that already.'

'That was the Oath of Allegiance.'

'Do you reckon they'll be filming us tomorrow?' Joanie said. 'I mean, at least we have morning drill followed by an exercise icebreaker. Can you imagine if it was today? The whole world watching us queuing, and not even a royal coffin at the end of it.'

Fish was still glaring at him. 'Is that all you have to say?'

'Seems like it.'

'Fine, that's the last time I take you to the Balloon Fiesta.' Fish stomped a wide circle back to the buffet table. 'My head is cold, and touching it weirds me out.'

'My uniform feels like I got a cheap duvet,' Joanie said.

'Just because I'm beyond stoked about being scouted by WØLF, doesn't mean I'm not beyond annoyed with you, Joan. I'm fit to storm off like a drama, but they told us we can't leave the room.'

'You could storm off to the toilets,' Joanie said. 'Establish what degree of privacy being accompanied by a studio runner entails.'

Fish looked around the room. 'Come with me then.'

'Okay.'

'And you.' Fish shoved a finger at Hubert Frank. 'Hollow and you, The Hubert, don't start talking about anything till we get back, mind. And hands off the pumpkin ravioli.'

'I can't tell them something,' Joanie said into her shoulder.

'I know, babe.'

Hubert Frank watched Fish and Joanie leave, nodding an acknowledgment to Hollow. 'What you gaming, bru?'

'I don't play computer games,' Hollow said.

From there, there was little-to-no likelihood of Hollow Quinn and Hubert Frank talking about anything, or indeed eating any pumpkin ravioli. They sat at opposite sides of the seating area and ate in silence. Everything in the whole world had changed. It was still Tuesday.

8

There can't be two people with that name

Jeep headlights threw a fake sunrise around the bunkhouse, but the night was already softening into a new day. Hollow held the white feather between her fingers, turning it until it glowed with artificial light. A few times in the night she'd heard Fish asking if she was awake, but it was just another noise in a room full of noise and Hollow didn't answer. All four of them had mulched around the reasons not to join *WØLF*, and not one of them with any intention of turning it down. By eight o'clock that same night, base personnel had been informed that fixed rig cameras were being installed and filming would commence the following afternoon. There was only one instruction: *WØLF* is not here. Too basic an instruction perhaps, but the army wasn't one for icing the cake. Subsequently, when the four of them had rocked up at the mess hall for supper, the base personnel just carried on like they were every other scared kid one day into army training. As contracted personnel of Plug Productions, they'd been given their own dedicated bunkhouse, but they'd watched *WØLF* long enough to know it wasn't a fame thing. Elspeth Hart had talked them through filming procedure and taught them the best way to avoid looking at the cameras. She'd advised them on how to interact with other troops and how to act like they weren't being filmed. Mostly she'd talked about what to expect and what not to expect. The legal representative had painstakingly taken them through an interim contract that was comprehensive, legally binding and utterly immaterial. It might as well have been a tick box; if they wanted to be on the show, all they could do was agree.

Fittingly, it had been Major Hyde who'd snagged the last word. '*Bello te Prepares*: prepare yourself for war. This is the motto of all British army training centres. Put aside aspirations of fame or fortune. Concentrate on what you came here to do. Become the best soldier you can be. And prepare yourself for war.'

Hollow lay with her eyes closed and thought about how she'd left her house keys in the little blue bowl by the front door.

'What day even is it?' Joanie asked fifteen minutes later, stretching out the ravenous urge to talk about *WØLF*.

'Today,' Hollow said. Two nights without sleep and she should have been dead on her feet. Instead, she was just dead. More specifically, Hollow Quinn was dead. This wasn't her life any more; it was a cinema afterlife, a life that belonged to a production company. So she got up. Washed in the communal bathroom. Put on her uniform. Tied her bootlaces, tidied her bunk and waited to be told what to do along with every other new recruit on the base.

The parade ground was square and still damp from overnight rain. The drill sergeant stood them in lines, facing away from the sun. 'Phase One of initial training will teach you how the army works. You will improve your health and fitness levels, you will learn individual skills and you will learn team skills. You will learn survival and fieldcraft skills, you will learn first aid, and you will learn how to use a rifle. Above all these things, you will learn what it means to be a soldier. And being a soldier always starts with drill.' The drill sergeant paused in front of the four new *WØLF* recruits, adjusting Fish's collar to make a perfect V in the centre. 'I suppose you may be asking yourself why we are standing here, wasting our time with drill when we have an enemy to fight. And I will tell you why so you get it fixed in your head right from the start, because if you do not understand this, everything else is a waste of your time.' Each clipped word, each clipped step, was measured, calculated, controlled. Taking in the length of them, their uniforms, their posture, their breathing. Holding the anticipation of an answer just long enough to make them want it more than resist it. 'Drill is the single most important thing you will learn in the army. Drill turns a squad of individuals into a single unit. And you might be the smartest recruit we have ever had here, but smart means nothing on the battlefield. In the ten seconds it takes your smart brain to figure out the best thing to do, you are already dead. Drill does not need thinking. Drill just does. That is why drill will save your life. And if you are still doubting me, remember that drill is as old as the army, and the army is as efficient as a machine can get. If drill did not work, drill would not be in the army. You learn drill because drill works. And before you learn drill, you learn how to Stand at Ease. And before you learn to Stand at Ease, you learn to Stand to Attention.' The drill sergeant mimicked the movement of each word as it was said, like it was too deep in the muscle memory to stop it.

Joanie was the first one called forward.

'When you hear the command Attention, you fix both feet flat and firm on the ground. Heels in line and touching. Knees braced. Arms straight, held tight to the body. Forearms behind the hip bones.' The drill sergeant moved Joanie's arms back a little. 'Fingers touching just behind the seam of the trouser. Wrists straight. Hands closed. Thumbs vertical and facing front. Shoulders down and back. Head up. Neck touching the back of the collar. Eyes open, looking just above your own height. Chin raised. Mouth closed. This is the correct position for Attention.'

Joanie stood there, keeping it all in like he'd won a medal and swallowed it, not even needing a camera to feel like a superstar as he chanced a look at Fish and rejoined the line. But Fish had her eyes fixed on the drill sergeant. They all did. *WØLF* didn't matter much in the big picture.

'I will now ask for questions,' the drill sergeant said. 'This will be followed by a practice run-through. When I am happy that you all know how to stand in the correct way, I will call you to Attention. A strong chain depends on every single link. Do not consider yourself above needing correction. Do not consider yourself better for not needing correction. You are the squad; the squad is you. If you cannot willingly stand with every single one of your colleagues, regardless of their rank or ability, then do not take the Attestation Oath this afternoon, because you do not belong in the army. Is that understood?'

'Yes, Sergeant!'

The drill sergeant waited without speaking for longer than it took to process the words. 'As this is your first time standing to Attention, you can expect it to feel awkward, but within a few days this command will become so second nature, you will even do it in your sleep.'

Once they'd mastered Attention, they moved to Stand at Ease. Each step of the position was demonstrated and explained, right down to the finest detail. Not even their breath was left to guesswork. Then they moved to transitioning between the two, collectively, individually, over and over until there were no mistakes.

'This is the end of the lesson for this morning,' the drill sergeant said. 'You now know the positions for Attention and Stand at Ease. Next you will learn the first dressing movement. I am happy with what I've seen today. Keep this standard up and you will do well here.'

No one looked around. No one smiled. They stared straight ahead, necks touching the back of their collars. Looking just above their own height. Chins raised. Mouths closed. Part of something old and sacred, and big enough to take care of them all.

'Squad, Atten—tion! This is your standard position as a soldier. From now on, you will Stand to Attention in the presence of an officer unless you are told otherwise. At the end of each lesson, I will call you to Stand at Ease, and you will return the call, One Stop. Understood?'

'Yes, Sergeant!'

'Squad, Stand at—Ease.'

'ONE STOP.'

The drill sergeant span on one heel, marching away across the parade ground like everything that had needed to be said was said.

SMART SLATE

Whiskey-Zero-One-Foxtrot/s3e2/REMI IP link PP confirm: EFP rig/crew
Producer: *Elspeth Hart*
EXT/INT. GBR. BOOT CAMP – DAY

Scene: New *WØLF* recruits intro. *Fish Nazari, Hubert Frank, Joanie Magrath* and *Hollow Quinn* are on the sports field when Hollow attacks a physical training instructor. Fixed rig and crew cameras stay with Hollow as she's marched to the punishment block by the Provost Staff – continuous

Punishment was a square room, no bigger than a Portsmouth lounge with all the furniture ripped out and painted the colour of nothing.

'Hand on the back wall. Floor. Front wall. Back wall. Floor. Ceiling.' Provost Staff took up the space like no one else had a right to it. 'Floor. Back wall. Left wall. Faster. Right wall. Ceiling. Hand on the ceiling. Front wall.'

The bleep got closer as Hollow got further away, arcs that crossed like swords, and there was only ever one winner. Provost Staff didn't have a name, just a pace stick and a black peaked cap pulled below the eyes. But they could still see Hollow, in all the places she was weakest.

'Faster. Back wall. Front wall. Floor. Floor. Faster. Ceiling. Right wall. Ceiling. Right wall.'

ITM SCENE
COMMENTARY
FISH NAZARI:
We'd just done our first drill on how to stand in the two basic positions. It was only an hour, but we were so high on adrenalin, we didn't need any pumping up for the exercise icebreaker. And I'm not lying, Hollow was buzzing just like we all were, I mean, as much as Hollow can. We're just heading out to the sports ground when we come face to face with the physical training instructor. Next minute, Hollow's being dragged off to the punishment block.

PRODUCER:
What happened?

FISH NAZARI:
I don't even know. The PTI didn't do anything, he didn't speak or anything. I was there and I don't know what happened. Like I said, we were buzzing. Maybe he looked at her the wrong way or something.

JOANIE MAGRATH:
It all happened so quickly, it was a bit of a shock, to be honest. They had to drag her to the reprimand block. It was all a bit of a shock.

PRODUCER:
Hollow attacked the PTI, Joanie.

JOANIE MAGRATH:
She must have had a good reason. You don't just attack people for no reason.

HUBERT FRANK:
We the living dread generation, all one alongside ourselves.

Provost Staff leant in, too close to Hollow's face. The audience watching at home didn't need to be there to smell the sour milk and warm tea. 'Get your hand on the fucking ceiling, Quinn, before I snap it off and wipe my arse with it.'

Hollow was fitter than she'd ever been in her life, but there'd been too many nights without sleep and her body was burning dry. 'I can't.'

'Jump!'

'I can't.'

'JUMP!'

'I CAN'T!'

All the time, the bleep just kept on coming. And Provost Staff, watching from the eyeless dark of the black peaked cap as Hollow struggled to stand. To breathe. 'Have I broken you?'

'No.'

Provost Staff leant in again, taking their time with it. 'No, I don't believe I have.'

ITM SCENE
COMMENTARY
HOLLOW QUINN:
Yesterday felt like a school trip, like we had a packed lunch and a coach home after. Today, we're every person who's woken up into the reality of a decision they made.

And you were right, Elspeth, when you said that we'd been standardised. They don't even give us separate shower blocks or changing areas in the bunkhouses. You'd think it'd be embarrassing, except we all just get on with it. Embarrassment is irrelevant now. Gender is irrelevant, alignment is irrelevant, shame is irrelevant, body con is irrelevant.

You also said *WØLF* wants people who are naturally unique, which is ironic, because anything unique is obviously irrelevant in the army.

PRODUCER:
What happened with the PTI, Hollow?

HOLLOW QUINN:
I didn't get much sleep lately. There's a lot to think about, and my mind won't switch off. You know like when you're boss-level crabby, and it's so bad you're not even noticing it. I was a spark away from catching fire all morning. The PTI was just in the wrong place at the wrong time, that's all.

PRODUCER:
Do you think it's important to challenge authority?

HOLLOW QUINN:
I mean, sure. But not the army's kind of authority. There's only right or wrong here. If it looks good, it is good. If it doesn't look good, it gets ripped out and started again. There's no angsty grey areas, no should I, shouldn't I decisions to make. You know where you stand with that.

From what I can see, being in the army is easier than not being in the army.

PRODUCER:
That's the first time I've heard anyone describe the punishment block as easy.

HOLLOW QUINN:
I don't mean that sort of easy, I mean like…it's harder, when you don't know where the lines are. But the army is standard issue. Everything has a rule. Everything has a place. If it can be ironed, it's ironed three times. Every single part of life is folded, numbered and arranged in size order. Every moment from when you wake up in the morning to when you go to bed at night is scheduled. There's no I in army, Elspeth, even the I in khaki is an E.

It's easy to colour inside the lines here…that's what I meant.

PROVOST STAFF:
Conversely, there is a ME in army. And that's what needs dismantling on occasion.

PRODUCER:
Is that why you tried to break Hollow?

PROVOST STAFF:
That kid was broken long before she came to the army.

'Ezra!' Sheila Blake hammered a pummelling on the bedroom door. 'Ezra, you have to come and see this, you have to come quick.'
    'Not right now, Mum.'

'Quick.'

Ezra flicked back to the microphone. 'Sorry, guys. Mum in distress. Carry on playing without me.'

Sheila hammered again. 'Now!'

'Yes, I'm coming.'

'It's Hollow,' Sheila was already halfway back downstairs, 'Hollow is on *WØLF*.'

'No way!' Ezra scrabbled then, catching a knee on the banisters and not even stopping to feel the pain of it. 'It's too early, did they change the time?'

'It's a trailer,' Tulip Blake called from the front room. 'She's on tonight's show.'

Ezra skidded through the door. 'Pause it, wait for me.'

'I'm already recording it, kiddo.'

'A lot of the background soldiers look the same,' Ezra said. 'Are you sure it's her?'

'She's not a background soldier.' Sheila grabbed a cushion, budging Tulip over so Ezra could sit between them. 'She's on *WØLF*.'

'Like an interview?'

'Like part of the squad,' Tulip said. 'The production team have selected four new recruits to join the existing cast. Hollow is one of them.'

'Shut up!'

'They just announced it, just now.' Sheila took hold of Ezra's hand. 'She looks different, sweetheart, but it's her. And they called her Hollow. There can't be two people with that name.'

'No...' Ezra sat like a slow-motion demolition '...maybe.'

On the screen, the trailer flickered in a crescendo of images: Mika Kamari dragging Mattoo Bolte from a flaming truck. Caster Dupont staring down the stone-chipped barrel of an assault rifle. Stan Dobresnski crouched against a container unit, clutching an accordion like it was all he had left in the world. Sylvie Stevens holding the hands of a smoke-blackened woman, coaxing her away from the tiny bodies no mother could bear to leave behind.

And Hollow Quinn, struggling to stand, struggling to breathe as Provost Staff leant over her. 'Have I broken you?'

'That's her!' Sheila yelled, jabbing at the screen. 'That's Hollow.'

'They sent her to Afghanistan!'

'No, no, it's boot camp,' Tulip said. 'We still watch what's happening with the existing cast in Afghanistan, but we also get to see the new *WØLF* recruits as they go through their Phase One basic training here in the UK. I must admit, it'll be interesting to watch their transition from civilians to soldiers in a time of war.'

Sheila shot her a look. 'It'll be nice to know how Hollow's doing.'

'Mum's right, kiddo.' Tulip wriggled an arm behind Ezra. 'At least this way you get to keep watch over your friend. Despite everything that's going on in this dreadful world, you get to keep watch over your friend.'

9

This isn't the petrol station

M ac Eden peered through the yew trees, nothing more than a scarecrow of shadow and moonlight in the ancient forest. This prey was old, confused, struggling to keep her balance on the filleted network of tree roots. For a seasoned killer like Mac, it was a wretched, defenceless thing to witness, and she didn't even blink as the moon faded and rain fell heavy on her eyelashes. More by fate than any human reason, the old woman had stumbled on the only serviceable trail out of the tangled trees. She'd lost one of her slippers; there were twigs in her hair; she was flinching around like a startled pheasant. Pity would spare her from this night of predators, but there was no pity now. There was only moonlight and monsters.

Keeping her eyes fixed on the target, Mac tucked the missing slipper into her belt. The stink of it clung to her like a kitten, crawling her flesh through two layers of utility workwear and a sensible vest. With the next swell of wind, Mac slid between the flaking branches and tried not to breathe through her nose. All she could do now was wait out the numerous agonies of impatience as the rain slowed to a tuneless melody and the old woman tottered away from the squirming dark of the yew wood.

Effie Cox raked her hair into an untidy clump, tucking it behind her ears as she walked. Always keeping to the chalk trail, always keeping the trees behind her. Along the ancient pathways, granite bones cut the throat of the sky. A chalk embankment marked the first boundary between the woodland and the Neolithic hillfort. Effie buttoned her pink dressing gown through the wrong holes, catching the final fragments of rain on her oversized glasses as she looked up at the steep incline, breathing like she was at Everest base camp and there wasn't even a queue.

A courageous ten minutes' worth of climb-slip-stagger later, and Effie was a victim profile in the lunar spotlight. Breathing harder now. Hands to her mouth. Playing the part. 'Oh dear,' she said, 'this isn't the petrol station.'

Clouds owned the horizon. Moonlight would last a few more minutes at most. Effie made a show of elderly fidgeting, wrestling a hand under the frilly hem of her nightdress on the pretence of scratching a rash. Torches were barred from the side character field kit, but the bejewelled penlight had made it through on a trinket technicality. Effie chanced another look around, groaning with her knees as she propped the penlight against her foot. A nightingale was singing in the downland pastures, and she let her fingers linger on the chalk and brittle earth. She knew it was coming for her: the scent of summer rain on tarmac, a memory of feathers on her skin. Effie closed her eyes and thought about crochet as the last beaded moment of moonlight ran dry.

Darkness took her like a cloak. Silent as an owl to a mouse. A child's hand in her hand. 'Are we lost, Granny?'

'Damn,' Effie said. There were rules to the game, but they came with the player. And the Mandolin always used your own rules against you.

'I'm scared, Granny.'

'You just hold on tight now.' Effie squeezed his hand. 'Granny's friend will make it quick.'

'Will it hurt, Granny?'

'No, bairn, not if she does it right.'

A netting trap always came before the sound of it, but the high-frequency, teeth-clenching shriek was never the worst part. Neither was the uplift of black dust that consumed everything within a two-metre radius of the net. And it wasn't the metallic taste of iron, or the nausea, or even the cold efficiency of a traffic light system that told Effie when the trap had successfully neutralised its contents. It wasn't any of that. Effie rolled backwards into an awkward crouch, choking for air as the writhing, wailing creature fell away from her. There wasn't much to see in a netting, but the screams could tear your whole heart out if you paid them a mind.

'Granny's friend?' Mac disarmed the netgun, swivelling the pistol head so she could scan the barcode on the trap. 'That's a first.'

Effie coughed, pulling a tissue out of her pocket. 'Grandson.'

'Don't let it mean anything,' Mac said. 'Bastards mimic whoever they figure will hurt us the most.'

Effie coughed again, spitting the blackened layers of a micro-dust filter into the tissue. 'I love that wee bairn more than life itself.'

'These young ones are entry-level extremists.' Mac shoved the netgun into a bag-for-life, not even ashamed of the irony. 'They ain't interested in improving their ranking; all they want is a haunting legacy. Don't let it mean anything.'

Effie straightened up, dusting off her nightdress and several decades' worth of old woman. 'Who'd you see?'

'Woah!' Mac rounded on her. 'You know we never ask each other that question.'

'Aye, and maybe we should ask it.'

'And maybe you should shut up before you say something I'll regret having to listen to.' Mac grimaced, rubbing at her shoulder. 'I ain't kidding about that. I'm supposed to be at work right now.'

'In the middle of the night?'

'Not down to my choice.' Mac rubbed her shoulder again. 'Fabian Evirate House added me to the nightshift cleaning rota, on account of a level-two spillage from the second-floor balcony.'

'The semi-mortal clock again?'

'Ain't it always,' Mac said.

'There's some twiddly plasterwork below that balcony, mind.' Effie took a deep breath, nodding to the slipper tucked in Mac's waistband. 'I see you found it, then.'

'Fucking thing stinks so bad I found it before I got there.'

'My old mam swore by the mature slipper.'

'Better than seaweed for hiding your scent in.' Mac looked at her watch. 'I could've stalked a pack of police sniffer dogs while I was at it.'

'Aye.' Effie drew a line in the black dust with her big toe. 'Poor wee bairn was scared.'

'Result.' Mac fake-punched Effie's arm, dropping back when she saw the look on her colleague's face. 'Too close to see. Too simple to understand. Too familiar to remember. Just like you're always telling me.'

'Except we do see and we do understand.' Effie straightened a faded cord tied around her wrist. 'And we do remember.'

'No, we don't,' Mac said. 'That's the playground rules out here.'

Effie was still looking at the faded cord. 'The day he was born, I vowed I'd never see any harm come to him.'

'Did I mention I have to be back at work?'

'You best be off then.' Effie said the words but her body didn't agree with them. The trap was still now, a chainmail of blackened metal illuminated in the manuscript of torchlight. 'He was wearing that stripy bobble hat I knitted for his third birthday.'

Mac frowned. 'Effie?'

'Gaaagh.' Effie snapped away, kicking the netting trap down the slope. 'Eight months, and nothing but celebrities to show for it.'

'HEY!' Mac yelled, scrabbling backwards. 'Go fucking careful with that.'

'Stop your fretting. It's already burned down to ash.'

'Even a single drop of Mandolin blood is a risk up here,' Mac said, as solid as she could muster. 'The distress flare goes off in an untouched place like this and nobody's gonna be talking about Afghanistan. You know that, Effie Cox.'

'Aye…' Effie said '…I suppose I do.'

'We can't get complacent with their blood, not never.' Mac pulled the slipper out with her fingertips, plopping it on the ground like a full stop. 'And you can put that back on before it breeds with a rat or something.'

'It'd be a rabbit up here,' Effie said, staring down at the slipper.

'It's the pink dressing gown, mate,' Mac said. 'We wouldn't be having this conversation if you was in a floral tabard.'

Effie looked up at Mac, all wide eyes and slightly unnerving. 'What if it's too late, lass?'

'They're just popular in gritty crime fiction right now,' Mac said. 'Give it a year or so and the tabard will be back on the side character camouflage list.'

'I'm not talking about tabards.' Effie was pacing again, but the ramparts of Haifengate were weatherworn and treacherous with age. She caught her foot in a ragged hole and stumbled forward, grabbing Mac's arm to stop herself from falling. 'Eight months and the war isn't won. They didn't get bored, Mac. The Mandolin players didn't get bored.'

Mac might have been a long way from decent, but she wasn't insensitive to a sister in distress. She took hold of Effie's clenched hand, slow, careful with it. 'You remember why your old mam swore by the slipper?'

Effie looked down at her hand, trying to focus. 'There's nowt between a nose and an angled mirror.'

'She was no fool, your mam. Took me a while to figure it out…' Mac cleared her throat. 'You can't fool a nose with visual trickery. Smell is smart beyond anything the other senses have got, and right now I can smell a stale gloom on you, even above all the piss and rot. Why don't you head off back to my car, there's a blanket on the back seat big enough to comfort a blue whale. I'll finish up here. We can have a proper chat when I'm done.'

'A blanket?' Effie growled, drawing up close to Mac. 'You think I need a comfort blanket?'

'Entry level players take the game to religion level.' Mac dropped her hold on Effie's hand. 'And this was a real mean one. You need to step away, Effie.'

'Feck off.'

'Damn sure you're burning through my recently acquired score of ninety-five per cent for the Co-workers and Empathy Online Training Module,' Mac said. 'Took me seven attempts and a website crash before Dave hopped in.'

Effie wrinkled her nose. 'What'd he drop the five per cent on?'

'Counter-Sympathy and the Appropriate Use of Tissues.'

'Aye, well, that's not really Dave's fault.' Effie finally stepped away, sliding her foot into the soggy slipper. 'The whole of that section was badly worded.'

'You're telling me. Dave struggled to keep it professional when that question came up on different types of four-ply.'

'Everything's changing, Mac, and we have to change with it or we'd just as well go away with the dinosaurs.'

'They had a stonking great meteor land on them. Change don't always make room for survival.' Mac sighed then, long and hard. But her breath was just another loss to the desolate landscape. 'There's change coming, but nothing changes. Remember who told me that?'

'Aye, and maybe I was wrong.'

'This ain't like you, Effie.' Mac looked into her eyes, searching her out. 'You sure you're alone in there?'

'Stop giving me the look. You'd rather see a psych-jacking than listen to the truth.'

'I'd rather see your ozone exposure.'

Effie snatched a string of plastic beads from under the collar of her nightdress. If they'd come with a paper crown and a joke, they'd have looked classier. She shoved them at Mac. 'Red. Minimal. Happy?'

Mac took a steadying breath and thought about having to resubmit the Co-workers and Empathy Online Training Module. 'This ain't about me being happy, mate.'

But Effie was looking at the faded cord again. 'He was so scared...'

'As it was,' Mac drew herself up to her full height, 'and is.'

Effie snapped to Attention. Heels in line and touching. Knees braced. Arms straight, held tight to the body. Forearms behind the hip bones. Fingers touching just behind the side seam of her dressing gown. Wrists straight. Hands closed. Thumbs vertical and facing front. Shoulders down and back. 'And always will be.'

'State your side character single command function.'

Effie kept her head up. Neck touching the back of her frilly collar. Eyes open, looking just above her own height. Chin raised. 'Shield the non-player characters from the game.'

'We did what we came here to do,' Mac said. 'We successfully shielded a coach trip full of NPCs from the game. The rest ain't nothing but a dream about beasts.'

Effie relaxed all the way down to a slouch. 'You got any tea in your car, lass?'

'Passenger-side door.'

'I'll be away then.'

Mac gave a brief nod and pulled two spray cans out of her boilersuit like she was a gunslinger or something. 'I'd best drench the whole area, in case there's some leftover residue sparking around. Make it look like someone lit an illegal bonfire up here. There's not much can't be covered up with a bonfire. I once covered up a bonfire with a bon—'

'I just need a nice cup of tea,' Effie said, turning away before Mac could finish her co-worker reassurance.

The net had gone tripping and bumbling over stumpy mounds and chalk-resistant grasses, finally coming to rest in a ring of pale mushrooms. Mac Eden kept her eyes fixed on the horizon. She'd avoided looking directly at the despicable thing since she'd netted it. There were only so many times you could kill the people you loved before something in you snapped.

10

We were all fish once

Ezra shuffled a handful of sick bags into their designated holder, waiting respectfully as ten fat maggots bumbled free of a coiled cylinder and crawled to their genetically allocated places on the tattooed glass of the clock face. It wasn't so much a digital time display as a lesson in chubby choreography, each tiny movement marking the seconds to 10:01am as the wrinkly maggots turned themselves around and wrinkled their wrinkly way to the clock's lower pupation chamber. Most people didn't bother to watch the whole fleshy minute, but Ezra had been sighing for a solid hour and the dubious magic of maggot metamorphosis promised to lighten the mood. For its part, the semi-mortal clock groaned and moaned the opening notes of a lament to lost companions.

'Stop it,' Ezra said, frowning at the clock.

According to the localised systems manager, the Fabian Evirate House timepiece was in good spirits and there were no reported overnight issues, but the way the semi-mortal clock frowned back suggested that the localised systems manager needed to update its assigned parameters for the word issue.

'All right, fine, I feel like crap if you must know,' Ezra said. 'It was seeing Hollow on *WØLF* last night. And I'm not saying it's her fault, it was just a bit of a shock, that's all.'

The semi-mortal clock added a gothic counterpoint.

'FYI, I did tell the D&D group. Not that it's any of your business,' Ezra said, dismissing an amber notification alert on the LED screen that had popped up next to the souvenir pencils. 'Hollow enlisted in the army and she didn't want to talk about her reasons, so I honoured her privacy. When she wanted space, I gave her space. I even respected her decision to not tell me when she was quitting uni. Every single step of the way, I've acted with understanding and integrity.' Ezra slumped against the clock. 'Mostly because of the underlying sense that she'd made a massive mistake and I could be there to help her when she realised that. Except now Hollow's on TV, and Hollow has friends, and judging by social media's reaction to her soulful commentary, Hollow is set to be the next WØLF darling. It's all so utterly incompatible with reality.'

The semi-mortal clock looped the lament down into an elongated sigh.

'I know, I know,' Ezra said. 'I can't exactly complain. A GiFT at Fabian Evirate House is like finding a winning lottery ticket on your way to cashing in a winning lottery ticket. Normally, I'd have self-sabotaged my way into missing the application deadline.' Ezra echoed the clock's sweeping sigh around the phylactery information-station. 'But I had emotional altitude sickness from climbing so much moral high ground.'

Ezra knew that Emporia had considered a position at customer reception, but when the semi-mortal clock welcomed the newest GiFT donator with a fanfare of trumpets and a generous puff of ant powder, there wasn't any room for arguing. The view from the second-floor balcony sailed high above the triple-terraced arrivals lounge and was wholly delightful, except for the fact that Ezra's Bakelite information-station was also permanently, and often threateningly, overshadowed by two tonnes of carved oak, iron, coal, handblown glass and the bones of several extinct species of giant lizard. There was nothing tangible to give the semi-mortal clock life, but sometimes it died, and the clock argued that nothing could die that hadn't once been alive. Most people thought of the clock as a golem, which seemed to help them sleep at night. And all day, every day, the great stomachs of the monstrous clock tick-tocked down the hours, minutes and seconds of worldly life with all the reassurance of an undetonated explosive device. It also had a knack with background music.

'As you can imagine, I'm a confliction of emotions,' Ezra said, answering a buzz on the in-ear monitors. 'Ezra, copy.'

'Ezra. Ezra. Base. Confirm ten o'clock status.'

'Base. Base. Ezra.' Ezra did a quick visual check of the balcony. 'Phylactery clear.'

'Base received.'

'Oh, I nearly forgot,' Ezra said, squinting at a neatly written list, 'Mum just dropped some cupcakes off at the back door.'

'Copy that.'

Ezra squinted at the list again. 'Any update on the VIP arrival?'

'Imminent. Clear IEMs and wait on Emporia.'

'IEMs clear.'

'Base over and out.'

'Imminent,' Ezra said, patting the semi-mortal clock. 'Which is why I especially appreciate you denying entry to that last group of visitors. Two of them snuck into the antechamber anyway, but they didn't hold on to their breakfast long enough to find out what a phylactery is.'

The clock's reply was deep, ominous and decidedly bilious. It was accompanied by a flashing ruby notification alert.

> # FLY-FULL
> ### IMMEDIATE
> ### ATTENTION REQUIRED

'Seriously?' Ezra chanced a glance down the meandering

balustrades of the nearest staircase. 'You couldn't have waited?'

There were five flies crawling across the clock face; all five were grinning.

'This better not be wind.' Ezra slipped an arm behind the clock, opening a concealed hatch just enough to unclip a miniature dustpan and brush. 'Lucky for us, it looks like Emporia and associated VIP have been delayed by the mandatory reading of the precautionary notices. No doubt they're answering the three random precaution-related questions in order to level up to the next staircase. Unwittingly embellishing their immersion experience of impatience if Dicky reset the wrong answers again.'

Ezra swept up as many dead flies as the short brush could cope with, rushing more than the training had advised. Lately, all the flies had been black. Some of the smaller flies had ventured along the brown part of the evolutionary spectrum, but it was obvious from the miserable way they collected in the corners that they were thinking about black. Black was the coolest colour, even for dead flies. Most of the live flies were flying around the arched vaults; a few were crawling figure eights on the engraved runes. Some of the older flies skulked among the dead. The clock whistled an old music hall tune.

'Oh, and I didn't tell you the worst of it.' Ezra squirmed further inside the narrow gap; a wayward stretch short of shoulder dislocation. 'Apparently, Hollow is a better person without me around. And that isn't a nice guest at anyone's thought table.'

'Hi, I have an appointment...'

Ezra jolted upright, smashing the fly-filled dustpan against the wall and slamming the hatch shut in a single graceless move.

'...with Emporia.'

The young man stood in the cacophony of wings and things, and when he smiled, it felt like the sun coming out. Ezra began to blush, fumbling the miniature dustpan and brush under the desk like a semi-pubescent, hopelessly awkward schoolkid would if they were avoiding looking directly at their crush. Unlike Ezra's former crush, Atticus Valentine didn't instigate an Instagram follow and subsequently ignore every comment Ezra left, but instead asked what the sick bags were for.

'Sick,' Ezra said.

'My dear Mr Valentine, welcome back.' Emporia's trilling authority intervened. 'What an absolute delight it is to see you again.'

'Emporia,' he said, 'I tried not to be early.'

Emporia curtsied several times. 'And so it is that you have indeed arrived at the perfect time.'

'Perfect!' Ezra squawked.

Emporia gestured towards Ezra like she was unveiling a plaque. 'Our newest recruit, and appointed guardian of the marvellous phylactery. A clock favourite. Gifted Free Time. Mandatory perhaps, but a keen mind nonetheless. Wonderful with our visitors. Student, I might add. A bright addition, some would be reminded of a comrade to dearest TS Eliot, although comrade is more verb than noun, perhaps. And indeed, far more I could say, if we but had the time. Donating something to the social sciences. Dead flies, by the look of it. Ha ha ha.'

'Great to meet you, Ezra,' he said.

How he'd managed to excavate a usable name from Emporia's cryptic crossword introduction was a mystery, but excavate it he had. And when he stepped away from the little reception desk it was like losing something. The clock sneezed, burped and farted. Ezra pulled out a can of pine air freshener, smiled sweetly and sprayed everything that wasn't the clock. Whatever punishing gods stalked the corridors of Fabian Evirate House, you could bet your boots they were thanking themselves that Emporia was in charge.

What Ezra hadn't realised was that Emporia was also struggling to hold things together. 'And so, we shall away… to the phylactery. This way if you please, young sir,' she said, offering her arm to Atticus Valentine as if he were a gentleman come to take her for a stroll along the promenade.

A look of horrified embarrassment immediately blazed across Emporia's face. Ezra had recently completed the Co-workers and Empathy Online Training Module and was contractually obliged to rush to her aid. But the arm was out there like a malfunction on an international space station, and there was no going back. For his part, Atticus Valentine took Emporia's arm like it was the sort of thing he did every day. Ezra could have kissed him for that. Ezra could have kissed him for lots of things: the sun coming up; the moon not flying out of orbit; hydrogen and oxygen teambuilding their way through the periodic table. The explosive popularity of *WØLF* had catapulted Atticus Valentine's production company into a media empire overnight, but most people still expected the chief executive officer of Plug Productions to resemble a rather mature-looking goat. Turned out Atticus Valentine wasn't a mature-looking goat. In fact, he was wildly young and so exceedingly un-goatlike that most people forgot what goats looked like when they met him. Plus, he had one of those beautiful mouths that rested on the threshold of a smile. Ezra could have kissed him if he'd taken a poop on the desk and covered it with a welcome leaflet.

'At long last we have arrived,' Emporia said with a chortle, having escorted Atticus Valentine the full six and a half steps to the clawed entrance of the phylactery antechamber. 'For this rather startling façade leads us to a rather startling room, which leads us to another... room, where we have collected, together... some symbolic artefacts, here at, Fabian, Evirate House. That, might indeed, help. With your rather intriguing I might, add, mission.' It wasn't eloquent and the blasted commas were all over the shop, but at least she'd stopped curtsying.

In keeping with the Victorian tradition of gratuitous masonry, a huge onyx bird encompassed the vaulted entrance, along with a handful of dismembered figures. Several more of the

Pompeiiesque statues struggled forlornly between the demonic claws of the bird. Their petrified struggle was often mistaken for a warning but was in fact only demonstrating the limitations of the one-way entrance system. The architect of its creation had also figured that nothing was made worse by the addition of fresh entrails. An assortment of available innards dripped from the mantled beak of the onyx bird like the contents of a carelessly lidded liquidiser before pooling into a Latin epitaph set unobtrusively into the floor. The epitaph roughly translated as *I hate you all* (had there been any remaining doubt). Still, curiosity was as ubiquitous as fear. The neo-classical pick of the day was a small part of what kept the phylactery squatting near the top of the visitor attraction list. And, as anyone viewing the spectacle for the first time was inclined to remark, we were all fish once.

Atticus Valentine took it all in his stride. 'I'm no stranger to inexplicable decisions.'

Emporia's laugh exploded like a DIY firework display. 'Not to everyone's taste, I'll admit. But we like to think that… something…we…yes…goodness, is that the time?' She squinted at her phone, curtsied out of Atticus' arm and squeezed between the entrance claws.

Ezra smiled reassuringly as the roof above the balcony flooded with light and the nearest of the infamous Fabian Evirate House windows glistened a full spectrum of teeth and talons across the floor between them. 'It's best to keep everything closed for the first part.'

Atticus grinned.

'Anyway,' Ezra said, returning to the sanctuary of shuffling the already neatly shuffled stack of sick bags, 'I'll leave you with Emporia. Good luck, and use the back of your hand where possible.'

'You're not coming in?'

'Um, I mean, I'm,' Ezra shuffled, 'I'm probably… I should probably, have to stay at the desk. Probably.'

'Oh, okay, sure,' he said.

Along with a request for help in identifying the origins of a family talisman, Atticus Valentine had just donated an outrageously large amount of money to Fabian Evirate House. The entire staff had been updated on how to avoid accidentally quizzing him about *WØLF*, and instructed to politely help him with whatever he wanted. Needless to say, what Atticus Valentine wanted had already been decided by several lengthy meetings and a strategic report from a representative of the subcommittee.

'I mean... I can,' Ezra said, 'I can come in with you, if you want.'

'I'd appreciate the company,' Atticus said, pulling back slightly from the claws, 'and for you to go first.'

Ezra plucked a sick bag from the pile and fluttered it like a fan. 'Then I shall indeed join you, kind sir.'

The semi-mortal clock rumbled their departure through the opening notes of *Robin Adair* with all the subtlety of a regency mother, ten unmarried offspring and a country garden in need of muscular attention.

If the internet had been a room instead of a bewildering network of networks, it would've been a phylactery. Every surface, every cabinet, every nook, and most certainly every cranny, was filled with amulets, talismans and charms.

Atticus bit his lip. 'Goodness. I'm not sure my brain can process all this.'

Ezra had almost tripped him up negotiating the double-bend entrance. 'Look at the things directly in front of you and think of England.'

'Don't encourage me.'

'Poppycock!' Ezra said.

Atticus took a tentative look around the nine-sided room. 'So this is the famous heart of Fabian Evirate House?'

Unexpectedly saying the word poppycock had sent Ezra spiralling towards a System-32 failure loop that required a reboot and several cups of sweet tea to recover from. Emporia should have been waiting to take up the tour, but the public liaison officer was too engrossed in an important handkerchief fumble to notice they'd arrived at all. Ezra took a steadying breath and gathered up into something that might have been an adult. 'In answer to your question, Mr Valentine, yes, this is the famous heart of Fabian Evirate House. At least in the sense that it's been constructed at the place where the heart would be if Fabian Evirate House were indeed a person. Which, according to several online sources, it may well be... And, in contemporary fantasy games, a phylactery is an object that protects a soul from death. If that helps at all.'

'Isn't it also a vial of blood, used to track down a mage?'

'We have a vacancy in our D&D group,' Ezra said, at a pitch only replicated by bats.

'And all that out there is protecting this room?'

'Ironic, I know,' Ezra said, 'to put such creative effort into protecting the objects of your own protection.'

'Like nuclear weapons.'

'If only,' Ezra said, nudging past a stumpy wooden figure with hundreds of black nails hammered into it.

'It's the weather,' Emporia said.

Atticus turned a slow circle, taking in the mahogany cabinets full of decorated rod wands. Calcite. Hippo ivory. Ebony curses rolled in lead and papyrus. Stones with holes. Pale blue stones. Amber. Coral. Mother of pearl. String charms. Wooden charms. Iron charms. Copper charms. Tin charms. Witch bottles. Word squares. Magic word crosses. Hands. Feet. Knives. Thunderstones. Totems. Figurines. Bones. Horseshoes. Masks. Sacred hearts. Juniper. Yew. Ash. As many rowan sticks as you could shake a stick at. There was even a disco ball of sorts, suspended at the centre of the phylactery, glass and reflective paint to ward off witches and warn of danger. But Atticus Valentine didn't stop to look at any of them; he stopped to look at a wooden panel that didn't even belong in the phylactery to begin with. 'You put this in with the desire?'

'The desire?' Ezra glanced at a whole articulated display case of evil eyes.

'The getting what we want.'

'Right,' Ezra said, still half waiting on Emporia. 'Are you interested in Nordic cryptology?'

'Nordic?' Atticus ran his hand over the wooden panel like his fingers could read the rough lines cut into it. 'That's interesting.'

'Yes, we do,' Emporia said.

'Jötunvillur, to be exact,' Ezra said. 'It's the only example in here, but we have others. In the submerged atrium. Which is on your tour, if I remember rightly.'

'They told me to bring a warm coat.'

'Did they warn you about not carrying food?'

'No...' Atticus said.

'And who are we to argue.' Ezra picked up an amulet that had been delicately carved with three dots and a triangle. 'What I like most about the phylactery is that out of context it's hard to know the reason for anything.'

'Even in context, to be fair,' Atticus said. 'If you sent my last dm a thousand years into the future, it's anyone's guess. I wrote it and I'm not entirely sure what I meant.'

'And indeed nursery rhymes,' Emporia said. 'Here comes the candle to light you to bed.'

'Here comes the axe to chop off your head,' Atticus said, the tips of his fingers still resting on the panel.

'Chopper,' Ezra said. 'It's a... chopper.'

Atticus grinned. 'So it is.'

'I for one,' Emporia finally produced a violet embroidered handkerchief, 'would favour a confusing dm over an amusingly shaped vegetable any day.'

'You're kinder to me than I deserve, Emporia.'

Emporia bothered her way around his words, flicking at the moment as though she was shooing away a mosquito. Her name usually sounded like a vape flavour, but on Atticus Valentine's lips it conjured up golden lands and temperate goddesses. The very next minute, he seemed so young and sweet that she felt the need to snuggle him up and put the cartoon channel on. Emporia turned away, hastily reorganising a group of grotesque figurines into date order. 'Poppycock. Me? Kind? Well, I suppose you'd find many in agreement with you there, or indeed later I'll wager.' Honestly, the words barely made sense. Emporia moved along the display shelf, absentmindedly picking up a piece of broken masonry stone with a figure carved into it, cleaning out a crevice before realising she was dusting the vulva of a Sheela-na-gig. To her credit, Emporia didn't break her stride. 'And never let it be said that I allow a primordial gate to go undusted. Ha ha ha. Certainly not on my watch.'

'They won't hear it from me,' Atticus said.

Emporia curtsied, returned the stone to its original place, and began surreptitiously making her way towards the exit. 'Evil safely averted. For another day. And not a moment too soon by the looks of the witch ball. Which suddenly reminds me, that I must do something...that I have just this very moment recalled. Apologies all round. Can't be avoided. If you'll excuse me for a minute or two, Mr Valentine, and I will meanwhile leave you in the young, capable, young hands of our dear young, Ezra's... young hands. For a minute or two.' She glanced apologetically at Ezra, waved her handkerchief, and fled.

Ezra shot a look at the witch ball, and for a reason that escaped explanation, topped it off with a creepy little chuckle. It was all very upsetting. Fortunately, Atticus Valentine had also been intrigued by Emporia's parting words and was now looking up at the disco suspended object as if nothing more alarming than a dull reflective surface had happened. With any luck, Emporia would only be gone for a minute or two, just a minute or two to keep focused, to maintain the proficient and professional conduct required of any representative of Fabian Evirate House. A measly minute or two until Emporia returned and the handsome Atticus Valentine went handsomely on his handsome way.

Unfortunately, a minute or two is a terribly unreliable unit of measure when confronted with a handsome man. Atticus looked over to Ezra. 'Do you fancy grabbing a coffee?'

'A what now?'

Atticus smiled, sweet and soft as late spring snow. 'I can't imagine the coordinated network of random meetings will permit me to drink coffee alone. Think of yourself as a human shield.'

His request was simple, not unexpected considering the time of day. But a visit to the teashop wasn't on the VIP schedule, and it certainly wasn't acceptable for any member of staff to leave their work zone unattended for such a transferable request. In a billion alternative timelines, Ezra remembered the precarious nature of a Fabian Evirate House GiFT, made a bunch of totally legitimate excuses, and went on to write several books on slum tourism in the nineteenth century.

'Sure.'

But not this one.

11

If the maths is to be believed

The Great Exhibition of Enchantment sounded like the fun kind of visitor attraction people could take their children to at half-term. What they found on arrival, however, was the entirely immersive and often challenging experience of visiting their own mind. Some of the installations were pleasant. Some were difficult. Some came close to compassion and then crashed into pride at the last minute. Some of the best ones were hard to understand and some of the worst ones were so easy to understand they could make you cry. The lilac gallery entrance was a small wooden door. Simple and unmemorable as gateways go, and certainly it was nothing compared to what awaited visitors on the other side. The air was brighter, the colours more colourful, the wondrous sight of the great white banners that hung floor to ceiling between the pale carved pillars of a mirrored walkway was more wondrous than any wonder previously experienced. But the gallery's soft drifting beauty delivered more than a pleasant distraction; it delivered an instant antidote to any suffering it encountered. And that wasn't just pleasant; that was bliss. As the longest room in Fabian Evirate House, the lilac gallery dropped down a series of shallow steps which were easily traversed and often overlooked at the time. As were the assemblage of drooling gargoyles that oozed and dribbled a life essence of faint glowing braids around the ever-dimming pillars like a dark-web maypole dance. And all around a concealed terrace, the paratech windows sent lightform insects scuttling endlessly across rust-black alchemy symbols inlaid in the hematite floor. It was a hard space to negotiate. Some visitors never made it beyond the small wooden door. Some had to be removed by force. Fabian Evirate House wasn't one for sugar-coating the experience of addiction.

Atticus wrapped his jacket tight around him as they reached the steep climb out of the lilac gallery and tried not to look at the leg-heavy thing that clung to his chest. 'Addiction certainly has a unique appeal.'

'Unique, yeah,' Ezra said. Yep. It was actually going okay. Emporia would buzz through on IEMs any minute now and everything was going okay. Meanwhile, all Ezra had to do was stop repeating everything Atticus Valentine said.

'Are the alchemy symbols important?'

'Important, yeah.' Damn.

Ezra had done a fair amount of online dating. Every bio included a list of preferred historical periods, favourite books, aspirations and life heroes. Every site submission form had intellectually interesting ticked as the primary selection category when looking for a match. And yet here was an intellectually interesting man and all Ezra's brain could come up with was how beautiful he was. How no light could tame the colour of his eyes.

'It's like, none of it would matter if they weren't there,' Atticus said. 'Luckily, the suffering comes back anyway.'

'Luckily, yeah.' And what was up with his hair? His hair couldn't have been more attractive if it had rushed into a burning house, rescued twelve children and then gone back for the cat.

'Imagine the paperwork if you were trying to build something like this today.' Atticus risked a quick look over his shoulder. 'We had enough trouble persuading the local council that growing trees on a roof terrace was structurally safe.'

'Safe, yeah...' Honestly, it wasn't like Ezra couldn't snap out a witty reply quicker than a panic buyer in the tinned goods aisle, but it was hard to think of anything witty when the underwear of everything you believed about yourself had just fallen down around your ankles. 'And so, here we are. Ha ha ha,' Ezra said, trying not to sound like Emporia, and sounding like Emporia. 'We've reached the rite of passageway that leads us to the teashop. Please attach the safety strap provided, and keep focused on your destination or you'll end up back in the lilac gallery. And whatever you do, don't look up.'

Atticus didn't look up. Which was a successful rite of passage in itself. Instead, he took a strap from the dispenser, snapped it around his wrist and attached it to an etched rail that guided valiant visitors to a pastry-based experience. And all the time chatting away like they were old friends or something. 'The local council insisted we could only plant elm and native oak, but they have some deep-rooted problems.'

'Problems. Shit. I mean, damn. I mean...crap.' Ezra sighed heavily. 'Obviously, I failed the training module on showing celebrities around.'

'People usually think I'm the intern.' Atticus unclipped himself from the handrail, dropped his safety strap in the deposit station, and tagged himself on the end of the teashop queue. 'I've turned up to all sorts of reactions. You're doing fine.'

'Am I, though?' Ezra sighed again. 'I was instructed to stay at my post and make sure the clock behaved itself. Which it didn't, clearly.'

'You accompanied me at my request.'

'Yeah, I suppose.' Ezra checked IEMs were still working. 'And Emporia will be here in a minute. Because she's great, and I'm on a GiFT. Honestly, I'm beyond stoked to even be here... At Fabian Evirate House. Not with you. No, I mean, I do also love being here with you. And I love coffee. I do love coffee. What I mean is...' Ezra had taken to waving an arm around '... it's great that the GiFT programme can still support this kind of placement. Especially because there's so much pressure to do a military GiFT right now... And finding something you don't mind doing for a year is difficult enough, let alone finding something you can't wait to turn up for. Some people would sell their soul to get a GiFT here, that's what I mean.'

'Did you?'

'Did I what, now?'

Atticus didn't answer; he just looked up at the menu board. And the thought that the throwaway drivel of an accidental word-vomit had upset him, well, suffice to say it dumped an incendiary of embarrassment through any catastrophe that had preceded it. The desire to casually mention Hollow being on *WØLF* was circling like a rescue vulture, but Ezra had also been briefed on the nefarious manifestations of panic quizzing, and advised to resort to mindless chit-chat if necessary. 'Interesting fact: If you combine the ages of all the Fabian Evirate House staff and multiply by seven, you get the exact circumference of the earth.'

'The average employee's age is ninety-seven?' he said. And even though he was still looking up at the menu, his smile set loose a flotilla of butterflies inside Ezra's stomach.

'If the maths is to be believed.'

Atticus turned and leant against the counter. 'I listened to a podcast that claims this building took on human form and spoke to the founder in person.'

'A lot more people than you'd imagine believe the building will awaken at a time of great need. It's the massive sword.' Ezra drummed a tune on the handrail. 'Did you do that maths in your head, or has someone told you before?'

He had a sweet habit of chewing his lip. 'Having recently spent fourteen months and several decade's worth of carbon footprints discussing the environmental impact of upgrading a set of automatic doors, I can add up pretty much anything in my head.'

'Impressive.' Ezra turned away, catching the attention of a woman serving behind the teashop till. 'Hi, can I quickly introduce you to Mr Valentine. He's having a look around Fabian Evirate House today.'

'Welcome to the teashop,' Mac Eden said. 'What can I get you folks?'

'Coffee, yes,' Ezra said, 'that's why we came here.'

But Mac wasn't looking at Ezra. She was looking at Atticus with the same sideways kind of look that a lot of people seemed to use. Unlike a lot of people, the expression on her face wasn't that of a love-struck teenager. Indeed, Mac's face suggested it had seen more attractive life forms hanging around hydrothermal vents. 'Identify yourself.'

'This is Mr Atticus Valentine, he's visiting with us today,' Ezra said. 'And I'm Ezra, from the GiFT placement.'

Mac didn't answer; she just pulled a black plastic necklace out from under her collar, shaking it like it was faulty.

'Is everything okay, Mac?'

Mac shook her necklace again.

'Ha ha ha.' Ezra's laugh carried as much credibility as an estimated exam grade. 'Classic teashop team, always chancing a joke. It's the gargoyles.'

Mac didn't clarify it as a joke in any way imaginable. She tucked the necklace back under her collar, dragged her sleeve across a puddle of spilled milk and blew her nose in a tea towel, silencing the teashop and breaching a dozen health and safety protocols at the same time. 'This place is a failsafe.'

Ezra nodded along, smiling at Atticus, pretending it was all part of the visitor experience. 'The coffee is actually really good here. They use it to descale the pipes.'

'Descale the vermin,' Mac said.

Despite the obvious complexities of being a side character in a game no one knew about, Mac Eden delivered a bullish kind of ambiguity. To everyone at Fabian Evirate House, she was good old Mac. A zero-hour employee who was always grateful for work and did whatever she was asked to do. Some days, she could be found thoroughly cleaning the urinals. Other days, she was thoroughly covering the teashop till. Honestly, she was dead reliable, and not at all the sort of person who glared at customers like she might shove their faces through the baguette slicer.

'So, coffee?' Ezra said, hopefully.

Keeping her eyes locked on Atticus, Mac reached down and produced a heavy metal ladle, smacking the rusted utensil twice on the counter in an overly dramatic fashion. 'Access denied.'

'Oh, right.' Ezra turned to Atticus, shrugging apologetically. 'Apparently, there really is a problem here. Plan B, we have a nice coffee machine in the staffroom, if you don't mind a sofa tragedy.'

Atticus didn't say anything; he just reached around Ezra and gently took the ladle from Mac, placing it on the counter next to a little basket of calorie-free brownies.

Mac looked down at the ladle as though it had just revealed a cure for cancer through the medium of modern dance. Then she looked back at Atticus. It was almost as if nothing had happened. Which was exactly what had happened. Mac blinked twice. 'What can I get you folks?'

'Just a regular black for me,' Atticus said.

'Same for me,' Ezra said, 'except a coconut latte.'

'A regular black and a coconut latte,' Mac said. 'Is that everything for you?'

'Yes, thank you,' Ezra said. 'And a triple chocolate muffin. For Emporia. She'll be here in a minute.'

'That'll be nine hundred and fifty pounds,' Mac said. 'Tap the top for contactless.'

'Could you just…check the amount?' Ezra said.

Mac looked at the till again. 'Nine pounds fifty.'

'My treat,' Atticus said.

'Take a seat, folks…' Mac was shaking her head '…I'll bring

your order over when it's ready.' And honest to God, she went to hand him a customer receipt, but she just couldn't seem to let it go.

Ezra leant on the rail and tried not to throw up.

There'd been recent speculation that the teashop was an experience of awakening because it'd been built inside out by mistake, citing photographic evidence of a faded decorative menu and several line drawings of coffee beans still visible on the outside of the building. The question of moving the teashop to a more desirable location had been raised several times, but the desirable location was four miles away, with off-street parking and a spectacular view of the harbour. Besides, the way the great hematite walls rose up like a late-night drunken chorus of the hokey-cokey, well, honestly, you didn't need to be in marketing to understand why that sort of thing encouraged more cake sales. Ezra sank into one of the upcycled chairs by the window, sighing like someone who'd just sat their final exam and didn't get the result for three months.

Atticus placed a glass of water on the table. 'You're sure you don't want a first aider?'

'No, honestly,' Ezra said, 'I feel better already.'

'I've been trained in seven types of running to get a first aider.'

'I probably skipped breakfast, that's all.' Ezra managed a laugh. 'It seems like a long time ago. And thank you, for looking after me. Emporia's right, you really are a jolly good egg.'

'A jolly good egg?' Atticus said.

'According to Emporia.'

'I don't know what that is, but it sounds great.' Atticus looked around the teashop. 'You're a student, I hear. What are you studying?'

'History. Medieval Europe, through to Enlightenment.'

'I say!' A mid-fifties woman, daisy jumper and hat to match, waved from two tables away. 'I say, excuse me, my friend was wondering if you're him.'

'Usually,' Atticus said, to a round of giggling and a deal more looking from nearby tables.

'My friend was wondering, with these four new people coming in, is Sylvie leaving WØLF? Only there's chat all over social media that Sylvie is leaving WØLF.'

'Okay,' Atticus said.

'So it's true!' The daisy jumper woman gasped dramatically. 'Sylvie Stevens is leaving WØLF.'

Even the building leant in to listen.

'Do you think it's true?' Atticus said.

'Me?' The woman flustered around her friend. 'That's not really for me to say. I'm not part of the WØLF production team.'

'Me neither,' Atticus said. 'I just pay the bills. Which is probably for the best, because I'd bring them all back home.'

A firmly buttoned woman with a disinclination to speak at normal volume hustled into the conversation. 'An honest and admirable sentiment, young man. But, unfortunately, the WØLF cast are also enlisted soldiers, and we are at war. As much as one might want to, one cannot just up and bring our troops back home willy-nilly.'

'So they tell me,' Atticus said. And when he smiled, it was hard to remember anything else.

'Could my friend get a photograph with you?' the daisy jumper woman said.

'Sure.'

She thrust a phone at her friend, scrabbling next to Atticus and grinning like she'd won the euro millions and wasn't sharing it with any relatives. A flurry of comparable requests occupied the table for a while. Ezra tried to keep out of the way, but it wasn't necessary. Other than a cursory smile here and there, the person sitting with the CEO of Plug Productions was of no interest to anyone. Atticus Valentine had successfully achieved all the things society promised would make him happy. And he didn't just embrace that; he personified it. Even from the tormented bliss of the lilac gallery, it was hard to tag Atticus Valentine in any picture of suffering at all. Ezra sat back, watching the lightform of a honey badger scrounge for crumbs under the table as the photograph flurry slowed and finally faded away.

Atticus picked up a discarded spoon from the table and spun it through his fingers. 'Why history?'

'Oh, you know, the usual lifelong obsession with the past.' Ezra blagged an offhand casual laugh. 'People haven't changed much, not really. That's interesting to think about when you study history. We want the same things our distant ancestors wanted, and we mess up in all the same ways. Like Brexit and Silbury Hill, they're not much different when you look at the reasons for them. Not forgetting Isambard Kingdom Brunel, of course.' Isambard Kingdom Brunel was often the best exit strategy when you'd lost track of what you were talking about. Ezra laughed again, hastily manoeuvring the conversation away from any questions about civil and mechanical engineering. 'Have you been to Fabian Evirate House many times before, Mr Valentine?'

'Only once, to meet Emporia.'

'Oh, I thought because...'

'Because I threw my money at it?'

'Because you came here to find answers.'

Atticus looked down at the spoon. 'They made me an honorary associate.'

'Yes.'

'I'm not sure I deserve to be an honorary associate.'

'Oh! Oh!' Ezra said, clapping like a seal. 'Honorary associates have open access to everything. They can basically go anywhere they want. Like, you could go to the towers. Or use the staff toilets. If you want.'

'I'll bear that in mind.'

'The staff toilets are lovely, by the way. Also haunted. By a dog ghost. For ages, people thought it was a stable lightform but then someone pointed out that there aren't any windows in the staff toilets. It's sweet, though, and if you have biscuits, it brings you a ghost tennis ball. Don't ask about the towers. Plus, you get a free tote bag at the gift shop.'

'And the jolly egg?'

For all the staffroom whisperings of this man, no one, not one single person, had warned Ezra of the exquisite conflict in him. It came like shipwrecks and a sunlit sea. 'This research means a lot to you, doesn't it?'

Atticus leant forward, running the edge of the spoon along the table as if he was writing a poem. 'Do you believe people can be cursed?'

'What, like something really bad will happen to them?'

'Well,' his voice was quiet, 'I guess that depends on what you mean by bad.' And he looked up with his beautiful, turbulent eyes, trapping Ezra's reflection like an insect in amber.

12

We did Kafka

Mac Eden dropped the tray of drinks onto the table with all the subtlety of a last-minute sick note. She wasn't sure what had happened, but she was damn sure it wasn't going to happen again.

'Oh, thank you,' Ezra said, kinder than Mac deserved.

'Whatever,' Mac said, ruder than Ezra deserved.

'How was your holiday, Mac?' Ezra grinned, nodding extra chirpily. 'The weather was great.'

Mac pulled the black plastic necklace out again and held it towards Atticus. 'I suppose.'

'Did you get to walk any of the Jurassic Coast?'

'Nope.' Mac stuffed the necklace back and set to half-heartedly clearing a newly vacated table.

'Mac's just back from a week in Lyme Regis,' Ezra said to Atticus. 'We went there all the time when I was little. There are loads of dinosaur-themed places, and fossils to look for, and one or two things you thought were fossils but were actually a plastic model of Clint Eastwood. It was my favourite place in the whole world. Which, if you go with early experience theory, would probably turn out to be the real reason I like history.'

'Clint Eastwood?' he said.

'In a poncho.' Ezra sighed happily. 'They had loads of these little tourist-trade gift shops, crammed so full of tat they could barely keep it in the door. And not just any tat. The ugliest, most useless tat you can imagine, then covered in shells. My parents had to put up a shelf. Mac, please tell me those little shops are still there.'

'Some.'

Ezra sighed again, laying back into the chair. Too caught up in nostalgia to read the room that was Mac Eden. 'I bet your children loved them, didn't they?'

'Some.'

'How old are your children?' Atticus asked.

Mac screwed her cleaning cloth into a ball, turning on Atticus like he'd threatened to steal her babies, eat them, use the leftovers to create clones and then eat them as well. She leant close to him, more venomous than a rattlesnake. 'All smugly sitting there like a smug advert for smugness. But whatever stunt you pulled back there, it's not going to work again, do you understand?'

Ezra glanced around the teashop. 'Mac, what are you doing?'

'No, it's fine,' Atticus said softly. 'I understand.'

'Good, it's good you understand.' Mac smiled then, so close to Atticus she was almost on his lap. 'Because your kind are forbidden here.'

Ezra stretched and stood up. 'A quick word, Mac.'

'Which one,' Mac said, still glaring at Atticus, 'Piss or Off?'

Ezra smiled, linking arms with Mac and hauling her chummily into a *trompe l'oeil* tunnel situated adjacent to the teashop exit. The tunnel masqueraded as a double drainpipe and ran underneath the teashop via a series of uneven steps, before looping around an upper balcony, dropping into a tiny subterranean garden and back up a steep incline until it finally emerged from a *trompe l'oeil* tunnel masquerading as a double drainpipe adjacent to the teashop exit. There wasn't enough room for the accustomed social distancing, so Mac had to stand inside one of the lightforms.

'What are you doing, Mac?'

'My job.'

'And this is standard teashop procedure, is it?'

'You don't know anything.'

'No, I don't,' Ezra squeaked. 'I shouldn't even be here. But I am here. And you're here. And a VIP guest is here. And this configuration of people doesn't seem to be working out terribly well.'

'May as well not even have a failsafe...'

'And I can see this is really difficult for you, but you should have come to the staff briefing.'

'...or a necklace.'

'I'm trying to understand.' Ezra went to pat Mac's arm but chickened out. 'What's going on here, Mac?'

'Nowhere near enough, it seems.'

'You know if he puts in a complaint, we're royally screwed. Both of us. And I don't know if that even means anything to you, but it would be a total disaster for me. People who get thrown off their GiFT don't get second choices. They get automatically transferred to the military service programme to learn about discipline. And I'd be a terrible soldier. I'd probably just get killed at boot camp. Like accidentally shooting myself with live ammo or something. Or immediately when I got to the war. And I really, REALLY don't want to get immediately killed when I get to the war. I'd honestly rather get immediately killed by accidentally shooting myself with live ammo at boot camp. Is that what you want, Mac, for me to rather I get immediately killed by accidentally shooting myself with live ammo, at boot camp?'

It was a soliloquy of sorts. Mac was unmoved.

'We can still pull this back,' Ezra said, 'but this is some serious-level rudeness we're trying to sidestep here. Luckily, it transpires that Mr Valentine is a jolly good egg. And I think it might be okay if you apologise. We can pass it off as a bad day or something, because he does seem like he's a jolly good egg.'

Mac remained unmoved.

'Fine, have it your way.' Ezra went to tap IEMs.

'I never figured you for someone who'd snitch on their co-workers.'

Ezra almost choked. 'Reporting gross misconduct isn't snitching. It's acting with professional integ—'

'Gross misconduct?' Mac said. 'I'd immediately lose my job.'

'That's what I've been saying.'

'Right.' Mac looked down at her feet. The lightform had wrapped its stumpy claws around them like a pair of hairy slippers. 'So you're saying that unless I go back in there and apologise, you'll report me?'

"Locker cleared and escorted off the premises.'

Mac bobbed around awkwardly, trying to jump into the understanding pool. 'What if I just went back to the till?'

'To be honest, Mac, I'm not sure an apology will be enough. But it's worth a shot, right? To save our jobs. And I've got A Level drama, so I can put in a noteworthy performance explaining things for you.'

'Right.'

Ezra softened to accomplice. 'Okay, the plan is, we go back to the table. You quickly dip in with an apology and head back to the till. Meanwhile, I ramp up the chirpy but totally out-of-their-depth GiFT donator. Mr Valentine and I neck our coffee. I take him down to the towers. He forgets his own name. Job done.'

'The towers?'

'Exactly. So we have a plan?'

The lightform snuggled itself around Mac like a ceremonial bearskin. She looked up then, desperate. 'What if I can't get the apology to come out?'

'People think this job is a breeze,' Ezra said. 'When Emporia suggested moving me up to front of house, I was like…working with the public, yay, that'll be fun. Turns out, it's really hard. But as Dicky once told me, when you're on the frontline, you see things no person should ever be allowed to see.'

'He mention the Sebastian Incident?'

'Yeah.'

'Dicky had a full beard back then,' Mac said. 'The whole thing fell out the next day and never grew back.'

'Indeed.' Ezra could almost see the finish line. 'And whatever this is, at least it's not as bad as the Sebastian Incident, right?'

'We found little bits of hair in the staffroom kettle for weeks after,' Mac said. 'Like they weren't sure where they should be.'

'I can imagine.'

'I could probably manage a fake apologise,' Mac said, running her fingers over the links of the black plastic necklace. She tried to chase out an accompanying smile, but it wasn't ready for meeting people yet. 'But if that bastard thing ever comes anywhere near this place again, lose my job or not, I'll rip its stinking guts out with my bare teeth.'

'That's the spirit.' Ezra nodded an encouraging look towards the teashop.

Mac shuffled awkwardly and cleared her throat. 'Now I come to it, finding the actual apology words ain't easy. I mean, how do you randomly fake something like that?'

'Look, you're overthinking this,' Ezra said. 'Just fix your eyes on his right ear and stick the word sorry after everything you say.'

'Right ear?' Mac cleared her throat again. 'I see.'

'Great. Let's get fake apology done. And no more threatening him.'

'Fine.'

Ezra smirked. 'Because I couldn't bear it.'

'No, I appreciate that.'

'And it might get a bit grizzly in there.'

'Yeah,' Mac said.

'Right, well, good luck, soldier.' Ezra took a deep breath. 'See you on the other side.'

'Who said I was a soldier?'

'No, it's a figure of speech.'

'It's a figure of people minding their own business before their own business finds itself without a business. That's what it is.'

'Noted,' Ezra said.

Atticus Valentine was talking on his phone. He raised his hand to show he wouldn't be long. 'No, that's perfect. I'll let you know when to switch them over.'

Ezra could sense Mac inflating like a gelignite balloon. 'The new floor lighting in here is quite effective, surprising really, considering the fuss the bishop made.'

'Is it?'

'Mac?' Ezra shuffled slightly closer. 'What exactly happened with the Sebastian Incident?'

'You weren't there, you wouldn't understand.'

'I could give it a shot.'

'No, you couldn't.'

'Was it like an accident, or something?'

'No.'

'A hostage situation?'

'No,' Mac said.

'Vampires?'

'No.'

'Does it have anything to do with the thrupenny bit?'

Atticus stood up, touching his hand to Mac's arm. 'Forgive me. Business never did have a sense of timing.'

Mac froze like he'd infected her with Ebola.

'Mr Valentine, Mac has something she would like to say.'

Mac took a few steps on the same spot. 'Sorry.'

'Sorry for...' Ezra nudged her.

'Sorry for the piss off. Sorry.'

Well, it was more than Ezra could have hoped, and at least

127

Mac hadn't added the *you fucking bastard* that hung in the air between them like an accident in a chemistry lab.

'There really is nothing to apologise for,' Atticus said. 'You should see some of our imprint meetings.'

'Well, you're very kind.' Ezra nudged Mac again. 'Isn't he, Mac?'

'KIND,' Mac said, staring at Atticus' right ear like she was trying not to accidentally bite it off. 'Sorry.'

'I know it's probably not worth anything,' Atticus said, 'but sometimes my name runs around making all sorts of trouble without me.'

Mac recoiled. 'I've done what I was told. If you think you're getting anything else from me then you're an idiot as well as a fuc—'

'Marvellous, thank you, Mac!' Ezra said. 'And we don't want to hold you up any longer.'

Mac snatched up the cleaning cloth, growled the word sorry and left. Apology or not, if her face had possessed a middle finger, it would have hoisted it like a flag.

'She's a bit off today.' Ezra slumped into the chair like a sack of primary school beanbags. 'Sorry.'

'Please don't worry about it.'

'But Mac's a great person. She's just having a tough time of it at the moment. I'd tell you about it, but she's also a private kind of person and it's not something she'd want me to say anything about, not directly. Sorry.'

'Really, it's fine.'

'It's pretty awful, that's all I can say.' Ezra nodded a whole load of implied awfulness. 'Really awful, actually.'

'So many people have lost partners and children to the war, they want someone to blame, so they blame us for making WØLF.'

'Grief is a…sad thing.'

'It certainly is,' Atticus said. 'And at least she didn't spit in my coffee.'

'Gosh, no, Mac would never do that.' Ezra sat forward, earnest with it. 'Because that would be unhygienic, and Mac is very fastidious where cleaning is... And she has adorable children, who she endlessly worries about, obviously, because she's a great mum. Her partner grows vegetables for the community food bank, you know?'

'Oh, okay.'

'At the community allotment. And Mac does loads of extra jobs around here, for free. Even with the super-tough time she's going through right now. She says it helps her to keep busy, which is understandable. And, now I come to think about it, she's lost a brother or something to the war...' Ezra moved a grain of sugar along the table '...because that would make a whole lot more sense.'

'I'm not going to complain.'

'Ah,' Ezra said. 'Busted.'

'It was good acting, though.'

'We did Kafka, for our final exam,' Ezra said, in an offhand kind of manner that suggested a relaxed and yet respectful attitude to the potential PR disaster that had recently erupted, and that Atticus should find his own way to Kafka. 'Places like this attract unique personalities, but we're also a tight team, we look out for each other.'

'Of course.'

'Talking of,' Ezra said. 'I was thinking I could buzz through and get Emporia to meet us at the towers. Strictly speaking, they're not scheduled on your tour, or indeed any tour, but if you happened to mention to me that you'd really like to see them, what else could I do? I mean, you're an honorary associate, and I'd be failing in my duty if I didn't immediately take you down there.'

'The towers?'

'I've only been in one through three,' Ezra said. 'They get progressively postmodern, so don't expect much sense out of them beyond the flying saucers.'

Atticus leant towards her. 'How do I ask you for help?'

'No, it's fine, they give you an alarm lanyard to wear.'

'With the research, how do I ask for help with the research?'

'Oh, gosh, sorry, your research, of course, sorry.' Ezra grimaced. 'Emporia has blocked out some time after the tour. To get you set up at least. They moved her in with the furniture, not the sofa tragedy, obviously, but the rest of the furniture. Did I mention that she's great? I think I did. I'll buzz through to Emporia now, shall I?'

'You,' he said, 'how do I ask you?'

'Me?' Ezra laughed. 'I'm a GiFT donator, Mr Valentine. I've only been allowed to open the staffroom fridge since Wednesday.'

'I never underestimate anyone.'

'You're very sweet.'

'So they tell me.'

'And…um…' Ezra picked up the triple chocolate muffin and peeled the wrapper away '…the towers aren't usually open this time of day, so it'll be a new experience for me too.'

Atticus swirled coffee around his cup. 'You didn't answer my question.'

'I thought we already…' Ezra inhaled, coughing and dribbling triple chocolate muffin across the table and onto the floor '…with the staffroom fridge example.'

Atticus fished a pale-blue cotton handkerchief from his pocket like he was all too used to people dribbling baked goods. 'I'm sorry, I didn't mean to startle you.'

'No, no, it's just a lot of chocolate.' Ezra took the handkerchief and folded it neatly before mopping up the spillage with a paper napkin. 'In all seriousness, Emporia is the best person to work with. Or Dicky. Dicky is brilliant with the entomology of symbols. I'll call through for Dicky. He won't mind, and he's super-interesting to talk to once you get over the thrupenny bit.'

'I'd rather it was you.'

'Poppycock,' Ezra said, with an Emporia-like chuckle,

flapping the soggy napkin around, and plopping bits of it across the table. 'Also, I seem to have contracted the word poppycock.'

'Have a think about it.' Atticus looked around the teashop. 'A nineteenth-century midwife foreshadowed postmodernism?'

Seriously, it was like trying to choose what to watch on TV when someone was flicking through the channels too quickly. 'You know about Maudie Clump?'

'A little. There's not much written about her.'

Ezra gathered up all the soggy napkin bits, pressing them together into an unplanned heart. 'Foreshadowing postmodernism is a postmodern distortion of time in itself, when you think about it. Did you know that she met—' A double buzz on IEMs cut into the conversation. 'Excuse me, Mr Valentine, I just need to get this. It'll be Emporia looking to catch up with us.'

'Ezra, Ezra, Emporia. What is your twenty?' Emporia used coms like she was a truck-driving American police officer who'd been to finishing school and unexpectedly found themselves landing an aircraft.

'Visitor teashop,' Ezra said.

'Ten-four. Do you have any information regarding the current whereabouts of our missing VIP?'

'Visitor teashop.'

'Ah,' Emporia said. 'Understood. Confirm situation under control, copy?'

'Copy that.'

'Remain at current location, repeat, remain at current location. Copy?'

'Copy that.'

'ETA ten minutes,' Emporia said. 'Copy.'

'Um…copy that.'

'Emporia over and out.' IEMs hissed for a few seconds. 'Ezra. Ezra. Emporia. Confirm over and out.'

Ezra fidgeted the grain of sugar along the table again. 'Ezra over and out.'

There are moments in life when it's like you're watching yourself from a distance. Detached, baffling moments when your mouth carries on talking without you. But this moment wasn't like that. Ezra knew exactly what was happening. 'I've thought about it.'

Atticus sat forward. 'You'll help me?'

'Yep, apparently I will.'

Back in the teashop kitchen, Mac Eden looked at her phone in disbelief. 'You think this is game fatigue!'

'...'

'Yes,' Mac said, calmer this time. 'Of course I know the building is made o—'

'...'

'I don't know! It must be faulty.'

'...'

Mac pulled the black plastic necklace off, threw it in the sink and watched it disappear into the bubbles. 'Yeah, and maybe the alarms are faulty too. Maybe I picked up the wrong ladle. And maybe that sounds like a lot of malfunction coincidences, but I'm telling you straight, this was a Mandolin player. A high-rank player by the way it was manipulating everyone.'

'...'

'Oh, is that right? And what about our grandmothers? They didn't have no fancy, colour-changing, ozone-detecting necklaces telling them what something was and wasn't. They learnt it in their blood.'

'...'

'How it sounds? I'll tell you exactly how it sounds. It sounds like a great deal of fretting about the judgement of an experienced side character and nowhere near enough fretting about a major breach to the failsafe!'

'...'

'Since when did we have solicitors?'

'...'

'Fine, you set up a cell meeting for tonight, and I'll find you the unequivocal evidence.'

Mac put the phone down carefully. She even hummed a tune as she fished her necklace out of the sink, rebooting it through the factory setting and drying it off with a blue paper towel. 'It's not game fatigue,' she said.

Still, there was something toxic in the words, something Mac couldn't dry off with blue paper towel. That night up on Haifengate, the look she'd seen on Effie Cox's face. Game fatigue took the best of them, and it took them slow enough to seem like it came out of nowhere. 'It's not game fatigue,' she said.

Mac went back to humming the tune as she screwed the paper towel into a ball, only cut short of popping it into the compostable waste bin by a yellow WARNING notice stuck to the top with duct tape. Bin notices weren't unusual, but this one had footnotes. According to a cross-department email from Downstairs Lesley (see attached), fifty cupcakes had been baked and hand-delivered by Ezra Blake's mum in time for a primary school visit. The cupcakes came ready decorated with scarlet veined icing and cherry eyeballs, lifelike enough to make you think twice about putting them in your mouth. And while Dicky conceded that Sheila Blake's gesture showed splendid community spirit in a time of war, he also made the executive decision to keep them back, what with allergies and potential lawsuits and everything. Which the governing body agreed was a sensible precaution considering a) most six-year-old kids had only been outside twice in their life and b) the eyes on the cupcakes not only followed you around the room, they also suggested they'd follow you home and kill you in your sleep. Subsequently, the donated cupcakes had been left in the staffroom for people to help themselves. A couple were eaten out of guilt, but most ended up where all unfathomable things ended up – the IT department document shredder. Which had been a bit of a shock for Downstairs Lesley, who'd gone to shred an urgent request for IT assistance, only to find the shredder clogged with icing and a hundred bloodshot eyeballs staring up at her like a compound nightmare. Downstairs Lesley had immediately unleashed a cross-department email (see attached) and flooded the entire shredder with foam from an electrical fire extinguisher, because the Sebastian Incident had changed them all, and Downstairs Lesley was no longer the sort of person who ran screaming from something that hid in the bottom of a shredder and had fifty pairs of bloodshot eyes.

Mac peeled the notice off carefully, still humming away as she bent forward and stuffed her whole head into the bin. 'It's not game fatigue,' she said.

Granted, she hadn't found the right words to explain to the Operating System why this nothing much of a thing felt so utterly terrifying, but that didn't excuse the lameness of their response. The only thing you could trust in the whole goddamn world was iron. That was the first and last rule of the side characters. Fabian Evirate House was built on hematite and out of hematite. The architectural stages leading to the main entrance channelled iron on iron. And iron took the Mandolin down like arsenic took down rats. It was the south coast failsafe. The Great Exhibition of Enchantment, built by Maudie Clump to hide its true purpose in plain sight. One hundred and fifty years of somewhere impenetrable for side characters to meet, to know with absolute certainty that no Mandolin lurked among them. The bastard thing should have been half dead before it got across the threshold. But it wasn't half dead. It was all the way in the teashop queue waiting to buy a coffee. Mac straightened up, flicking a teabag off her cheek. 'It is NOT game fatigue,' she said.

The Operating System had agreed that something wasn't right, but according to them that something was her. Honestly, if she could write a list of all the things she was pissed about, that would be second to top. Mac pulled a banana skin out of her hair and dropped it in the bin. She'd followed side character protocol. She'd reported an incident. She'd even held back and requested an emergency cell meeting when what she'd really wanted from them was to invite Mr Atticus Valentine to Porton Down for a tour of the facility. Stick it under electron bombardment. Disrupt the magnetic field. Deionise its bastard DNA. Slice it until there was nothing but feathers to look at under the microscope. And in return, the Operating System had just wanted to know everything she'd done. Every shameful, embarrassing second like she'd messed up a worst-case tactical event.

Mac picked up her phone, hit ICE and waited for an algorithm to throw her signal around a bit. 'Hi, it's me,' she said, 'we have a code white.'

'…'

'No, no, I'm fine. But you need to get the kids out of school and go stay with your mum for a bit, okay.'

'…'

'No, right now, Dave. Go right now.'

She'd relay the matter to her cell meeting tonight, play it like the Operating System wanted. Meanwhile, she'd subtly gather more intel, subtly find out exactly what this Atticus Valentine thing was, maybe subtly rough it up a bit, maybe subtly shove a netgun down its throat and subtly pull the trigger. Cos the bastard thing had asked about her children. And that was personal. That was top of the list.

13

Did she cc me?

Anyone with cleaning utensils had open access to all the hours a day could provide, and it wasn't unusual for Mac Eden to be the last person in the building. She made her way to the myriagon vestibule, angry enough to chance a punch at one of the echo-based lightforms that hung around in that part of Fabian Evirate House. The room was reputed to be a polygon with ten thousand sides, but for the most part it was a circle. At the centre of the myriagon, a robot cleaner with a broom had been programmed to contain a large oil spill. An impossible, unending, unbearable task that triggered a visitor experience of pity, despair, frustration, even joy, if they were that way inclined. Mac tripped the robot up and trod oil across the floor to a top-secret access portal positioned just below the self-service defibrillator. As top-secret access portals went, it wasn't like they tried to hide the thing; it even had a grade II listing as a utilitarian 1970s interior fitting. It was also so entirely bland it made the magnolia skirting board look exciting. People would swear the myriagon vestibule had no dumbwaiter, often while leaning on the dumbwaiter. Mac braced her foot against the wall and took hold of a painted wooden handle with both hands, yanking it several times before she finally got the hatch open. The Operating System had authorised an upgrade, but no amount of state-of-the-art security could beat a sticky knob when it came to bypassing curiosity.

The interior of the dumbwaiter was small, basic, seemingly never intended to carry much more than a hearty breakfast tray. It sagged unnervingly as Mac climbed in, splintering and clunking like it might plummet its occupant to their death at any moment. But that was as much a part of the deception as the dust-knotted cobwebs and the cheesy smell. Mac pulled her foot backwards to clear the door, negotiating the specific way of sitting that allowed passengers to press the soggy black button concealed in a soggy clump of black mould at the lower left corner of the dumbwaiter. Keeping one hand braced against each wall, Mac emptied her lungs and cursed as the contraption dropped four levels like a cherry sinking through thick custard. There was certainly time to relax, browse through a newsfeed or something. Unfortunately, the compartment was also network dark, no wi-fi, and not even a naked lightbulb to pass the time by.

As the dumbwaiter reached the lower, lower level, it rang a little bell, signalling destination arrival and an open hatch exit slowly scrolling into view like a dial-up network search. The room itself was solid hematite, long and high, and as much square as you could get from an oblong. A row of fluorescent lights ran the length of the ceiling, desks in neat rows, a dozen women in faded sweatshirts who put their screens to sleep as Mac walked past. There was nothing to say, nothing to see and nothing to hear but the squeaking of her own trainers as she headed towards the far end of the room.

'Dolly,' Mac said, finding the chair with her name on it and sitting down next to a little old lady. 'How you holding up?'

'Oh, I'm very well, dear.'

'You come in past the myriagon vestibule?'

'I did, dear.'

'See the robot installation?'

'Oh yes. Apparently, the artist made it for us, dear,' Dolly said, all soft perm and gravy evidence on her cardigan. 'As a

137

metaphoric representation of our endless struggle to contain a toxic spill.'

'Is that right?' Mac flicked a friendship nod to Effie Cox. 'I probably shouldn't have tripped it up then.'

'Any idea what this meeting is about?' Dolly said.

'Every idea, seeing as I called it,' Mac said. And nothing more until all the side characters of the south coast cell had taken their seats.

Side character cells didn't have a leader as such, but Beverly Smith had stepped into the role of cell facilitator like she'd been re-elected with a large majority and a bunch of flowers. Unconventionally, Beverly hadn't taken the downward career route but had instead opted to remain in a position of relative authority within HMRC. She had, however, micromanaged her whole department into a state of emotional insolvency and created a gravitational productivity loop so dense even a black hole couldn't escape. People avoided contact with her like she was a blanket off a plague ship. In many ways, Beverly Smith had achieved more invisibility than any other side character in game history.

Beverly walked around the group of mismatched women, straightening a chair and making a note of it in the notebook she was holding. She waited for them to fall silent. 'As it was, and is.'

Each one of them came to Attention, feet flat and firm on the ground. Heels in line and touching. Knees braced. Arms straight, held tight to the body. Forearms behind the hip bones. Fingers touching just behind the side seam of their various camouflage uniforms. 'And always will be.'

'Thank you all for coming in at such short notice.' Beverly waited for them to take their seats. 'As you know, calling an emergency meeting is an extra-ordinary event.'

Mac stood back up. 'I ain't wasting nobody's time.'

'An extra-ordinary event. And as meeting facilitator, I am

bound to respect procedure. But I would be failing in my duty to you if I did not also include any outstanding cell business in tonight's agenda. Shelly, if you would be so kind.'

Shelly Manchin handed a wad of papers to the woman next to her. 'Take one for yourself, love, pass the others on.'

'And thank you,' Beverly said, 'to those of you who let me know that they'd received the minutes of the last meeting. It saves a great deal of time if I don't have to chase you up. As I have received no comments or objections, I move that we accept the minutes from the last meeting as they appear. Would anyone like to second?'

A woman who looked a lot like Mac put her hand up.

'Seconded by…Linda. Thank you, Linda. Shelly, if you could make a note of that in the minutes.'

Mac was still standing. 'I said, I ain't wasting nobody's time.'

Beverly carried on checking over the minutes from the last meeting, and took long enough about it to light a fire under anyone. 'If you turn to page eleven, you'll find a copy of the agenda for today's meeting in case you didn't have time to print one off. I've also included an interim financial report on the biscuit fund. Projected only as, Claire, you haven't sent me today's figures. On page twenty, you'll find a spreadsheet overview of all required and available training. If you can fill that in and return it to me before you leave, that would be appreciated. I've also included a hardcopy of the email I sent earlier explaining what a spreadsheet overview of required and available training is, and how you should approach filling it in.'

Mac picked her chair up and threw it across the room. 'The Mandolin have breached the failsafe. Bastard thing got all the way to the teashop and not so much as a nosebleed to show for it. Where's the tick box for that on your spreadsheet overview of required and available training, Beverly?'

Beverly sighed and wrote something lengthy in her notebook. 'Having acquired a first-attempt score of one hundred per cent for the Co-workers and Empathy Online Training Module, I understand that some people can act violently out of frustration,' she said. 'I also understand that throwing the chair just now was done out of an inability to control your anger, Mac. But had you read through the agenda, you would be aware that I have pencilled you in to speak to the group about your experience later this eve—'

'Did you fucking hear wha—'

'Sorry to speak while you're interrupting me,' Beverly said, 'but we have a lot to discuss tonight, and you will have your time in the spotlight after the main topic for discussion and before Paula's presentation on knitting socials. Shelly, do we have any apologies?'

'Sue's stuck on the Chichester bypass,' Shelly said.

'Did she cc me?'

'Her son just messaged me now…to say she's stuck on the Chichester bypass.'

'I'm sorry, but an apology can only be an apology if I am cc'd,' Beverly said. 'Make a note of that in the minutes, Shelly.'

'Shall I put Sue in as an unofficial apology then?' Shelly said, already losing the thread of her own role priorities. 'Because her son did message me.'

'Do what you think is best.'

'What do I think is best?'

'Did she cc me?' Beverly said, writing something that could have been Shelly in her notebook.

'No.'

'Well then, you have your answer,' Beverly said, managerial and overly disappointed with it. 'Now, if we can move on to the main reason for calling this meeting. Underneath your chairs you will find an emergency meeting pack. Inside the pack is an updated list of recommended reading for side characters, along with a brief overview outlining what we'll be talking about tonight. You'll also find a set of appendices based on my observations of the brief overview outlining what we'll be talking about tonight. Paper and pens in the red pencil cases provided. If you have any questions, write them down and put them in the envelopes, also provided. Shelly will collect up your envelopes, and we can discuss any common themes after the tea break.'

'Finally,' Mac said, retrieving her chair and barging a space next to Effie Cox. 'I was close to losing my natural politeness.'

Effie just shrugged, handing Mac an emergency meeting pack. It had two words written on the front: GAME FATIGUE.

In the time it took for Mac to realise what was happening, Beverly had launched into the pre-introduction to the introduction to the briefing. 'If you could open your packs and turn to page one.'

'Sorry,' Mac said, 'I think I've come to the wrong meeting.'

'Mac Eden.' Beverly sighed sternly. 'Many of us have had to cancel important events to attend this emergency cell meeting tonight, a meeting that you yourself instigated. At least have the decency to wait until your allotted time to speak.'

'Is this game fatigue crap coming from the Operating System, or you?'

'Game fatigue is a growing concern among side characters,' Beverly said. 'The Operating System take our mental health extremely seriously.'

'As seriously as a breach to the failsafe?'

Beverly sighed again. 'Would you like to tell us who came into the teashop today, Mac?'

'Since when did we call them a who?'

'Just tell us the name, Mac.'

'I'll tell you this, whatever Mandolin came into the teashop today, it wasn't like anything we've seen before. And if I'm right, it might turn out to be the deadliest player we've faced in all our history.'

Beverly indulged Mac, and was obvious about it. 'And the actual name of this catastrophic terror is?'

'The...name?' Mac hesitated, looking around the room. 'Ain't no one permitted to speak their true name.'

'I am not asking for the...true name.' Beverly squirmed uncomfortably. 'I am asking for the name used by this particular individual, in this particular instance.'

'Right...' Mac said. 'In this particular instance, it might have particularly called itself, Atticus Valentine.'

'Atticus Valentine?'

'That's what I heard, anyway.'

'Mr Atticus Valentine.' Beverly turned to the rest of the cell members. 'The same delightful and undeniably talented young man, risen from parental adversity, to found a highly successful production company. That Atticus Valentine?'

'No,' Mac said. 'Pretty sure that's a hard no.'

Beverly pulled a well-thumbed photograph from her notebook. 'Perhaps this might help.'

'That...that there!' Mac pointed triumphantly. 'That's exactly what it looked like when it came into the teashop. It weren't using mimicry, more like some kind of mass deception. I ain't seen anything like it. All sorts of people were swooning and fawning and whatnot. That means it's got to be a high-rank player, the highest I've ever come across. I'm figuring it's got itself a fraud identity set up somewhere close. Somewhere it can keep an eye on us.'

'That's certainly one theory,' Beverly said. 'Myself, I have followed side character procedure and confirmed with the Operating System that the aforementioned visit was arranged through all the correct channels. As to your accusations, Mac, I would suggest that the aforementioned visitor bore a remarkable resemblance to Atticus Valentine, because he was indeed, Atticus Valentine.'

'I know what I saw.'

Beverly handed Mac several sheets of paper. 'I have provided a choice of accompanying evidence.'

Mac flicked through, her frown rapidly progressing into bewilderment as she checked the papers a second time. 'It says here Plug Productions.'

'That is correct,' Beverly said.

Mac stared at her. 'That's the same people what make *WØLF*?'

'They do indeed. Although, from what I understand, Atticus Valentine is more the people,' Beverly said, 'than the make.'

'No, you got that wrong.'

'Do you need me to spell this out? Atticus Valentine is the chief executive officer of Plug Productions. Google it, it's no secret,' Beverly said, all undeniable evidence and pleased with herself.

'Shit,' Mac said. 'Shit, shit, shit. Fuck.'

Beverly winced. 'A little constructive feedback, Mac. If you could keep your language clean, that would make things much clearer for Shelly.'

'Bastard thing strolled itself all the way to the fucking teashop, and it didn't even have the fucking decency to die touching old iron. Now you fucking tell me it's somehow got itself a fraud identity giving it control of the company making *WØLF*. Fucking sure we need a new fucking containment strategy, and fucking quick about it or everything we've fucking fought to prevent all these fucking years is finished. Is that fucking clear enough for you, Shelly?'

Beverly drew several exclamation marks in her notebook. 'Thank you for bringing this to the attention of the cell, Mac.'

'Yeah, well,' Mac said. 'Single command function, it's our responsibility to report these things.'

Beverly flicked to a clean page in her notebook. 'Now, if you'll all turn to page one in your packs, you'll notice that I have included a brief history of game fat—'

'It picked up my ladle,' Mac said, talking over her. 'My iron ladle that's six hundred years old. And made from a ladle that came before it. There's seasoned blacksmiths won't go near that ladle.'

'Yes, thank you, Mac.'

'Iron triggers a catastrophic deionisation in them,' Mac growled. 'We've all seen it with our own eyes. Every time, every bastard time. Even the entry level players aren't stupid enough to go beyond the threshold of Fabian Evirate House. This thing should have been dead ten times over, except it wasn't. If the Mandolin really have found a way to tolerate iron, then we're fucked. There's no way left to kill them that doesn't mean spilled blood, and we all know what that fucking means.' Mac threw her meeting pack on the ground loudly and with a great deal of frustration. 'Lucky for us, the Operating System scheduled an emergency cell meeting on game fatigue.'

'Or perhaps because of,' Beverly said, kind almost. 'The job we do, there's no shame to be found in game fatigue. It finds the best of us.' She looked to Effie Cox then. 'Effie, perhaps this is an opportune moment for you to say a few words.'

'Sit down, Effie,' Mac said.

'Will you listen to what I have to say, lass?'

'The Mandolin caught us with our pants in the wash when they hosted that nuclear firework display in Afghanistan,' Mac said. 'And yeah, I awaited further instructions. I downplayed this *WØLF* malarkey. I kept my mind fixed on the job because I imagined the Operating System would be putting some sort of futureproof strategy in place. But I don't see no evidence of futureproofing, and somehow our pants are still in the wash. We're sat here talking about game fatigue when the enemy push this fucking game further and further towards the impossible ending. How long do we have left before the Mandolin go and reveal their true name on social media? God help us all then.' Mac ignored Effie's pleading look. 'Did any of you read the new public gameplay strategy the Operating System uploaded?'

'I have a list,' Beverly said.

'I read the whole thing through three times,' Mac said. 'And not even in the footnotes does the strategy recommend the use of wokeness as an effective weapon in containing the Mandolin.'

'Fortifying the mental wellbeing of side characters is not wokeness,' Beverly said. 'Never is it wokeness.'

'Great Exhibition of Enchantment,' Mac mumbled. 'Great Exhibition of Wokeness, more like.'

'Corrupting the vision of Maudie Clump, blessed be,' Beverly crossed herself reverently, 'is a cheap shot, Mac. And it doesn't do justice to your loyalty and service.'

'I weren't—'

'In her capacity as midwife, our beloved benefactor withstood many difficult labours,' Beverly said. 'She knew when to push and when to yield. At present, the Operating System sees Afghanistan as a time to yield.'

'A time to yield?' Mac looked around the room. 'Maudie Clump, blessed be, didn't yield to Jack the Ripper, but we're happy yielding to some suited-up Mandolin player that dares to tread a foot on our turf? Our turf. Ours. And I know that means something to this cell, because it means something to me. We take our orders from the Operating System, but when the scummy filth hits the south coast fan, the south coast fan hits back. I say we send the Mandolin a message, and we make it loud enough for the whole of their sorry history to hear: This is our land. You are not welcome here. Not now. Not never. Access Denied.' It was a stirring speech. Mac waited on a rallying cry, but all she got was more sympathy like she was at an AA meeting and still in denial. 'So what, we live in a fucking Beverly echo chamber now?'

Effie lifted her hand, soft to Mac's shoulder. 'Just listen to what I have to say.'

'Shit, you all think I made a mistake,' Mac said, scraping her chair backwards out of the group. 'All of you, you think I made a mistake.' And her hands screwed into her hair, too much frustration to know what else to say.

Dolly picked up her chair and moved to sit next to Mac. 'Bev means well, dear, she just finds it hard to disagree with herself. I once suspended a startled young man from the top balcony of a block of flats, convinced he was Mandolin. As it turned out, he was the new window cleaner.'

'Yeah, we've all done that,' Mac said, 'but I appreciate the sentiment.'

'What I'm really saying,' Dolly touched her fingers to Mac's hand, 'is that it doesn't matter how much game experience we have, we still make mistakes. And that's good, because if we stop making mistakes, then we stop learning. And I wouldn't want to live in a world that had stopped learning.'

Mac stood up again, hair all twisted up and face to match. 'Do I look like someone who has game fatigue?'

Beverly had let go of the meeting reins for long enough. 'If you wish to address the group, Mac Eden, you must bring your chair back into alignment.'

'What I wish, is for you to tell the Operating System...' Mac took hold of the hand Dolly had offered. 'You know what, Beverly, you do whatever the fuck you want.'

Well, it wasn't the first time Beverly had heard those words, and it certainly wouldn't be the last. She made a note to look up borderline personality disorder when she got home, and set about restoring calm with a well-structured agenda. 'As you can see from the diagram on page forty-nine, what we side characters might refer to as game fatigue, has existed in one form or another for as long as Homo sapiens have experienced trauma.'

Effie Cox put up her hand. 'Shall I still say a few words, Beverly?'

'I thought you already had,' Beverly said.

'Did I?'

'I'm the one asking you?'

'I'm not sure,' Effie said, fading.

'I'm afraid only you know the answer to that,' Beverly said. 'Now, article one, page two. What is game fatigue?'

'You coming, Dolly?' Mac said, quiet enough now to go unnoticed.

'I'll stay here,' Dolly said. 'For the young ones. Some of them have no resilience for spreadsheets.'

As the meeting closed, Dolly caught up with a disappointed Paula. 'I'm sorry we didn't get to see your presentation on knitting socials, dear. Will you bring it along next time?'

'I made everyone a pair of socks.'

'Lovely.'

'Beverly said there might not be time at the next meeting,' Paula said. 'I suppose I could just give everyone their socks anyway.'

'Why don't you come along to Bingo tomorrow?' Dolly said, accepting Paula's offer of a steadying arm to hold. 'It's none of that phone nonsense, real chairs and tables, real people too, and prizes galore. You get a cup of tea if you buy five strips. Last week, I won a family picture frame. It came with a set of pictures already in the holes. A family. They seem just lovely, and they have a dog, fancy that. Two children and a dog. They don't look old enough to have two children, but everyone looks so young these days. I had a nail already in the wall where that print of Venice was hanging, and I asked the new orderly if she could pop it up there for me, just to give me something nice to look at. I call the dog Spot, for a bit of fun, you know. *Hello, Spot, who's a good boy then?* I suppose they had the dog before the children, but the children must remember to be gentle, because Spot is an old boy now.'

Paula slowed her walk to match Dolly's shuffle. 'Dolly, do you ever wonder if we worsen the stereotypes?'

'Worsen, dear?'

'For women, for age.' Paula looked down at her cable-knit jumper. 'For knitting.'

'I heard knitting was fashionable,' Dolly said.

'That's because men and young people do it now.'

'Women and age are such underpinned strongholds of discrimination, dear,' Dolly said. 'I was chatting to a lovely ninety-two-year-old woman at the last 10k charity run. I doddered around for half a kilometre. In a buttoned coat, of course, with everyone clapping and telling me how inspirational I was. She, on the other hand, was dressed appropriately and smashed the time record for the over-seventies.' Dolly sighed. 'Several people posted that a sports bra and tight shorts were not suitable for a woman of her age, and no one sat with her when we had our coffee.'

'So we compound the discrimination?'

'We do what we have to do, dear,' Dolly said, squeezing Paula's arm. 'Our fight is elsewhere.'

14

Forty per cent of George Washington's blood

The army had a way of teaching some things down to the minutest detail and leaving others so short of instruction it felt like being lost in the woods without a torch. The first fieldcraft lesson was reputedly an ease-in for town dwellers, except this one had *WØLF* crew cameras, riggers, drones and four up-and-coming superstars to ignore. Nothing about it felt like an ease-in. Settling them came down to Sergeant Naleigh. Former SAS, he'd reportedly killed twenty-five people with a paperclip before losing both legs to a suicide attack. It would have been easy to assume his way of walking came down to prosthetic augmentation, but the sergeant walked among them like he owned a small island, brandishing the oak walking stick he'd brought with him. And when he went climbing up the long barrow they'd be sleeping in, thumping a kerb stone like he was a god fixing fire to the earth, all of them knew it wasn't the sort of walk you could blame on prosthetic augmentation. The trainee soldiers dropped their packs and set their camp, keeping their backs to the cover stone of the Neolithic burial chamber, still daylight and not even the *WØLF* crew riggers anxious to go inside.

Whiskey-Zero-One-Foxtrot/s3e5/REMI IP link PP confirm: EFP crew

Producer: *Elspeth Hart*

EXT. GBR. DEMDYKE LONG BARROW – DAY

Scene: New *WØLF* recruits *Hollow Quinn, Joanie Magrath, Fish Nazari* and *Hubert Frank* experience their first fieldcraft lesson. Crew cameras on *SGT Naleigh* – continuous

Sergeant Naleigh inspected the small pile of branches they'd collected. 'Not bad for a first attempt. As you will have noticed, firewood is a scarcity on a chalk plain. Who brought the gorse?'

'Sergeant.' A sun-freckled recruit stepped forward; his hands already covered in fine scratches.

'Gorse burns hot as charcoal, especially when it's dry. But you gotta watch it, and I'm not talking about the thorns. One wayward spark and the whole plain goes up in smoke, and no one wants that, especially a soldier trying to keep their mission under wraps. Save the gorse for wet days where smoke can be lost in the fog.' Sergeant Naleigh picked a seed-heavy grass stalk from the pile and stuck it in the corner of his mouth. 'Give me some ideas as to what else you could use, something that will last you overnight, and no smoke to give your position away.'

He waited out the silence.

'Right, you lot,' he said, 'it doesn't matter if an officer is briefing you on what socks to wear or a dream they had where nothing happened, you better listen like it's the most important thing you ever heard.' He chewed the stalk to the other side of his mouth. 'But there's listening, and then there's brain dead. You see a gap in our conversation, recruits, you better fill it, or I'll be forced to engage you in some impromptu singing.'

Joanie fought the urge to put his hand up. 'I heard you can

go three months without food, but that allows for snacks, right?'

'Survival question?' The forbidding mountain that was Sergeant Naleigh succumbed to a half-smile. 'You read my mind, kid.'

'Sorry,' Joanie said.

'Lesson One: the fear is in the question. Can't say I blame you. Three months without food has got to scare the desire to survive out of anyone. Truth is, surviving without food can be a lot shorter than three months, especially if you're in a hurry to get somewhere. If you preserve energy, you've got weeks rather than days. But there's usually something you can eat, and hardly anyone dies of starvation in the field.' Sergeant Naleigh straightened up. 'And seeing as you kicked us off on this topic, kid, give me some things that'll kill you before starvation.'

'Thirst?'

'Correct. You only get a few days without water, so water always takes priority over food. What you can't survive for long is the elements. Cold will kill you before you know you're in trouble. Same goes for heat. It doesn't matter what environment you find yourself in, shelter is your top priority.' He looked around the group of recruits. 'Quicker than exposure?'

'No oxygen,' Fish said.

Sergeant Naleigh's laugh startled the birds. 'Well now, that's true enough, so don't go putting a plastic bag over your head to keep the rain off.'

'A bullet.'

'A year ago, I'd have agreed with you, but most of the bullets you'll come across now are soft-casing iron powder. They'll make a mess of your uniform, but they won't kill you. Not unless there's a cuckoo nesting among you, eh?' Sergeant Naleigh flicked the grass to the other side of his mouth, grinning more than he ought to. 'And who needs live ammo when there's all sorts of nerve toxins out there, and I'm not just talking about the ones they manufacture in a lab.'

Hubert Frank was a few steps away from the main group. 'We joined the boy scouts now?'

Sergeant Naleigh carried on like nothing untoward had been said. 'There's innocent-looking plants that'll stop your heart dead, even if it's just using their twigs to roast your supper on. Then you've got snakes, insects, frogs, all manner of marine life. But all the above is just a matter of knowing what you're doing, and that's not what I'm talking about here. So, answer me this, my little rainbows, what is the biggest threat to your survival on this whole goddamn earth?'

'Boredom?' Hubert Frank said.

'What's your name, son?'

'The Hubert.'

'The Hubert?' Sergeant Naleigh smiled, but every single micro expression said otherwise. 'Well, seeing as you're feeling so bored, The Hubert, you're our latrine queen for the duration.'

'Whatever you say, you're the man,' Hubert Frank said, and cocky with it. 'The Hubert don't shy from no shit.'

Sergeant Naleigh reached into his top pocket, pulled out a paperclip and casually pushed it onto his collar like a rank insignia. 'You might've noticed we keep the ozone scanners running twenty-four hours a day. Solar, wind, biomass, backup generators for the backup generators. Three rank, rotating authorisation for basic maintenance. Offsite evacuation procedure. Every double-check you can think of gets double-checked. And the reason for that precautionary overload leads me back to the single most important question you'll get asked in your time at army training camp.' He fixed a look on Hubert Frank. 'What is the biggest threat to your survival on this whole goddamn earth?'

'The Mandolin.'

'Wrong.'

'The Hubert has a question.' Hubert Frank kicked his heel through a clump of tall grasses. 'What's with the idle time?'

'You think fieldcraft is idle time?'

'Ain't nothing personal, bru, but wind us up and let us do what we came here to do.' Hubert Frank eyeballed the group like there was solidarity to be found there. 'Hubert Frank ain't no wait-around skank.'

'How old are you, son?'

'Sixteen years,' Hubert Frank said.

'Sixteen?' Sergeant Naleigh shook his head. 'Hell, at sixteen it still feels like you're the primary guest at the table of life. I hate to break it to you, son, but you have no idea how far off the primary guest you are. And while I appreciate your youthful honesty, you're talking down to an officer. In my day, you'd be back home already, and an advisory letter to your parents. But we're all modern sensitives at army training camp now. Shit, we even call it boot camp so it sounds more accessible. And apparently accessibility also runs to teaching Phase One recruits how to respect authority. Consider yourself duly enlightened. I catch any of you talking down to an officer again and you're on report.'

'Permission to speak candidly,' Hubert Frank said, with a salute.

'You're treading a fine line there, son,' Sergeant Naleigh said. 'There's more etiquette involved in saluting than dining with the king. Until you've been trained to salute, you do not salute. The Hubert, what I see in you is an appetite for attention and general ignorance. General ignorance is down to us to fix; craving attention, that's all on you.'

'Do I get a question, bru?'

'Not your bru.'

'Do I get a question, Sergeant Naleigh?'

'Ask your question, son.'

'Not...' Hubert Frank started like he might challenge the sergeant, but he never quite got there. 'We headed to desert warfare, why you teaching us to build sandcastles?'

Sergeant Naleigh took his time to answer, leaning for a while on his walking stick. 'All wars smell the same. And it's not smoke or gunpowder. I was an old soldier before you lot were even born. Does that make me too old to know much about this new kind of war with its adaptive technology and its fashion-forward soldiers? Damn right it does. But you better believe me when I tell you that how old you are means nothing when you see your first body floating down the same river you're drinking from. All wars smell of death. You taste it in your food; you smell it on your clothes; you cough it out of your lungs until you're not sure you can remember what it smells like to be alive any more. And humans, they're more liable to brutality than you'd ever think possible. If you can keep your moral compass intact, you probably weren't there.' Sergeant Naleigh chewed the grass stalk back across his mouth. 'So maybe The Hubert here is right. Maybe a new kind of war means fieldcraft should be about showing you how to access your uniform interface when the wi-fi has dropped out. Except this isn't a new kind of war we're fighting, it's good old-fashioned slaughter. And the International War Agency are rammed so tight up the cooperation route, they've lost sight of the army.'

'Sergeant Naleigh?' Joanie said.

But Sergeant Naleigh was already too full into the rant-roll to stop. 'Believe me, there's more than localised radiation about using a dirty bomb. Never, not in all our bloody history, have we used one of those bastard weapons. But the Mandolin, they go and introduce themselves with it. Not a major city, not somewhere that would kill hundreds, just a low-rank military base in Afghanistan. That bomb was nothing as far as mass casualty strikes go, but it was as psychologically damaging as the notification hack. And maybe they've already played their ace. Maybe the ace is still out there somewhere. There's no way to know. All we know is that us humans got caught on the back foot. Still on the bloody back foot. Too much arrogance for our own good. If we're to stand a chance, we need to get back to basics.' Sergeant Naleigh nodded towards Hubert Frank. 'That's not just Phase One of initial training, that's back to the things that have been handed down since the birth of war. And these sandcastles, as you call them, they're teaching you how to survive. God knows you'll all need to believe that's possible.'

The group flickered through enough reactions to fill an old cinema reel, but only one could bring themself to say the terrible thing. 'It's not them,' Hollow said, 'it's us. We're the ones being slaughtered.'

And maybe it was that even the *WØLF* production crew hadn't wanted it said, because when Sergeant Naleigh roared with laughter and held his hands up in mock surrender, they laughed too.

'Now that's on me,' Sergeant Naleigh said. 'Special forces is special forces. A mosquito comes too close, we take it down like it's a grenade drone.'

'We're doing okay, though?' Fish said.

'We're Homo sapiens, kid. We didn't dominate the earth because we're the smartest or the fittest; we dominated because we're the rats of the human evolutionary tree. We eat anything, we live anywhere and we breed like there's never enough of us. Anyone who knows anything about rats knows that they'll survive when most other creatures would fail. Hell, I've seen full-grown rats crawl out of a bucket of water after five hours of forced drowning.' Sergeant Naleigh winked at Joanie. 'That's something to remember when the lights go out.'

Hubert Frank laughed, but he'd found something in Sergeant Naleigh's rant that he put a value to, and the laugh was sweeter for it. 'Which SAS unit, Sergeant?'

Sergeant Naleigh just grinned. Grabbed his walking stick, and owned the ancient landscape like he was born to it. 'Right then, my little rainbow recruits, how about the rats catch themselves some vermin for supper?'

Following the network of grass-flattened runs and covering their scent with rabbit dung, they set a dozen snares around the bank of warrens a half mile from camp. The sergeant showed them how to identify a moss that would keep the fire burning overnight, and then sent them to find it. Several times, Hubert Frank tried to hook the sergeant into a conversation about Special Air Services, but he didn't get a bite. In the end, he found some allies among the older recruits. They spoke too loudly to go unnoticed, but Sergeant Naleigh left them to it.

Away from camp, Joanie and Fish drifted from their leisurely search into a reflective standstill. There was a gentle warmth to the air and no wind to chase it away.

'Rats?' Fish looked towards the silhouette of Hubert Frank. 'It's not a leap.'

'Some rats are quite lovely,' Joanie said.

'For disease-infested pests.'

'Fish…' Joanie spoke slowly '…I can't tell you something.'

'I know, babe.'

'I want to tell you.'

'It's okay.'

'No, Fish.' Joanie teared up. 'No, it's not.'

'Shit.' Fish took hold of his shoulders. 'Breathe it through. Breathe it through. Remember when we were coming back from Edinburgh, and you confided in me about sleeping with Jeremiah. And you were confused about how you were feeling, because it was your first time, and Jeremiah was a hairy lumberjack from Connecticut. Remember how I swore on my honour that I wouldn't tell anyone, but I already told Eli and Felicia before we got off the train.'

Joanie looked down at his boots. 'Yeah.'

'You can't tell me.'

'I can't tell you.'

'Is it bad?'

'It's really bad, Fish.'

'It was bound to be triggered by being here, mind.' Fish dropped away from him, walking a slow circle, searching the rough ground for something that wasn't there. 'So I'm freaking out, obvs, because I got reminded of that waiting-for-you-to-go-extinct message.'

'Yeah, we all tried to forget about that.'

'Now I have to forget the slaughter thing as well.'

'I know.' Joanie sighed it all out. 'Back at boot camp, everyone's saying the war will be over before we finish our training. It's hard to know what to believe.'

'Do we still get an active service medal if the war's already over?' Fish said. 'Plus, The Hubert is annoying me beyond.'

'He's scared,' Joanie said.

'He's a dickhead, Joan. An arrogant, obnoxious dickhead.' Fish paced a gap between them. 'I can't believe Sergeant Naleigh let him get away with talking shit like that.'

'Sergeant Naleigh?'

'Yeah, well, it's not my place,' Fish said.

Joanie tilted his head. 'Since when?'

'What can I say, I'm a hot mess of mental polarity.'

ITM SCENE
COMMENTARY
FISH NAZARI:
Hubert Frank is a spanner. None of us know what level yet, but it's probably boss-level. Except I'm stood there thinking, yeah, he's right, we should be doing more than talking about moss. Next minute, I'm crapping myself even thinking about this training being over.

PRODUCER:
Is Joanie hiding something?

157

FISH NAZARI:
No, sake. I mean, not like hiding it…hiding it. Joanie's book is so open, it's a motivational placemat. Except, he has this thing he can't talk about. And he's not that sort of person, so when he wants to talk about it, he tells people he can't talk about it.

PRODUCER:
What sort of thing?

FISH NAZARI:
You know, like a thing…thing. That he can't talk about for some reason. It's a bit weird, but it makes sense to him and that's all I care about.

PRODUCER:
And if the thing is better spoken about?

FISH NAZARI:
I mean, sure. And he'd tell me if I asked him, but he also knows I can't keep it secret.

PRODUCER:
Can't, or won't?

FISH NAZARI:
No, can't.

PRODUCER:
Whatever he's keeping secret is big enough to hide from his best friend. He might tell you something you don't want to hear, Fish. Maybe it's easier for you to avoid it.

FISH NAZARI:

You know what, Elspeth, there's nothing Joan could tell me that would stop me loving him. It's me that's the problem. I'm scared of what I'd do with it, and terrified of how much I'd hurt him because of that. Which is why I remind him of how he can't trust me. By constantly telling people his darkest, dirtiest secrets.

Mostly it's gossip about his parents, but it's the thought that counts, right?

Fish took a step away from Joanie, away from the answer maybe. 'Joan, what if we actually have to kill someone?'

'For fieldcraft?'

'Don't even joke.'

Joanie closed the gap, wrapping his arm around her. 'You know what Sylvie Stevens always says in situations like this.'

'It might be a war zone, but we can still look after our teeth?'

Joanie laughed for both of them. 'Don't use up your whole heart crying about things that haven't happened. Besides, we're Medivac. We should be more worried about body fluids. And not just blood.'

'Everyone knows about Mandolin psych scams.' Fish took a deep breath. 'About how they make you kill your own friends.'

'I didn't enlist in the army to kill people,' Joanie said. 'I enlisted because I wanted to save people from dying.'

'What if I was trying to kill you, Joan?' Fish struggled to keep the words straight. 'God, what if I killed you.'

Joanie took a while to answer. 'Let's both stay near Hollow.'

'Yeah, yeah, that's probably the best thing.' Fish pulled away from Joanie. 'But you have to promise me something, Joan.'

'No.'

'I haven't even told you yet.'

'No, I won't promise it.' Joanie backed away, further, faster, until he came to a stop against the immovable object that was Sergeant Naleigh.

'Can I assume from your inaction, that you two rainbows have found what I sent you to find?'

'Sorry, Sergeant.'

'Sorry, Sergeant.' Sergeant Naleigh leant in. 'And don't think I haven't seen the biscuits.'

When the recruits returned from checking the empty snares, there were three skinned rabbits, ready skewered and dripping fat onto the fire. Sergeant Naleigh didn't welcome them back; he just carried on setting up the ozone detectors, building a ring of them into the ditch that encircled the long barrow.

'We all know about dinosaurs,' he said. 'We know what their skin was like, what they ate, what they sounded like. We know they lived on this planet for more than one hundred and fifty million years. Most of us assume we always knew about them, but George Washington never knew about dinosaurs. Imagine that, being born in a time when no one knew about dinosaurs. It wasn't like the evidence didn't exist; it was the thinking that didn't exist. Everyone went about their lives believing in giants, just like their parents had.' Sergeant Naleigh stepped back, flicking a switch to run a system error scan through the ozone detectors. 'Doctors took forty per cent of George Washington's blood trying to save him from a throat infection, and killied him quicker than the throat infection. Humans are serial thinkers. We think we know everything there is to know, but all we know is what we know right now. There's nothing to be gained in denying that. Here in the army we teach the same basic rules of survival that kept every single one of our ancestors alive long enough to be our ancestors. Foraged subsistence is simple enough: You eat WHEN you can. You eat WHERE you can. You eat WHAT you can.'

One of the older recruits put up her hand. 'Permission to ask about the ozone detectors?'

'Granted.'

'Why do we need them, Sergeant Naleigh?'

'Because you're never sure when your next meal will be.'

She persevered. 'If there's no Mandolin footfall beyond Afghanistan, then why do we need them?'

'If you won't eat everything until you'll eat anything, it's already too late,' Sergeant Naleigh said. 'And you bloody well trust your commanding officer like your life depended on it, because one day it will.'

ITM SCENE
COMMENTARY
FISH NAZARI:
The rabbit meat was bloody grim, mind. Dry, earthy, intense, and bloody grim. I would have passed, but Sergeant Naleigh just gave us the talk, and you get the impression that refusal isn't an option in the army. I tried thinking about it being a piece of old carpet, except old carpet would have been nicer. No one was happy eating it, not even Hollow, and she's like, completely switched off since she had that run-in with the PTI corporal.

PRODUCER:
What makes you think Hollow has switched off?

FISH NAZARI:
I mean, yeah. Can't you see it? I thought it was obvious.

JOANIE MAGRATH:
It's everyone's first night without a phone, so I stashed four packets of chocolate digestives and some hand sanitiser in a heart-shaped outcrop by the latrine. Sergeant Naleigh didn't confiscate them, maybe he

figured we could all do with something comforting. There was hardly any meat on the rabbit, everyone is starving, but there's still two packets of biscuits left. I think we'll be okay.

The ozone detectors hummed softly, and the sky was as clear as it could get with a ribbon of light pollution smudging a glow along the horizon. For most of the recruits, their first night ignoring a camera crew would have been anxiety enough, but they had a bite of hunger in their bellies, and none of them were used to the eerie quiet of a wild place. Sergeant Naleigh picked Joanie for first watch and sat with him, guarding the entrance of the long barrow while the others crept inside to sleep. None of them had experienced the death-dark cold of a Neolithic burial chamber before, and they moved slowly with it. Their boots scuffing the thresholds, their gloved hands on rock worn smooth by touch, and each arc of torchlight trespassing the intimacy of silent square tombs. There was nothing to see, but still they saw it: the foetal curl of lost bones in the house of the dead. They didn't speak much beyond finding a way to the central chamber and laying their bivvy bags close together. The air was damp and heavy with incense. Melted wax marked the shrine points. Spices, feathers and beads. And the slabs of ancient rock, stacked and suspended above them in an unyielding perseverance of stone. Too used to darkness, too used to sacrament to rest easy with their childish whisperings. Lights-out had four of them scrabbling back outside. The first rasping bark of a fox brought the rest. For all his bluster, Sergeant Naleigh stayed with them, every hour, every watch, keeping the fire alight, keeping the monsters at bay. And sometimes he sang, low and melodic.

> *"I might try*
> *to hold the moon in the sky*
> *one last night to ease my sorrow,*

but the birds of my homeland
still bring me the sun,
still bring me tomorrow."

The next morning, Sergeant Naleigh met their waking with a dangling rabbit. It was all eyes and terror, not even kicking any more . 'War,' he said, 'isn't about denying your rage; it's about making it work for you. Anger is a resource, just like petrol is a resource. Use it. Respect it. Don't throw it around at a party.'

When the time came, Hubert Frank volunteered to kill the poor creature, but everyone could see the sergeant wasn't looking for volunteers.

'It's your lucky day, Quinn,' Sergeant Naleigh said, handing the rabbit over to Hollow. 'Let's see if you live up to your name, shall we?'

The rabbit was silent and small, and the beautiful grey of a soft spring mist. It looked like it should have been a pet. Hollow stroked its head with the back of her finger and snapped its neck.

'I guess you do, some part of it at least,' Sergeant Naleigh said. 'And seeing as you're on a roll, Quinn, perhaps you'd also like to enlighten us as to what the biggest threat to your survival on the whole of this goddamn earth is.'

'My own mind,' Hollow said.

15

Not foreign affairs

Ezra's reflection pirouetted in the glass witch ball, every part of it cut to pieces and put back together again. The phylactery was the heart of Fabian Evirate House, a heart crammed full of outdated superstition and fear. But Atticus Valentine hadn't called it fear; he'd called it desire. Which made far more sense, because desire was at the heart of everything. The lightforms were smaller in here, and they stayed the same no matter what the light was like. Squatting toads, frogs, snails, lizards, serpents on the upper levels, unchanged since the building had been built. Twelve hours ago, Ezra had seen Hollow snap the neck of a rabbit. Everyone agreed that it was probably war that made it seem okay. Apparently, war could be blamed for lots of dodgy things now, including why Ezra had agreed to help Atticus Valentine. There'd been time to stop it before Emporia arrived, but Atticus hadn't stopped it, and there was nothing about it that Ezra wanted to stop. Not for the GiFT, not for the rules, not for whatever kind of payback was waiting at the end of it all. In a way, Ezra had snapped a rabbit's neck along with Hollow, a less gruesome morality event horizon perhaps, but a morality event horizon nonetheless.

In the teashop, Ezra had waited on Emporia's arrival like they were trapped in the final few minutes of a sand timer.

'This symbol has been with me my whole life,' Atticus had

said. 'I'm hoping Fabian Evirate House can help me find the answers I can't find anywhere else.'

'We'll help you figure this out,' Ezra had said, watching Atticus twist the cord of a pendant he'd pulled from his pocket like he wasn't sure he should show it to anyone. 'I promise.'

'My life is public property. I can't get up in the morning without someone having an opinion about it. And if I speak to Emporia or Dicky, then this becomes...'

'Public property too.'

'Yes.'

'Fear not, I shall remain the epitome of discretion.'

'Thank you,' he'd said, taking hold of Ezra's hand. And when he'd let go, the pendant was there. Cold in the heat and black with age. A few strips of iron forged to form a crude basket shape. Suspended from a faded leather cord. Straightforward forge welding. Indeterminate date. Basic. Simple even. Harmless.

'The best place to start is the in-house database,' Ezra had said. 'There's one-click access to the Smithsonian and British Museum if you can't find what you're looking for on our system. You don't even need to create a separate account. All public space access is triple authenticated, but we also have some private rooms you can use.'

Atticus Valentine had smiled softly then. 'I don't need a private room.'

'Sure, okay. And you can always change your mind,' Ezra said. 'The security firewall lets most things through, apart from the usual. There will be no hacking government departments or looking at dodgy things here at Fabian Evirate House. Apart from our own dodgy things, obviously. And it's worth bearing in mind that the parameters for dodgy were set out by the board of trustees, so basically a gentleman wearing a loose t-shirt on a windy day qualifies as dodgy.'

Ezra had tried to hand the pendant back then, but Atticus turned it away. 'I've done enough research to last me a lifetime.

And no matter where I look, I just keep running into the same wall. I was hoping a fresh set of eyes might make a difference.'

'A fresh set of eyes?'

'Your eyes.' His words had been soft, careful, as though Ezra was a suicide-tourist on the edge of a cliff.

'Ah, got it.' To be fair, there was no way Atticus would have seen the volcano of emotions that erupted in that one perilous moment. 'I could try a basic timeline sweep,' Ezra had said. 'Considering the research you've already done, I doubt it will solve the mystery, but it might flag up a place to start.'

He'd nodded then, fleeting, heartbreakingly young. 'Thank you.'

'And you think it might be connected to a curse of some kind?'

'Of some kind.'

'Is it a protection charm?'

He'd scuffed over a little laugh. 'No.'

'Crap, it's not the curse, is it!'

'No, no.' Atticus had scooped up Ezra's hand to close around the pendant, quick to reassure. 'It's fine, I promise, it's not a curse.'

'Right. Stand down red alert.' Ezra had said, embarrassed and awkward. 'And the wall you keep running into?'

'Finding it is easy.' He'd looked over to the counter then, to the place where Mac Eden had been. 'It's getting past it that's the problem.'

'Enigmatic. It's a family piece, yes?' Ezra had said.

'Sure.'

'Did anyone in your family ever tell you anything about it, like even if it didn't make much sense at the time?'

'I'm sorry, I know it's not much to work with.'

'Honestly, don't worry,' Ezra had said. 'Sometimes, having no place to start works out for the best anyway.'

'Thank you, for not pushing it. And it's okay to freak out. You'll understand why when you get there.'

'The mysterious wall?'

He'd turned away like he was looking for someone. 'Yep.'

'Mysterious.'

There could have been more said between them, but Emporia's estimated time of arrival had been unsurprisingly accurate. She'd come blustering into the teashop, fully scheduled and in charge. Atticus had welcomed her like she'd turned up at just the right moment, all sweetness and charmingly apologetic. But Ezra had been stretched with the elastic band of normality, and when it snapped back into shape, the shock of it was like surfacing too quickly from the bottom of the ocean.

'Sorry,' Atticus had whispered as he leant in to finish his coffee, 'I wish I could tell you more.'

'No, I love a mystery.'

It was true. Not only in matters of history, but in matters of everything. In many ways, it explained why Hollow's company could act like a pick-me-up. But Hollow was an obvious mystery; she came with an untamed sort of dangerous you could spot a mile off. Atticus Valentine wasn't like that. If anything, he was the antithesis of dangerous. Except that didn't sit right either. Mac Eden's reaction might have been upfront weird, but it also felt weirdly apt. There was something intangible about him. Something that meant he could randomly turn out to be the most dangerous person Ezra had ever met. Whatever way you looked at it, Atticus Valentine was a mystery with mysterious bells on.

Ezra walked a meandering route to the Jötunvillur panel, casually wrapping and unwrapping the pendant from its leather cord. History always had time on its side, day after day gradually levelling out the knocks and edges, turning even the bumpiest things into something as smooth as silk. Fortunately, the marks on this panel were deep set enough to survive the ironing board of time. There were traces of decoration, abstract shapes filled with wood resin, blue pigment caught under the ridges. Fragments of a carved framework had been gilded, delicate, hopeful in the borders. Jötunvillur was usually cut into rough timber or bone, lines like a tally, not anything near precious enough to be carved or gilded. In unguarded moments, Dicky talked about finding something in the panel that everyone else had missed. He'd even reiterated his induction day promise that the discovery might provide Ezra with something more permanent than a GiFT certificate at the end of the year. Ezra took a deep breath, dangling the pendant at arm's length. Hoping at least for a lantern, or a compass, to show the way.

'See these mud runes,' Ezra said to the pendant. 'These little guys relate to eternal, pre-existent forces. Esoterically bewildering; contextually grounded. But you, you're not a rune. You're just a few strips of iron forged to form a crude basket shape. Straightforward forge welding. Indeterminate age. Basic. Simple even. Hanging there looking all harmless like a crescent moon, or two straight lines, or a plain black flag. Without context, it's impossible to understand your power. So what's your story, little one, what am I looking for?' Ezra turned a full circle, accidentally tap-tapping the pendant against a winged talisman. 'Where in this mess of desire do you fit?'

Keeping hold of the pendant had been Atticus Valentine's idea, but it was down to Ezra to know just how forbidden it was for staff to take items into their personal care. It was a blatant transgression of duty in a series of less blatant transgressions. From there, the absolute wrongness of hiding the pendant as Emporia Precipice Mantlepiece bustled her way across the teashop had seemed like the right thing to do. And just like that, events had paddled so far up the creek, it seemed a waste of time to bother about something as inconsequential as a morality event horizon.

A whole three floors down, and a whole four times more pissed off with the mystery that was Atticus Valentine, Mac stuffed a packet of sponges into her cleaning trolley. The emergency cell meeting had been a full-blown lesson on what not to do when the Operating System was incompatible with current events. But such things occurred from time to time, and she could still do this on her own. Her priority now was intel, which meant she needed to get closer to the bastard thing. Fortunately, it looked like Ezra Blake might have won its attention, and Mac could turn that unfortunate win to her advantage. Civilian recruitment was restricted to extreme circumstances. Unauthorised civilian recruitment carried a custodial sentence. Still, there wasn't always time to follow correct procedure in the field, and when it needed to happen, it needed to happen. Today if possible. By accident if Mac could engineer it.

It was long past closing time when Samuel buzzed through on IEMs, asking how much longer Ezra might be and suggesting they partake in an escorted departure. Ezra wasn't sure what projected expectations came with someone agreeing to an escorted departure, and wasn't waiting around to find out. The phylactery hadn't shed much light on the origins of the pendant, but the organic shape was comparable to Thamudic runes and petroglyphs. It was a solid next step in the research process, and more than a good step towards seeing Atticus Valentine again. Ezra shouldered a rucksack and headed to the staff exit, taking the longer, less desirable route through the lunar harvesting corridors to avoid meeting Samuel. The walls of the corridors were lined with thousands of solar spheres and populated with eldritch lightforms that hid in the shadows and jumped the living daylights out of even the hardiest employee. It was a desperate soul who chose to walk the lunar harvesting corridors at night, and by the time Ezra reached the glittering epicentre of the power-generating network, even the sight of Mac Eden and her cleaning trolley brought an unexpected surge of relief.

Mac was focused on chasing down the origins of a red crayon mark that had meandered itself into the shape of a large dog. Humming a showtune, she stood back to look at her handiwork, accidentally knocking her cleaning trolley across the icy smooth of the crystal floor and accidentally blocking Ezra's path. 'Well, I'm blessed,' she called, sparkling innocently in the fractal moonlight as she skated gracefully to join her trolley. 'That's a bit of luck, just the person I wanted to see.'

'Oh, hi, Mac, I thought everyone had gone home.'

'Crayon dogs might not seem like much, but it means we're running below capacity on a clear moon like tonight. It all adds up, and one unscoured crayon dog can tip us into power deficit come the darkest days of winter.'

'Of course.'

'Only, I wanted to apologise.' Mac looked at Ezra's left ear. 'Sorry. For what happened in the teashop yesterday. Sorry.'

'It's all sorted. He was great about the whole thing. Honestly, I'd already forgotten about it.'

'Well, that's decent of you,' Mac said, not even flinching as a phantom screeched through the cleaning trolley. 'And I can see you're in a hurry.'

'Yes, I am,' Ezra said. 'Sorry.'

'Of course, of course, I won't keep you,' Mac said. 'Only I wanted to make sure you were all right, that's all.'

'Yes, thank you.'

'You know, after your...coffee,' Mac said, leaning forward ominously.

'Completely fine. Thank you for asking.'

'Well, that's great, I'm relieved.' Mac ran her fingers over the crystal-ball contours of the nearest wall like she was reading Ezra's future. 'I hoped you would be.'

'Me too.' Ezra tried to edge around her. 'Goodnight, then.'

Mac lifted a plastic spray bottle and scouring sponge from her trolley, drenching the nearest solar sphere in bleach and scrubbing intently at a green crayon mark while somehow still managing to block Ezra's exit with her trolley. 'And all that stuff with the ladle and the swearing and the...you know, take no notice.'

'No notice taken,' Ezra said.

'And I assume the thing you were with, it went back where it came from?'

'The thing?'

Mac struggled through various replies. 'The Atticus Valentine...thing.'

'I left Mr Valentine in the teashop, with Emporia. It's not our business to check up on him.'

'Bastard.' Mac hadn't meant to say it; it just popped out like a testicle in a tight pair of shorts. 'And by bastard, I mean this bastard crayon mark here,' she said. 'Not the other...bastard. Sorry.'

'Anyway, I'd better be off.'

'And will the Atticus Valentine be returning to see us anytime soon? Only, I'd like to be prepared.' Mac waited as a drooling apparition scuttled across the crystal ceiling. 'With my apology. Sorry.'

'I don't know, Mac. I'm not in the loop.'

'Hmm. Because that's a piece of information that should have been said about.' Mac scratched her chin with the scouring sponge. 'I heard you all went to the phylactery.'

'We...' Ezra sidestepped a small child carrying a teddy bear '...did.'

'I was wondering what the Atticus Valentine wanted from a room like that.'

'Mac, I'm just here on a GiFT, I don't get told anything. I was at the phylactery because it's my designated workstation. I had a coffee with Mr Valentine because Mr Valentine wanted a coffee and Emporia had this emergency thing. I honestly don't know what else I can tell you.'

'Ah, I guessed as much.' Mac scoured around a contorted face straining through a solar sphere. 'I wonder, might you perhaps consider knowing a bit more, say, if your country was in need?'

'If my country was in need of what?'

'In need of assistance with the ongoing battle.'

'Is this about recycling?' Ezra said.

'I'm asking if you might consider helping,' Mac looked around subversively, 'with the…ongoing battle.'

'The war?'

'Homeland,' Mac said. 'Not foreign affairs.'

'Oh, shit, you're a…?' Recent events tried to add themselves up. 'Shit.'

'And speaking to you as a…' Mac said. 'We seem to have a need of your skills, so to speak. Would this be something you might consider?'

'My skills?'

'So to speak.'

'Like my history skills?'

'History!' Mac gagged on the word. 'History is what got us in this mess. No, this particular mission has need of skills much closer than history, so to speak.'

'Skills much closer than history?'

'So to speak,' Mac said, with a reassuring smile. 'What do you say?'

'If you mean seduction, then absolutely not.'

'Seduction!' Mac choked.

'What then?'

'Intel.'

'Intel?' Ezra said. 'Intel connected to Mr Valentine?'

'Yes,' Mac said. 'Possibly no. But most likely yes.'

'In what way?'

'I can't say unless you're on board.'

'Why would I get on board with something without knowing what something I'm getting on board with?'

Mac hadn't had much coercion experience, but it wasn't working out as well as she'd hoped. 'Even if I was to reiterate that it's for assistance with the ongoing battle?'

Ezra let it all wash around for a bit. 'Honestly, Mac, the whole visit was organised through Dicky and the board of trustees. Somehow, you've got hold of the idea that I was more involved. I barely met Mr Valentine. All I can tell you is that Plug Productions screen the single most effective propaganda machine ever created. If the Ministry of War want to talk to him, I'm sure he'd be accommodating.'

'The Ministry of War can do what they fucking like.'

'I'm not saying they can't. I'm just saying that sometimes the best solutions are the most obvious. If the Ministry are upfront with him, I think he'd be happy to help in any way he can.' Ezra slid an ungainly circle, trying to manoeuvre around the cleaning trolley. 'It all sounds super-exciting, though. Unfortunately, I'm not the right person for what you want.'

'I ain't told you what I want.'

'Is it dangerous?'

'Such creatures most dangerous,' Mac said, all scouring sponge and eyebrows.

'Then it's definitely a pass from me.'

'Right.' Mac was nodding as she dropped the scouring sponge into a tub of bleach and unclipped a mop from the trolley. 'Cos you'd be doing your country a great service.'

'I'm fine doing my country a great service where I am,' Ezra said, waiting for the drooling apparition to scuttle back across the crystal ceiling. 'But thanks again, for the offer.'

'Don't mention it.'

'Great.'

'Not to no one.'

'Oh no, of course,' Ezra said.

'And I won't hold you up no more,' Mac said. But as Ezra went to slide past, she thrust her mop across the exit like a last-minute ticket inspection. 'If you're really serious about not knowing nothing, and you're not interested in helping with the ongoing battle, then it's really important for you to not go nowhere near the Atticus Valentine, not ever, do you understand?'

'So…that's quite a lot of negatives to negotiate.'

Mac did soften a little then. 'Hey, all I can do is warn you. In the end, it's up to you. It's just I'd feel awful if I stood back and said nothing and then something horrible happened. Probably something ghastlier than you can ever imagine. And I'm talking pretty grim for those who'd have to clean it up.' Mac nodded a silent claim to that.

'Noted,' Ezra said.

'You've got my mobile on the staff contact pages. Don't be afraid about ringing me if you need to, even the night time.' Mac finally dropped the mop barrier. 'And make sure you pay attention to the things that don't want to be paid attention to, because sometimes it can feel like you're going mad.'

'It certainly can.'

Mac patted Ezra's arm. 'Just keep what I've said in mind.'

'I certainly will think about it, yes.'

'Or phone me anyway, if you want to. It don't have to be about anything gruesome.'

'Ah, ha ha, sure.'

'We could do a coffee or something?'

'That would be really great.' Ezra was already slipping away through the nearest exit. 'I mean, I'm quite busy at the moment, but, yeah.'

'See you later,' Mac called after Ezra, her voice fading as the empty silence of lunar light and several chain-dragging wraiths closed in around her.

Back home, Ezra flopped forward onto the bed. The choice Hollow had forced that day in the drop-in centre had seemed so done and done with. The idea that you could stay home and still be actively involved in the war hadn't featured anywhere, not until now. Now it felt like existing inside a submarine and the war was cracking the windows; too much pressure to keep from breaking in. Frankly, it was okay to be downright mad at Mac Eden for that. It was also okay to be downright madder at Hollow for being famous, and better, and not here to talk to about all the Ministry of War secret-service weirdness that had just happened like they were in a middle-grade spy novel. Ezra sighed, pulled out the pendant and let it dangle over the edge of the bed.

'Twinkle, twinkle little star, how I wonder what you are.'

The pendant swung hypnotically, back and forth. The marks were hand tooled; the folds were hand forged; the patina looked genuine.

'Up above the…' Ezra sat up. 'Shit.'

In the time it took for the laptop to boot through all the cybersecurity programmes and software updates, Ezra had paced the room enough times to trigger an active exercise commendation from the Ministry of Health. Even typing the word Mandolin felt dangerous. There were the obvious news stories, conspiracy theories, part matches, obscure articles, video footage of the phone hack, the war in Afghanistan. Nothing came close to being remotely relevant to Ezra's symbol search. If the Mandolin had a flag, they weren't bothered about showing it. The whole thing was a categorical dead end, but it had successfully done what Ezra wanted it to do. It had eradicated even the remote possibility that the pendant was usable intel connecting Atticus Valentine to something treasonous.

'Apparently, civic duty is a way more comfortable concept when you don't have to do anything uncomfortable,' Ezra said, ignoring the ping asking if a recent search was anything the Ministry of War could help with.

Mac Eden sank into the scarce shadows of a neatly clipped privet hedge. Conqueror Square was posher than she'd expected. Not the falling to pieces since the Reformation sort of posh, more a heated pool and double entrance driveway sort of posh. Mac zipped her sweatshirt up over her chin. The accidental meeting with Ezra Blake hadn't gone as well as expected. If anything, things had ended up worse than they were before. Not because Ezra Blake had said no and walked away, but because she'd let Ezra Blake walk away with no idea of just how bad this situation could get. Mac shrugged off a moth and sank further into the shadows. In her heart, she knew there wasn't much likelihood of the Atticus Valentine turning up at Ezra's house, but you never knew with Mandolin players. And if it did turn up, well, she'd be right there, making sure it encountered an unexpected turn of events. Mac shooed another moth away and set an alarm ringing on the house opposite. Catching a Mandolin player was the easy part; finding somewhere inconspicuous to wait was the real challenge. Gated communities were paranoid before the war.

16

See who's afraid of the big bad

SMART SLATE
Whiskey-Zero-One-Foxtrot/s3e6/REMI IP link PP confirm: EFP crew/IGH test
Producer: *Elspeth Hart*
EXT. GBR. DEMDYKE LONG BARROW – DAY

Scene: New *WØLF* recruits *Hollow Quinn*, *Joanie Magrath*, *Fish Nazari* and *Hubert Frank* begin the second day of their fieldcraft lesson. IGH with action. Crew cameras on *SGT Naleigh* – continuous

'Something brought you here,' Sergeant Naleigh said. 'Something inside of you that couldn't sit back and do nothing. And I admire that, I honestly do. But the beautiful rainbow that left home won't make it through a war. And I'm not talking about death here, I'm talking about change. You all want the outcome, but you want to stay the same. Maths like that doesn't add up.' Sergeant Naleigh held another scrabbling rabbit by the ears, parading it around the group. 'And right here we have another opportunity for change. So who's stepping up to this one?'

The recruits stood in silence. None of them had slept much,

and although they'd tried to normalise what Hollow had done, the shock of it stayed on their faces like a faded Polaroid.

'No one?'

'I'll do it,' Joanie said.

'Joan?' Fish pulled him back, but he shrugged her away, already taking off the microphone pack strapped around his waist.

Sergeant Naleigh carried on walking around the group, finally stopping in front of Joanie. 'Make it a quick kill, recruit. Don't let your heart get in the way of kindness.'

'Not here,' Joanie said. 'Not with everyone watching.'

'You gonna let it go, son?'

'I can't do it if everyone is watching me.'

Sergeant Naleigh flicked a nod to the long barrow, handing the rabbit over. Joanie took it without speaking, cradling it into his chest as he walked away from the group. It wasn't down to Sergeant Naleigh to interact with the *WØLF* crew cameras, but he gave them a look that made it clear the filming stayed right where it was.

Everyone expected Joanie to say the rabbit had accidentally escaped, but he brought the limp, dead thing back to them. Passing it straight to Sergeant Naleigh, his face as pale as the mist and a fleck of blood on his cheek.

'Good lad,' Sergeant Naleigh said, slipping his fingers under the skin of the rabbit and pulling in opposite directions to turn it back through. 'You can fight each other for the pelt of this one.'

ITM SCENE
COMMENTARY
FISH NAZARI:
Not gonna lie, I'm a bit confused.

JOANIE MAGRATH:
Last night, Sergeant Naleigh was saying that Demdyke

long barrow is seven thousand years old. That's like, unimaginable, but also imaginable.

FISH NAZARI:

Not even confused, bulldozed. But Joan's got a good reason for what he did. Like, if he was saving me from doing it or something. Yeah, that's probably it. He was saving me from getting picked to do it.

I mean, Joan volunteered for the army to save his parents' marriage. That's just who he is. Yeah, he definitely volunteered so I wouldn't have to get picked.

HOLLOW QUINN:

Sure, I'm surprised about Joanie, but it was an initiation, and that's what initiations are designed to do. They tear you down and change you without you even having to try. If you can't cope with killing a rabbit, you really shouldn't be here.

SGT NALEIGH:

Right now, they think it's harder to kill a wild rabbit than it is to kill another human. Guess they played too many video games.

Twelve hours ago, they'd thrown rabbit bones on the fire. Now they just left everything where it fell. When it came to the turned-out rabbit skin, it was Joanie who stepped forward and took it for a trophy.

'Squad, Atten—tion!' Sergeant Naleigh roared, energy enough to snap them out of the bewildered funk they'd settled into. He walked the rank, correcting their posture, straightening their sleep-crumpled uniforms. 'Today is all about implementation. The Hubert, take the shovel and cover the latrine. The rest of you, move this camp inside the long barrow,

179

and be respectful about it. You might find yourself thinking that it's a waste of time, considering we'll be back here in a few hours, but every time you leave a site, you take it back to looking like it did before you arrived. And I mean *every* time, not just when you're hiding your tracks. Respecting the land will heal your soul more than any church.'

Joanie muddled around the camp, close to the fire, picking up sticks and bones here and there. Super-busy clearing up, gradually moving away until he was out of sight of the others and their voices were only sometimes on the wind. He knelt then, gently moving any insects that crawled through the grass and dug a hole with a piece of flint he'd found in the long barrow. Down until blood dripped from his fingers, down until the earth grew cold, down to the network of roots and mycelial fungi. When the hole was dug, he pulled the rabbit pelt from under his shirt and whispered something into the soft grey skin. He lined the hole like a nest, and placed each tiny bone carefully into it. He stayed for as long as he dared, covered the hole, turf tucked down tight and droppings scattered around like only rabbits had ever been there.

'I'm sorry, little one,' he said.

ITM SCENE
COMMENTARY
PRODUCER:
Why did you volunteer to kill the rabbit, Joanie?

JOANIE MAGRATH:
It was going to die anyway. Someone had to do it.

PRODUCER:
Fish thinks you did it to save her from being picked. But that's not the truth, is it?

JOANIE MAGRATH:
Please don't ask me about this any more. Because I'll
tell you, Elspeth, I'll honestly tell you. And the reason
is so unspeakable.

Implementation wasn't a word to make things easy. It was
obvious the recruits had no idea what to expect, and Sergeant
Naleigh didn't care to enlighten them. As they walked out onto
the desolate plain, Hubert Frank hung close to Hollow, not all
obvious about it, more craft and stealth, like he was trying to
catch a virus or something. In the end, Hollow turned on him
and told him to back off. Of all the recruits, Hubert Frank wasn't
one to back off quietly. He shoved past Hollow, knocking against
her, spitting a line about lesbians.

'Piss off, The Latrine!' Fish shouted after him, grabbing a
look at Hollow. 'Don't let him get to you.'

'He didn't get to me.'

'Everything we've been through in the last ten years,' Fish
said. 'What's it gonna take for something to change?'

'Things have changed,' Joanie said. 'Especially for The Hubert.'

'He's a misogynistic pig.'

'Then talk to him about it.'

'Um, so you're supposed to be on my side.'

'I am on your side.'

'Act like it much?'

Joanie looked at her. 'What do you want me to say?'

'You saw him with Hollow, behaviour like that isn't
acceptable.'

'So we auto-delete the conversation?' Joanie looked over to
where Hubert Frank had tried to buddy up with a group and
failed. 'Every day, he's thrown out of the dickhead party for
being a dickhead.'

'Misogyny is like an octopus, Joan. It'll find a way into anything.'

'And it's handsy,' Hollow said.

'They say the Mandolin don't care what Homo sapiens think,' Joanie said, falling away from them. 'Doesn't that make his opinions worth something? Even if you don't agree with them.'

'Don't you put this back on me, Joanie Magrath!'

'Where else do I put it, Fish?'

'On yourself. On the sodding patriarchy. I don't care. I'm not wasting my time on him.'

'And that's the truth of it.'

'Joan!' Fish shouted after him, but he'd already dropped into step with Hubert Frank and didn't respond.

'The kid's right,' Sergeant Naleigh said, striding on past Fish and Hollow. 'And there's more grief than anger to be found in that if you'll let yourself see it.'

'Sake, I'm not saying all men are misogynists.' Fish looked to Hollow for sisterhood, but it wasn't the right place to look.

'Every baby that draws breath is a selfish bastard,' Hollow said.

Sergeant Naleigh's instructions were simple enough. Take everything you've learnt and put it into practice. The day was already overcast, which meant the mist came creeping in slowly, stealing away the landscape without making a fuss about it. With their eyes down looking for moss, kindling, animal tracks, anything that might be useful, the trainee soldiers didn't notice the mist until it was right on top of them. Sergeant Naleigh disappeared back to the long barrow two kilometres away and only called them home when they had no way to find it.

'CAMP!' His yell was faint, but it pulled them from what they were doing. The sergeant held back on a second call.

ITM SCENE
COMMENTARY
SGT NALEIGH:
The new bogs are treacherous; the old crows aren't

fussy. These Phase One recruits are all busy with their eyes on the ground, but I've been watching the horizon since I sent them out. A mist like this is a teaching gift. Not a real life-ending danger, but close enough for them to remember what it tastes like.

HOLLOW QUINN:
I'd separated myself from the others even though Sergeant Naleigh told us to stay with at least one other member of the group. It wasn't me being stupid, I just needed some headspace, and there's not much of any space in the army. I fixed a tripod of landmarks, I paid attention to the terrain and established where I was in relation to the camp. It was a solid plan, except for the landmarks and the terrain, and everything else that got obliterated by the mist. One minute it's all okay, the next it's not.

JOANIE MAGRATH:
Sergeant Naleigh sent us off with just our utility uniform and a whole load of stories about people who've disappeared on the plain. Not spooky disappeared, not even real stupidity disappeared, more accidental stupidity disappeared. Wearing the wrong clothes. Not bringing a map and compass. Forgetting to check the weather. Forgetting to respect too many years of climate change. He told us that sometimes their bones turn up, and sometimes they don't. Everyone thought he was just trying to scare us, but when the fog came down, we knew he wasn't.

FISH NAZARI:
When I looked up, I couldn't even see Joan. And he was stood right next to me. It's supposed to be a mist, but

all we could see was this thick, damp whiteout. Joan said it was like looking in a bathroom mirror after you had a shower. He made me laugh, rummaging around for a towel to wipe the mist away. I think he felt bad. I mean, I felt bad too. Like, I get what he's saying, about other people's opinions being worth something. It's just really, really hard to remember that when other people are being a misogynistic dickhead.

HOLLOW QUINN:
Sergeant Naleigh's voice was the only solid information we had. There were whistles and shouts all around, and I wanted to run towards them, but I knew I had to just keep listening for Sergeant Naleigh.

It was still the morning but blurred down to this grey half-light. There was rain too, but not falling from the sky, it was coming up from the mist. It was the weirdest thing.

PRODUCER:
Were you scared?

HOLLOW QUINN:
Of course. I think that's the point of this training.

SGT NALEIGH:
I get these kids out here telling me that fear is good, that fear keeps us alive. I act like I'm listening out of respect for their woke upbringing, but it's all bollocks. Fear doesn't keep you alive. Fear makes you stupid. Fear freezes you to the spot when a tiger jumps out at you. It's understanding a situation that gets you out alive, not fear.

The sergeant's call came again. 'CAMP!'

Fixing his position was easier the second time. Hollow walked a left-foot bias, eyes on the fog, not looking down, always waiting on the next call. She almost tripped over Hubert Frank before she saw him. Low on the ground, arms pulled tight around his legs. His chin resting on his knees.

'Come on,' she said, 'get up, it's this way.'

He just shook his head.

'Come on, it's this way.' She went to grab his sleeve, but he twisted away, still shaking his head. Hollow crouched down next to him. 'I guess we wait here, then.'

Fifteen minutes later, Sergeant Naleigh called again. This time, he used a flare. Red-bright and unmissable.

Hubert Frank stood up. 'It's this way.'

Back at camp, he told everyone he'd stayed to look after Hollow. Sergeant Naleigh raised a questioning look, but Hollow didn't bother to correct it.

The recruits were cold to the bone and emotionally deflated. It took a hard command to stand back and watch their failing attempts to establish a campfire. Sergeant Naleigh set to rally them with a song, boisterously harmonising with the frail smoke of their fire to start a whole new fire that roared like it was burning dry tinder.

> *"The soldier awoke*
> *looking up at the sky*
> *buckled and tightened again*
> *So watchful, so wasteless*
> *of battle, some say*
> *and his cry*
> *was the silence*
> *of doom*
> *of doom*
> *His cry was the silence of doom."*

185

The sergeant stomped with the chorus, pacing the words, pulling them into the rhythm. It should have reset their spirits, but the ground was running wet to mud and they'd seen first-hand just how little they knew about survival. Twice, Sergeant Naleigh offered them shelter in the dry of the long barrow, but none of them took it.

ITM SCENE
COMMENTARY
FISH NAZARI:
It could have been a test, or probably just human kindness, but nothing changed the fact that all the uncomfortable dampness outside was beyond preferable to the creepy silence waiting for us inside that long barrow. And the sergeant wasn't shy about the rabbits he was holding either. We all knew what was coming next.

HOLLOW QUINN:
Sergeant Naleigh did his best to pump life into us, but we were done in. And yeah, we were all grateful for Joanie's secret stash of biscuits, but at this point, nothing short of a pizza delivery would have brought us any comfort.

PRODUCER:
Why didn't you correct Hubert Frank when he said he'd stayed behind to look after you?

HOLLOW QUINN:
Every day, he's thrown out of the dickhead party for being a dickhead.

PRODUCER:
But he lied.

HOLLOW QUINN:
That's why I knew how much it mattered to him.

'Tomorrow is our last day together,' Sergeant Naleigh said, 'and I have my Phase One army-approved schedule to teach you all there is to know about surviving in times of modern warfare. You'd think this would include me telling you a bit more about the Mandolin, but I also have my instructions not to talk to recruits about the Mandolin.' Sergeant Naleigh watched a blue-green beetle crawl away from the fire and crushed it with his boot. 'Makes no sense to me, but we're not ones to question decisions in the army. However, suppose tomorrow morning, you were to ask me about how I lost my legs? I suppose I'd have to tell you about it.'

Those who'd managed to sleep woke before the sun. Whispering in groups, buzzing with the question they'd been left to sleep on. The mist had lingered, close to the earth and delicate with spider webs. Somewhere in the night, the army had dropped off a metal coffin. Sergeant Naleigh didn't have to wait long to explain it.
    'How did you lose your legs, Sergeant?'
    'Gather in, my little rainbows, and I'll tell you a tale of my first encounter with the Mandolin.' Sergeant Naleigh knocked on the coffin like he was warding off bad luck. 'Sangin settlement, Northern Helmand Province. Every single operative wanted to make a difference to the people living there, but most days it felt like we were making it worse for them. We're heading back from a stalemate recon when we get a call that a dead camel is contaminating a local water source. And those calls, those everyday improvement-of-life calls, they come like a sweet tonic to any war. Fucking thing stank like it'd been there for weeks. We hauled it out, doused it with petrol and set it on fire. But what with the water and the decomp, the bastard thing was too wet to burn. Two litres of fuel didn't touch it. So my captain, he pulls

out a live grenade, kneels down and stuffs it inside the ribcage. We're backing off, choking on the stink, waiting for him to tell us to retreat to cover. Except he doesn't, he just says, 'Fuck.' That's all the warning we got. Next thing the captain is running at us, grenade in hand, pin pulled out, screaming at us to shoot him. My captain was a damn good field officer, but he was finished the moment he touched that camel. As it was, the grenade took out half a jeep and a third of my body.'

'It was a psych scam,' Fish said, finding Joanie's hand.

'Mandolin scams trick you into seeing what's not there. They're full of malicious intent, but mostly you get out alive. No, kid, there's more than scams to these foul creatures. One of them gets control of your central processing unit and you may as well be locked in as an NPC role in a virtual reality wargame.' Sergeant Naleigh grinned and switched the ozone detectors off. 'You'll notice I learnt some lingo from the last lot of rainbows that came through here.'

There'd seemed no need for the ring of slim detectors before, but as the humming stopped, it felt like more than just silence, it felt like a warning. The trainee soldiers drew closer together, looking for answers without any questions.

'Was a psych jacking,' Hubert Frank said. 'My bru Edgar went that way, hear what I say. Some nights, I dream he walks with me, and we talking, young and free, not wanting much beyond this company. It's come to me in more than pieces, in the creases I can't cry in, no use denying another day, hear what I say.'

'I hear what you say, kid.' Sergeant Naleigh gave them a moment before snapping a lock open on the box. 'Right then, my little rainbows, time for the interactive part of the story.'

'It's not your legs, is it?' Fish said.

'In a manner of speaking.' Sergeant Naleigh laughed, but not long enough with it to seem like it mattered. 'In their wisdom, the army has decided that any talk of the Mandolin should be kept to a minimum. However, you lot stepped up when your country called, and I figure you've earned the right to see what sort of creature you'll be facing. So I pulled a few strings.'

It wasn't just Fish who stepped back. 'There's a Mandolin in there?'

'Sedated.' Sergeant Naleigh scratched his chin. 'Hopefully, they used enough this time.'

'We've only just started boot camp, Sergeant,' the sun-freckled recruit said. 'Is this allowed?'

'Not even remotely.' Sergeant Naleigh unclipped the last lock, flipped the lid back and peered inside. 'Yep, we're good to go.'

All but one of them crept forward, looking tentatively into the slate-grey darkness of the sinister box.

'Problem, son?' Sergeant Naleigh asked.

'I'll have a look when there's more room, Sergeant,' Joanie said.

'Suit yourself.' Sergeant Naleigh turned back to the others. 'What do you think of the Mandolin, then?'

'Is it in a gas state?' Fish said.

'You tell me.'

Hubert Frank stuck his hand into the coffin shaped box, shaking it around the empty space. 'Ain't nothing here but echoes.'

'Sure about that?'

'You testing us,' Hubert Frank said, tilting a nod to Joanie. 'See who's afraid of the big bad.'

Sergeant Naleigh rustled a smile from somewhere not very nice. 'Sensory information is how we understand the world. It's not perfect, but our dear old human brains are used to filling in the information gaps. The Mandolin use neural decoding proteins to hijack host information. Their psych scams piggyback optical, audio, tactile, olfactory, even gustatory receptors. You find yourself face to face with the Mandolin, I guarantee that

189

whatever you can see, hear, smell, feel and even taste, should it come down to it, is entirely dependent on what the Mandolin is letting you see, hear, smell, feel and taste. And the only one of you who stands a chance right now is standing over there by the cover stone, waiting to see what happens to the rest of you.'

'Move,' Hollow said, shoving Fish away and half stumbling into the fire.

Sergeant Naleigh closed the lid of the coffin. 'As you were. There's no Mandolin in this box. There's a lesson if you want to learn it, but that's up to you. Put that fire out before you set yourself alight, Quinn. Magrath, fetch us that crate of gawks from the long barrow. Out of all the senses, eyesight is primary. It's also the most unreliable. Let's see how well you rainbows get on clearing the camp without your primary sense.'

'Sergeant,' Joanie said, 'I wasn't...'

'I know you wasn't, kid.'

'The Mandolin attack our minds, yeah?' Fish said, a half-look towards Joanie. 'Will the army teach us Buddhist meditation or something?'

Sergeant Naleigh was walking around the ozone detectors, turning each one back on and synching the circuit. 'I was already in service when this war started. They gave us enough tactical training on the Mandolin to make us sick of hearing about them. We learnt all there was to know about their physiology, their attack strategies, their territorial ambitions, their weaknesses. We even learnt how to meditate under a Zen master so we could protect our minds from them. We knew them better than they knew us, and it should have given us the war, but it didn't. The Mandolin took all our training like we'd handed them the launch codes to a mass destruction weapon. That's when we came to learn that good old basic army training was a hundred times more effective than anything else we had.'

'So why tell us about the Mandolin at all?'

'Hey, you rainbows asked how I lost my legs,' Sergeant

Naleigh said, grabbing up his walking stick and thumping it into the ground. 'Now get those gawks set to one hundred per cent blackout. The Hubert, a reminder that you're still on latrine duty.'

Later that day, Sergeant Naleigh boiled a caddy of water and took them to find an ant nest. 'See this nest, it's not doing much harm. But if we were sleeping here, it might be an inconvenience, correct?'

'Yes, Sergeant.'

Sergeant Naleigh poured the whole kettle of boiling water over the nest, making them all watch as the ants went scrabbling over the scorched grass, trying to get the eggs out, dying in their trying. It was like an ant apocalypse.

'These ants here, they have no concept of the creature behind the boiling water. They just know the boiling water. But if you look, you can see how hard they fight to protect their home and their future. They work together, and they do what they've been trained to do. A lot of them die, but the nest survives. Superior power doesn't guarantee a win. In my experience, it's often the opposite. Mostly, it comes down to what you're fighting for, and if you've got your whole existence at stake, that's what wins out in the end.'

17

Like we went to the fairground

Phase One of initial training lasted for fourteen weeks. It was brutal, intense, progressively challenging and, for the most part, enjoyable. It was no real surprise to anyone that Hollow rated top in combat marksmanship and fieldcraft, top five in everything else. She didn't tell her mum about the passing-out parade.

SMART SLATE
Whiskey-Zero-One-Foxtrot/s3e59/REMI IP link PP confirm: EFP rig/crew
Producer: *Elspeth Hart*
INT/EXT. GBR. BOOT CAMP – DAY

Scene: Passing-out parade. *Hollow Quinn, Joanie Magrath, Fish Nazari* and *Hubert Frank* stand in rank, ready to walk out onto the parade ground. Fixed rig transition to crew cameras as the soldiers wait for the drums to start – continuous

Bello te Prepares. Prepare yourself for war. The drums beat through them. Every boot on the beat. Two-Three-Four. The band playing behind them. Two-Three-Four. As they marched to the stand where the families were. Two-Three-Four. Salute. Two-Three-Four.

So many friends and family had come, it was impossible to pick out a single face. Still, the cheer came like a roar, over the drum, over the band, over the thump-thumping of their hearts. The passing-out parade was over in a matter of minutes, but even the TV audience felt the power of it.

ITM SCENE
COMMENTARY
FISH NAZARI:
I'm Private Nazari now, it's so weird. And Joan, he's Private Magrath. Ha, that's so bloody weird, mind.

JOANIE MAGRATH:
We spent the whole week leading up to the ceremony polishing and ironing our number two dress uniforms. We knew what to do, when to do it, where to do it, and why we should be so proud of what we've achieved. And that was how we waited, silent and rank ready. When the drums started, every one of us took a breath before we took a step. Things like that stay with you for the rest of your life.

You can't imagine how much we were looking forward to seeing our families. Except when Hollow told us that her dad is caught up in Canada, and her mum tested positive for a new COVID variant that makes your front teeth fall out. We all felt bad for her. She seemed okay about it, though.

FISH NAZARI:
Hollow kept talking about how far we'd come and what the ceremony represented. She said it didn't matter that her parents weren't there. But you can't be okay with that, can you? Not with everyone else

having their family around. And we're her friends. We couldn't just ignore that. We couldn't leave her to spend the day on her own.

JOANIE MAGRATH:
Me and Fish, we were looking around for Hollow, but she'd already gone.

Hollow hung back, watching as Fish and Joanie were engulfed by their families. The moment they were out of sight, she started walking like she had to go somewhere. Always heading back towards the bunkhouse and always keeping the crowd between them.

'Not your cup of tea, Private Quinn?'

Hollow snapped to a halt. 'Not really, Sergeant.'

'As you were.' Sergeant Naleigh fell awkwardly into step with her. 'No family?'

'Unfortunately, they couldn't make it, Sergeant. But they've arranged a party for when I go home. It's all over so quickly anyway.'

Sergeant Naleigh laughed. 'Weeks of preparation and it's finished in ten minutes. Every op I've ever been on.'

'Yes, Sergeant.'

'Tell me about the incident with the PTI.'

Hollow didn't answer straight away. 'Everyone thinks I must have looked at him the wrong way, Sergeant.'

'Is that so?'

'Maybe I did.' Hollow flicked Sergeant Naleigh a look. 'Permission to speak candidly.'

'Go on.'

'Personally, I think it's part of an overarching psychological strategy. If the punishment is harsh and we don't know what we did wrong, we get programmed to look outside of ourselves for instruction.'

'Enlightening.' Sergeant Naleigh altered his stride, slightly, imperceptibly, just enough to upset Hollow's pace. 'And is bullshitting one of the strategies you'd normally use to shift attention away from any question you don't want to answer?'

'No, Sergeant.' Hollow lowered her head. 'I mean, sometimes. I just…I find it hard to talk about things. Even to think about things, most of the time. It's so much easier, I guess.'

'Easier than what?'

'Easier than letting my mind be the biggest threat to my survival on this whole goddamn earth.'

Sergeant Naleigh paused like he was going to laugh, but he didn't laugh. 'You're a bright kid, Quinn, I'm not the only one who sees the seed of something in you. Whether that seed is a good seed or a rotten seed, that's for you to decide.'

Hollow kept her eyes fixed ahead, walking a straight line. 'The PTI reminded me of someone I don't know.'

'Someone you don't know?'

'I mean, I know who he is, but I've never met him.'

'And you mistook the PTI for this man?'

'No,' Hollow said, still walking a straight line, not even trying to match Sergeant Naleigh, 'I knew it wasn't him.'

'Myself, I always favour the good seed,' the sergeant said. 'Losing my legs, that could have turned me sour. Instead, I came out singing. Get all that fury under control and it'll serve you for the rest of your days. But if you let it control you, you're nothing more than a walking effigy to whatever bastard messed you up so bad you want to sucker-punch a PTI for not being him.'

'Yes, Sergeant.'

Sergeant Naleigh altered his stride again. 'You ever think about special forces, Quinn?'

'Not that I can recall, Sergeant.'

'Do your time in the field. If it's something you're interested in at the end of your tour, get in touch.'

'Thank you, Sergeant.'

If Sergeant Naleigh had more to say, it was silenced by a squeal. 'Holl! It's me. Wait up, Holl!' Gemma came teetering, all nails and heels too fancy for the occasion. 'Didn't you see me by the pillar? I was waving like mad.'

'Gemma.'

'Ah.' Sergeant Naleigh stepped back and away. 'I'll leave you to it, Quinn.'

Gemma smiled, waiting on him to stride into the crowd. 'I've been chasing you halfway round this bloody place. It's like you're avoiding me or something.'

'Shit.' Hollow took off the peaked cap she'd brushed and polished that morning. 'You came.'

'Of course I came.' Gemma beamed. 'What sort of mum do you think I am? I'd never miss my little girl's parade.'

'I didn't think you'd want to come.'

'You're telling me,' Gemma said, strategically looking around the parade ground, finding her best side for the crew cameras. 'I only found out where it was happening from that Henri down the drop-in.'

'You asked at the drop-in?'

'It's lovely that you were protecting me, in case I felt too exposed. And you know me and parades, Holl. But that was quite something.' Gemma looked around again. 'What a thing, eh?'

'Yeah.'

'What a thing.'

Hollow stared down at her boots, a shine bright enough to see her face in, and just the grey empty sky reflected back. 'You got hair extensions?'

'They had an offer on at the nail salon.'

'It's like mine.'

'Um, I don't think so,' Gemma said, patting Hollow's newly shaved head.

'Like it used to be.'

'It's nothing like it, silly.' Gemma laughed, unconvincing and hesitant with it. 'I got you a twenty per cent discount voucher. You can use it for nails, if you want.'

'Everything okay back home?'

'Yeah, not too bad. The sill under the bathroom window fell out.'

'Oh, that's not good.'

'I got a builder coming to do a quote.' Gemma fixed her hands to her hips, scooped another cheesy smile from somewhere. 'Come on then, aren't you going to introduce me to your friends?'

'I don't have any friends.'

'Private Hollow Quinn,' Fish said, linking arms with Hollow and Gemma, and steering them a half-circle back towards the crowd. 'I'm afraid that's where you're wrong.'

ITM SCENE
COMMENTARY
GEMMA QUINN:
It was lovely to surprise Hollow like that. Did you see her face? She was right taken aback that I came, what with her not telling me it was on. She tries to protect me, but I wasn't going to miss this. And I can hardly recognise her, even though I sort of see her all the time. It's not the same to actually see her.

PRODUCER:
How did it feel to have your mum turn up, Hollow?

HOLLOW QUINN:
Like we went to the fairground. Not in a clown and freakshow way, it was nice of her to come and all. It was more like she was trying to win me a stuffed bear on the coconut throw, and I don't want a stuffed bear.

I'm not sure it was about me, that's all. But that's as good as it gets with Gemma sometimes.

GEMMA QUINN:
She's grown up so much. I think this army training has been good for her. I always told her she had it in her to do something worthwhile with her life. I always said that.

18

The camel would bite it off

Boot camp taught them practicalities and trade training taught them necessities, but only war could teach them what it meant to be a soldier. They stood in ranks as the postings were read out, front, centre and rear. An interval of one arm's length between them. Directly in line with the person in front, beside and behind. Afghanistan was a land already too familiar with war; the posting came as no surprise. All Hollow could remember thinking was how Ezra would learn about it on TV.

The pre-deployment base was sixty miles away. Years older and years more rundown than boot camp. There were no WØLF cameras. No wireless body mics. No fixed rig technology. Their DAF lorry was kept at the drop barrier while the guards checked through their papers, calling for clearance from one of the grey square huts. A tall razor wire fence ran the whole perimeter of the camp, broken only by the incongruous beauty of the slender ozone towers. Inside a lower fence, the accommodation buildings weren't much more than block-built huts. Cold War ugly, metal-framed windows that didn't shut properly, broken tiles, dented lockers, shower rooms covered in limescale and graffiti. The neglected grimness of the buildings should have disheartened them, but it didn't. This base wasn't a home; it was a temporary port. Luxury was immaterial and comfort was for everyone they were leaving behind. They were at the base for eight weeks. Four phase training of increasing intensity. The camera crews stayed away. There was no mistaking fieldcraft for sandcastles; there was no mistaking their WØLF status for anything else but war. As the date of deployment got closer, they had their temp QRID tattoos inked into permanent identification markers. They had their final haircut, blood review and more vaccination shots: cholera, typhoid, diphtheria, multiviral booster and rabies. They were issued with iodine tablets to block the absorption of radiation. They took antimalarials to protect them from the new malaria mutations and a biochemical cocktail to regulate their mood. They were lectured on the procedure for minimising the risk of contracting breakbone fever and taught enough Pashto to tell if a local was asking for help or just saying hello. A week before deployment, their posting documents arrived, along with their chameleon combat uniforms and dog tag ID discs.

'How do you work the chameleon mode?' Fish said, twisting her arm as the reflection of overhead light vanished into the unnerving dark of her combat uniform.

The quartermaster signalled Hubert Frank forward to demonstrate. 'Cookie-dough desert camos are still the most effective camouflage you'll be issued, but everyone is waiting on the chameleon skins. This combat uniform remains on the matt black neutral setting until activated.' He walked slowly around Hubert Frank, keeping an authoritarian lid on the excitement that bubbled around the walls of tech dispatch. 'Radiation-resistant, ozone-reactive and a nano material that adapts to mimic surroundings. Each one of these suits is covered in millions of chromatophores, just like a cuttlefish. Unlike a cuttlefish, these suits are made from silicone and they cost a bloody fortune to produce, so if you break this suit, you'll have me to answer to. The on switch is in the collar stud.'

'The Hubert in an aqua suit, bru,' Hubert Frank whispered.

'This isn't an aqua suit,' Fish whispered back, as the suit flickered to match the grey walls. 'This is a bloody sci-fi novel.'

Joanie was looking around for something that wasn't military green or military grey. 'Dibs on the tie-dye sweatshirt back at the bunkhouse.'

'Will it work with your face?' Fish said.

Joanie caught a look from the quartermaster. 'These aren't toys, Fish,' he said, adjusting his sleeve.

'Where's Hollow anyway?'

'She got called back,' Joanie said. 'For new orders or something.'

'What new orders?'

'I don't know. Something about our travel arrangements.'

'We should all be invisible,' Fish said. 'She'll think we left.'

'Ozone strips are colour coded,' the quartermaster said. 'Black through to white, with tonal emphasis to compensate for any colour blindness. Afghanistan will generate a range from indigo to green as a background reading. Anything past that is a Mandolin proximity alert.' He slowed his voice down then, but his words had already hushed them. 'Radiation exposure triggers an audio warning. The closer the beep, the higher the exposure. Don't ignore this warning. The suits provide moderate protection, but they won't protect you from prolonged levels of exposure. The alarm goes off, you get yourself to a decontamination shower immediately and seek medical help.'

The quartermaster gave them half an hour to familiarise themselves with the chameleon combat suits, waiting until the excitement had died down before handing out their ID discs. 'Name. Service Number. Blood Group. Religion. These discs are to be worn around your neck at all times. Do not remove them for any reason. Not when you shower. Not when you exercise. Not when you have carnal relations with a local. And not when you're home on leave. QRID is fallible, and these stainless steel discs contain all the personal details the army needs to know in a form that can be read without a scanner. If you lose them, it generates a delay. There's only one thing that irritates a quartermaster more than an unscheduled delay, and that's an unnecessary unscheduled delay.'

Hollow arrived at the provisions depot ten minutes later, handing over her papers to the quartermaster and squirming into her matt black suit. 'We've been assigned to a temporary squad. We leave at two o'clock tomorrow morning.'

'Two o'clock?' Joanie said.

'The rest of today, we're helping pack up an ISO shipping container with everything the squad will need to set up a build-from-scratch camp on arrival.'

'Two o'clock in the morning?'

'None of the squad know each other, so it shouldn't be too weird.'

'It's real, then.' Joanie looked over to Fish. 'We're going to Afghanistan.'

'It's always been real,' Hollow said.

'I don't know, it didn't feel real until now.'

'You'll be fine, Joan,' Hollow said, patting Joanie's arm. 'Sylvie Stevens might not be, but you'll be fine.'

The experienced soldiers were keyed up and ready to go. The others picked up on their confidence and followed their lead. Some days, it was hard to forget they were heading out to join the rest of WØLF. Some days, it was hard to remember. Private Elliot Mason met the four of them in the departure lounge at Heathrow Airport, escorting them to a quieter section of the seating area. As a regular reservist, he'd been recalled to the army after fifteen years, and was the only soldier in WØLF with any combat experience. In an army of newly qualified fresh faces, Elliot Mason looked like the map at the start of a fantasy novel. He'd probably been white at one time in his life, but it was hard to tell what ethnicity he belonged to now.

'Call me Jar,' he said, like they wouldn't already know him from the TV. 'It's a joke in case you missed it. Private Elliot Mason. Mason jar. That's a screw thread glass jar, for preserving, named after John Landis Mason, who patented it in 1858. And before you tune out, it can also double as a cocktail shaker.' Jar strolled along an aisle of red plastic chairs and slumped into the centre seat. 'Can't trust Gen-Z to care about pickles.'

'Um, we're not Gen-Z,' Fish said.

Jar answered with an unhurried look around the departure lounge. 'How you kids holding up with all this?'

'Not too bad,' Joanie said, sitting next to him. 'Good, I guess. I got a suntan at pre-deployment, Hollow got star pupil, Fish got scabies, The Hubert got the look.'

'Studio make you do those in-the-moment scene commentaries yet?'

'Commentaries?'

'For WØLF?'

Joanie dropped to a whisper even though none of them was wearing a wireless mic. 'We're not supposed to talk about this.'

'I do them occasionally,' Jar said. 'When I feel like there's something to say. Bastards gave up on trying to make me do them. Now they mostly follow me around and we get some smokes in.'

'The legal representative said we couldn't talk about it to anyone,' Joanie said. 'I had a dream where I talked about it and had a panic attack.'

'Lawyers think they can put the fear of hellfire into you.' Jar pulled a pen out of his top pocket and picked his nose with it. 'Once you've seen your own insides close up, it's all just white noise.'

'So, Jar,' Fish said, beating Hubert Frank to a seat next to Joanie, 'are you here representing the army, or the...other thing?'

Jar just shrugged, which kept both possibilities alive. 'You get the biochemical cocktail?'

'It's required meds, right?' Fish said.

'Fucking mind control. Making us do what we're told.'

'Soldiers,' Hollow said, still walking around the seating area.

Joanie shrugged. 'I read that biochemicals have already reduced PTSD cases by seventy per cent.'

'So say the mind controllers.'

'Sake.' Fish tipped her head to rest on Joanie's shoulder. 'It's just a new form of medicine, that's all. People got freaked out by vaccines back in ye olde days. It didn't mean they were something bad.'

'I poured the cocktail down my leg.' Jar wiped the pen on his sleeve and put it back into his pocket. 'Told them I pissed myself.'

'A case in point,' Fish said.

They already knew from watching Jar on TV that his mood rested somewhere between gnarly depressive and reluctant father figure. It was a situational call on how to approach him, but the offhand way he talked about *WØLF* was oddly reassuring. They sat together on the red plastic chairs, waiting to be called to their flight along with two hundred other troops. No passports. No tickets. London to Cyprus. Cyprus to Kabul.

SMART SLATE

Whiskey-Zero-One-Foxtrot/s3e91/REMI IP link PP confirm: EFP single crew - *Bassie*
Producer: *Elspeth Hart*
INT/EXT. GBR. HEATHROW – EARLY AM

Scene: New *WØLF* recruits arrive at Heathrow for deployment to Afghanistan. *Hollow Quinn, Fish Nazari, Joanie Magrath* and *Hubert Frank* meet the first member of their new squad. Single crew camera commences on *Jar* – continuous to Bagram

Jar leant across and nudged Joanie, flashing a photo up on his phone. 'Hope you got your balls insured.'

'What the!' Joanie flinched away. The soldier in the

photograph was wearing the old-style desert combats and holding up an insect the size of a cat.

'This here is your camel spider. So called because it fixes itself to the underside of a camel while it munches the stomach out.'

'No way,' Fish said, grabbing the phone. 'The camel would bite it off.'

'Bite enzyme numbs the site,' Jar said. 'Digestive fluid liquefies it. Bastard thing just sits there, sucking everything up like a milkshake. And the poor camel don't know a thing about it till its guts plop down between its legs.'

'Now I'm more scared of the wildlife than the war,' Joanie said.

'There's no half-measure with camel spiders,' Jar said. 'Fuckers can run too. Last rotation in Helmand Province, I saw one chase down a Taliban, cracking its jaws and screaming like a banshee. By the time we caught up, it'd eaten the poor sod's face clean off. Don't get me wrong, I love a dying Taliban, but that was the fucking worst thing I've ever seen.' Jar leant across, taking his phone back. 'This ain't just Afghanistan we're headed for, kiddies, this is Helmand. And Helmand ain't anything like you can imagine.'

The single crew camera stayed with them as they arrived in Afghanistan, filming Kabul with its ribbon of snow-capped mountains, the plane shadow circling a huge dust bowl. From the air, it looked like the whole nation was on fire.

'Is this it?' Hubert Frank said, and some panic to it. 'Is this the war?'

'Stand down, it's the Kurdish festival of Nowruz,' Fish said. 'New Year is on the spring equinox. The bonfires are supposed to represent light winning over darkness, but now it's more about a way for Kurds to remind themselves that they survived.'

PRODUCER:
How does it feel to come back to Afghanistan, Fish?

FISH NAZARI:
You know, I still dream about the day we got evacuated. I was so scared we wouldn't get on a plane. There were thousands of people at the airport, and they didn't have the right papers. I wouldn't let go of my dad because I thought they'd make him stay behind.

I remember there was a woman with flowers. She was handing them to the soldiers and they wouldn't take them. They wouldn't take the children.

Humans fighting humans seems epically insane now.

Fish nudged Joanie in the ribs with her elbow. 'Better wake up the sleeping beauty, we'll be landing soon.'

Joanie leant over, best cabin crew accent. 'Excuse me, miss, weren't you supposed to get off at Kabul?'

'I'm just waiting for the people sat next to me to leave,' Hollow said. 'I've been trying to ditch them since boot camp.'

'Oh, those two, they got bumped up to first class on account of them being too beautiful for economy.'

Hollow stretched out a laugh. 'Did I miss anything?'

'Jar went supersonic in the toilet,' Fish said. 'Multi-terrain coverage, all portals. We could hear it from back here.'

'He also took photos,' Joanie said.

'And video.' Fish puffed a look around the plane. 'That was worth a good hour of anyone's time.'

'Sweet.' Hollow stood up, flexing her back. 'Which toilet do I avoid?'

PRODUCER:
It's thirteen hours from London to Kabul, Hollow. Did you really sleep the whole way?

HOLLOW QUINN:
I needed some time to think.

PRODUCER:
What takes thirteen hours to think about?

HOLLOW QUINN:
Did anyone ever ask why it's *WØLF*? Whiskey, Zero, One, Foxtrot. Where does the One fit? It should be WØ1F, right? We should be WØ1F Squad.

JAR:
All squads get to pick their own name. Two letters and two numbers. It was Stan's idea, using the number one as a letter L like the old password trick. When he brought the flip chart out, none of us had the energy to argue.

Anything else you want to know? Only my gut just exploded out my arse and I'm kinda busy with that.

From Khwaja Rawash Airport they caught a military transport shuttle to Bagram Air Base where they were security checked and sent to a holding area. The base was at the foot of the Hindu Kush mountains. Air-conditioned gyms, restaurants, coffee shops, even a post office run by volunteers. Bagram suited a country recovering from years of conflict, but Mandolin hostility and the subsequent influx of international troops had stretched it way beyond capacity. For Hollow and pretty much everyone else, Bagram accommodation had returned to the overcrowded B-huts and overused tents of previous conflicts. The air base should have been a chance for them to acclimatise, but the weather was damp and depressingly like home, and the failing infrastructure meant there was nowhere to go to avoid it. The soldiers spent fifteen days in dull lessons, soggy cots and rain-flattened scenery, getting used to their uniforms, the time zone and each other. When the clearance order came, they were given their papers, issued with iron powder ammo clips, and deployed to Camp Bastion. This time, they were dressed in chameleon combat uniform.

ITM SCENE
COMMENTARY
FISH NAZARI:
The further we got from Bagram, the more the world around us changed. The light is different, the sand is different, the air is different. Even the Russian signs inside the Mi-8 helicopter remind us that we're foreigners in a foreign land.

PRODUCER:
Except you were born here, Fish. You have Afghan nationality.

FISH NAZARI:
I'm also a British citizen. And it's where you grow up that makes a place your home. You should be asking me about Bristol, because that's where the story is. I'm a person from Bristol, sitting in an Mi-8, flying out to a military base in the middle of a desert. Minted.

Also, I'm hot, I'm tired and I'm thirsty, thank you for asking. Afghanistan is an ad break in a film, that's how much I care about it.

Camp Bastion was a four-mile-long, two-mile-wide army fort built on the flat emptiness of an Afghan desert. Filmed from the air, it looked like the circuit board blueprint of a lost civilisation. The transfer sergeant steadied herself on the rigging as the helicopter banked and prepared to land. 'Each and every one of you needs to be aware that you are about to enter a white zone. Gloves and gawks to desert setting. Chameleon on. Weapons ready. Await the order to disembark.'

And even though they'd been through it over and over, the instructions had never felt more necessary. They sat in silence, guns loaded, burn gloves on, UV goggles set to desert level five as the nano material identified and adapted to mimic the interior of the helicopter, and the ozone strips across their bodies faded from indigo to blue. Every soldier on the flight had been waiting on the order to disembark since the moment they'd stepped inside the helicopter.

The shape of a solitary DAF lorry parked a half-mile from Camp Bastion marked their landing spot. The Mi-8 came down in a choking uplift, obliterating everything. No one spoke. They just sat inside the clicking, grumbling helicopter, waiting for the blades to stop, waiting for the uplift to settle, waiting to see the land that was to be their home. When the settle finally came, they wished it hadn't. The DAF lorry appeared in drifts of pale sand like the scenery from a wargame. All the canvas had been stripped back and an iron grid soldered to the ribcage. The only kind of shade came from the general-purpose machine gun fixed to the roof of the cab. Everything about the military vehicle was drenched in overuse and as ugly as a machine could get without being torched. When the order came to disembark, they disembarked. Hubert Frank was first off and the DAF lorry was the only place to run to, so he ran. They all ran. Guns and boots and heartbeats, thudding and clinking in a land that wouldn't hold their footprints.

ITM SCENE
COMMENTARY
FISH NAZARI:
You might not think a DAF lorry could even be a

landing marker, except everything else is sand, so it works.

We're all desperate for a drink of water at this point, but we don't drink, we don't even speak. We just sit there inside the helicopter, waiting for the order.

HUBERT FRANK:
The DAF lorry. Shit, that's one army relic, bru. We hold tight in the dust storm, wait for the desert to hand back the controller.

JOANIE MAGRATH:
You have to appreciate, it's like an industrial oven inside the helicopter. All I could think about was getting out into the fresh air, but when I got down onto the sand there's no fresh air, just more heat, slamming into me like a freight train. And even though I know it's heat, my body can't make sense of it so it just feels like terror. That's why we all ran, because it felt like terror.

HOLLOW QUINN:
I think Jar walked to the DAF with the transfer sergeant, but the rest of us were barely keeping it together. As soon as Hubert Frank ran, we all ran. Joanie was with me, but we lost Fish somewhere between the helicopter and the lorry. I guess I was searching her out before I even knew it mattered.

PRODUCER:
What mattered?

HOLLOW QUINN:
I don't want to be alone here.

'Get yourself straight, soldier!' the transfer sergeant bellowed at Joanie, pushing past him and climbing up the iron grid to stand next to the gun. She even kicked her heel three times on the cab roof because another set of dents weren't gonna make a lot of difference. 'Minds closed. Eyes open. Weapons ready.'

The engine spluttered into life and every combat uniform changed to match the surroundings. From the back of the DAF lorry, the single crew camera filmed the delicate, shifting sands of an endless white desert as though it had been somewhere beautiful once.

'You doing okay, Joan?' Hollow said.

'I can't breathe.'

Hollow was holding her rifle tight to her chest. 'Me neither.'

'It's too much.'

'It's a half mile to camp. That's like five minutes. Just keep it together for five minutes, Joan.'

'It's too much.'

Hollow looked away, but she could feel Joanie's panic all the way through to her bones. The soldiers at Bagram had filled them full of spook stories. Suicide Nation. No way to tell who the enemy is, except they don't breathe. Watch to see if they're breathing. Hollow saw the trucks before she knew what they were, pointing at them with the butt of her rifle. 'Sergeant.'

Hubert Frank stood up in his seat. 'What they doing?'

The transfer sergeant kept looking straight. 'Sit down.'

'Is it them?'

'Sit. Down.'

'Should we be doing something?'

'You should be sitting down, soldier.'

Hollow kept her eyes fixed on the transfer sergeant, hugging her rifle as the jingling chaos of Hi-Lux trucks came too close, all colour and noise and rectangular troughs filled with large oval-leaved plants. Joanie had slumped against the grid, his head lolling with the movement of the DAF lorry. She pulled him straight, keeping her body pressed against him so the transfer sergeant wouldn't see that he'd passed out. 'Keep it together, Joan,' she hissed.

Hubert Frank sat down shabbily, laughing everything off. 'Always take your drugs with you.'

'*Nicotiana tabacum*,' the transfer sergeant shouted down. 'There's no ready-made benzidine strips for Afghan civilians, but ozone turns tobacco leaves brown. It makes them as good as a canary in a cage.'

'Afghan people love flowers,' Fish said, her feelings unscripted and sadder than expected. 'I remember that.'

The trucks crossed paths all around them, radiating away from the DAF lorry like lines on a compass. Under all the colour and noise, the Afghan trucks had the same iron grid protection, and the people looked as scared as they did. Everyone in the whole scenario was holding their breath.

Except for Jar. His uncensored commentary was bolstering around somewhere near the back of the truck. 'Ain't no roads here, you gotta make them up as you go. If we shot every bastard who did that, we'd have run out of innocent bystanders years ago.'

It was hard to imagine that they'd processed any of it as they hit Camp Bastion. Rolls of razor wire, fencing thirty feet tall, blast walls, cameras, motion sensors, air and ground radar, guards on high alert along an S-shaped corridor. Three lines. Three barricades. Questioning who they were and why they were there. Evaluating every movement, every soldier, every single part of the eaten-away truck like they weren't on the same side. Hollow and the rest of the new arrivals were checked in and decanted into a country so used to war it didn't want anyone.

ITM SCENE
COMMENTARY

HUBERT FRANK:

Those jingly-jangly trucks, they keep getting closer and closer. Sharks to blood bait, bru, and we the blood bait. That's a lot of heat to stay cool with, know what I'm saying.

JOANIE MAGRATH:

It was all too much, I couldn't breathe. I'm so glad Hollow was there. I could hear her telling me to keep it together, but I couldn't keep it together. I don't know what I'd have done if Hollow hadn't been there.

JAR:

All the elements of hell are here. But this isn't hell. This is a waiting room where every door leads to the worst thing that can happen to you.

Welcome to Helmand, bitches.

19

That's a lot of life for just one man

At one time, Camp Bastion had been home to over thirty thousand troops and bragged more flights than Gatwick Airport. When the conflict ended, the fort was decommissioned, abandoned and stripped out to stop the Taliban making any use of the site. Returning to Bastion meant a whole lot of starting again, but it didn't take a military genius to figure out that returning to the site was more than fixing a strategic foothold in the south; it was a calculated propaganda strategy.

The new *WØLF* soldiers had expected to be met by the overseas production team. Instead, they were handed over to a warrant officer and told to unload the equipment along with the rest of their temporary squad. Camp Bastion was expanding and there were already three more divisions than when the war had started. As UK troops, they were automatically stationed at the old Camp Viking site in Bastion One. The single crew camera who'd stayed with them since London stopped filming, disconnected their body mics, and headed off to the static remote integration studio where IP links were already streaming content to Plug Productions. As the designated representative of *WØLF*, Jar disappeared five minutes after they'd opened the ISO shipping container, so the four of them just carried on setting up camp without him. There was nowhere to put their kit, and nowhere for them to get out of the sun, but they'd practised putting up and taking down the green tents so many times their bodies knew it more than their memory did. Within an hour, they'd built a bunkhouse, a rudimentary stove and somewhere they could grab some shade and change into the lighter weight, lighter familiarity of their cookie-dough camos.

Joanie set his chair down next to Hollow, puffing a look around the 4x4 tent. 'The ambient light in here is lovely.'

Hollow was busy searching through the last of the equipment boxes. 'How's your head now?'

'Better,' Joanie said, but he was still pale and his hand shook when he brushed sand off his knee. 'They gave me some meds.'

'Did they say it was dehydration?'

'Yeah,' Joanie said, 'and also from when I fainted in the DAF lorry.'

'Don't worry about it, Joan. The soldier next to me wet herself. None of us will be winning performance awards for our arrival in Camp Bastion.'

'You'd win an award.' Joanie sighed, leaning into Hollow's shoulder. 'You were brilliant.'

'If you say so.'

Fish barged her chair between them. 'Do we stay in this squad now, or what?'

'It's where the army put us,' Joanie said. 'Someone from WØLF will eventually come and tell us what to do.'

'Yeah,' Fish said. 'It's a bit weird, though.'

'The squad seem okay,' Hollow said. 'We'll muddle through.'

Hubert Frank was mooching around them. 'The Hubert don't muddle.'

'Nailed by The Hubert,' Joanie said. 'We belong here, because this is where we are. When they come and get us, we'll belong there.'

'Imagine if they don't come and get us, though.' Fish poked a boot at the hexi stove. 'Like, not ever.'

'Not ever?'

'Because they said not to talk about *WØLF* and we SO talked about *WØLF*.' Fish leant forward and unpacked four tea mugs, lining them up by the stove. 'And now the crew camera just left us. And Jar just left us. Maybe they know something we don't know.'

'Jar would have told us.'

'Yeah...' Fish didn't look convinced enough to sound it '...or maybe the production lawyers told him not to.'

'Jar?'

Fish finally grinned. 'He'd have definitely told us.'

'Guys,' Hollow was still raking around, 'did anyone see the instruction manual for the stove anywhere?'

Hubert Frank nodded to his bunk. 'The Hubert has the book.'

It was a simple, sweet moment. Twenty minutes later, Jar turned up. 'What are you lot doing in here?'

'Settling in,' Joanie said. 'We put up the tents.'

'Congratulations, I ain't carrying anything.'

Fish poured another tea. 'Thanks for clearing that up, Jar.'

'It's okay,' Joanie said, 'you don't have to look after us. We're already used to production days, and we did our radiation and medical evacuation training back in the UK. It's not field experience, but the army aren't expecting us to be up to your level yet. Once we get issued with our work schedule, we can be pretty much self-sufficient.'

'You won't even notice us,' Fish said.

'I forgot till just now.' Jar walked a slow circle around the 4x4 tent. 'You've done it up nice in here. Shame you're moving to the bunkhouse.'

'The bunkhouse?'

'Pack up your bags,' Jar said. 'You're in with us now, pumpkins.'

'We're in the *WØLF* bunkhouse!' Joanie blurted it out, staggering his chair sideways into Fish.

'Just like on TV,' Jar said.

'Just like on TV,' Joanie said, clutching hold of Hollow. 'I have to get undressed in front of Sylvie Stevens.'

'Worse than that, kid,' Jar said, 'she gets undressed in front of you.'

'Yeah, no, it's fine, it's fine.' Joanie stood up, bobbing around. 'I can go three years without a change of uniform.'

Jar laughed too long, watching them pack up like they'd picked the fast scanner at the supermarket checkout. 'Nell got some shore leave. The rest of the squad are off base for a few days. We set you up with some cots. Put them wherever you want as long as it's far away from me. And get your heads out of your autograph books. We're not influence divas, we're army soldiers, just like you lot are army soldiers. The more uncomfortable you make it, the more uncomfortable it'll be.'

'Everyone's down with us being here, though?' Fish said.

'Four more to the squad means we run with a full unit in reserve. And if you can hog the cameras off us occasionally, what's not to be down with.'

'The Hubert obliges.'

'We can get by with three,' Jar said.

He didn't hang around to help, so they set their beds at the front of the WØLF bunkhouse, grouped together because it all felt weird and intrusive. They were used to fixed rig cameras and mic receivers, but this was proper WØLF, three seasons deep and next-level superstars.

'It's a bit hot up this end of the tent, mind,' Fish said, 'but I was talking to some of the regulars, and they said the nights get cold here.'

'And there's less shadows,' Joanie said. 'Camel spiders like hiding in shadows.'

'We all shadows.' Hubert Frank wandered around the tent, grabbing up a pearl-embellished accordion by its shoulder straps. 'Caught waiting too long on the sun.'

217

'Don't,' Fish said. 'That's not yours.'

'She belongs to the squad,' Hubert Frank said, wriggling into the straps like he was trying to figure out a parachute. 'And we the squad.'

'We're not the squad.' Fish snatched it away from him. 'We're the second generation.'

'Any ways, many ways.' Hubert Frank shrugged and went back to looking around the bunkhouse. Prodding things and poking about until he spotted a long table with a wooden screen fixed at one end.

'Sake, if he breaks anything, they'll hate all of us.' Fish put the accordion back carefully. 'And FYI, camel spiders aren't even spiders. A couple of squaddies set it up ages ago. There's a bunch of myth-breaker channels if you want to see how they did it. Spoiler, it's forced perspective.'

'Like I haven't already looked,' Joanie said. 'The scale is fake, but not the digestive enzyme thing.'

'Sake. Tell him, Hollow.'

Hollow shrugged. 'We all looked them up.'

'No, they don't jump or scream or eat people's faces,' Fish said. 'You can't say it's not bogus just because they look like that. I might as well photograph a cockroach and tell everyone they speak Italian and ride around on skateboards, except for the scale.'

'And the digestive enzyme thing,' Joanie said.

Fish dumped her kit on a bunk. 'And the gullibility thing.'

'I'm just trying to keep us safe.'

'Whatever.' Fish leant in close to Hollow under the pretence of arranging a sleeping bag. 'It's not actually the camel spiders. Joan can't cope with being near Sylvie.'

'It's true,' Joanie whimpered.

Fish swanned around Hollow's bunk. 'Also, I swapped The Hubert's kit onto Jar's bed. For entertainment purposes.'

'The Hubert a frequency for all channels,' Hubert Frank

called from the table, eyeing a hand-drawn map like it was a dropped fifty-pound note and he was waiting until no one was watching to pick it up.

Hollow arched her back, stretching out the relentless heat of the day. 'Can we at least call them wind scorpions?'

'If they're not allowed to be spiders,' Joanie said, 'they're not allowed to be scorpions.'

'I mean, you have to admit, wind scorpion sounds cool, mind,' Fish said. 'Like a pack of them already ate your face off.'

'It's a cluster of spiders,' Joanie said, 'not a pack.'

'They're not spiders.'

Jar turned up half an hour later. His uniform was wet with what could have been sweat, except for the smell that came with him. They'd expected him to shower, but he just pushed Hubert Frank's kit on the floor and flopped forward onto his bunk, one arm hanging off the edge, staring at a spot on the far wall like he could almost see something. When Joanie tried to include him in the conversation, he just pulled his shirt up over his head and left it there.

'Should we do something to help him?' Fish whispered.

'Not today,' Hollow said.

Joanie opened some ventilation. 'He'll ask for help if he needs it, right, Jar?'

'Some days,' Jar said. 'Today, I'm good.'

'Um, you're obviously not good,' Fish said.

'Some days, people ask if you need help and you say you're good. And people should respect that.'

Fish spoke for an audience. 'It gets me when these old guys still won't admit that they need help, like struggling to cope is something to be ashamed of. And being who he is, he could be an example. He could show everyone it's okay to talk about mental health, no matter who you are. It's a wasted opportunity, that's all.'

'Not today,' Hollow said.

'Why?' Fish flounced up close to Hollow. 'Why not today?'

'Today, he needs so much help he doesn't know where to start.'

'Who you calling old?' Jar said.

SMART SLATE

Whiskey-Zero-One-Foxtrot/s4e1/REMI IP link PP confirm: EFP rig/ crew
Producer: *Elspeth Hart*
EXT/INT. AFG. CAMP BASTION – DAY

Scene: *Jar* gets to know new recruits *Fish Nazari*, *Hubert Frank*, *Hollow Quinn* and *Joanie Magrath*. Fixed rig and crew cameras commence on *2LT Felicity Sampson* as she walks towards the bunkhouse – continuous

At the bottom of the officer ladder, a squeaky clean twenty-three-year-old Second Lieutenant Felicity Sampson had her work cut out for her the moment she set foot in the *WØLF* bunkhouse.

'As you were,' she said. 'This is an informal visit. How are you all settling in?'

'We good, Lieutenant.' Hubert Frank nodded to the D&D table at the back of the bunkhouse. 'They unlock the lich.'

'Good, good. I don't profess to know what that means, but perhaps one day you can teach me.' Lieutenant Sampson accepted Fish's offer of tea. 'Now, I'm sure you've all been told to trust your commanding officer like your life depended on it. I would add that we also carry a sense of camaraderie in the army that transcends even rank. The way we treat each other is the way we become. I want you to remember that.'

'What happened to old Davenport then?' Jar said, drying his feet on Joanie's bunk. 'Alma left a note on my cot, saying we had a replacement.'

'Lieutenant Davenport was killed in action a week ago.'

'You're shitting me!' Jar saluted the reprimand before it landed. 'Begging your pardon, ma'am. For the swearing.'

Sampson dismissed his exaggerated acknowledgement with more grace than it deserved. 'And you must be Private Elliot Mason. RR. Having a member of the squad who has already done a tour here is our good fortune.'

'Jar,' Jar said.

'Indeed. Your familiarity with the landscape and environment is invaluable. These days, even the Taliban will admit that they are fighting the country as much as the enemy,' Sampson said, stirring five teaspoons of sugar into her tea. 'And, Mason, it's been a while since the army insisted on addressing a commanding officer by their gender. Best not make a habit of it, eh?'

Fish handed over a tin. 'Biscuit with your tea, Lieutenant?'

'Ah, thank you, Private Nazari. As you can see, I've brought myself up to speed on the squad. It's good practice to know a bit about the soldiers under your command.'

'Just turn on the TV,' Jar said.

Sampson maintained the jovial road. 'And, in return, it seems only fair that you learn something about my background. The military runs in my family, too many generations to mention. I've had more homes than phones. I enjoy cricket and old-school sci-fi novels. I can pull a reasonable tune out of a reasonable guitar, and an unreasonable tune out of any violin. I might even be persuaded to pick up an accordion, should the occasion arise.'

'You'll have to fight Stan for it,' Jar said. 'He fusses over that thing like it's something alive.'

'As I said, should the occasion arise.'

ITM SCENE
COMMENTARY
FISH NAZARI:

It was decent of Lieutenant Sampson to tell us about herself, but I've read more exciting online profiles. I really wanted to ask her about the wedding ring. She kept tapping it against her mug.

I would have asked about it, except, she's my commanding officer, and the ring looked too new and out of place on her hand to belong to a good story. Some things are private. I'll ask Jar.

JAR:
How the hell should I know?

Okay, so she's got this request for leave on the table, and she ain't been here more than two weeks. Talk is, her brand-new husband done the dirty, and now there's a stray kid in the can, but you didn't hear that from me.

Lieutenant Sampson switched topics, as neat with it as she was with her uniform. 'Now, as you've probably noticed, the heat here can be a bit of a shock to the system. Drink more than you think you need, hot black tea works wonders, and as much sugar in it as you can cope with. Our construction timetable fits in around the worst of the sun here at Bastion, which means a three o'clock start tomorrow morning, I'm afraid. It sounds frightfully early but you'll be thankful for it soon enough. You'll start with unpacking the rest of your equipment out of the ISO container. Once it's empty, we'll use it to extend the ward capacity of the second field hospital. The lightness of these standardised shipping containers makes them terribly useful for any kind of bolt on unit, but it also leaves them vulnerable to the desert storms. You'll need to weigh it down with sandbags before we move the next section in, so a great deal of shovelling sand for the first week or so. Not the most pleasant of tasks, but it can't be helped.'

'We're here to work, Lieutenant,' Joanie said.

Jar grabbed a handful of biscuits and lined them up on his knee like the keyboard of a piano. 'Says the new kid.'

Sampson downed her tea and accepted another. 'If you get a chance, have a walk around the base this afternoon, get your bearings. There are plenty of things to do here at Bastion One, and there's a bus service if you want to go further afield. Heroes is the closest we have to an English pub. No alcohol, of course, but it has all the UK TV channels and they run a decent karaoke on a Thursday night if you're interested in that sort of thing. The gymnasiums are air conditioned, so bear that in mind. The army has also reconstructed the replica Afghan village here at Bastion One. It's set up only a few blocks away, and designed to prepare you chaps for how it feels outside of a military base. To our unending good fortune, it's still run by local vendors. They have a bread oven to die for if you're up and about early enough, and a marvellous food market. There's always plenty of kahwa tea, and the hospitality alone is well worth the visit.' She looked over to Jar. 'Anything I've missed, Mason?'

Jar was tapping his knee, silently counting the lined up biscuits. 'Jar.'

'Thank you, Lieutenant,' Joanie said, 'we'll have a look.'

'Good, you do that. And make sure you get yourselves acquainted with the rules and regulations around here. Mason can help you with that.'

'Jar.' Jar stopped counting and picked up one of the biscuits.

'Is this a medical problem, Mason?'

'Jar,' Jar said, through a mouthful of crumbs.

Sampson fixed him with a stare that would have unnerved a portrait of Henry VIII. 'Loyalty. Duty. Respect. Selfless service. Honour. Integrity. Personal courage. These values are fundamental to every British soldier, regardless of their situation. Do not expect less of yourself than you deserve.'

'Already trying, Lieutenant.'

'Make sure you do,' Sampson said, not dropping her stare until Jar shrugged and turned back to silently counting the biscuits. 'The rest of you, if you're not sure about anything, it's advisable to check with the warrant officer first. A fort this size operates more like a city than an army base. There may not be any roads, but inside the wire the speed limit is twenty-four miles per hour. Anything more than that will kick up a storm of dust to choke us all. You'll also notice that all the standing lights are sodium vapour. It makes us look like an old-fashioned London, but climate change is on all our minds and we get more than our fair share of UV radiation out here in Helmand. Sodium vapour light is the best we can do to cut it from output. We keep to blackout after nine o'clock. Make sure you have your chameleon skins on charge by eight and everything else you need by eight-thirty. There's no curfew as such, but the nights are cold here, and anything cold is sacred to us this time of year. The last thing we want is a new arrival stumbling around looking for a spare recharge interface.' Sampson drained the last of her tea and turned the cup upside down. 'Well, I'll let you chaps get back to settling yourselves in. Private Quinn, a quick word outside, if you would.'

Sampson was waiting in the shade of a pop-up Bar & Grill a few metres from the bunkhouse. 'At Ease, Quinn. It's nothing to worry about, just a chat. Find yourself a bit of shade.'

Hollow moved her left foot to the side, fingers interlocked behind her back. Chin up. Looking straight ahead. 'I'm fine here, Lieutenant.'

'As you wish. Look, I've been doing a bit of homework regarding the squad, and I didn't want to mention this in front of the others...' Sampson waited for a couple of soldiers to walk by, returning their salute. 'I hope you don't mind if I speak candidly.'

'Of course not, Lieutenant.'

'Going over the reports from boot camp, I noticed several insubordination marks against your name. Now, Quinn, this isn't a dressing-down, this is just an impromptu evaluation point, for both of us, if you like. We learn a lot about authority at Sandhurst, but I get a sense that this was never an authority issue. Am I correct?'

'I don't know, Lieutenant.'

'I think you do, Quinn. Rank isn't about obedience; it's about trust. You have to trust me. I have to trust the rank above me and so forth until we reach the top. Any break in that chain and the whole system falls apart. Unfortunately, Afghanistan isn't the sort of place that allows for second chances. And that means finding a solution before we have a problem. Let's start by exposing insubordination as a coping mechanism that doesn't work in your favour. How does that sound?'

'Good, Lieutenant.'

'You need to trust the army with your life, Quinn, and I'm not sure that's something you're very good at. But we must be prepared to be bad at something before we can be good at it. I find reflection and evaluation to be useful.' Sampson looked down at her boots. 'I'm brand new to this, Quinn. I'm not sure if I'm making myself clear.'

'Very clear. Thank you, Lieutenant.'

'We'll see each other through, eh?'

'Yes, Lieutenant.'

'Have a think on alternative strategies, as will I. We'll give it a week and check in on how it's all going, agreed?'

'Agreed, Lieutenant.'

'Meanwhile, you know where I am. Or perhaps confide in one of the others. Mason might be a rough sort of fellow, but he's faced enough inner demons to allow safe counsel. Captain

Dupont is a good option, by all accounts. And there's Sylvie Stevens, of course. The saviour of us all. Your squad is your family now, Quinn, if you'll only let them in.'

Fish was sat with Jar and Hubert Frank, picking sand out of her boots with a pair of tweezers. 'Everything okay?'

'The lieutenant was just asking me about biomechanics.'

'Biomechanics?' Jar nudged an already smirking Hubert Frank. 'Guess she's looking to grease things up, eh?'

'Yes,' Hollow said, 'in effect, she is. Biomechanics are mostly associated with elite sport performance, but they can just as easily apply to any form of physical movement. The momentum, motion, force, lever and balance of our bodies has to adapt to meet the environment. Matching the acute variables makes a lot of sense in a climate like this.'

'Shit,' Jar said. 'I'm surprised you made it back from that conversation alive. Chips here thought you'd been up to something suspect.'

'Um, that was you.' Fish clipped the back of his head with one of her boots. 'And you can quit with the Chips. It's not that kind of army any more .'

'It's always that kind of army,' Jar said.

Hollow was busy searching through videos on her phone. 'It's not just the physical terrain, the extremes of temperature here mean that the body has to adapt quickly. It's easy to pick up an injury without knowing it. If you're interested, I can forward you some videos on kinetic alignment and temperature.'

Jar held his hands up. 'No, you're good. Why'd all that crap need to be taken outside anyway?'

Hollow shrugged. 'I guess Lieutenant Sampson thought it warranted a private conversation.'

'You ain't kidding.'

Fish brushed past Hollow, rough with it. 'Since when did you get so smart?'

'Since I was interested in something.'

'I suppose you just surprised me,' Fish said, 'what with the sports and all.'

'Sports psychology isn't what you think,' Hollow said.

'So how come Sampson was asking you about biomechanics? I'd have thought she'd be better off speaking to one of the physios over at the gym.'

'This place is getting to me,' Hollow said. 'I just made a joke.'

ITM SCENE
COMMENTARY
2LT SAMPSON:
Afghanistan trespasses on the ancient Silk Road. For hundreds of years it's been a hub for trade and migration routes, and a way-station on the hippie trail across Asia. As a country, it welcomes everyone like a long-lost cousin. As a battlefield, I suppose it welcomes this war like it has welcomed every other war that came before it. The last round of conflicts dragged on for thirty years and ended in civil war. Let's hope this war will deliver a brighter outcome for all of us.

HOLLOW QUINN:
Sampson seems okay. And she was trying to help. Not all the officers would do that.

PRODUCER:
Do you think Lieutenant Sampson was right about the reasons behind your insubordination?

HOLLOW QUINN:
She was so far from being right, she'll need a map to find her way back.

JAR:

They haven't had the paperwork come through yet, but last time I was home I changed my name to Jar Audie Murphy Jar by deed poll.

Audie Murphy. By the time he was twenty, he was the most decorated American soldier in World War II. Then he went to Hollywood and made forty-four films. Mostly westerns, in case you ain't been watching much daytime TV. And he was a successful songwriter. That's a lot of life for just one man.

I read he had PTSD.

20

There's a pirate joke in there somewhere

SMART SLATE

Whiskey-Zero-One-Foxtrot/s4e6/REMI IP link PP confirm: EFP rig/ IGH remote
Producer: *Elspeth Hart*
INT/EXT. AFG. CAMP BASTION – DAY

Scene: *Hollow Quinn, Hubert Frank* and *Jar* sleep off the hottest part of the day. Fixed rig and IGH as required. *Fish Nazari* returns to the bunkhouse – continuous

Fish casually shook Hollow awake. 'Pretend you're not listening.'

'Done.'

'Yeah, but also listen.'

Hollow checked her phone. 'It's one-thirty in the afternoon. Why are you even awake?'

'Me and Joan, we were talking to Fred at the gym. No one knows yet. But Fred does. He made us promise not to tell anyone, mind.' Fish flung herself down on Hollow's bed, grinning her face in half. 'Ask me, go on, ask me, ask me.'

Hollow pulled a makeshift curtain away from the window,

flinching at the glare of the sun. 'I thought Fred told you not to say anything.'

Fish totally failed at keeping a lid on her excitement. '*WØLF* is back filming in Helmand tomorrow. They want to do some scenes at Camp Bastion. No one knows which unit yet, but the extras coordinator is here already, signing up people for background drilling, loading ambulances and stuff. Can you believe it? We're actually going to meet *WØLF*.'

'None taken,' Jar said, from under a sheet.

'You don't count.'

'Do me a favour and fuck off,' Jar said.

Hollow shoved Fish off the bunk with her foot. 'And when you get there, fuck off again in case you didn't fuck off far enough.'

'Come on, Hollow, you must be excited that we finally get to meet them for real. Joan already sweated through three shirts. We can go down and watch the filming. Come on, it'll be weird watching someone else on camera. Joan's gonna die. Imagine him trying to act all normal soldier if it's Sylvie Stevens.'

'Ask me tomorrow,' Hollow said.

Fish sat back on Hollow's bunk. 'None of the on-duty troops have permission to sign up as extras yet, and everyone off-duty is sleeping. The extras list is first come, first seen. By soldier two hundred, the agency scouts will be bored to death of looking at the same face.'

'Them and me both.'

'Me and Joan are gonna go and look at the queue.'

'Enjoy.'

'Come with us, come on,' Fish said. 'Everyone from England loves a queue. Remember the queue to see the old queen's coffin? That had its own social media.'

'I'm not getting up at one-thirty in the afternoon to look at a queue.'

'Come on, it's a queue. It's written in your DNA. You know you want to.'

'Balls, I actually do.'

'I love you, you're the best!' Fish grabbed Hollow's foot, dragging her out of bed. 'But we have to go now.'

ITM SCENE
COMMENTARY
FISH NAZARI:
We might be in a white zone, but honestly, nothing happens at Bastion outside of work. It's just the same old people talking about the same old things. Everyone who's lived through the COVID lockdowns knows what a buzz it is to have fresh stuff to talk about.

By the time we scooped Joan up and went to look at the queue, the news was all over camp.

PRODUCER:
How did it feel, watching it all from the inside?

FISH NAZARI:
The queue was epic entertainment, obvs. It stretched all the way back to the gyms. They couldn't sit down, because of the excitement. And the heat. Most of them didn't have their gawks so they were making protective eyewear out of their socks. Then the extras coordinator went and told them to keep the laughing down. Honestly, you couldn't want more from a queue.

JOANIE MAGRATH:
When they put the extras into groups of eight, it felt like something was happening, but they were just getting their uniforms checked and adjusted by the

costume team. The extras coordinator was telling them to minimise activity and try not to sweat. Like that's even possible here. In the end, they put them in an old ISO and gave them a complimentary meal. Tuna sandwiches, I think.

Hollow leant back against a studio-commandeered shipping container. 'It's sad when a queue comes to an end.'

'A good queue is like reading a book series,' Joanie said. 'When it's finally over, you don't know what to do with yourself.'

'Except we do know, because...' Fish jumped up and down on the spot '...we're gonna meet WØLF tomorrow.'

'Please stop talking about it,' Joanie said.

Fish closed her eyes. 'Imagine if they're all like Jar.'

'We can but hope,' Jar said, sliding into their group chat without an invite.

Overnight, the ISO was invaded and subsequently infested with camel spiders. They weren't as big as the photograph suggested, but they were a great deal bigger than any insect back home and they had jaws that made up a third of their body. It wasn't hard to see why the stories still clung to them, and despite assurances that the creatures were more scared of the soldiers than the soldiers were of them, no one was happy about sharing a confined space with a whole load of segmented insects the size of a small puppy, snapping their jaws and running towards them at ten miles an hour. The ISO was sealed up and scheduled for chemical extermination.

The extras coordinator grumbled and groaned and eventually gave her permission for the extras to remain on set for the duration of filming. 'I know it's all very exciting,' she said, 'but this isn't a red-carpet event. You are professionals working with professionals. Don't gawp at the cast. Don't take photos. Don't do anything at all that might distract the cast or crew.

Don't speak to or interact with the runners unless you're called forward. This is a live set broadcast. Keep still. Keep quiet. Keep out of the way.'

The talk was designed for civilians, and they were soldiers. They'd messed around in the thrill of it all, but the extras coordinator was issuing new orders, and in Camp Bastion an order was an order. They sat where they were told and waited on some final words from Producer Elspeth Hart like they were at a mission briefing and she was the commanding officer.

'At Ease,' she said, 'and thank you for your support today. I don't need to remind you that being selected as an extra is no guarantee of a role within the show.' Elspeth Hart stepped into the Afghan sunrise, adjusting an oversized gardening hat to shield her shoulders and create a natural halo. 'However, Bastion has always been our hometown. It's an honour to share this day with you, and I hope to repay that honour by including each and every one of you in today's filming schedule.' She gave the extras a brief wave and headed back to a seat behind the primary screen.

'Three cheers for Elspeth Hart,' a soldier called.

Elspeth met the cheers with a shy smile, a hearty wave, a sincere nod. 'It's a rare treat to have a live audience on set,' she said to the crew. 'Let's give them a day to remember.'

While Hollow and Fish listened to a stream of instructions on what the extras should do if they needed to leave during filming, Joanie snagged them a prime spot. Sandbags to sit on. A good amount of shade when the sun got going. Full view of the set from all angles. He sat waiting for them, all proud like he'd scalped the best tickets at a sold-out gig.

'And you'll notice,' he said, 'we're directly in line of sight for the producer. Should it be necessary to call us onto set, we'll be straight up.'

'I thought we were here to enjoy the watching,' Fish said.

'In case, though.'

'You think there's time to grab my gawks?' Hollow said.

'No.'

'I can grab yours while I'm there.'

'I'm not looking at Sylvie Stevens through any kind of filter.'

Fish glanced at Hollow. 'You know this might not be Unit One, Joan?'

'It will be.'

'I'm just saying, it might not be. You shouldn't be disappointed if it's Hamid, Stan and Alma.'

'Except, it won't be Hamid, Stan and Alma.'

Hollow went to stand up. 'They're right by my bunk, I'll be back in a minute.'

'No.'

'I'll ask one of the runners.'

Fish kicked her boot at Hollow. 'There's no point in messing with him when he's like this. He's too easy today.'

'Yeah, I guess it really is love.'

Fish just shrugged. 'Do you think they'll come in the Ridgeback?'

Beside her, Joanie staggered through something inaudible, not even making it to a full pointing-out that as the sun rolled into the sky, and the camp settled itself into a new day in Helmand Province, the soldiers of *WØLF* Unit One had arrived on set. It wasn't that they were different. They were just a better, more astoundingly unique version of something a soldier could be if they'd been born that way. Hollow wasn't even sat next to Joanie, but she still felt him tense as Sylvie Stevens stepped down from the iconic patrol vehicle, taking off her gawks, adjusting a drawcord on her armoured Osprey vest, wearing every bit of standard assault body armour like it was made for her.

'She so...' Joanie choked back into the shade, covering his mouth to stop any more words getting out.

'...just another member of our squad?' Fish said.

Hollow laughed along, but it wasn't true. They were weeds and Sylvie Stevens was an English rose. She couldn't take her eyes off her; no one could. Sylvie was the soldier everyone wanted to be, or date, or daydream about when they were supposed to be listening to a work podcast. Her episode ratings took down everything that had come before, and when she disobeyed orders and pulled a two-year-old Afghan out of a burning hut, the whole world fell in love with her.

SMART SLATE

Whiskey-Zero-One-Foxtrot/s4e7/REMI IP link PP confirm: EFP rig/ crew/IGH remote
Producer: *Elspeth Hart*
EXT/INT. AFG. CAMP BASTION – DAY

Scene: *WØLF* Unit One *Sylvie Stevens, Mattoo Bolte* and *Mika Kamari* return to Camp Bastion with a critically injured Taliban fighter. Sylvie stays at the Ridgeback. Fixed rig and crew cameras on Mika and Mattoo. IGH stays with *Hollow Quinn, Fish Nazari* and *Joanie Magrath* – continuous

It was altogether obvious to the onlookers that the Taliban soldier had a nasty gut wound. *WØLF* electronic film production was always stylistic and beautiful, but it never shielded TV audiences from death or injury. Part of the appeal of the reality series was that it didn't try to hide what war really was.

'The Taliban have a unique set of skills,' Mika said, jumping out of the Ridgeback to grab the end of the stretcher. 'I can't imagine what it's like going that deep inside enemy-occupied zones.'

'Hence why they've landed themselves a bit of a mythical rep.' Mattoo let the stretcher roll the full length of the runners.

'I've only seen two others since we've been here, and they were both P4.'

'It's got to be an uneasy elephant in the room, though,' Mika said. 'Too many returning soldiers on both sides to make it simple.'

'A life is a life.' Mattoo dropped down behind the stretcher, holding the weight of it as Mika locked the wheels in place. 'We pick them up, we patch them up. We don't ask for evidence of what side they're on.'

'Still, the way things are, I'm not sure I'd want to be a Taliban spending my recovery in a high-dependency ward full of soldiers all secretly hating me for not dying.'

'You don't need to be Taliban for that, Mika.'

'Rude,' Mika said.

Mattoo was taking his time now, checking the wounded soldier was stable enough to move. 'You remember that poem I wrote?'

'Should I?'

'When I was sick with the dysentery.'

'Ah, yes,' Mika said. 'The poem.'

'And I was really upset when someone took it.'

'We need to get this guy out of the heat.' Mika pulled the stretcher away, heading towards the hospital. 'We can talk about this later.'

Mattoo grabbed hold of the other end of the stretcher, steering it straight. 'You told me it was Stan who took it.'

'Well then,' Mika said, 'I guess it must have been Stan.'

'I caught up with Stan at the IWA holding facility in Washir District,' Mattoo said. 'I went in hard, and he accused me of using my rank to scapegoat him. I haven't seen that level of fury in him for ages.'

'Don't take it personally,' Mika said, struggling to push the stretcher through an overnight drift of sand. 'That place spooks the civility out of everyone.'

'He'd seen the poem, but he swore he didn't have it any more.'

'I really do wonder what that boy does with things,' Mika said, shoving the stretcher to a stop. 'He could lose a firework in a box of matches.'

'Right,' Mattoo said, checking on the wounded soldier again. 'Except he didn't lose it, he gave it back to you.'

'If that's what he said, then he's bullshitting you.' Mika crouched down, clearing sand away from the front wheels. 'I told you to watch him for that.'

'Yeah, you did,' Mattoo said. 'That's why I asked if he had any proof.'

'Proof?' Mika straightened up. 'So now you're accusing me of lying?'

'What's the deal with you, Mika? You know that poem wasn't written to be read. I thought you were my friend?'

'I am your friend.'

Mattoo grabbed Mika's sleeve. 'Then why does it feel like you're always punishing me for something?'

'It's pushing thirty-five degrees out here, Lieutenant.' The sun was in his eyes, but Mika didn't turn away. 'We need to get this soldier to the hospital.'

Filming concentrated everything on the emerging drama, with nothing much more than a brief handover at the hospital before Mattoo showed Mika some video footage and everything kicked off.

Back at the Ridgeback, Sylvie was pacing, tuneless and unsettled.

Joanie ate a lump of sugar. 'If aliens landed, they'd laugh at us.'

'Reckon they'd pick the other team,' Jar said, shooing a wasp and sitting himself next to Joanie.

'Um, you're not allowed on set once the cameras are rolling,' Fish said. 'You shouldn't be here.'

'So I keep telling them,' Jar said, sticking a cushion behind his head.

Joanie snagged himself a share of Jar's cushion. 'Did you know *WØLF* is the first reality series to win a choreography citation? I read it's because Elspeth Hart has a background in contemporary dance.'

'You don't say,' Jar said.

'*WØLF* is required study for every film and media degree in the country, already. Every part of it is cinematic, and amazingly beautiful, but then Elspeth Hart still manages to make it as close to a personal experience as a viewer can get. Without them having to be here.'

'You're wasted on this war, kid.'

Elspeth Hart was true to her word and every extra had their moment of screen time as the action moved seamlessly around the set. Filming eventually wound down with Sylvie Stevens as she talked to a wounded soldier about going home. In the drama of things, it wasn't much, but Sylvie was often at her best in the quiet moments.

'Is there any news about when this might be over?' the soldier asked.

Sylvie just shook her head. 'I'm sorry.'

'It'll be over soon,' the soldier said. 'I don't mind that I'm going home early. My misses does a blackberry crumble to die for.'

'Oh my goodness, I haven't tasted fresh blackberries since I was a little girl.'

The soldier scratched the place where his knee had been, staring at his hand like it might not be there either. 'There's a bramble hedgerow that runs along the back of the road I live in. The squad will be right jealous of me being able to pick blackberries off the back of the road.'

'I'll speak to the head chef before I leave. You never know, we might be able to get some shipped out to them.' Sylvie went to say goodbye, but instead she stopped. 'If it's the right season.' The scene felt like it should end there, but there was still some screen time left on the clock. Sylvie turned away from the soldier, her helmet slowly dropping through her fingers. 'I don't remember,' she said, 'is it September?'

'Are you okay, Sylvie?' the soldier said.

'I don't remember.'

'When the blackberries are in season?'

'Did we have September already?'

'Not for two months.' The soldier squirmed awkwardly, half an eye on Elspeth Hart. But she just gave the briefest of signals to keep the cameras rolling.

Off set, Joanie was watching Sylvie. Without even thinking, he ran to her, collecting her up as she fell to pieces. 'I've got you,' he said. 'It's okay, I've got you.' And wrapping her in his jacket, he took her to the *WØLF* bunkhouse, gently tucked under his arm as though he was walking her home.

Joanie expected a runner to follow them and say that Sylvie was needed for an in-the-moment commentary, but it was Elspeth Hart who turned up to take Sylvie away.

'We don't censor the reality of war because it's too painful to film, Joanie,' she said. 'We film it because it's real. Often, the most painful moments turn out to be the most important scenes you'll ever film.'

'Then I'm staying with her,' Joanie said, his arm still tucked around Sylvie.

'She has to do this on her own.'

'No one has to do anything on their own,' Joanie said. 'Not even poop, if you're in the army.'

Sylvie laughed then. There wasn't much to it, but it was a step away from the edge. 'You're Joanie Magrath,' she said. 'They told us you'd be here today.'

'At your service.'

'It's been a tough week, that's all.' Sylvie wiped her face. 'The commentaries can be quite cathartic.'

'We'll look after her.' Elspeth placed a reassuring hand on Joanie's shoulder. 'Sylvie will be back before you know it.'

'I'll stay right here, then.'

Sylvie leant across and kissed his cheek. 'It's good to have you with us, Joanie Magrath.'

By the time Fish and Hollow burst into the bunkhouse, Joanie was curled on the floor next to his bed. 'Sylvie Stevens knows my name.'

'Get a grip,' Fish said, breathless from panic running. 'Mattoo and Mika are heading over here right now.'

'She knows my name,' Joanie said. 'Now I can't move my legs.'

Fish dragged him upright. 'Sake, Joan, is this the first impression you want to get stuck with?'

'Sylvie Stevens knows my name.'

'This is our big intro to Unit One of WØLF. If you ruin it, I'll sign the restraining order myself.'

'Come on, Joan,' Hollow said. 'How about I run some water in the sink and hold your head under until you think you're gonna die.'

'You're a good friend,' Joanie said.

'I'll wait here for Mattoo and Mika, shall I?' Fish said, struggling through several versions of how to appear like she was catching up on downtime, just a normal member of a normal squad, normally chilling in the WØLF bunkhouse.

Mattoo didn't acknowledge Fish when he came in. He just threw his helmet on his bunk and headed to the shower. It was Mika who sat down beside her. 'Hey, how you going? I'm Mika.'

'Fish.'

'We figured this must be weirder for you guys.'

'Uh-huh.'

'Moving in with the original cast, and all that.'

'Uh-huh.'

'So, we keep standard bunkhouse rules. No smoking. No making moonshine. No overnight guests. No touching anyone else's stuff.' Mika nodded over to the accordion. 'Or at least have the sense to make it look like you haven't touched it. If you break something, it's your job to report it to the quartermaster. Respect everyone's working hours. Don't be a dick, basically.'

'Uh-huh.'

'The best advice I can give you is to make yourself a space that feels like a home. If you tread on any existing territory, we'll be sure to let you know.'

'Uh-huh.'

'And don't let the endless drama fool you. We're much more boring than you'd imagine. Most of us at least.' Mika looked around the bunkhouse. 'Did Jar come back with you?'

'Uh-huh.'

'You know where he is now?'

'He's back in the damn hellhole,' Jar said, barging past Mika. 'Put out the fucking flags.'

'We put them out when you went home,' Mika said. 'How was Uxbridge?'

'Cold.'

'They cleared you to come back then?'

'They said *WØLF* was too boring without me.'

Mika flicked a look towards Fish. 'But you're doing okay, though?'

'What Mika here is edging around and subsequently drawing attention to, is that I had myself a full-blown Chernobyl while you four were at boot camp.' Jar scratched his crotch. 'The footage has gone viral, if you want a rewind. Bunch of content creators got a million views out of it, so that's something. Personally, I'd have put me down with a rifle, but the army figured otherwise and sent me home for some good old R&R. An RR sent home for R&R, there's a pirate joke in there somewhere.'

'You know your trouble, Jar,' Mika said, 'you think you have the ownership deal on mental health. The whole squad's been running on empty for months. It may not be as glamorous as stripping off and running a laxative through the officers' mess, but we're all defending our mental health in whatever way we can.'

'And defending your mental health is what got you passing round that poem, is it, Mika?'

'Hey, now that was a genuine mistake.' Mika winked at Fish. 'Show some respect, will you.'

'You show some respect and keep your proverbial beak out,' Mika said. 'This is between me and Mattoo.'

'This isn't me getting a beak in; this is me calling you out on disrespect. Causing trouble like that for no reason, you'll drag us down to a reality TV drama fest.'

'Steady, Grandpa.'

'You know what, Mika, fame don't make you, it shows the world what you are. And Mattoo, he's in love with Caster. Not just some stupid infatuation, real love. And instead of putting all the responsibility for that love onto Caster, he's invested it in the purity of keeping his gob shut.' Jar patted Mika on the head, too rough to be affection. 'Anyone with half a heart can see how much it costs him.'

Mika sighed. 'Uxbridge's gain is our loss.'

'And while we're on topic, Mattoo's running up close to burning himself with this. So close he can't bear to see himself in anyone else. If you think this squad will stand back and watch while you put him through another round of your adolescent bullying, you just try it and see what happens.'

'Who died and made you the DM?'

'Oh, I'm no dungeon master, Mika, I'm just a roll of the dice.' Jar grinned. 'And FYI, you better get your little soldier shit together, cos you're in with me now, kid.'

'What are you talking about?'

'I'm talking about you and Nell swapping places for the next rotation.'

'Yeah, right,' Mika said.

242

Jar leant in towards Fish. 'Between you and me, Mattoo is made up to be working with Nell.'

'You want fries with that bluffing?' Mika said. 'It's beyond your paygrade to move squad personnel around.'

'It's not beyond me persuasively suggesting it to Sampson, though.'

'You better be winding me up,' Mika was shaking his head, 'because there's no coming back from crossing that line, Jar. Not for either of us.'

'Already crossed it,' Jar said. 'And that bloody poem better be back on Mattoo's bunk before he's out that shower, or I'm persuasively suggesting that Sampson makes it a permanent transfer.'

'You'll regret this, Jar.'

'In so many ways.'

Hubert Frank strolled in, no embarrassment in meeting the WØLF star. 'That your D&D game, bru?'

'I'll just...' Fish slid off her bunk and legged it to the washroom.

It should have been a place of sanctuary, but Joanie still had his head in the sink. Hollow was still holding him under. And the honourable, courageous, breathtakingly unique in a world of standardised beauty Mattoo Bolte, was stark naked and taking a shower.

Ezra stood in the doorway between the kitchen and the lounge, watching WØLF without committing to it. Sylvie Stevens was having some sort of slow-motion breakdown on camera. No one knew what to do, except for Joanie Magrath, who put his arms around her and walked her back to the bunkhouse. Hollow held his head under water. She cared about him. Ezra leant against the door and for the shortest of times imagined how different things could have been.

21

Water from hell

Sand wasn't the right name. This was dust. A fine, prickly white dust that didn't compress and didn't stay put, and poured into the top of their boots every time they took a step. For six more days, the new *WØLF* soldiers shovelled the uncooperative sand into ammo sacks, each one four and a half metres tall and near impossible to move once it was full. They repeated the same task over and over until they had enough bags to weigh down the shipping containers. The work was relentless and exhausting, and it only took a sandstorm to undo everything. Physically, mentally, emotionally, extending the field hospital took up every single part of their lives. And Sampson pushed them hard. There were times when they stressed about sharing a bunkhouse with superstars, but mostly they got up at three in the morning and went to bed at seven in the evening without thinking about anything beyond work and sleep. Hubert Frank ditched their company by day two, scoring a D&D interview with Hamid, Alma, Mika and Nell, and moving his bed closer to the dedicated game zone they'd created at the back of the bunkhouse. Hollow, Joanie and Fish hung around together and didn't venture much further than the shower block. In the end, it was Mattoo Bolte who shoved the three of them out of the door, telling them to take a look around the local sites, because all work and no play made them shit bunkmates. Jar tagged along as their tour guide at the last minute, and they were too worn out to reason why he shouldn't.

Beyond the personnel sections, Camp Bastion transitioned into plant machinery, utility services and more shipping containers – twelve thousand of the standardised units, stacked nine high and left behind after the last war in a neat chronological dockyard. Jar's tour started at the incinerator.

'My first posting here,' he said, 'we had eight of these waste-dragons on site. We burned anything that couldn't be reused. The smoke bellowed so high it could've choked the gods.'

'Hence the climate crisis,' Fish said.

'Couldn't be reused, judge and jury. The army don't like to throw anything away, including ex-service personnel who should be tucked up at home right now.' Jar looked around. 'Oh, and that food warehouse over there. That used to be the second-biggest building in Afghanistan.'

Joanie made all the appropriate noises. 'So, did they just rebuild the whole base exactly like it was before?'

'There weren't any decontamination blocks last time I was here. Any bastard insane enough to use nukes would've taken out the major cities.' Jar leant against a designated bus stop. 'No sense wasting your high-yield weapons on lighting up a few soldiers. I heard they trashed the place when they left, but it seems like most of it's been put back the same. Reuse is better than recycle, and the army's not one for reinventing itself.'

'Interesting,' Joanie said. 'Do you ever get used to the heat?'

'In winter, you'll be begging for it, kid.' Jar looked up, searching the sky for familiar stars. 'And it sure is something to wake up to your first desert snowfall. But a few days in and you're suffering the cold as much as you were suffering the heat. There's not one part of this bastard country can make up its mind about which side it wants to be on. Personally, I never could figure out why war keeps on coming back to this place.'

'Can we just do the tour already?' Fish said.

'Fun fact,' Jar pulled out a cigarette, 'Bastion dug boreholes so deep you can hear screams from all the souls in hell. You ask me, that's what this is all about.'

'Hell?' Joanie said.

'Water. Water keeps the enemy stuck out in the mountains. The Taliban try to starve us out; they're the ones who die.'

'Um, so the Taliban are on our side,' Fish said.

'Good for you.' Jar tucked the cigarette behind his ear and flagged down an approaching bus. 'The bastards chased you out of your home, not sure I could be so generous.'

'There's nothing to be generous about. I'm putting the past behind me and getting on with my life.'

'Ah, still running from them,' Jar said. 'I get that.'

'So, it's something called emotional maturity, actually,' Fish said. 'You should try it sometime.'

'This bus route takes us past the water bottling plant.' Jar waved to the driver and skipped up onto the footplate. 'All aboard who's coming aboard.'

Hollow jumped onto the footplate next to him. 'Water from hell?'

'As much as you can drink, kid.'

'I'm not running from anything,' Fish said. 'I'm here to do my duty for king and country. And that's Bristol, before you ask.'

Jar wasn't one for putting glitter on a turd. 'You've been avoiding Afghanistan since you got here, Chips, and God knows I'm not judging that. But anyone with half an eye can see how this land is stalking you. It hangs around you like a hungry lion, and a hungry lion don't do well with being ignored. You want my advice? You better figure out how to stop avoiding it before it chases you down and eats you.'

'Which just goes to show that you know nothing about me at all,' Fish said, turning away and crossing her arms.

'Guess I must have made a mistake,' Jar said to the driver. 'Well, ain't that something. Ain't that really something.'

246

'FYI,' Fish said, 'I don't feel anything coming back here. Not one single thing.'

'Yeah, you should get that looked at,' Jar said. 'Now, you two Gen-Z coming, or are we just gonna stand here chatting all night?'

Fish stomped her foot. 'Gen-Alpha.'

'Joan?'

'I'll give hell a miss.'

'Suit yourselves.' Jar shoved Hollow ahead of him. Sprawling across the front two seats like he'd just arrived home after a long day.

'Arsehole,' Fish said, leaning into Joanie.

'You think maybe he struck paydirt?'

'No.'

Joanie took a while to answer. 'You're my big sister. I love you more than anything. And you leaving Afghanistan meant I got to have you in my life, but I wish it hadn't happened to you. I wish that with all my heart.'

'How do I embrace this bloody country, Joan?'

'As I recall, there was no mention of embracing. Jar just said to stop avoiding it.' Joanie looked around the mathematical precision of empty shipping containers like he was trying to fit them to a graph. 'Being stuck on this base doesn't help. Camp Bastion isn't Afghanistan; it's the British army.'

'So, we could try the replica Afghan village?' Fish said. 'And don't tell Jar we talked about this.'

'He told you out of respect,' Joanie said. 'And respect is about love, not malice.'

'Love!' Fish laughed the whole thing down. 'Sake, Joan, how do you get to be so fucking nice all the time?'

'I'm not being nice,' Joanie said. 'I'm just being...me.'

ITM SCENE
COMMENTARY
FISH NAZARI:
They should put Joanie in charge of the whole world.

247

It'll probably be Hollow, though. Hollow's all sorts of complexities, like a jigsaw puzzle. It's the complexities of monsters that draw us in to people like that. Joanie is totally uncomplex. He's like the picture on the front of the puzzle box. He's always been that way, right from that first day we met. Like he'd decided I was his big sister from that first day. And he's my little brother. He'll always be my little brother.

PRODUCER:
You think Hollow is a monster?

FISH NAZARI:
I think she could be, or she could already be. Or I could be a million miles off the mark. It's hard to tell with all the complexities. And what's even a monster in a war? Maybe it's someone who turns bad things into acceptable things, so good people don't feel so bad about doing them.

Yeah, I'm not sure which one is the monster in that scenario.

Jar kicked Hollow's leg with the side of his boot. 'Why'd you go and ditch your friends like that?'

'I prefer your company.'

'Understandable.' Jar squirmed into a more comfortable position. 'By the way, I accidentally forgot to say in front of the others, Alma got us a boardgame version of Dungeons and Dragons.'

'Alma got us a boardgame?'

'Me, you, Joan and Fish,' Jar said. 'As a welcome to the squad, slash, sorry about your mental illness, gift. It would have been for The Hubert too, but he already made it into their tabletop game, so that's a bullet dodged.'

'And you accidentally forgot to mention this welcome gift while Fish and Joan were around?'

'It's the army drugs.'

'Do we want a Dungeons and Dragons boardgame?'

'You ask me, no one in their right fucking mind wants a D&D boardgame,' Jar said, 'but I haven't been in my right mind since I got back here, so I'm not qualified to pass judgement.'

'Are we thinking of playing it?'

'Alma's a good kid,' Jar said. 'Me and her had a thing for a while. She never sits comfortable in her own body. It's like she's showing you around a short-term rent agreement. We should at least open the box. Dibs on Elf.'

'You're a locked-room mystery, Jar.'

'Get Tiefling if they have one.' Jar laid back, eyes closed and not even a trace of humour on his face. 'I can see you as a Tiefling.'

'I guess it wouldn't hurt to try it,' Hollow said.

'So why'd you really ditch your friends?'

'I wanted to see the hellhole.'

'Need to find all the exits before you sit down, eh?'

'If you say so.'

'A bit of fatherly advice,' Jar said. 'You'll never win against the army, but you can bite them with their own teeth. Take the Jar Audie Murphy Jar thing. Every time an officer has to call me Jar, that's a small bite of victory. Private Jar, on the other hand, that was an unforeseen and most agreeable bonus.' Jar broke into a grin. 'Private Jar sounds like a place one might keep one's officer condoms.'

Back at the bunkhouse, Jar produced the D&D game like it was an appointment to have his teeth removed. While Alma, Fish and Joanie tried to persuade him to give it a go, Hollow went to ask Lieutenant Sampson if an early evening run around the perimeter of Bastion One might make a good alternative coping mechanism. For someone who'd pictured herself as

Hollow's mentor, Sampson was more than happy to agree. Beyond a lecture on adequate hydration and sodium-electrolyte fuel, Sampson's only condition was that the run didn't overlap with the dedicated boardgame time Jar had already requested to boost squad morale.

It took Hollow a couple of rounds to coordinate the duration, the time and the most unnoticed section of the camp. After that, she just went straight to the pump station behind the water bottling plant and smoked until it was time to leave. When Sampson offered to come with her, Hollow said that running alone seemed to be helping. She kept to the routine for a few more days then told Sampson she felt much better. She would've bailed on the D&D boardgame, but Jar protested his participation loud enough to wake the dead, and that battle was already lost.

There were no weekends at Bastion. They got up and they worked, and nothing existed beyond the work. It took another seventeen days to secure the containers and make them fit for purpose, and by then coughing sand out of their lungs was as mundane as emptying it out of their boots. Sampson checked the site over and brought in the duty doctor to inspect the new wards. Their work was signed off that same morning. There should have been a sense of accomplishment, but now the work was gone and all they had to think about was what happened next.

Ambulance shifts ran twenty-four hours on, twenty-four hours off. Each rotation lasted three weeks. Hollow was put into Unit Three, teamed up with Hubert Frank and whichever on-duty officer was available. She wore her gun like she wore her uniform, but shooting someone was an impossible thing to think about, so Hollow didn't think about it. She paid attention to the training and kept herself focused on learning all the case scenarios as if a written exam and a certificate were waiting at the end instead of something else.

SMART SLATE

Whiskey-Zero-One-Foxtrot/s4e21/REMI IP link PP confirm: EFP rig/crew

Producer: *Elspeth Hart*

INT/EXT. AFG. CAMP BASTION – DAY

Scene: *WØLF* Unit Three *Hollow Quinn* and *Hubert Frank* are called to their first mission briefing. *2LT Felicity Sampson* is the officer on duty. Fixed rig and crew cameras in briefing room – continuous

Medivac. *WØLF* Unit Three. P4. Friendly. The mission briefing could have been a case scenario. Three French soldiers picked up by locals. Four weeks in a hot zone. Unit Three to meet and greet. Hand over payment. Bring the soldiers back to Camp Bastion. Every part of the return was covered, including what to wear, how to approach the village, how to walk, how to stand, how to hold their rifles and how to leave.

> ITM SCENE
> COMMENTARY
> 2LT SAMPSON:
> I assigned myself as the on-duty officer. This sort of return usually demands male authority, but the army is no longer willing to indulge that particular brand of respect. What the army does continue to respect, however, is that there will always be an exchange of money.
>
> PRODUCER:
> Did you assign yourself as the on-duty officer to provoke a reaction?

Look, this is the first time outside the wire for Unit Three, except that's not the worst of it. They know P4 means dead.

And, unfortunately, no mission briefing can prepare you for the sort of death war can bring. The least I can do is be there when they come out on the other side of that.

The village was small, stone and mud buildings and enough sand to blur out the edges between them. Sampson shook hands with the elder and placed her right hand on her heart. She collected the handover information and delivered payment along with an official thank you on behalf of the French army.

There were seven body bags laid out beside the elder, and each one of them stretched to full capacity. Hollow was close enough to Hubert Frank to whisper to him. 'I thought there were three bodies?'

'Guess we'll be packing and stacking.'

'Shotgun,' Hollow said.

Sampson waited for the elder to disappear back into the village before she signalled to Hubert Frank. 'Get yourself into a CBRN suit and bring the Geiger from the truck. They were picked up close to the contamination zone.'

'Radiation?'

'Unlikely, but it's best to check before we transfer them to fresh bags.'

'All seven?'

'Three,' Sampson said.

Hollow stepped forward. 'Do you want me to call in for another crew, Lieutenant?'

'What on earth for?'

'The others.'

'There are no others, Quinn.'

Hubert Frank had turned towards the field ambulance, shockingly young and so far out of his depth he looked like a different person. It was hard to watch, but the army wasn't one for handholding anyone, not even the audience back home.

'Hurry up, Frank, we haven't got all day.'

ITM SCENE
COMMENTARY
2LT SAMPSON:
We must remember that this isn't our country. Every war has tried to dislodge these little villages. At best, they tolerate us. But it's a fragile alliance. Payment is a mark of respect, on both sides.

PRODUCER:
This is a huge transitional step for Hollow and Hubert. Would it have been preferable to start with an easy return?

2LT SAMPSON:
There are no easy returns. You learn to adapt quickly out in the field.

PRODUCER:
And if they don't adapt?

2LT SAMPSON:
It's my job to see that they do.

Hubert Frank donned the reinforced nylon suit like he'd done a dozen times in training, but his hand was shaking as he held the Geiger counter close to the first bag. 'Zero point five mSv, Lieutenant.'

'Not enough to trigger the alarms. It's probably sand contamination. Quinn, get into CBRN and check the others, will you.' Sampson took the Geiger from Hubert Frank and handed it to Hollow. 'Anything above one mSv gets a red flag and is left for the specialist unit.'

'Yes, Lieutenant.'

Hollow didn't think about it, she just did as she was told. Every movement precise, calculated, following the protocols of radiation training like she'd written them. Establish your base reading. Approach upwind of the site. Scan each item in turn. Top to bottom. Right to left. Keep your eyes fixed on the needle. Listen for exposure warnings. Mark any contaminated material and withdraw.

Sampson turned back to Hubert Frank. 'This will need a steady hand, I'm afraid. Three deep breaths usually do the job. You'll need to let the tension in the zip guide you. Keep it slow and steady. Give the gases a chance to get out first.'

'You want me to...?' Hubert Frank stumbled backwards, almost tripping over his own feet.

'Gloves off. It's best to hold the zipper with your fingertips,' Sampson said, like she hadn't seen the panic that boiled through him. 'Pull it open gently, a bit at a time.'

'Can't we just transfer them as they are, Lieutenant?' Hollow said, circling slowly around the next bag.

'These poor souls have been waiting on a pickup for two weeks and, unfortunately, biology has us beat on this one, Quinn. One untoward jolt of the truck and the existing bag can unzip itself, as it were.'

Hubert Frank was still breathing hard. 'I can't do it.'

'It's best not to think too much about it.'

'I can't do it.'

'Come on, there's a good chap.'

Hubert Frank turned away, crashing into Hollow. Ready to run and nowhere to run to. 'I can't.'

Hollow handed him the Geiger. 'I'll do it.'

Hubert Frank didn't wait for Sampson; he just set to scanning the next bag for radiation like he'd got the okay.

Hollow ditched her CBRN suit, crouched down next to the bag and rooted her feet in the sand to get her balance. The metal zipper was dull, rough to touch, corroded out of shape. It broke with a snap. Hollow froze, not daring to breathe, holding the broken zipper like she'd accidentally pulled the pin out of a grenade.

'It happens,' Sampson said. 'Just take your knife and pierce some holes in the bag. Careful about it, or we'll be in a fine old mess.'

'You want me to make some holes?' Hollow said.

'Use the tip of the knife, like a curry in the microwave.'

Hollow pulled her knife out, kneeling now to keep her hand steady. 'A curry in the microwave.'

'Good, that's good,' Sampson said, tucked behind Hollow as she carefully pierced each hole. 'Releasing the gases has given us a bit more room. Now cut the rest of the bag away. Easy as you go.'

It was an upper torso. The soldier's eyes were fish eyes, skin waxy and paler than the remnants of a cheap latex sex doll. The camera crew did their best to film it, but it wasn't an easy thing to translate into anything but art.

ITM SCENE
COMMENTARY
2LT SAMPSON:
The CBRN suits are lined with charcoal infused felt, and are lightweight enough to wear in combat. They provide protection against chemical, biological, radiological and nuclear exposure.

We are all acutely aware of the psychological threat the Mandolin pose, but we cannot forget that they have already used a nuclear device. Subsequently, we must assume they are also capable of using chemical and biological weapons.

Even knowing that feels like a form of psychological warfare.

HOLLOW QUINN:
Training isn't anything like this, but it prepares you for moments like this. You listen to what to do so you don't have to think about what to do. Lieutenant Sampson talked me through the steps, and I was just doing the next thing and then the next thing.

I guess, as something in me disconnected, something else stepped up.

The smell was…worse than the worst vomit you've ever smelled. SO much worse. My brain was like, you should throw up. But I didn't. So that's good. And Lieutenant Sampson, she was all everyday about it. I kept thinking, it must be okay then. It must be okay.

PRODUCER:
Lieutenant Sampson asked Hubert Frank to do it. Why did you step in?

HOLLOW QUINN:
I was watching The Hubert panic, and I kept thinking about this tobacco I got the day I enlisted. It sounds stupid, but the tobacco was bad. And by bad, I mean, rank. All the time I was smoking it, I was thinking, this is really horrible.

Like I even knew what horrible was.

Hollow stepped back to catch her breath. 'That's all of the bag cut away, Lieutenant.'

'Well done, Quinn.' Sampson turned and spoke to Hubert Frank like nothing had gone before. 'We'll need you over here for this bit, Frank.'

And that was exactly how she talked them through the handling protocol. Calm. Clinical. Respectful. Instruction by instruction and word by word, she changed something unbearable into something normal. Once they'd transferred the torso into a fresh body bag, they opened another, doing their best to match up the pieces. Then they loaded the bags into the field ambulance, burned what was left, and drove back to camp with the doors open. Sampson gave them five minutes of silence, still guiding them through their first mission even if they didn't know it. 'Rather a grisly introduction, I'm afraid,' she said.

'Yes, Lieutenant.'

'Although, I have dated online.'

Hollow and Hubert Frank laughed, more out of requirement than humour.

'And the bag didn't pop,' Sampson said. 'Which is a tick in the success box.'

'Do they often pop, Lieutenant?' Hollow said.

'More often than one would hope.'

'Right,' Hollow said. 'I'm glad I didn't know that.'

'Sometimes, they go shooting around like an unknotted balloon.'

Hollow choked on her own laugh. 'No way.'

'Which is most unfortunate,' Sampson said. 'Especially if it chases down the village elder.'

Hubert Frank nodded along. 'That ain't the sort of meet-and-greet anyone wants.'

Sampson's laugh was unexpectedly untamed, raw and loud. 'You'll be relieved to hear,' she said eventually, 'that I'd strategically positioned myself so that Quinn would have taken the worst of it. Can't have a British officer coming back covered in French juices. It would be terribly bad for morale.'

As they got closer to the camp, Sampson dropped the mood down, easing them back to their duties just like she'd eased them through everything else. 'You'll take these three soldiers straight to the refrigerated ISO, and be respectful about it. We owe them everything, never forget that.'

'Yes, Lieutenant.'

'And get yourselves over to the decontamination block. No radiation to speak of, but it never hurts to scrub the dust from your bones after a job like this.'

The heat haze of a cloudless sky shimmered a lake along the horizon. Their tyre tracks were already fading as the fine white sand drifted in waves across the endless desert. The ocean was still there, but the sea had been evacuated.

ITM SCENE
COMMENTARY
HOLLOW QUINN:
It felt good to get them into the cold. The duty doctor told us to take them out of the body bags and put them with the other bodies. I don't think he knew what they were. We didn't take them out. We just left them inside the bags.

I think we must have been trying to protect them. It sounds stupid, they're dead. But the rest of the ISO was too ghastly to look at, even for a corpse. And at the back, there was this place, this...

...sorting place.

I think maybe I'm losing touch with what's okay and what's not okay. In the field ambulance, it was like we'd been doing the worst thing you could imagine, and we were laughing all the way back to camp. I guess there's some things you can never get out of your mind, so you don't even bother to try. Yeah, you don't bother to try.

2LT SAMPSON:
Hollow Quinn listened to instructions, and she trusted me. I'm pleased with how she handled herself today.

PRODUCER:
And Hubert Frank?

2LT SAMPSON:
Although I talk about Quinn handling herself well, I want you to understand that there was no opposite, no failure on show here today. We can be caught out by our own behaviour, especially in extreme situations. This experience gave Hubert Frank a realistic baseline to work from. By the time we'd finished the procedure, he was working at the required level of competence. How could there be any failure in that?

Hubert Frank held the door open for Hollow, restless and more than ready to leave the refrigerated ISO.

'Three.' The doctor looked exhausted, thin as a runway model and paler than the bodies he cared for. 'Pass me that clipboard, will you.'

The folded metal clipboard was propped up on a steel table next to the exit. Hollow handed it over. 'Anything else, Captain?'

'Names?'

'Private Quinn and Private Frank.'

'Names of the P4.' The doctor sighed. 'ID discs, if you please.

The barcodes can be useful for reconstruction, but they're often damaged in battle.'

'We have to go to the decontamination block,' Hubert Frank said.

The doctor recoiled, scrabbling to check a rectangular panel on his white coat. 'What the hell are you doing, bringing radioactive material in here!'

'It's advisory, Captain,' Hollow said. 'There were traces at the pickup site.'

'Level?'

'Zero point five mSv.'

'Sand,' the doctor said. 'The explosion from that blasted Mandolin bomb scattered radioactive debris no more than a few hundred yards, but the wind has carried contaminated sand for hundreds of miles. A year on, and the whole desert is a radioactive zone. Fortunately, iodine tablets are enough protection at these levels. If your suit isn't squealing, there's no need to put yourself through a decontamination procedure.'

'Yes, Captain.'

'Well, this only needs one of you,' the doctor said. 'Frank, you're dismissed. And for pity's sake, shut that door behind you. It's hard enough keeping this place cold as it is.'

Hubert Frank stood on the threshold for a second, then turned away, closing the door and leaving Hollow behind.

'Don't just stand there, Quinn, get me the names.'

Hollow unzipped the first body bag, fumbling the ID discs, dragging at the flesh. 'Yes, Captain, I have it.'

The doctor had the decency to notice. 'I haven't seen you in here before.'

'It's our first pickup.'

'Unfortunately, you do get used to it.'

'Yes, Captain.'

'Name?'

Hollow was staring at the disc. 'It's in French.'

'This isn't a GCSE oral exam, Quinn. Do your best.'

'*Caporal-chef Maël Florian Blanchard.*'

'Religion?'

'*Catholique,*' Hollow said. 'Catholic. Blood group—'

'No need for blood groups in here.'

'Sorry, Captain.' Hollow unzipped the next bag, slow and respectful like she'd known how to handle the dead forever.

'There are only two official causes of death in this war,' the doctor said, drawing a delicate hummingbird next to his signature. 'Friendly fire and induced suicide. But I've seen a slower death, a death that keeps you alive...'

Hollow zipped up the last bag. 'Permission to return to duty, Captain.'

'Denied,' the doctor said, snapping the clipboard shut. 'I need some help in here today, and it might as well be you.'

'I'm on ambulance crew until eight. They'll be looking for me.'

'Who's your CO?'

'Lieutenant Sampson.'

'I'll clear it with Sampson,' the doctor said, heading towards the back of the ISO. 'It's not the most pleasant of jobs, but these poor souls have done their best to defend the human race. In return, we do our best to get them home in one piece.'

ITM SCENE
COMMENTARY
HOLLOW QUINN:
All the king's horses and all the king's men, there were
body bits laid out on table after table. Soldiers, Afghan
civilians, old people, babies. All jumbled up together
like a serial killer's basement. Seeing something like
that sorting place could break you.

PRODUCER:
And if you're already broken?

HOLLOW QUINN:
I guess you're fine, then.

PRODUCER:
Are you fine, Hollow?

HOLLOW QUINN:
Apparently, the army really does take all the jumbled-up pieces and put them together in a way that makes sense.

Hollow didn't ask where all the pieces came from; she just did her best to help the doctor put them together again. Back at the bunkhouse, she plugged her uniform into a reboot outlet, ripped off the wireless microphone pack and ran the shower hot until her skin burned.

'Cold water is better.' Sylvie leant around Hollow, adjusting the heating on the shower. 'It still hurts but you can sleep after.'

'Does it get the smell off?'

'First body?'

'Every part of me stinks of it. I can literally taste it in my mouth.'

Sylvie smiled a little, more from understanding than humour. 'You can't have two enemies, sweetie.'

'I'm just getting the smell off.'

'And I said the exact same thing a year ago,' Sylvie said. 'There's no right or wrong way with WØLF, but sometimes it can get lonely. They tell me I should confide in someone, except it's not easy finding someone you trust enough to catch you.'

'Sure.'

'If you ever need someone to talk to.'

'Sampson already suggested Jar.'

'Sometimes, I think Jar is the best of us.' Sylvie almost laughed. 'Mostly, it's a good day if he finds his own socks.'

'Sylvie, I get that you have this drive to save everyone,' Hollow said. 'But rescuing people is always about the rescuer, and I'm fine with being left behind.'

'Some battles are played to be lost in the game between angels and men.'

'Whatever.'

'There are two sides to fame, sweetie. The side of you that wants it and the side of you that's terrified of it.' Sylvie leant in again, close enough to the running water to mask her voice. 'And in-between is where you get to live.'

Sylvie had gone by the time Hollow got dressed. She grabbed some notepaper and went to sit behind the hospital toilet block, writing a letter to Ezra, and then ripping it up.

ITM SCENE
COMMENTARY
HUBERT FRANK:
We all been playing at soldiers. Up till today, we been playing at soldiers. Then we went and got our first look at the war. Except, it's not the right war.

The Hubert's been to the training. Trusting the method, just like Sergeant Naleigh says. And Sergeant Naleigh, he got the right war. Sergeant Naleigh got to be the soldier.

This ain't how The Hubert's supposed to be. The Hubert ain't no background wuss. It's the wrong war, bru.

They sent The Hubert to the wrong war.

22

Is that some kind of landscaping term?

Ezra was done with the whole mysterious thing. The symbol
was unique enough to stand alone and simple enough
to give nothing away. All the glorious research avenues had
narrowed and dwindled into cul-de-sacs. More importantly,
Atticus Valentine had said he'd be in touch in a few days, but
the untouched days became a week, two weeks, eventually
two months, and not so much as a friendly message asking
how things were going. Even the wall he'd said was easy to
find remained stubbornly undiscoverable. Ezra's flirtation
with clandestine research had officially reached a dead end.
It was time to return the pendant, along with a polite note
explaining the situation, apologising for the delay. Telling
Mr Valentine not to give up on his search and thanking him
for the opportunity. Today would be best. Or tomorrow. Or
perhaps it would be safer to hand-deliver it to the reception
desk at Plug Productions next weekend. For the attention of
Atticus Valentine.

'If they're open.' Ezra ignored the semi-mortal clock as it
thundered through a drum solo. 'They're probably not open on
the weekend.'

And it wasn't as if Ezra always wore the pendant like a
favourite necklace, or went indulging a daydream that Atticus
Valentine might happen to be in the foyer of Plug Productions

next weekend. Maybe he'd suggest another coffee and their hands would touch, sending him into an instant marriage proposal. Ezra coughed and straightened the guide books, embarrassed that a daydream featuring an instant marriage proposal had slipped so smoothly into work time. More especially, a particular moment of work time when a tweed-embellished woman had presented herself at the wrong desk.

In fact, Blessing Woodworm wasn't at the wrong desk at all. She was at exactly the right desk. Unlike, as she was often heard to say, most of the other people who worked at Plug Productions. Atypically, forty-six-year-old Blessing Woodworm had risen like a dandelion through the manicured lawn of attractive staff, often embodying her weedy defiance so magnificently that the manicured lawn secretly wished it was a whole field of dandelions. When Atticus Valentine had taken an interest in Fabian Evirate House, Blessing Woodworm had insisted that she be the initial contact, as eccentric places needed a fair degree of common sense to negotiate. She'd then added, not unkindly, that Atticus Valentine might not recognise an ounce of common sense if it came up to him at a club, bought him a drink and then suggested they find somewhere quieter to talk. The fact that Atticus Valentine had taken it upon himself to go ahead and visit the place anyway only served to prove the point.

'Woodworm.' Blessing Woodworm presented a business card. 'I find two names unnecessary.'

'Woodworm,' Ezra said. It was hard to think of anything else to say, as Blessing Woodworm did indeed have the brusque look of someone who'd never found a practical use for her first name. Ezra managed to drag a smile from somewhere, but it was an achievement of strength more than courtesy. Atticus Valentine hadn't been in contact, and now he'd sent someone else to pick up the research. This was so far from an instant marriage proposal that it lived in a monastery.

'I would prefer to get straight to the matter,' Blessing

Woodworm said, running her index finger along the edge of the Bakelite desk. 'I find chit-chat unnecessary.'

'You've come to collect the pendant.'

'Collect the pendant?' Blessing Woodworm frowned. 'Does my business card suggest that I am in courier collection?'

'No...'

'No.' Blessing Woodworm picked up the smart little document case that she'd placed neatly on the floor beside her. 'Well, lay on Macduff.'

'With the?'

Blessing Woodworm circumnavigated the desk like a sensible asteroid, pointing to things, scribbling notes on her phone with a glass stylus, and generally mumbling to herself. She finally came to rest, tapping the stylus several times next to the word inadequate. 'I hope you don't agree with all this nonsense.'

'Remind me of the...nonsense.'

Blessing Woodworm didn't speak for a while; she just held the glass stylus against her lip thoughtfully. 'Fortunately, I find disappointment unnecessary.'

'How can I help, Woodworm?'

'Perhaps you can.' Blessing Woodworm gestured towards the words written at the foot of the phylactery entrance. 'If you wouldn't mind translating that inscription, you would be a legend.'

'The epitaph?'

Blessing Woodworm made a strange little noise which unexpectedly turned out to be a laugh. 'Ah, you'll have to excuse my sense of humour,' she said, patting at the corner of her eye.

'I find a sense of humour unnecessary,' Ezra said.

Blessing Woodworm inwardly applauded Ezra's harsh response to her moment of weakness, although she certainly wasn't going to say so. She wandered around the clock, less flinchy than most, making notes and photographing several features to show the *team* back at Plug Productions.

The clock was quieter than usual, and a shade of pink around the uppermost glass panels, as the unexpected visitor continued with several more photographs and some stern tutting at her phone's determination to tag a fly as her mother. It even succumbed to an indulgent puff of ant powder as Blessing Woodworm informed Ezra that someone would be in touch shortly and made her own way back down the staircase.

First thing Monday morning, Emporia was disturbed from occupational salsa dancing by a phone call from someone called Myxy.

'Hi there, this is Myxy calling from Plug Productions, ya?' Myxy left a question mark at the end of everything and made a popping noise through some sort of chewing gum. 'How are you today?'

'My dear child, an enquiry as to a lady's wellbeing requires a discreet calling card and several days of mandatory silence,' Emporia said. 'How may I assist you?'

'Hi there, this is Emporia, ya?'

'There has obviously been some kind of confusion. I think you'll find that I am Emporia.'

'You, ya?' Myxy said, with a giggle.

'You require a You-Ya?' A group of children had left fingerprints on the frosted glass swing outside Emporia's office, and one of them had licked it. She was not in the mood for anyone under the age of thirty-five. 'Is that some kind of landscaping term?'

Myxy had only been at Plug Productions for three weeks, and two of those weeks had been spent at a health spa retreat in Croatia. He decided to start again. 'Hi there, this is Myxy calling from Plug Productions?'

'I'm sorry, there is no one by the name of Myxy here,' Emporia said with a flourish, because the continent that was Emporia Precipice Mantlepiece was not going quietly into the night.

'Atticus Valentine,' Myxy said, swallowing his gum and carefully repressing an upward inflection by squashing everything into a single sentence, 'has left a message for me to call Emporia at Fabian Evirate House, to ask if an Ezra Blake might be available for an early supper meeting tonight…ya?'

'Young Mr Valentine?' Emporia blushed slightly. 'Well, of course, why didn't you say so, child? I'm sure Ezra Blake would be perfectly delighted to accept. If you care to hold the line, I shall enquire this very moment.'

Ezra carried on arranging a set of souvenir pencils into a rainbow as Emporia delivered the invitation, fixing a smile somewhere between flattered and professional, and yet still managing to look six days of constipation and a laxative short of holding it together.

Sheila Blake arrived home to discover there'd been some kind of controlled explosion in Ezra's wardrobe. 'First things first,' she inhaled, 'are there any wounded?'

'If I even had his phone number, I'd cancel.' Ezra's face resembled an onion that had been peeling onions. 'By text, obviously.'

'Have you informed the bomb squad?' Sheila edged around the door.

'So I was thinking, maybe you could go down to the restaurant for me,' Ezra said. 'I can give you the link to the research I did. And I've got the personal property he left with us. You'd just need to hand it all over to him. Tell him I've been taken sick. He'll be fine with that. Honestly, I think that's the best thing.'

Having made a note of all the things not to do in every film she'd ever watched, Sheila was great in a crisis. 'You lost me after restaurant.'

'It's not even a lie, Mum. I feel really sick.'

Sheila held a hand to Ezra's forehead. 'Anxiety?'

'Maybe...' Ezra had regrettably done some stalker-based research on the bus '...I mean, he dates models and actors.'

'You're meeting Atticus Valentine again?'

'For work.'

'You said he was a jolly good egg,' Sheila said. 'And Hollow's on WØLF now. I'm sure he'd be interested to hear some stories about you and Hollow growing up together.'

'We can't talk about WØLF to him. I had the training.'

'What if he talks about it?'

Ezra flung both arms around like naked hand puppets. 'I don't know, Mum. All I know is we're not allowed to talk to Atticus Valentine about WØLF.'

'He might want to talk about it, poor chap.' Sheila leant down, curling her little finger around the collar of a fluorescent shirt that still had its tag on. 'Are you wearing this?'

'I don't know,' Ezra's voice was hovering in the no-man's-land between a sob and a laugh, 'I'm incapable of making a decision.'

Sheila folded the shirt in half and covered it with a crochet-edged poncho. 'What we need is a little music.'

'Mum, I don't want any music.'

'No music?' Sheila put her hands on her hips. 'You like this guy!'

'No, shut up.'

'You're not doing anything wrong by liking him, sweetheart.'

'Mum, I'm super-stressed because he's an important Fabian Evirate House customer and I have to tell him that I got nowhere with his research. I also need to manage his understandable disappointment. Which I should have done before I started.'

'But you do like him?'

'Poppycock!' Ezra squealed.

'Poppycock?'

'I say that now, apparently...' Ezra picked at the sequins of a green scarf. 'I do lots of things now, apparently.'

Sheila sat on the edge of the bed. 'Does he like you?'

'He's a customer, Mum.' Ezra twisted the scarf into a noose. 'I have an early evening work meeting with a customer.'

'Well then, I guess we'd better make this an early evening work meeting to remember.'

'OMG,' Ezra said. 'I don't want this to be an early evening work meeting to remember. I want this to be an early evening work meeting so forgotten we can't even remember talking about forgetting it.'

'Sweetheart, there are so many awful things happening in the world right now, we're all having to make choices that even a year ago would have seemed impossible. The choices might not be the same, but they always come down to the same thing. Courage.'

'No, you're right, it's courage,' Ezra said, slowly crumpling into a ball. 'Hollow didn't hesitate. You should have seen her at the armed forces drop-in centre, Mum. She was amazing. And she's so brilliant and brave on TV. Every time I see her, she's doing something even more brilliant and brave. And I'm...not. I'm getting myself in a state over some stupid work meeting. What does that say about me?' Ezra looked up, all undried tears and desperation. 'Should I enlist, Mum?'

'Enlist?' Sheila frowned. 'I thought we were talking about a work meeting.'

'It always comes down to courage,' Ezra said. 'And I should force myself to do something I don't want to do.'

'That's not courage, sweetheart, that's fear.'

'Okay.' Ezra nodded it out. 'Fear is good. I can work with fear. Sergeant Naleigh said that fear makes us do something stupid, and I don't want to be doing something stupid, not in the middle of a paraspecies war.'

'If I recall correctly...' Tulip Blake leant against the door frame '...Sergeant Naleigh also said that understanding a situation is what gets you out alive. Although why we're suddenly basing our future conduct on *WØLF* doctrine is slightly concerning.'

'He certainly didn't mention courage,' Sheila said. 'So no panic enlisting.'

'Courage is the opposite of being afraid.' Tulip smiled softly. 'What are you afraid of, kiddo?'

'I don't even know...' Ezra took a deep breath. 'Things not turning out how I want them to, I guess.'

'You've got this,' Sheila said.

'I've got this.' Ezra sat up, puffing through nineteen years of angst and rebounding into a hopeful grin. 'Or you could tell him I have monkeypox.'

'Monkeypox?' Sheila threw herself back on the bed like a seal that had become entangled in a charity shop donation bag. 'Unless you have a medical diagnosis, the household policy on dishonesty remains unchanged.'

'No, no, hear me out,' Ezra said. 'I actually do have this weird rash thing on my leg, and it might be monkeypox. Should we risk taking a notifiable disease to a restaurant full of people? Plus, no one ever asks any questions if you mention monkeypox.'

'What sort of weird rash thing?' Tulip said.

Sheila shook her head. 'Did you do your best with his research project?'

'Of course.'

'Then you've got this,' Sheila said. 'And ask for Angela if he turns out to be a creep.'

'Did you do a rash scan on the NHS app?' Tulip said.

'It's a heat rash, Mum.'

Reservations weren't mandatory on a Monday evening, but if you'd booked ahead, the door thanked you for it. The maître d' escorted Ezra to a table, discreetly mentioning that Mr Valentine had been slightly delayed. Ezra asked for water and stared at the table for ten minutes. It was a lovely, lovely table, all tucked away and secret in the corner. An enhanced candlelight of ambient fragrance drifted in delicate curls over the timeless beauty of walnut. It was the sort of artisan table that required years of experience, an organised workshop and a hundred grades of sandpaper.

'I'm so sorry,' Atticus said. 'The more I tried not to be late, the worse it got.'

Ezra hadn't even heard him arrive. 'Oh no, honestly, no, it's fine. I haven't been here very long.'

Atticus loosened his tie and sat back. 'It's good to see you again. How's everything at Fabian Evirate House?'

'I met Woodworm.'

'So I hear. She said you weren't incompetent.'

Ezra grimaced, took a deep breath and bungee jumped into the conversation. 'I'm not embroidering this for sympathy or anything, but I tried to get my mum to tell you I had monkeypox. She obviously refused on account of defending the truth or something. Then she forced me into a taxi or I wouldn't be here either. Her name is Sheila. She's my best friend. Not my pact best friend, just my general best friend. Sad, eh? But not sad, because it's also adorable. She did my hair. All the extra bits of neon were her idea. Not that I don't like them. She's so great. Even with the disco. And the horror. And...Christmas. My other mum is obviously my best friend too, but in more sensible circumstances.' The words just kept on coming. It felt like driving a car in a computer game. Hopefully, Ezra wouldn't hit anyone. 'She was named after her paternal aunt, Lady Tulip Splendid-Underpinning II, who accidentally sailed naked down the Thames on an inflatable crocodile during the regatta. It was the crocodile that sparked a media frenzy.' Ezra picked at a bit of nail varnish that had escaped removal. 'The naked bit didn't seem to bother anyone.'

'You made a pact with someone?'

'Yeah, okay, yeah. Yeah, I did, yeah,' Ezra said, eventually. 'And a pretty comprehensive one, considering we were, like, twelve. It's got living arrangements and relationship strategies, and a whole section on… It's a boring story. Anyway, she signed up for the army, just randomly at the bus stop. And it wasn't even a military GiFT. She enlisted for the full tour. Three years. Which wasn't in the pact at all. And she didn't say anything about enlisting before, like it just came out of nowhere. I don't even know where she is now. Well, actually I do. Because she's on a reality TV show. In Afghanistan. I can't tell you which exact reality TV show in Afghanistan, because I had the training.'

Atticus sat forward. 'She's on *WØLF*?'

'I know, right. It's an ongoing shock situation.'

'Wow, that's awkward.'

'Is it, though?' Ezra said. 'I mean, it's not like I've been messaging her about you coming to Fabian Evirate House. I actually haven't spoken to her since she enlisted. And she hasn't contacted me, not one time, even though she broke the pact and by all rights it's down to her.' Ezra sighed. 'The pact was supposed to be binding, but right now it's hard to remember anything except the paper and the blood.'

'One of the new recruits?'

'Yeah, see, they didn't cover this scenario in the training.'

'Is it Fish?' Atticus said.

'It's Hollow.'

'Hollow?'

'We've known each other since preschool.' Ezra stared at the table again. 'Sorry, I should have told you.'

As if on a misinformed cue, the maître d' swanned between them with a bottle of water and two menus.

'I had a really late lunch,' Ezra said.

'Same,' Atticus said, 'and then they put the biscuit plate in front of me at the last meeting.'

The maître d' smiled like it belonged to someone else. 'The evening air is daringly sweet. May I suggest, Mr Valentine, that we retire your table to the garden for coffee? A small selection of antipasti, perhaps?'

Atticus looked over to Ezra. 'Sounds good?'

'Sure.' Ezra took another deep breath. 'I've already told you about Hollow. I suppose I'd better tell you what else I should have already told you.'

The restaurant garden greeted them with a sincere and wonderfully fragrant embrace. Its paving delicately laced by an assortment of alpine perennials, each one a graded compliance to the symmetry that unified the seating areas without compromising their individual beauty. And all around them, stone-carved mirrors gathered the softening glow of the evening sun in amber starlight. As an outside seating area, the restaurant garden was as close to perfect as you could get with a five-hundred-thousand-pound budget and a penchant for Pre-Raphaelite art.

Atticus sat next to Ezra, close enough for conversation, but leaving his phone on the bench between them like an uninvited third wheel. 'Having your friend on WØLF, that must be incredibly difficult,' he said.

'I want to say yes, but if I'm honest, it's better than her just being in the army. At least I only have to turn on the TV to know she's doing okay.' Ezra picked at the nail varnish again. 'Or not doing okay. Mostly, I'm not thinking about it.'

'I understand,' Atticus said.

Ezra sat up straight, wrung out enough to sigh with it. 'I've put all the pendant research up on the Cloud. I can make you an appointment to look through it, or I can just send you a secure link.'

'We can talk about WØLF, if you want to.'

'I promised you a timeline,' Ezra said. 'Unfortunately, nothing comparable is itemised at Fabian Evirate House or any of our sister sites. There were some promising leads in Thamudic runes and petroglyphs, but every trail I followed ended up taking me further away. That doesn't mean to say the answer isn't in a dusty old database somewhere. Things turn up under floorboards, and manuscripts are being discovered all the time.' Ezra tried to look at him but made a hash of it. 'Or it could be that there just aren't any answers out there. Most of our everyday history is already lost.'

'Everyday history...' Atticus moved to allow room for a spider to crawl across his phone '...like a throwaway thing.'

'Not like household rubbish, like a piece of art,' Ezra said. 'It could be a pattern inspired by organic shapes found in nature. It could even be a stylised set of initials or something. Meaningful, unique and most probably treasured. But without its creator, it's almost impenetrable.'

'You think it's a piece of art?'

'No, no, I'm not saying it is. It could just as easily be a lost rune or an abstract representation of something amazing. Something we don't know about yet. But I've gone as far as I can with this, I haven't got anywhere left to try. I'm so sorry, Mr Valentine, I know it's not the result you wanted from this.'

'It's me who should apologise.' Atticus looked down, watching the spider spin the first lines of thread like cracks across his phone screen. 'I should have got back to you sooner.'

'Honestly, the last thing you want is someone constantly asking for updates when you're busy researching something.' Ezra sighed, blagging the shady line between telling a lie and telling the truth. 'You gave me time to look everywhere, and I appreciate the opportunity so much.'

'I took an old computer apart once,' Atticus said. 'One of those massive tower ones that everyone used to have. By the end, its components fitted into a shoebox. Eighty per cent of the computer was nothing. Just a whole load of empty space keeping the computer cool enough to stop it destroying itself.' He was still watching the spider. 'Sometimes nothing is the most important thing you find.'

'It is.' Ezra stared at him. 'That's one of the fundamental

truths of all research. And I forgot it. I was so busy trying to find an answer, I forgot a fundamental truth.'

Atticus shooed the spider off his phone. 'Let's assume you've already done an image search.'

Ezra frowned. 'Of course.'

'Try this one.'

Ezra took his phone, studying the image. 'I already tried this, Mr Valentine, like a hundred times.'

Atticus didn't answer.

'There's no match,' Ezra said. 'There's nothing to find.'

'Did you find the wall?'

'I'm sorry.' Ezra tried to hand his phone back. 'You can still try Emporia or Dicky, they would be discreet, I'm sure they would.'

He tilted his head. 'Be creative.'

'How?' Ezra said. 'There's nothing to be creative with.'

'Come on, there's always something.'

'Don't make me ask for Angela.' Ezra sat back, closer to him without being all obvious about it. 'Okay. Think creative. Think outside the shoebox. Okay. Okay. So, that day in the phylactery, you said something odd. Something that didn't make much sense at the time. You said we'd put the Jötunvillur panel in with the power and magic.'

'I did.'

'But this symbol isn't Jötunvillur. It's nothing like Jötunvillur...' Ezra paused. 'Except, no one really knows what Jötunvillur is. There's a theory that it might be...games.'

Atticus finally smiled. 'Games.'

'Ha!' Ezra sat up. 'Hanging it on a bit of leather cord makes it look like a symbol, but what if it's actually a puzzle?'

'You're pretty good at this.'

'So it's a puzzle, yeah?' Ezra pulled the image up again. 'And puzzles always have the solution built into them. With a jigsaw, you put the pieces together, but this image is already solved. I need to work backwards.' Ezra grinned. 'I need to take all the pieces apart.'

'Maybe,' he said. And then he winked, which was horribly unfair considering Ezra was trying to solve a puzzle.

'Okay. Let's start with the basics. I can see a letter T, maybe a Y. The arches could be a U and an N. Wait...' Ezra frowned. 'It can't be that easy.'

'Some answers are designed to be too easy,' Atticus said. 'We're inclined to overlook them.'

'UNITY, these are the stacked letters of UNITY.' Ezra looked sideways at Atticus. 'Except you already knew that.'

'I thought I'd found the solution,' Atticus said, 'but it was only another piece of the puzzle.'

'UNITY.' Ezra tapped the phone for a few seconds. 'U.N.I.T.Y. Like an acronym, maybe? Something to do with the United Nations?'

He smiled, looking down at his hands. 'Try it.'

The acronym brought pages of nothing, not even a random university article predicting the end of the world. 'Okay...' Ezra cleared the search again. 'What piece of a puzzle is so important you can't get anywhere without it?'

Atticus grinned. 'Can I get you a drink?'

'A password!' Ezra laughed, taking in the beautiful restaurant garden like someone might arrive with a genius certificate at any moment. 'Oh my God, this is a password.'

'Yes.'

'So where do we put the password?'

'Too easy,' he said.

'Too easy.' Ezra looked down at Atticus' phone. 'All we have is this image... Is that it? Is that where the password goes? In the metta tags?'

And yep, Atticus Valentine just sat there, his arm resting along the back of the bench, looking for all the world like he was in a magazine for high-end restaurant gardens.

Ezra took several deep breaths. Opened the image metta tags. Added the word UNITY to the empty field. Clicked on the search-generated link. Grinned. Stopped grinning. Put the phone face down on the bench. Picked the phone up again to check the link was cut. Pushed it back towards Atticus like it was an unexpected clump of tuberculosis growing on a half-eaten bacon sandwich. 'Fucking hell.'

'Welcome to the wall.'

'Ezra was staring at the space where a genius certificate had almost been. 'Muh.'

'Did I mention it was okay to freak out?' Atticus said.

'Muh.'

'Breathe in through your nose, and—'

'Seriously!' Ezra spluttered. 'You would have let me find that on the Fabian Evirate House database?'

'You didn't find it.'

'Right, right,' Ezra said.

'This only comes back to me. It's on my phone.'

'Does it, though?' Ezra said, as a ping lit up the pocket of a fluorescent shirt and the inevitable truth of warfare in a time of technology.

**YOU HAVE BEEN IN CLOSE CONTACT
WITH SOMEONE ATTEMPTING TO
ACCESS A WEBSITE SEIZED BY THE
INTERNATIONAL WAR AGENCY UNDER
THE PREVENTION OF TERRORISM ACT**

**PLEASE FOLLOW CURRENT GOVERNMENT
GUIDELINES VIA THIS LINK**

23

They were time-travelling coat hangers

Ezra sank the Tequila shot, and nothing but a lime twist was left. 'It's probably treason. I got pinged looking at treason.'

'I did say it was okay to freak out.'

'Yes, yes, you did,' Ezra said. 'So that's fine then.'

'If I'd told you about the website at the beginning, you wouldn't have agreed to help me.'

'Help you with what?' Ezra said, sarcastically. 'Finding out all the stuff you already know?'

'Getting past it.'

'Oh, of course.' Ezra stood on the second attempt. 'And here's me thinking it was just treason.'

'It's not like that,' Atticus said, standing up with Ezra, but only in the sense that they both stood up.

'You sat there, all lovely and kind and listening to me babbling on about Hollow. And all the time you're waiting on an opportunity to trick me into finding that. What even is that?' Ezra stopped him before he could answer. 'No, don't, don't tell me, I don't want to know anything about it… Except I know the password. If I get tortured, I know the password.'

'No one will torture you.'

'I've had a ping from the International War Agency!' Ezra stared a whole selection box of emotions at him. 'That's not just here, that's like the Russians and the Americans, and everyone. Belarus. I just got pinged by Belarus.'

'The ping was from the Ministry of War.'

'That's all fine then!' Ezra yelled, but just above a whisper because this was some serious shit going down. 'Except, the Ministry of War, they don't even need a reason to lock you up and throw away the key. I honestly don't know how I'd cope being in treason prison. And what if I *had* found it at work? We're flagged up by government spyware and the Ministry of War are suddenly taking an active interest in what we're doing at Fabian Evirate House. Some of the installations are hard to explain at the best of times, and I'm pretty sure Downstairs Lesley once belonged to the communist party.'

'It's not that bad,' Atticus said. 'It would be obvious from the way you cut the link that nothing subversive was going on, I promise.'

'Alright then, mister innocent browsing history, what if the Ministry of War had a quiet week and decided to pop over and check us out? What if they were to, oh, I don't know, have a look around, ask a few questions, notice a GiFT donator merrily wearing a terrorist password around their neck?'

Atticus stepped back. 'You wore it around your neck?'

'You practically forced it on me, and all the time you knew what it represented, what it could have meant for me.'

'It would have been okay.'

'Would it?' Ezra was breathing through an urge to scream at full volume. 'Because if the Ministry of War even asked me my name, I'd crack. I'd immediately tell them that I know the password to a seized website. And I saw the words: *The First Mark*. What does that even mean?'

'It's—'

'OMG, don't tell me!' Ezra puffed it all out. 'I'd also rat on you immediately, by the way.'

'I can handle the Ministry,' he said, 'I would have protected you.'

'You don't even know me,' Ezra said. 'I once wrote a

short story about a family of coat hangers living in medieval Europe.'

'Wood or wire?'

'Wire.'

'The wire coat hanger was invented in 1903,' Atticus said.

'They were time-travelling coat hangers.' Ezra was a long way from smiling. Still, Atticus' outstanding knowledge of coat hangers had softened things a little. 'You made me look at treason.'

'Will you give me a chance to explain?'

Ezra took several steadying licks of the shot glass, sucked the lime twist, and sat back down. 'It's been a bit of a shock, what with the ping and all.'

'Of course, I totally get that.'

'Did you bring your car here?'

'I did...' Atticus spoke carefully '...it's in the car park.'

'And you really think you can convince me that this isn't what it seems?'

'I think so.'

Ezra spat a lime pip into the nearest cluster of delicate alpine perennials. 'How about if you give me a lift home, and I give you thirty minutes to explain?'

'A lift home?'

'Yes.'

'To your home?' Atticus was looking at Ezra like he wasn't sure which red wire to cut. 'In my car?'

'The taxi driver would ask me how my evening went. And Gran Lizeth says there's ghosts on the bus. I already look like I saw one, so it could get sketchy.' Ezra peered at him through the bottom of the shot glass. 'People will be asking to see my licence from the intelligence services.'

'I'll let the restaurant know we're leaving.'

'I might just pop to the loo.' Ezra turned the shot glass upside down and placed it on the arm of the bench. 'Except they probably call it a *guardez l'eau* or something.'

281

'Not since the Battle of Castillon.'

'Sweet. And I promise I won't hide in a cubicle and click on any government links or anything.' Ezra smiled more encouragingly this time. 'Meet you out the front, yeah? I'll be the one who looks like they've just been coerced into looking at an International War Agency seized website.'

Atticus didn't laugh; he just kept on looking back like he'd popped out to the garage for milk, and now a floodwater raged between them. Ezra smiled generously and waved another step towards the toilets, checking Atticus was out of sight before running back to the garden. Everything Mac Eden had said that night in the lunar harvesting corridor was making sense now, but instead of feeling relieved to learn the truth about Atticus Valentine, Ezra felt like the chalk outline after a homicide. Unfortunately, there was no knife or discarded gun in the slaughter of a beautiful daydream. Frankly, until all the evidence had been examined, it was impossible to rule out suicide.

At the far end of the garden, Ezra found a delivery bay that slipped down the side of the restaurant and out onto the road. It was a natural pergola of jasmine and sweet-smelling honeysuckle, and Ezra trampled the lower blossoms into pulp. Feeling like a chalk outline was grim, but it was better than feeling like you'd swallowed a whole bottle of wine without taking the cork out. Ezra had wanted the gorgeous, kind, sweet Atticus Valentine to be mysterious. The safe kind of mysterious. The intriguing kind of mysterious that kept you super-interested. Not the kind of mysterious that made you shit yourself. That sort of mysterious permitted you to run away from a restaurant. It certainly permitted you to scream at a guy throwing up on a knitted tribute to the Tolpuddle Martyrs. Running from the restaurant was by far the best thing to do in the circumstances. Away from the ping and the awkwardness and whatever brand of sedition Atticus Valentine was involved with. No one wanted their time on earth to be the terrible years that secondary school kids learnt about in history, and sometimes it was easier to be the chalk outline than it was to live and tell the tale. So Ezra kept on running, on and on in endless circles, because any step away from Atticus Valentine was like running the wrong way up an escalator.

The endless circles had widened and eventually coincided with catching a bus home. Ezra rang the bell and stood up. Rain raged against the window, reflecting the bio-luminescent glow of a Maddy's Hen Night sash. By all accounts, they were best friends now. The sash came with a complimentary plastic wand, but it had fallen into the footwell and Ezra didn't have the strength to pick it up.

Front door access needed two-factor authentication due to Ezra looking like an Egyptian mummy after they took the wrapping off. Sheila and Tulip were watching TV in the lounge. A pale light flickered on the walls. Jar's voice. Loud. Defensive. Ezra slipped along the hall and up the stairs, keeping to the edges and avoiding the creaks.

'Ezra?' Sheila called.

'Burglar.'

'You missed the start of WØLF.'

'I know,' Ezra shouted, 'they sent me a notification.'

'Hollow got her first pickup. Only, it's—'

'I'll watch it on catch-up.' Ezra kept climbing the stairs. 'I'm gonna grab a quick shower.'

'It's a P4, sweetheart,' Tulip called. 'Hollow's unit has been sent to a P4. It might be hard to watch.'

'It's what she does now, Mum.'

Ezra shut the bathroom door gently, standing in the glow of the Maddy's Hen Night sash like a deep-sea creature out of water. There was a decent argument for slumping in the corner until an emotion showed up, but that could take a while and there were company expectations waiting downstairs. So Ezra got changed instead, then clattered about in the kitchen and made a hot drink, finally arriving in the lounge doorway to catch the end of *WØLF*.

Sheila was clutching a pillow to her face, afraid to look at the screen, more afraid to look away. 'This war is full of such terrible, terrible things.'

'I don't care if it is your civic duty,' Tulip said. 'I'm not having you see that.'

'Such terrible, terrible things.'

'I wish…' Tulip held her hand out to Ezra. '*WØLF* promised us the real war, and this is the real war. This is what war is. And it's good that it still shocks us, because if it stops shocking us, then we're in real trouble.'

'Hollow wrote me a letter,' Ezra said, 'but I never got to see it.'

Ezra slept in late, batting away a parental wakeup call under the pretence of being up all night with a stomach bug. Fabian Evirate House was a gossip factory at the best of times, and Emporia wasn't one for keeping gossip in captivity. There'd be far too many excited questions, none of which would, should or indeed could be answered without spilling a whole can of potentially treasonous and almost certainly GiFT-destroying worms.

Sheila sat down on the bed. 'You know, it's okay to take a mental health day. You don't have to pretend you have food poisoning.'

'Except when you actually do have food poisoning.'

'Did you do a test?'

'I couldn't be bothered,' Ezra said, flopping away from Sheila. 'It'll just come back as positive for bacteria and make me send a poo sample.'

'You were quiet after *WØLF*.'

'Yeah, I already felt a bit iffy.'

'And that's all this is?' Sheila sounded about as convinced as a tutor on turn-it-in day. 'Because it was hard to see Hollow like

284

that. No one would think less of you if you took a day or two to process it.'

'Maybe you need the mental health day.'

Sheila hovered her hand over Ezra's head. 'I can take the day off if you need me to be around.'

'I'm fine, Mum. I just need to sleep this stomach bug off.'

Sheila hauled herself off the bed. 'Tulip's stuck with a set of intern interviews, so she'll be in the office all day. But she said to message her if you need anything. She can always pop back at lunch.'

'Thanks.'

'She's more shaken up than she'll admit.'

'Yeah,' Ezra said.

'Did the meeting go okay last night?'

'Yeah.'

'I can take a hint,' Sheila said, lingering. 'Try and get some sleep.'

She didn't get an answer.

Ezra waited for the front door to lock itself and phoned Mac Eden. Apparently, meeting at Mac's house was the best plan due to all the suggested alternatives not being as tech-secure. Ezra walked to the bus stop four roads away and took a while to answer when Sheila called.

'Hey.' Ezra spoke huskily, holding the phone close, trying to muffle the metallic yelp as a taxi clipped the pavement. A guy with a phlegmy cough had a face mask dropped down under his nose. A baby was grumbling for milk. Crows squabbled on a rooftop. A couple of women chatted and laughed. A dog was barking in the next street.

'Did you go out?'

'Yeah,' Ezra said. 'I thought some fresh air would help.'

'As long as you're okay.'

'I might wander down to look at where the flood defences flooded.'

'Take some pictures,' Sheila said. 'If you want to.'

'Love you.' Ezra hung up without waiting for an answer, leaning against a picture of Hollow as it scrolled the interactive wall of the bus shelter. The other occupants had bundled away from the coughing guy, and the coughing guy carried on coughing like he'd never heard of a highly transmissible, upper respiratory infection. Ezra stood somewhere between the two parties and waited for the bus. Lying to your mum felt like it deserved exposure.

Mac Eden's house was nothing much to look at. Quite nice, in a semi-suburban, semi-detached kind of way. The handy little porch that framed the old-style front door was filled with sticks, pebbles and small wellington boots. An iron horseshoe dribbled rust onto the doorframe. A nail in the archway fluttered with the tail ribbons of a kite. One of the double-glazed windows was steamed up like the seal had gone. The wooden slat blinds were pulled up unevenly. The windowsill was crowded with hand-painted cactus pots and a dancing donkey made of shells. The screws holding the house number on were the wrong kind of metal. The WELCOME mat had been scuffed into the corner of the porch. A dead wisteria had fake cobwebs from last year's Halloween. Ezra didn't need to ring the bell twice.

'Don't mind the mess,' Mac said, kicking a plastic sit-and-ride fire engine out of the hallway.

'Sorry, I didn't realise your children would be here.'

'They're not.' Mac picked up a battered yellow rabbit and lobbed it through a doorway at the end of the hall. 'The lounge is down there, follow the rabbit. You want a cup of tea?'

'Thank you. That would be lovely, thank you.' Ezra tried for something cheerful to follow on with, but all that flopped out was a shabby sort of sobbing noise. Atticus Valentine had haunted every minute since the restaurant. His body in the shape of other men, his style, his scent, his voice, his absence was everywhere, and he was nowhere at all. Something had broken between them, but it couldn't be put back together because there'd been nothing to break in the first place. Ezra wanted to tell Mac everything, but the tangled mess of it all felt impossible to explain using only twenty-six letters and a university education.

Mac sat Ezra down on a large sofa, moving washing, careful and mumsy about it. 'There's no rush, poppet, take your time.'

'I don't want to be a poppet,' Ezra said. 'I want to be a sensible adult.'

'Yeah, well, we all aspire to that.' Mac glanced towards the doorway. 'I ain't got no milk, by the way.'

'Why didn't you tell me, Mac?'

'Or tea,' Mac said. 'I been putting rum in hot water.'

'In the lunar harvesting corridor.' Ezra clutched hold of a striped beach towel. 'You said some weird things, and there was definitely talk of something ghastlier than I could ever imagine, but you didn't tell me properly.'

'Ah.' Mac sat on the coffee table. 'Right.'

'Why didn't you say it properly?'

'See...' Mac pulled a crayon from underneath her leg and threw it into a nearby biscuit tin '...you have to approach this sort of thing a bit carefully.'

'Not that carefully.'

Mac picked up another crayon. 'Just to check, we're both talking about...?'

'Atticus Valentine.'

'Thought so.'

'You were weird, Mac. And Mr Valentine wasn't weird. He was a jolly good egg. And I honestly wasn't expecting to hear from him again. When Emporia told me, I almost got the rainbow colours in the wrong order. Which, when you think about it, is probably why I just...agreed.'

'Agreed?'

'To meet him for an early supper. For work,' Ezra said. 'At a restaurant.'

'You met that bastard thing off site? Even though I expressly said for you to stay away?'

'You didn't say it properly,' Ezra said.

'When was this early supper?'

'Last night.'

'Right.'

'And at first it was okay, it was nice. But then it wasn't.'

Mac huffed out a suggestive grunt. 'I'll bet it wasn't.'

'Stop it,' Ezra said, 'you're doing it again.'

'Can you remember anything of what happened?'

'Um, yeah,' Ezra said, folding the striped beach towel into a manageable shape. 'Like I could die and be born again, and I'd still remember it.'

'Well, that's something.'

'And I never thought, not in a million years, I probably should have, except you didn't say it properly, you just said it weird. So I didn't. And it turns out he might be, probably is, almost certainly is.' Ezra flopped around. 'Now I'm not saying it properly.'

Mac sighed, absentmindedly playing with the links on her black plastic necklace. 'You think you should be able to spot them a mile off?'

'Yes!'

'That's not how they work.'

'But he's not some messed-up kid!' Ezra yelped. 'He's the chief executive officer of Plug Productions.'

'It ain't the obvious ones that do the real damage. It's the unobvious ones, the ones that go wherever they can do the most harm. Sometimes, they even pretend to be our friends, but that's just so they can get close to us. Close so we don't even know they're there. And when we do know, it's already too late.' Mac shook her head. 'You really should have listened to me.'

288

'Um, so I don't even want to admit this,' Ezra said. 'I mean, it's super embarrassing.'

'You thought it was interested in you?'

Ezra gripped the towel. 'For work.'

'These high-rank players, they give you just enough so you doubt yourself. They get you questioning your own judgement, and then you happily do all the work for them. Maybe they crush your spirit. Maybe they make you feel like you don't belong anywhere. Maybe they fill your head with too many thoughts…' Mac paused. 'Maybe they make you fall in love with them.'

'And blow things up,' Ezra said.

'But mostly it's falling in love with them,' Mac said, 'because, of all the torments, love is the cruellest.'

Ezra rolled the idea around for a bit. 'I mean, love does make us do things we'd never dream of doing otherwise.'

'They're total bastards, what can I say.'

'But ultimately it has a political agenda.'

'Can do.' Mac was philosophical. 'Can be just for fun. That's the nature of the game with no final whistle.'

'You think this was about fun?'

'In this particular instance?' Mac clicked her tongue. 'It's hard to say for sure, but probably, seeing as you went and fell in love with it.'

'No, no, that's even worse,' Ezra said, all dismay and hugging the towel. 'That's really, really, really… Not quite so bad, actually.'

'It's all bad.'

'Yes, like super mean. And arrogant. Super arrogant.' Ezra looked at Mac. 'How was I this stupid, though? I'm not someone who gets catfished for a laugh, I'm really not. I'm the person you ring up to check your email's not a scam. And I would never, ever, ever be someone who forgot one of the fundamental truths of all research. How did I get myself in this mess? I don't even know how I got in this mess.'

'It fucking is what it fucking is.' Mac shrugged through the roughed-up cliché. 'I suppose you want to know what to do next, then.'

'I, no, yeah, no, I do.'

'You do nothing.'

'Okay, yeah, I can do that.'

'Good.' Mac patted Ezra on the arm and hauled herself upright. 'Right then, I'd better make us that tea so we can figure out a plan for what to do while we ain't doing nothing.'

'Life without planning is just evolution,' Ezra said. 'That's what Mum says.'

'She bake us those eyeball cakes?' Mac was already halfway to the kitchen before Ezra could answer.

'No, that was Mum Sheila,' Ezra called, letting the sofa washing rearrange itself. 'Mum Tulip is the philologist.'

Mac came back with a primus stove and a couple of mugs. 'That a fancy name for something weird?'

'It's the history of languages. In Mum's case, the English language.'

Mac raked a clearing on the coffee table and set the primus alight. 'No disrespect to your mum, but there's some things we'd be best forgetting.' She balanced a camp kettle on the stove and topped it up with a glug of rum. 'I'd offer you a nice bit of cake, but I ain't got no cake neither.'

'Is your electricity out?'

'I'm keeping us IOT dark,' Mac said. 'You can't trust an electrical appliance at times like this.'

'Ah, of course.' Ezra took a long, deep breath. 'It's all a bit embarrassing really.'

'Embarrassment ain't nothing to be embarrassed about.' Mac sat next to the stove. 'It goes away on its own if you don't pick at it. It's what you do next that's the important thing.'

'Got it, do nothing.'

Mac shuffled her feet around a pile of socks. 'Nothing, till we figure out a plan.'

'Or doing nothing could be the whole plan.' Ezra leant in for a confidential. 'I think I just panicked, what with the ping and everything.'

'Right.'

'And obviously you know what this whole war paranoia situation is like,' Ezra said. 'I really don't want to click on the Ministry of War link, and then I'm freaking out about what'll happen if I don't click on the Ministry of War link. It's an impossible choice. Except I've explained it all to you now, and you can explain it to them. I still can't believe I fell for it, but lessons have been learnt.' Ezra sighed, resigned to reality and yet tentatively hopeful. 'Quite a few lessons have been learnt.'

'You want me to speak to the Ministry of War?'

'Thank you so much,' Ezra said. 'I can keep an eye on the kettle if you want to ring them now.'

Mac cleared her throat. Checked the camp kettle. Folded a unicorn duvet cover into its pillowcase. Picked up several towels and stacked them before starting on another duvet cover. 'The thing of it is, you've seen a little bit of something. And if I go ahead and tell you the rest, you'll never be able to go back to how your life is right now, not even if you want to.'

'Then don't tell me.' Ezra took the duvet cover from Mac and put it on the table. 'To be honest, I think all I really wanted was reassurance. And to curl up with my phone, watch a load of reels and not worry about the Ministry of War ping any more.'

'That's not down to me,' Mac said.

'But you're going to speak to them, right?'

'Like I said,' Mac lifted the kettle off the stove and poured two mugs of steaming rum water, 'that's not down to me.'

'So that's it then?' Ezra flopped back into the sofa. 'I'm left with the impossible choice. Whatever I do, the Ministry of War take all my details and stick them on a watchlist. I get to live with that hanging over me every single day for the rest of the war...maybe the rest of my life. All because I was a victim, Mac. How is that fair?'

Mac didn't say anything. She just held out a mug and quietly waited on the answer Ezra had dodged once before. And there really was no way out this time.

Ezra took the mug. 'I don't suppose that invitation to help with the war effort is still open?'

'Help with the war effort?' Mac let Ezra breathe the rum steam for a while. 'I suppose it could work.'

'Okay, I think I'll do it.'

Henri at the armed forces drop-in centre had responded to Hollow's enlistment with a respectful nod. Mac Eden didn't nod. She just closed her eyes like she'd ticked the wrong box and now there was a whole load of spam warnings and ninety-eight new emails in her inbox. 'Remember when you thought Santa was real?'

'Wait, Santa's not real?'

'Piss off, then,' Mac said.

'Sorry, nervous.'

'You were a kid once. You believed in Santa. You didn't question that you never had a chimney and Santa ate a billion mince pies in one single night. You just trusted the magic, right?'

Ezra nodded carefully. 'Sure...'

'Then the smug kid told you that Santa wasn't real and your parents just made him up, reindeer and all. That's what I'm talking about.' Mac paused. 'That tiny, world-changing moment when someone told you something and you couldn't unknow it, no matter how much you wanted to.'

'Because?'

'Because I'm gonna show you something,' Mac said, 'and once you've seen it, everything will change.'

'Am I officially working for the war effort now?'

'Welcome to the fucking team.'

Mac negotiated her way over to a tall bookcase in the corner of the room. The shelves were full of assorted picture books, ragged romance novels and several large DIY manuals, all stuffed together in the manner of children's libraries everywhere. Mac dragged a small plastic stool away from the wall to balance on as she took down one of the books from the top shelf. Even from the other side of the room, Ezra could see that it was painfully dull, and the way Mac blew the dust off it as she walked back to the sofa suggested it probably didn't get picked by many book groups.

'An old friend gave me this.' Mac looked at it lovingly, hugging it to her chest. 'And she knew a thing or two.'

The book supported all the orange and brown hallmarks of a 1970s classic. It even had the words IN COLOUR emblazoned on the front cover. Underneath, in smaller pipework letters, COOKING WITH GAS worked its way across a photograph of an insipid-looking kebab struggling desperately to outshine its boiled cabbage and mashed potato accompaniment. It was the sort of book that no one had ever wanted to flick through, not even when half a melon covered with tin foil was the height of culinary poshness.

'A cookery book?' Ezra ventured.

'I've had this book on show for ten years and no one has even asked me if they could look at it.' Mac shoved the washing aside and sat down next to Ezra. 'Too close to see. Too simple to understand. Too familiar to remember.' And when Mac handed Ezra the book, it was like she was handing over one of her children. 'Careful,' she said. 'Go careful.'

It was hard to make a call on the unexpected, but what Ezra found in the book was so totally unexpected it met itself while buying a coffee at the train station.

'Am I missing something?' Ezra said.

'More than you can even imagine.'

Ezra flicked through a run of age-beige pages detailing the rotational placements of a casserole dish when using it to cook an overnight bread and butter pudding. 'Do I need to spill blood on it or something?'

'Fuck off.'

'I mean, it's the perfect text for an uncrackable cypher code.'

'I suppose it would be,' Mac said, 'but it ain't.'

Ezra put the book on the table. 'I have literally no idea what this book has to do with the war effort.'

'Shhhhhh.' Mac glanced around the room dramatically. 'Keep it down.'

'I don't even know what I'm keeping down,' Ezra said, on the verge of not keeping it down.

Mac frowned. 'You said you knew.'

'About…?'

'The Atticus Valentine.'

'He tricked me into looking at a website,' Ezra said. 'The website had an International War Agency seizure notice on it.'

'Bastard.'

'I got the ping, as discussed.'

'Right.'

'And I obviously panicked,' Ezra said, 'because these days you panic if you accidentally get out of the wrong side of bed, and I thought he was trying to recruit me to a terrorist cause, or something.'

'A terrorist cause?'

'Or something.'

'Right.' Mac looked down at the book. 'I suppose that would explain the blowing-up bit.'

'But not the Santa bit.'

'No.' Mac wilted slightly. 'Not that bit.'

'So it's a relief, actually,' Ezra said, even though every micro-expression had already posted that notification.

'True enough you hit this sideways on. But sooner or later you would have found out anyway. Maybe it's better this way.'

'Or not,' Ezra said. 'We'll never know for sure.'

'Because this is old.'

Ezra shot a look at the book. 'I can see that.'

'Really old,' Mac said. 'Older than even a historian can think about.'

'1970?'

'You think you know all the stuff with your university education,' Mac said, 'but you don't know anything.'

Ezra sat forward. 'Just to be absolutely clear, we're still talking about the book?'

'It's always about the book.'

'Great.'

Mac didn't dignify Ezra's sigh with an answer; she just took the book from the table and flicked through the pages. 'Except this Atticus Valentine don't fit properly.'

'Maybe he has an electric hob?'

Mac lingered over a series of photographs highlighting the pros and cons of wearing hairspray while lighting an overhead grill plate. 'The Mandolin are bastard creatures, and that's especially true of the high-rank players. Day in, day out, they mess with your rules. But rules ain't the same as laws. And there's laws, scientific laws, that even the Mandolin can't break.'

'No, it's not the Mandolin, I already checked.'

Mac looked up then. 'Are you even listening to me?'

'I am, yes.'

'You think I'm showing you this book for fun?'

'Of course not.'

Mac stopped on a recipe for Irish stew. 'Because there's no fun in here.'

'Noted.' Ezra stretched like they'd just arrived at a holiday destination after a long and somewhat uncomfortable flight. 'I'm sorry to stop you, Mac, but I'm supposed to be getting some fresh air and I told Mum I was going to where the flood defences flooded. I should probably get some evidence of actual flooding before the waters drop. For when she asks about it. But thank you, Mac, for showing the book to me and clearing everything up. It's a lot to process. I should go and process. While I look at the flooding.'

'Be honest with me,' Mac said, 'does any of this seem a bit off to you?'

'I mean...'

'I suppose it could be a throwback, heaven help us.'

'Yes, that's probably it.' Ezra stretched again and stood up. 'And thank you for looking after me.'

'Except a throwback wouldn't explain the building. All technology can fail with a throwback, but not the building. The building's made from laws, magic laws. And magic laws don't have nothing in them to fail.'

'Magic laws?'

'Magic as was. Everything's gone scientific these days.' Mac spoke quietly, half-staring at a skanky book on preparing yourself for making dinners with a gas cooker. 'It took hold of my ladle. You saw it. You were there. You saw it.'

'Yes, I did. I did see it.'

Mac was searching for understanding in Ezra's face. 'We call them the Mandolin, but it ain't their true name.'

'It's not their name?' Ezra sat back down.

'And before you ask, we ain't permitted to speak it.'

'So why the Mandolin?'

'Because a beast without a name is a terrible thing,' Mac said. 'All sorts of unnecessary horrors and imagination belong to a beast with no name.'

'As opposed to the Mandolin?'

'Weren't my choosing.' Mac sighed. 'Look, I know you don't get the book, but maybe that's a good thing, maybe that's exactly why we need you. You could be more use than I thought.'

'Oh, right. The war effort. I forgot about that.'

'Easily done,' Mac said, 'and seeing as this is your first mission, I'll make it easy, to ease you in.'

'A mission, already?'

'Intel,' Mac said, 'not anything with iron.'

'I don't suppose you have any on-line missions available?'

Ezra said. 'Data analysis, spreadsheets, stalking people on social media?'

Mac stood up to close the door carefully like they could be overheard. 'I want you to arrange another coffee with the Atticus Valentine. Somewhere public, mind, not work. Somewhere I can keep an eye on you.'

'A coffee!' Ezra yelped.

'It don't have to be a literal coffee, I ain't micromanaging this. And we'll keep it to basic intel for now. Family history, backstory, hobbies, what it likes to do with its time of a Sunday evening. Use your imagination. You're better at this crap than me. And nothing too intrusive; we ain't talking ad trackers here. Just be yourself, like how you go about your inane chatter.' Mac flicked a fly away. 'Do that.'

'No, no, no, you don't understand,' Ezra said. 'He's Atticus Valentine. Atticus Valentine isn't someone you randomly call up.'

'We live in a time of war.' Mac leant in, her hands resting heavily on Ezra's shoulders. 'There's too much at stake for you not to find a way.'

'I suppose I could—'

'Good. That's sorted then. And if the Atticus Valentine has nothing to hide, it won't be getting nothing more than a pleasant chit-chat,' Mac said, in the manner of Big Brothers everywhere.

'I've got to be honest,' Ezra said, looking up at Mac like a puppy that had accidentally eaten half the couch, 'this isn't how I imagined my morning playing out at all.'

Mac's whole demeanour dropped into deflated mum as she sat back on the coffee table and tucked a pair of socks into each other. 'I ain't much good at this.'

'No, no,' Ezra said, 'it's me.'

'I'd tell you to take your time, poppet, but there's a bit of a rush order on this.' Mac finally managed a smile of sorts. 'And, at the end of the day, this is just you finding out if anyone is a fucking bastard, potentially mutated, unwanted infestation, that's all.'

'And it's fine if it's nothing?'

'Of course,' Mac said, all reassurance and cooking with gas. 'And that's what it usually turns out to be, nothing.'

'Okay, that's okay.'

'We're good to go, then?'

'Um, the betrayal, though?' Ezra said. 'How do I stop it feeling like a massive betrayal?'

'You never do,' Mac said, shooing the fly away again, with enough finality about it to end it there.

Ezra stuck to the food poisoning excuse, a gruesome and repeating narrative guaranteed to keep Fabian Evirate House insisting on sick leave, and everyone else a bucket distance away. Emporia telephoned mid-week, casually mentioning that Mr Valentine had phoned to see how Ezra was doing.

'Such a polite young gentleman,' Emporia said, popping round with a handwritten memo later that day. 'As you can see, he has telephoned again, this very afternoon, for an update on your welfare. He has also added his personal telephone number, should you wish to update him yourself.'

'He left me his phone number?'

'Highlighted.' Emporia nodded at the memo. 'Rationality can so easily be disturbed by illness. I myself have been known to telephone my own mobile number during periods of recovery.'

'I guess I have his phone number then.'

It wasn't like Ezra even had to chase the mission. Having Atticus Valentine's mobile number and an invitation to use it was as close to an open goal as an open goal could get. From here, messaging him was a simple enough thing to do.

It took two hours and three false starts before Ezra successfully picked up the memo.

24

We do this for them

Joanie passed the biscuit tin to Hollow. 'And when we get there, this guy has the whole bottom part of his arm blown off. Everything below the elbow. He was lucky the fire cauterised it or he'd have bled out.'

'And he's just sat there,' Fish said. 'Smoking a cigarette, waiting for us to arrive, with the bottom half of his arm laid on his lap like he's a trick-or-treat special.'

Joanie was nodding along. 'Fish is trying to find a vein to give him some morphine, and he keeps offering her the amputated arm, saying to try his good hand.'

'Lieutenant Sampson's keeping it low key, mind,' Fish said. 'And this guy is too full of adrenalin to feel anything. He's laughing like he's been waiting for an audience so he can crack the joke. No lie, he's chaos at the disco. And I'm thinking, please pass out before the pain kicks in.'

'It's weird, eh?' Stan said, a reminder of Cornwall beaches still rounding his accent despite ten years in exile and an affair with a vocal coach. 'They taught us about it at trade training, but the first time I saw it, it had me stumped.'

'Adrenalin allocates existing resources,' Caster Dupont said. 'It's not a painkiller as such. The pain is still there, but while a threat to life remains, adrenalin signs off on enough endorphins to keep the mind occupied.'

'Lancaster Dupont.' Stan hugged him. '*Par tout ce qui est sacré*, you are such sweet shelter for an innocent soul.'

'I mean,' Fish said, 'you have to hand it to adrenalin.'

'There's no arm in it,' Jar said.

Mika laughed a sarcastic entourage, spinning his impatience into frustration. 'What's keeping them?'

'They're only three hours late.' Jar wiggled the end of a glowstick into his ear. 'And no one can blame Mattoo and Sylvie for enjoying their time working with a decent human being in the third spot. They probably stopped off for some sightseeing.'

'Fuck you.'

Alma picked up a sock and chucked it on Jar's bunk. 'Tidy up after yourself, will you.'

'A man's got to air his feet in this climate.'

'You've been airing them for three hours.' Alma pranced around a dropped towel, enough cultivated spikes in her sun-bleached hair to shame a medieval weapon. 'You could have at least picked up your mess.'

'What's got into you, half-pint?'

'Three hours of you doing nothing about this mess, that's what's got into me.' Alma crossed her arms. 'We get a spot inspection now and we're all on report.'

'Whose idea was this group commentary anyway?' Jar said, scooting the sock off his bunk. 'No doubt the very same producer who thought making an anniversary special wouldn't be any extra fucking work for any of us.'

'Ain't no work,' Hubert Frank said, nudging Hamid awake with his boot.

Hamid jolted upright. 'Cast foresight.'

'My thoughts exactly,' Stan said, picking up the bunkhouse accordion and sitting it on his lap.

Hamid Zarif sat up, shielding his eyes from the glare of the sun. As a dancer, there was a promise of artistic prodigy in him, but it hadn't decided where to specialise yet. 'What time are we at?'

'We are at *WØLF* time,' Jar said. 'Twenty-four hours a day, seven days a week. No need to set an alarm, because you can never wake up.'

Mika didn't even bother with a sarcastic laugh this time. 'So speaks the sage of Bullshit Creek.'

'Moved in next door to you,' Jar said.

Mika smiled slowly, loading his words like he was arming a rifle. 'At death, we will be brought to face ourselves in the mirror: no cave, no shield, no sickness to cover the dreadful truth. You should think about that day, old man.'

Jar examined the end of the glowstick. 'Need some extra mind drugs with your tea, Mika?'

Caster stretched and stood up. 'I'm heading back to the hospital. Tell Elspeth she knows where to find me.'

'That's me out too.' Alma picked up a used tea bag and threw it at Jar. 'And clean this place up, will you.'

'I'll do it,' Joanie said.

'Sweetheart,' Alma said, 'why are you still single?'

'I'm more of a subscription service than a blockbuster,' Joanie said.

'They can clear up their own mess.' Alma hauled him to his feet. 'You're coming to the gym with me.'

'Hold up, troops,' Hamid said. 'It looks like there's a studio runner on the way over.'

'Unit One must have gone straight to ITM commentary.' Stan set the accordion down again. 'They could have told us.'

'It's not a runner...' Hamid said '...it's a major.'

Major Hyde never made house calls. 'As you were,' he said, taking off his service cap and tucking it under his arm. 'Find yourself a seat, will you.'

They sat in silence, closer than usual, ten heartbeats in the no-man's-land between innocence and tragedy.

'Look, there's no easy way to do this, so I'll just get on with it,'

Major Hyde said. 'Four hours ago, we received a report that Unit One had lost satellite signal during a sandstorm. Shortly after, the cartel controlling that sector issued a courtesy notification informing us that a British military vehicle had infringed the protected boundary of an active opium field.'

'Shit.' Jar stood up, screwing the glowstick tight to his head until it bent to the shape of his fingers.

'I don't understand,' Joanie said.

'It doesn't mean anything.' Caster was looking straight at the major. 'Mattoo is a good officer. If the satellite signal cut out, he'll have them holed up somewhere, waiting for the storm to pass.'

The major cleared his throat. 'The cartel surrendered three ID discs for collection from a village outside the protected boundary. We have a unit at the scene. Discs confirmed as Mattoo Bolte, Sylvie Stevens and Nell Cedric.'

Jar kicked a tea urn across the tent. 'The bastards fucking shot them.'

'They executed them?' Stan collapsed back into Mika, and found nothing but a brick wall.

'But they're Unit One of WØLF,' Joanie said. 'Nothing can happen to them, they're Unit One of WØLF.'

'The DM is taken?' Hubert Frank turned towards Hamid. 'Inside the circle they search for the map. But the DM is taken.'

'Ain't no fucking dungeon master in this place.' Jar snapped the glowstick, letting the contents drip over his uniform. 'It's just the same old storyline, time and time again.'

'The DM is taken.' Hamid tried to stand up. 'The game is over.'

The major cleared his throat again. 'As current agreements stand, any breach of the active opium fields results in immediate execution and incineration, regardless of who you are or why you're there. The rules are clear on both sides.'

'Both sides?' Fish said, her arm thrust around Joanie like she was ready to take all his grief into her own body. 'I thought we were all on the same side now.'

'You are relieved from duty for the remainder of the day,' the major said. 'The production company have set up a room for you away from base chatter. There's no protecting you once we go live with this, I'm afraid. But Plug have a bally line-up of people for you to talk to. Make sure you do just that. Consider it an order if it makes things any less awkward. You're all back on full duty tomorrow. War doesn't wait around for you to feel better, and you have more support than most. It's never easy to lose squad members to a cartel, but in situations like this we get by as best we can.'

'It's kind of you to deliver the news personally, Major,' Caster said, his voice not quite masking anything. 'The squad will need some time to process this, perhaps if we could give them a moment.'

'You are a part of this family, Caster,' Alma said.

'Understood.' Major Hyde saluted, clicking his heels like he was on parade, put his banded service cap back on and strode away from the bunkhouse.

'They can't be gone,' Joanie said.

'You didn't even fucking know them,' Mika said, shoving Stan away and storming out of the tent.

SMART SLATE

Whiskey-Zero-One-Foxtrot/s4se1.0/REMI IP link PP confirm: EFP studio cameras
Producer: *Elspeth Hart*
INT. AFG. CAMP BASTION – DAY

Scene: Studio. Camera on *MAJ Jonathan Hyde* – cut to Producer

    ITM SCENE
    COMMENTARY
    MAJ HYDE:

We were not welcomed back into this country. There were compromises to be made on both sides. One of those compromises is an agreement with the existing drug cartels to honour their territory and allow them to defend their property by whatever force they deem necessary.

In accordance with the International War Agency policy of cooperation, this cessation of hostilities agreement is binding and non-negotiable.

CUT TO
PRODUCER:
The army have informed us that at ten thirty this morning, a Ridgeback rescue vehicle driven by Mattoo Bolte lost satellite signal during a sandstorm and subsequently strayed across the protected boundary of an active opium field.

The penalty for crossing a protected boundary is immediate and without mercy. It falls on me to tell you that today we lost Unit One – Mattoo Bolte, Nell Cedric and Sylvie Stevens.

Their families back home, as well as their adopted families here in Afghanistan, have been informed of today's events, and are currently with studio counsellors.

After much soul-searching, we have decided to continue with tonight's scheduled broadcast. This one-year anniversary special was filmed over several weeks, and will include scenes that will be contextually difficult to watch.

It's no exaggeration to say that today we lost three of our dearest friends. We are numb, angry, desperately sad. But a year ago, Sylvie, Mattoo and Nell took an oath, and they died defending that oath. We will not hide their bravery behind our grief.

We do this for them.

25

Brace yourself

Minstrels Park was more of a massive walled garden than a park, and more of a gargantuan maze than a massive walled garden. Tourists often mistook it for a labyrinth and tried to trace a long continuous path to the centre. While this wasn't necessarily a disastrous mistake, it did add a few unplanned hours to the visit. Attempting to clean up the results, the council had recently installed more toilet facilities, vending machine stations, phone charging points and an SOS counselling service. In compliance with public liability insurance, there were no road signs directing traffic to the site, no designated car parks, no publicity material and no chirpy little teashops dotted around the neighbourhood. Instead, the yellow-striped warning sign fitted to the park entrance was military, unavoidable, and carefully worded with the same universal clarity as a nuclear waste disposal site.

> # DANGER!
> There is nothing of interest to
> be found beyond this marker
> This is NOT a safe place
> Leave now. Do NOT enter
> **NOTHING BUT DEATH**
> **AWAITS YOU HERE**

The council may as well have put up a FREE MONEY sign. Ezra fetched a packet of crisps from the vending machine and sat on one of the white stone benches, hoping whatever resolve had emerged would hold, and suspecting it had already let go. The outer paths of the maze were always cram-packed with people, and most of them eventually found their triumphant way to the false centre. The inner sanctum of Minstrels Park was nowhere near the false centre. It was a secret, disguised place, fingerprint protected, and only available with ID and proof of local residency. As a nominated meeting place, the glass fountain at the very centre was ideal. Always beautiful, generally private, especially able to be eavesdropped on by a weird cleaner who worked for some Ministry of War sideshoot.

'Hey.' He spoke lightly, but it still made Ezra jump.

'Mr Valentine,' Ezra said, standing up and then sitting down again. 'You got in okay, then?'

'I used to come here when they still had the Enigma machine.' Atticus sat next to Ezra. 'How are you feeling?'

'I'm fine.' Ezra ate a crisp. 'I mean, everyone's in total shock with what happened on *WØLF* last night.'

'Emporia said you've been unwell.'

'Yeah, I'm better now. And the fandom was saying how it must have been awful for the production company. Of course, you need to be at work. I absolutely understand that you need to be at work. Of course, and it's fine to do this another day. Of course, I don't mind at all.'

'To be honest, it's good to get out,' Atticus said. 'I don't feel like I'm much use anywhere at the moment.'

'Right, right, sure.'

'We always knew this could happen. They're soldiers fighting in a war. We've been living on borrowed time. We are prepared for it, we have all the protocols in place, but nothing can prepare you for when it happens.' Atticus looked down at his hands, a million miles from okay. 'Not when we lost them for something so worthless.'

'It was a horrible chain of events, but it wasn't worthless.'

'I'm sorry.' He looked up at Ezra then. 'Hollow is still out there. The last thing you need is me justifying Plug's part in all this.'

'No one should feel ashamed about talking honestly. And from an outside perspective, even though WØLF say all the time that they're real soldiers, I guess we've subconsciously presumed they'd be immune from the war. Yeah, it's been a wakeup call. But maybe we needed it.'

Atticus didn't answer.

'Hey, come on, have you seen the news? No one's angry at Plug for showing us the truth.' Ezra ate another crisp. 'Last night, I was thinking about how I might see Hollow die on TV. I don't know how that would feel. And I haven't said this to anyone, not even my mums, but it's like she's not my friend Hollow any more. She's an actor I recognise from another film.'

'I'm so sorry.'

Ezra paused, mid-crisp. 'No, don't be. What I mean is, she's different now. She's so much better around people than she was before. Sometimes, she even seems happy, which is a new experience for everyone. Honestly, I can't be sorry she's on WØLF, no matter how it ends.'

Atticus nodded, but it was barely noticeable. 'We have a good team of counsellors out in Afghanistan. She'll get any kind of support she needs.'

'Yeah, Hollow's not much one for counsellors,' Ezra said, 'but she's got Joanie and Fish. She talks to them far more than she ever talked to me.'

'She seems to have connected with Jar.'

'God help him.' Ezra offered a crisp. 'It's so weird talking about WØLF like it's something from real life.'

'That's the problem, WØLF is real life. Real life and real

death. Plug can justify its part in whatever way we want, but we can't escape the fact that we did this, we caused this to happen.' Atticus looked down at his hands again. 'I went to see their families. I don't think it helped.'

'It was kind, and kindness always helps.' The words sounded stupidly shallow. Atticus Valentine had all the things society promised would make him happy, but they hadn't made him happy, they'd just made him alone. 'It really helped me, when I heard that you'd called Fabian Evirate House to see how I was. Emporia even used a memo pad, which cheered everyone up. We thought they'd gone extinct.'

'Ezra, about what happened the other night. There's something I need to explain, something I—'

But Ezra didn't give him room to explain yet. 'I was thinking about how Hubert Frank said it was the wrong war. And Lieutenant Sampson was talking about being caught out by our own behaviour. Like, we're always surprised when we turn out to be much more of a disaster in real life.'

'Ezra...'

'I thought there'd be more bravery,' Ezra said. 'And less running.'

He grinned then. 'I really messed up, didn't I?'

'Just a bit.' Ezra peered into the empty crisp packet. 'Apparently, recruiting for an extremist cause isn't a straightforward evening out.'

Atticus sat forward. 'Can I show you something?'

Ezra folded the crisp packet several times and tied it into a knot. 'Is it an International War Agency seized website?'

'It's not an International War Agency seized website,' he said. 'But I do have to take my jacket off, and it does take some getting your head around.'

'Wait.' Ezra dropped the crisp packet, setting off several litter notifications. 'Are you going to kiss me?'

'No.'

'Is it wings?'

'No.'

Ezra reached down and retrieved the crisp packet, sliding it into the eco-disposal unit attached to the bench. 'Then continue.'

Atticus took his jacket off, unbuttoning his shirt like he'd turned up for his holiday jab. 'Brace yourself.'

'Never knowingly unbraced,' Ezra said. 'Oh...my... goodness.'

'Hence my dilemma.'

Ezra frowned at him. 'You got a tattoo?'

'Already had,' Atticus said. 'It was there when they found me.'

'The International War Agency?'

'No, no, in the hospital sink.'

Ezra frowned again. 'What?'

'It's not like it's a secret.' Atticus waited for a bunch of teenagers to run around and splash each other in the fountain. 'There isn't much of my life that someone somewhere hasn't traded.'

'They found you in a hospital sink?' Ezra said. 'Like a drunk thing?'

'Like a newborn baby thing.'

Ezra took a moment. 'Someone left you in a hospital sink when you were a baby?'

'Welcome to my family tree,' he said. 'Pretty grim, even without the tattoo. Now we're at war, and I'm the CEO of Plug Productions. It seems I've left it awkwardly late for laser ink removal.' He looked over to where the teenagers still splashed around. 'Thing is, it's always intrigued me. What is it? What does it mean? Why am I the only kid at primary school with a tattoo? When I stumbled on the word UNITY, it felt like the end. Everyone was happy and I had a great word to live by.'

'Except it wasn't the end.'

Atticus rebuttoned his shirt and pulled his jacket back on. 'I wanted to be happy, I tried to let it be enough, but why would you put the word UNITY on a baby and then abandon it in a hospital sink? It took me ages to work out that it was a password. When I found the website, I didn't tell anyone.' A maple leaf twisted the space between them. Atticus caught it. 'I convinced myself I was trying to protect them, but really I was ashamed.'

'But you were just a baby,' Ezra said, almost reaching out to touch his arm. 'You don't have anything to be ashamed of.'

'Growing up, I spent a lot of head time fantasising about it being the crest of a displaced royal family. Of course, they'd left me at the hospital to keep me hidden.' He turned the leaf between his fingers before letting it drop to the ground. 'To be honest, I think contacting Fabian Evirate House was the final part of that childhood fantasy. Maybe the symbol is also a spiritual talisman? Maybe it's an undiscovered rune? Maybe it's something, anything, that means my birth parents weren't radical extremists to the point where they'd tattoo a password on their own baby.'

'God, you poor thing.'

Atticus sat back then. 'I'm not often surprised, but you constantly surprise me, Ezra Blake. You honestly don't know the spellbinding backstory of Zara Seraphim's adopted son?'

'You're adopted?' Ezra's mouth would have dropped open if it hadn't already dropped open. 'By Zara Seraphim?'

'The one and only.'

'Zara Seraphim the filmmaker?'

'I know, right,' he said. 'Opinion is divided as to whether I took cuttings from the orchard of her genius, or had it all handed to me on a plate. I'm not even sure myself, to be honest.'

'No way!' Ezra squealed. 'I've actually met your mum. I mean, it was more of a staged photograph opportunity at the London premier of *Methuselah*. But I listed all her films chronologically and told her three times how much I love her work. We're practically chums.'

'I'm sure she was charmingly appreciative.'

'Wow, you're really Zara Seraphim's son?'

'I'm more Harry Valentine's son, if I'm honest.'

'Your dad?'

'Grandad,' Atticus said. 'He still runs the community repair shop in the town I grew up in. Zara was away from home a lot, so I hung around with him mostly. When I started creating reels for social media, he told me this story about how the great Zara Seraphim had been told by a psychic that she'd die on a mountain. And instead of avoiding mountains, she learnt to climb them.' Atticus looked down to where the leaf had fallen. 'Field maple.'

'Is that a mountain?'

'It's the only native maple tree,' Atticus said. 'I had a book on trees when I was seven, I never seemed to grow out of randomly identifying them.'

'You randomly identify trees?'

'Extremist recruiters randomly identify a lot of things.'

'We probably should stop joking about that,' Ezra said. 'Someone could be listening.'

'I know, right? Sometimes, I have lunch with my local MP. She brings a list.'

They walked the inner sanctum, familiar enough to be friends, but from a distance it was hard to tell what sort of friendship they shared. Ezra stopped, as serious and silent as the cavernous elm tree Atticus had just identified. 'I totally get how it must feel like you've been cursed, but your grandad, he shared that mountain story with you for a reason.'

'He told me Zara Seraphim didn't have a setting for running away.'

'And when you can't run away from something,' Ezra said, 'all you can do is run towards it. Did you ever track down your birth parents?'

But Atticus didn't answer, he just looked up through the

canopy of branches. 'Animals dominate our concept of life. We even make trees into something huggable. And trees, they just keep on being trees, cooperating with mycorrhizas, communicating information across vast networks, steadfastly reminding us that animals are just one small category of existence. When I was a kid, I had trees that were my friends. But not like pets, like trees. I wanted them at my birthday, so Zara gave my books away and told me to get another hobby.' He smiled then, as shy and sweet with it as he was with everything. 'I didn't get another hobby, I made a reel series on the way trees care for each other. There's this one tree in Japan that's supposed to be the—'

'Okay,' Ezra said, 'so now we're talking about hobbies?'

Atticus kicked at the path. 'I'm Zara Seraphim's adopted son. My whole life was a reality TV show, and I became the prize for every parental claim out there. Some repeat mother, churning out babies and too scared of Social Services to admit she was pregnant again, an addict popping out her kid and dead by teatime, prostitution, rape, religious taboo, some underage kid, too young to realise what was going on. There were enough nights when I lay awake, hoping the latest claim was true, hoping someone had come to take me home. And it never mattered who it was or why'd they'd left me, because going home was what I wanted more than anything. But now? The truth of who they are and why they left me feels like a huge mess of idealistic intentions. And me, the encrypted password protector, in the middle of it all. More afraid to go home than to stay where I am.' He kicked at the path again. 'Personally, I'm still holding out for the displaced royal family.'

'I'm so sorry,' Ezra said, because they'd driven up this road and now there was nowhere to turn around.

He finally stepped away from the path. 'I should never have dragged you into this.'

'You didn't drag me, Atticus.'

313

'That's the first time you've called me Atticus.'

'Is it?'

'You helped me when I asked for help,' Atticus said. 'I'll remember you, Ezra Blake. Of all the thousands of people I meet, I'll remember you. But this needs to be the end of the research trail for me.'

Ezra sighed. 'When you find yourself showing someone an International War Agency seized website in order to get answers, it's probably time to call it a day.'

'Please don't feel bad. Sometimes, all we're really looking for is an end to the search.' Atticus glanced at his watch. 'I should get back to work.'

'Thank you, for phoning about me, Mr Valentine. And thank you for taking the time to explain about the symbol, especially with what's happening on *WØLF*.' Ezra tried to yawn offhandedly but didn't quite succeed. 'Oh crap, I nearly forgot to ask, when would you like to collect your research property?'

'Woodworm wants to walk me around the lunar harvesting corridors,' Atticus said. 'I can pick it up then.'

'Oh, okay, so would that be at night?'

'We haven't organised a time yet.'

'Only, I might not be there,' Ezra said. 'If it's at night.'

He looked at his watch again. 'I'm sure we can figure something out.'

'Or we could meet. Outside of work. Somewhere easy for both of us. Handover rendezvous. Burn phones. No one saw anything, Officer.' Ezra looked up at the elm tree. 'What about meeting at Haifengate?'

'The Neolithic site?'

'The hillfort is Neolithic,' Ezra said. 'The stones are Mesolithic. A lot of people call it Heaven Gate, but Haifen comes from Hæfen, which is the old English word for Raven, so it should really be Raven Gate. And it's literally fifteen minutes from here. Maybe thirty on the bus. Forty if the ghosts are on all the stops. But the view is worth the trip. Plus, I could give you a lesson on hillforts that would keep you awake at night.'

'How can I refuse,' he said.

'Tomorrow evening?'

'I can't do tomorrow. This situation with WØLF has me booked out for weeks.' Atticus checked his diary. 'Sunday evening is currently cleared for scheduled downtime, if that works for you?'

'Sunday evening is perfect,' Ezra said. 'I'll bring a picnic.'

'I thought this was a handover rendezvous.'

'A picnic is our cover. In case the International War Agency are there.'

'Of course.'

'I'll message you the details,' Ezra said. 'And remind me to bring your research property with me.'

26

You mustn't wear the windcheater

Samuel was supposed to do a security sweep of the entire building before opening, but having already fed yesterday's phylactery entrails to the ravens and evicted a nest of disgruntled rats from the smallest of the nine great towers of Fabian Evirate House, the security guard was in dire need of caffeine. He punched the espresso button and stuck a half-full mug of coffee under the taps.

'Welcome back!' he called as Ezra tried to slip discreetly past the staffroom doorway. 'How's Typhoid Mary this morning?'

'Much better, thanks.'

'Are you permitted a drink?' Samuel held up a mug.

'I should probably report to Dicky first.'

'Then you're in luck on both counts, Dicky is on his way here.' Samuel negotiated a ragged packet from the back of the cupboard. 'I can do you a mint tea. Heads up, it went out of date in 2006.'

'Appealing to the historian in me?'

Samuel flicked the kettle on, turning away too fast and banging his head on the cupboard door. 'Just looking out for you, that's all.'

'Thanks.' Ezra dropped down into Part One of the sofa tragedy – a spongy three-seater named Orange. A retiring employee had kindly donated the sofa to the staff canteen on the understanding that they also took a larger, more upright sofa named Maurice, because Maurice and Orange were a couple, and separating them would be cruel. Part Two, however, turned out to be so big that for several days it had remained valiantly wedged, like a pale grey asylum seeker, in the neutral waters of the sorting area. It would have been there still, but Emporia had bluntly refused to slide underneath again and they needed her to discipline the coffee machine. Maurice eventually found safe harbour in the loading bay, and the best the staff could do was to place a photograph of Orange on the shelf next to it. Everyone pretended not to notice how sad they both looked. It was a very distressing story.

Samuel picked up the drinks and sat next to Ezra. 'That was a pretty rough bug you had by all accounts.'

'Yeah.' Ezra poked at the rectangular island of mint and dust floating unashamedly in the mug. 'I think I was a bit rundown, if I'm honest.'

Samuel swung a booted foot up on the table. 'Emporia said you went to a restaurant with Mr Plug.'

'It was a work thing.'

'You know he was found in a sink, right?' Samuel said. 'He could genuinely be anyone.'

'I can't imagine being abandoned like that.'

Samuel hid his sneer behind a swig of coffee. 'I'd say he got a good enough deal out of it. We'd all be running a production company if Mummy was a world-famous filmmaker, instead of doing funerals at the Co-op.'

'I think it must have been hard,' Ezra said. 'To grow up in her shadow.'

'Did you fuck him?'

Ezra shot a look at Samuel. 'What the actual?'

'Everyone said you had the chemistry.' Samuel took another swig of coffee, belching loudly. 'And the chemistry isn't something you can control.'

'No chemistry. Just history.'

'And some pretty attractive-looking biology, according to most everyone.'

Ezra wanted to laugh, but given Samuel's morose expression it felt unfair. 'I never was much good with the physical sciences.'

Samuel, on the other hand, laughed outrageously, all overcompensating and pretending not to be obsessing about it. 'Well, I guess that's my security investigation over. I shall report my findings to the gossip sub-committee.'

'Tell the gossip sub-committee I'll remember this next time they get called somewhere for work.'

Samuel yawned dramatically, sending a pile of Health and Safety at Work leaflets cascading to the floor in an informative waterfall. 'At least tell me you threw up all over his suit.'

'No can do.'

'I told Dicky it was too much to hope for.' Samuel picked up a handful of the leaflets and kicked the rest under the sofa. 'So, I expect Mr Plug has been all gold grapes and mopping your fevered brow.'

'Why on earth would Atticus Valentine be mopping my brow?'

'No reason.' Samuel drained his mug, looking back at the coffee machine like he might chance another. 'And I expect he was a bit busy, what with getting Sylvie Stevens executed and everything.'

'That wasn't anything to do with him.'

'It's not right losing Unit One like that. Plug Productions should have stepped in and paid a ransom, not left them to be shot for trespassing onto an opium field.' Samuel frowned into his empty mug. 'All three of them shot dead for drug money. That was too much.'

'The cartel just shot them,' Ezra said. 'There was no time for anyone to intervene. Even Jar said it's a risk they take every time they leave the camp.'

'You hear some crackhead got beaten to death in Chichester last night? People are angry, it was too much.'

Ezra sighed some breathing room into the conversation. 'I'm glad they showed the anniversary special, though. It felt like honouring them.'

But Samuel didn't need breathing room; Samuel needed a sense of punishment. 'The army should accidentally drop a few tonnes of heatseeking napalm on the poppy fields, that's what I say.'

'They were soldiers, they knew the risks.'

'You never nearly enlisted.' Samuel turned away. 'What do you know about any of it?'

All Ezra could do was sip tentatively at a drink that smelled like a packet of mints and tasted like hot water. 'You're right, Samuel, I don't know anything.'

'It's not like it's just you,' Samuel said. 'The trustees have been making a whole load of decisions based on AI predictions. Emporia is politely ignoring every update reminder. Downstairs Lesley is asking for whatever new tech costs the most. As for Dicky, that old dollop does whatever the trustees tell him, even if it makes no—'

'Ahem, if I may interject?'

'Mr Ipswich.' Samuel sat bolt upright. 'No, so I didn't actually mean…'

'At Ease,' Dicky said. 'And a welcome return to you, Ezra Blake.'

'I'm sorry I was away so long.'

'Can't be helped, can't be helped,' Dicky said. 'As to previous topic, a consultancy firm are currently advising us on how to appeal to a fluctuating visitor demographic. I would thoroughly recommend a visit to their website. Outstanding concept. Single-view access and not one piece of information pertaining to what they do. Why, I felt updated just for looking at it.'

'I will look, Mr Ipswich,' Samuel said, still sitting to Attention.

319

'Splendid,' Dicky said. 'Who's for a brew?'

'I'm good,' Ezra said.

'I say!' Emporia's voice pirouetted into the room. 'Is that young Ezra I can hear?'

'Hi, Emporia.'

'Are you recovered in all areas?'

'Absolutely.'

'Splendid news.' Emporia bustled around a shy acknowledgment to Dicky. 'These things can drain a person's resolve to do anything but look out of a window. I wonder, did you manage to speak to our dear Mr Valentine?'

'I did.'

'And?'

'Yeah, he was asking how I was.'

'Did he perhaps mention my message-taking efficiency?' Emporia said, all coy and offhand. 'I read it back to him several times.'

'He was most impressed with the memo pad.'

'Oh, nonsense.' Emporia bobbed a polite circle, heading towards a narrow staircase that led down to the baggage carousel. 'No need for me to mention it was the yellow one, of course, Dicky. Being a young gentleman, he would have assumed it would be.'

Ezra squirmed and stood up. 'I should check in with the clock.'

'A quick word,' Dicky said, waiting on a reluctant Samuel to follow Emporia out of the staffroom.

'Samuel didn't mean anything,' Ezra said.

'By its non-existence, I know it... Like the wasted light of a thunder moon, or the scent of elderflower on winter-cut hedgerows.'

'Did I do something wrong?'

'On the contrary,' Dicky said. 'The trustees are delighted with your continued dedication and unrivalled enthusiasm.

And as staff, we have certainly enjoyed having such a shot of positivity about the place. The clock itself has made several tuneful recommendations that we persuade you to extend your stay with us beyond the GiFT. Full steam on all fronts, what-ho.'

'Stay on?'

'Only if it would suit your plans,' Dicky said.

'At Fabian Evirate House?'

'Aforementioned.'

'Gosh.'

'There would, of course, be the customary remuneration agreement.' Dicky swished his hands in the air as though demonstrating the internal mechanism of a smoothie maker. 'Contract of employment, holiday allowance, dental, so forth and such like.'

'You're offering me a job?'

'To sweeten the pot, you may recall the mention of an intriguing project,' Dicky leant in, 'and several conversations regarding a certain Nordic anomaly.'

'The panel in the phylactery?'

'The very same.'

Ezra sat forward. 'You don't think it's Jötunvillur, do you?'

'Indeed I do not.' Dicky looked around the staffroom, leaning closer. 'I suspect it is something far older than Jötunvillur.'

'How much older?'

'Ah, but we must leave it there.' Dicky sat back, looking towards the kettle. 'I gather there is some peppermint tea available.'

'But I have my degree...' Ezra huffed and puffed around the angst of wanting two different things and only getting one of them. 'Can I think about it?'

'Time moves ever onward, Ezra Blake,' Dicky said. 'Seek advice from your loved ones, but linger not in the convenient caves of indecision, lest the sea come and steal the land away. Shall we say the end of the week?'

Samuel just happened to be walking the baggage carousel as Ezra emerged from the narrow stairwell above. 'So,' he said, spinning past, 'when are you seeing him again?'

'The end of the week.'

'I knew it!' Samuel slammed back into the central control unit, sending the baggage carousel into an undulating swing. 'I was right about Mr Plug all along.'

'Dicky, I'm seeing Dicky by the end of the week,' Ezra said, stepping onto the carousel and gripping the safety rope for balance. 'FYI, still about work.'

'Whatever.'

'No, Samuel, not whatever,' Ezra said. 'I didn't want to meet with Mr Valentine. I went because it was important for Fabian Evirate House. Now everyone's acting like he invited me to his yacht for supper or something.'

'You've been invited to supper with Mr Valentine!' Emporia squealed.

'On a fucking yacht,' Samuel said.

'I was illustrating a point,' Ezra said. 'There is no yacht, and I'm not having supper with anyone.'

'Now, you mustn't wear the windcheater,' Emporia said, walking against the carousel spin. 'Something more formal, I think, for supper. Perhaps a light jacket with red trim. French seam, of course. It can be choppy in the Channel, and no one wants to see an exposed pinking seam.'

'I like my windcheater.'

'Oh, my dear child,' Emporia said, gripping a rope to stop herself from toppling over at the thought of it. 'You must not mention this to Mr Valentine.'

'Believe me, there's no chance of this being mentioned to Mr Valentine.'

Emporia's delighted laugh fluttered like tropical butterflies around the baggage carousel, but Samuel just pushed Ezra aside, scrabbling to negotiate a short jump to the security section exit ramp. 'Better take some travel sickness pills,' he said. 'It would be a shame if you ruined it by throwing up again.'

Emporia bundled into the space Samuel had created to link arms with Ezra. 'Now don't you worry about that. Mr Valentine may be young, but he's no doubt an experienced seafarer. He'll keep the yacht on an even keel.' And then she added, 'Hello, Sailor,' because she really hadn't been herself since the phylactery.

Ezra kept steering everything back to the same old line. It was for work. It was for work. It was for work. There was no talk of top-secret conversations with Mac Eden, top-secret meetings in Minstrels Park, top-secret tattoos, top-secret intel gathering, or indeed top-secret unrequited daydreams. And that was a lot of lie to juggle for someone who found it hard to juggle even a small lie. What Ezra needed was Hollow. Hollow would have some lie-magician trick to make it simple. But Hollow wasn't here. Hollow was out in Afghanistan juggling catastrophic life events. And in a weird kind of way, that made the whole of the enormous lie Hollow's fault.

Sometimes, blame could be obvious. Sometimes, it crept up on you like an uncancelled subscription.

27

Like we're bloody Princess Diana

Filming didn't stop just because their loss was private. The
WØLF soldiers were a public commodity, even when they
were finding a way to carry on without Sylvie, Mattoo and Nell.
None of the squad had watched the programme for months. The
people watching at home couldn't look away.

SMART SLATE

Whiskey-Zero-One-Foxtrot/s5e1/REMI IP link PP confirm: EFP rig/ crew/IGH remote
Producer: *Elspeth Hart*
INT/EXT. AFG. CAMP BASTION – DAY

Scene: *WØLF* soldiers come together to rearrange the bunkhouse. Fixed rig and crew cameras stay with the soldiers. IGH as needed – continuous

ITM SCENE
COMMENTARY
CASTER DUPONT:
If war stopped when people die, it wouldn't be war. It
would be an absence of war.

Stan Dobresnski played a lament on the bunkhouse accordion, a misplaced, soulful sound that unhinged all the measures of their grief. In places, he even cried with it, the musician and the instrument as wild and untamed as the Cornish Sea. Jar stayed as far away as he could get while still being a part of it. Sitting in the bunkhouse doorway, cleaning boots like nothing had changed. The others hung about somewhere on the scale between them. Fish kept her arm locked around Joanie until the lament came to an end, and didn't let go when he tried to pull away.

'Hey, kid,' Jar called to him. 'Give me a hand with this.'

Joanie finally wriggled away from Fish. 'I'm heading out to the gym after, I'll see you tonight.'

'You don't have to pretend you're okay,' Fish said.

'Leave him be.' Alma pulled Fish back. 'If you can't work through this without him, then that's your problem, not his.'

'This isn't about me, you idiot.'

'Get your head out of your arse, Fish. This has been about you from the moment you arrived here.'

Fish glared at Alma. 'Did Jar go talking to everyone behind my back? Because Jar knows squat about me.'

'We've all seen how much you lean on that sweet boy,' Alma said. 'He holds the price of it more than is safe for anyone. Did you ever speak to him about that stuff with the rabbit skin?'

'What about the rabbit skin?'

'And that's the problem,' Alma said, turning away, 'that's the whole problem right there.'

Jar waited for Joanie to reach the doorway to shove a pair of boots at him. 'Get them cleaned up.'

'I'm okay.'

'Me too,' Jar said. 'There's brushes in the box.'

Joanie ran his finger over the name written on the tongue of the boots. 'These are Sylvie's.'

'Her old ones. I got them out of kit recycling. Took me hours rummaging through all them forgotten soles.' Jar shrugged, picking up a boot with Mattoo's name in it. 'Anyway, I thought her family might want them, seeing as it's just her ID discs and belongings to send back. And make sure you get every scrap of sand out the seams. They've served their time, and I'll be damned if those boots go home with even a trace of this bastard place left on them.'

'I didn't know her,' Joanie said, flicking a look over to Mika.

'It don't take much time if you have a real connection.'

Joanie hugged the pale desert boots and sat down next to Jar. 'You think that's true?'

'As much as I think anything's true,' Jar said.

'I feel like I shouldn't cry, like I don't have the right.'

'There's nothing wrong with tears, kid, we don't mind tears out here.' Jar passed Joanie a toothbrush. 'Our Stan, he's got a cry for all seasons. People say it's the music in him coming out.'

'How do I find a way through this, Jar?'

'You get those boots cleaned up,' Jar handed him a tub of bicarb, 'and I want to see your face in them before you're done.'

'They're mostly canvas,' Joanie said. 'It could take a while.'

'It'll take as long as you need.'

When Fish tried to sit with Joanie, Jar shooed her away, and was more gross about it than anyone wanted to see.

ITM SCENE
COMMENTARY
JAR:
The army don't have time for condolences, but you can find comfort in service.

PRODUCER:
It's good to see you looking out for Joanie.

JAR:
Saved me from cleaning them boots.

There'd hardly been time to cover the empty spaces when Sampson rocked up, sweat soaked and breathless from marching too quickly. 'We have a call,' she said. 'Unit Four, Quinn in for Magrath. Command want Captain Brooks on this. Full chameleon, briefing room at 14:30.'

ITM SCENE
COMMENTARY
HOLLOW QUINN:
They swapped me in for Joan. I'm a better shot. It's not personal, stuff like that. You just do your job.

FISH NAZARI:
It must be something bloody big, mind, for them to swap Captain Brooks in for this pickup. You could see Lieutenant Sampson was pissed about not being on the mission, but there was more relief dripping off her than sweat. I heard that Captain Brooks single-handedly squashed a suicide jacking and avoided mass casualties by throwing a water tank on top of her commanding officer. I bet she's amazing to work with.

I'll miss being out with Joan, but it makes a lot of sense for Hollow to be bumped over for something big. Maybe we got someone famous, like we're picking up the president of America or something.

PRODUCER:
How are you feeling about what Alma said to you, Fish?

FISH NAZARI:
Alma's trying to make out I don't know about the

rabbit skin, which I do know about, thank you. Joan took it so he could bury it with all the bones. It was decent and respectful, because he's like that. Alma met Joan, like hardly any time ago. What does she bloody know?

It's just the shock of losing Unit One stirring things up between me and Joan. Grief makes you hit out at the people you care most about, the people you know will take it.

PRODUCER:
Alma said you lean on him too much.

FISH NAZARI:
Me and Joan, we lean on each other. That's what friendship is. Now I'm supposed to start thinking there's something wrong with that? Everyone knows Almanac Johansson confuses sex with affection. What makes you think she knows squat about real friendship?

Major Hyde and Captain Brooks were waiting for them in the briefing room, with the mission already written up on the board. Medivac. *WØLF*. Unit Four. P2. Hostile.

The major kept his hands tucked behind his back and his eyes fixed on the far wall. 'We treat this like we treat any other return. We follow procedure. We do our job. P2 means this creature is badly wounded, incapacitated no doubt, but it doesn't mean dead. As you are aware, close contact with the Mandolin is a level white event. Ozone will be spiking at near lethal levels: breathers, gloves and gawks to be worn at all times, regardless of what your equipment is telling you.' He paused, looking at Fish and Hollow for the first time. 'Despite everything that's wrong with this bally war, a life is still a life.'

The rest of the briefing was cold, efficient, ordinary. At the end, Captain Brooks told Hollow and Fish to wait outside. It didn't take a military genius to guess the topic of her argument with Major Hyde.

Lieutenant Sampson kept them focused on the task, checking them for equipment errors and dumping a whole load of last minute advice on them like she was seeing them off on a backpacking holiday. 'You're both aware that Bastion has never returned a hostile alive before, but we have been involved in the transportation of their dead to the International War Agency holding facility at Camp Leatherneck for many months. Mandolin neural decoding proteins can scam us even after death, and this creature is badly injured. It's trying to survive. It will appear as whoever it needs to appear as, and that might well be someone you deeply care about. Keep focused on the mission and don't let your mind wander. The biggest danger is that it will feel like a standard P2 return—'

'I'll take it from here, Lieutenant.' Captain Brooks strode the gap between them. 'There's a damn good reason we teach troops to forget everything they think they know about the enemy.'

'Captain.' Lieutenant Sampson stepped back, but not away.

'How many times have these fucking breathers seen active service?' Captain Brooks grabbed Hollow's respiratory device and threw it on the floor. 'No second-use equipment on this mission. It's straight out of the manufacturer's box, and that includes chameleon skins. Humans are the weak link in this P2 return. We can't afford even a basic equipment error on top of that.'

Captain Brooks sat on a hexi block stool as Hollow and Fish stripped down to their underwear. She even organised herself a round of tea and biscuits while they waited for the replacement equipment to arrive.

'A Mandolin,' Fish whispered to Hollow. 'What do you think it'll be like?'

'I don't know,' Hollow said.

'Are you scared?' Fish risked a quick look at Captain Brooks. 'I'm scared.'

'I'm not thinking about it.'

'Soldiers,' Captain Brooks hollered, 'you have been told to wait in silence. I catch you two whispering again and you're on report.'

'Yes, Captain.'

Captain Brooks turned to Sampson, pulling her in close. 'The army agreed to cameras on this. I told them no, but I was overridden. Shit, I remember when Medivac was just a procedure. Now camera crews chase us around like we're bloody Princess Diana. This mission is on a knife edge already, there's no room for protecting arty civilians. They'll get us all killed.'

'Permission to speak off the record,' Sampson said.

'Go on.'

'If there's no room for protecting the camera crew, then don't.' Sampson looked around, making sure she was out of earshot. 'If the production company knows the full extent of the danger they're sending their people into, then protecting them is not your responsibility.'

'They know the extent all right.' Captain Brooks stood up, calling to Hollow and Fish. 'As soon as that equipment gets here, you get suited up. Meet me at the truck.'

'Yes, Captain.'

Captain Brooks nodded to Sampson. 'Cameras go in at their own risk, but I'll damn well blow that shithole to hell to keep those two soldiers alive.'

ITM SCENE
COMMENTARY
PRODUCER:
This is your first trip to an Afghan village, Fish. How are you feeling about it?

FISH NAZARI:
So, we didn't come from a village. My dad worked as a translator for the British Embassy. We lived in an apartment, in Kabul.

I mean, I get what you're saying. On some level, these are my people, and this is my country.

You want the actual truth? You really want the actual truth?

Helpless. I feel helpless. I feel confused, I feel lost, I feel scared. I can't even think straight. I want to cry all the bloody time. And before you say anything, it's not because of what Almanac Johansson said. I've felt this way since I got here.

Do you think it's okay to come home, Elspeth?

PRODUCER:
This isn't about what I think.

FISH NAZARI:
It didn't want us; our home didn't want us. What if it still doesn't want me?

Pulling up to the village, it was obvious that it wasn't just the soldiers of Camp Bastion who'd been unsettled. The village elder was already a hundred yards away from the last of the mud-built houses. He flagged them down, pointing to a square building at the centre of the village. Then he was on a bike and gone. The rest of the village was deserted, down to the last goat.

Hollow and Fish unloaded the medical containment unit from the back of the ambulance. They'd seen the coffin-shaped box once before, but this time there was no Sergeant Naleigh, no trusting excitement, no naive wondering about what war might be like. Gawks, gloves and breathers on. AS80 assault rifles strapped across the front of their bodies. Their dust-pale chameleon skins flicked to a deep grey to mimic the box. Along the mud-built walls of the village tobacco plants had faded to brown. The ozone strips on their uniforms were already close enough to yellow to tell them they hadn't come here for nothing.

Captain Brooks leant in as they dropped the box on the ground, checking the locks twice before starting again. 'We go in hot. Nazari, clear target on the hostile. Quinn, unlock a live ammo clip, keep your gun fixed on everyone else, and that includes the bloody camera crew.'

'Live ammo?' Hollow said.

'Thanks to our fretting Lieutenant Sampson, you don't need me to tell you that whatever you see in there is a scam.' Captain Brooks carried on checking the locks and lowered one of the sides. 'It doesn't matter if it's your mum in there, or your worst enemy, it's a scam. You pay attention to me, and just me. If I say shoot me, you shoot me. If I say shoot the camera crew, you shoot the camera crew. No hesitation, no second guessing, no messaging each other with questions. Got it?'

'You want me to shoot the camera crew?' Hollow said.

Captain Brooks looked straight at the camera. 'And that's an order.'

Fish pushed Hollow out of the way. 'With respect, Captain Brooks, as far as we know, this is still a P2. Are we prioritising shooting it over a return?'

'You put your gun where I tell you to put your gun,' Captain Brooks said. 'Believe me, I've seen this before, and the enemy won't be the worst thing in the room.'

'Yes, Captain.'

'Three to a team. One to cover you. One to shoot you.' Captain Brooks snapped her helmet on, dragging a tranquilliser rifle from the back of the truck. 'P2 injury is confirmed, but there's no intel on how close to P1 it is. If it's still conscious when we go through the door, it won't be for long. We drop it. Box it. Deliver it to the rendezvous site. Home in time for a celebratory tea.'

'Rendezvous site?' Fish said. 'I thought we were taking it back to camp.'

'We manage to take this thing alive, Washir District can come to us.'

'But if it's wounded...'

Captain Brooks threw a frustrated sigh. 'We pick it up, we hand it on. If it was down to me, I'd have nuked the whole damn country by now.'

'With respect, Captain,' Fish said. 'Major Hyde told us to treat this casualty like we treat every other casualty.'

'Command only stretches as far as the officer in front of you, Private.'

'What will happen to it?'

'You got yourself some sympathetic tendencies, soldier?'

'No, Captain,' Fish said.

'Follow my lead,' Captain Brooks said. 'That's all you have to do.'

'Will it be bad?'

'It's always bad with the Mandolin.' Captain Brooks snapped on an extra handgun and loaded three iron powder clips into her pocket. 'You just never know what kind of bad it's gonna be.'

Even with the breathers running at full air exchange, ozone took hold of their throats like an energy saving light bulb had blown. It was dark inside the building, but enough sunlight spilled in from the doorway to make out a small figure, huddled by the far wall. Younger than anyone could be prepared for, not much more than a toddler. His face was flushed and wet with a fever that had started long before they got there. Without even noticing, Hollow lowered her gun.

'Hold,' the captain snapped.

'Captain...'

'I said HOLD.'

The first dart missed. Captain Brooks cleared the tranquilliser rifle and loaded it again, edging forward an inch at a time, trying to focus the red target light. And the boy, panting with pain, pushing himself further into the shadows, all eyes and fear like he was waiting on abuse.

'Captain, he's too small, a dart could kill him,' Hollow said. She flicked a look at Fish, but Fish just stood her ground, gun pointed at the boy. Hollow took a step forward. 'I don't think it's a scam.'

'It's always a scam.' The captain was closer now, close enough to get a guaranteed shot. The boy covered his face, blood all over his hands. A piece of shrapnel, stupidly bright, some kind of aluminium cladding, was buried deep in his thigh. Hollow looked towards the door, gagging for a kind of air no breather could help with.

Captain Brooks spoke slowly. 'Quinn, how many times do I have to tell you to keep your arse still.'

ITM SCENE

COMMENTARY

HOLLOW QUINN:

I couldn't breathe, but it wasn't down to the ozone. This kid is so young, and the people in the village, they just left him behind for the enemy. Or maybe for us, I don't know.

All I saw was a terrified kid in a war that doesn't give a shit about how old you are. I already knew his leg would be no good, even if we saved his life. One more piece of flesh for the room of a thousand pieces. I thought I was going to break...

...but it wasn't me who broke.

Fish was running towards the boy, yelling at Captain Brooks, 'He's breathing. Hold your fire, he's breathing.'

'Back to your post!'

Fish twisted, putting her body between Captain Brooks and the child. 'Stop!'

'Stand down!'

But Fish didn't stand down. 'It's okay, little one,' she said, scooping the child up and hugging him to her body. 'It's all right. I won't let them hurt you.'

Captain Brooks spoke softer now, more in agreement. 'Put him down, Private Nazari. Just put him down so we can look him over, that's all.'

The boy choked on his own breath, hugging his face into Fish's chest and staining it the colour of rust. Fish shook her head. 'He's fucking breathing, what's wrong with you?'

'I can see that,' the captain said. 'And by the look of him, he needs a hospital.'

'You can't dart him, he's too weak.'

'No darts.' Captain Brooks was lowering the tranquilliser rifle. She dropped it on the floor. 'Let's see what we can do to make him more comfortable.'

Fish slumped, nodded, and almost put the boy down. Almost. Instead, she turned her gun on the captain. 'No.'

'Put the child down, Private Nazari.'

Fish screamed, shaking her head over and over. 'It's a setup, it's a setup.'

'It's not a setup,' Captain Brooks said. 'It's a P2 return.'

'No, I get it, I get it now,' Fish said. 'You don't need a hostile for this mission, you just need a victory.'

'Come on, Fish,' Hollow said. 'That doesn't make any sense.'

'No, no, it does make sense.' Fish was keeping her eyes on the captain, edging towards the door. 'Because all the terrified people in this village think he's Mandolin, just like all the terrified people back at camp think he's Mandolin. And that's what really matters. Killing one up close like this is good for morale.'

'We're Medivac,' the captain said. 'We're not here to kill anyone.'

'Like you didn't just piss all over that argument five minutes ago.' Fish took another step towards the light. 'I'm taking the truck back to camp. We can see what the doctors there say about him. You with me, Hollow?'

'I...' Hollow was switching focus between her commanding officer and her friend. 'I don't know.'

'You do know, soldier.' The captain was backing off in a slow circle that didn't look like a circle. 'Just like you know your strips are choking white on ozone.'

Hollow turned her gun on Fish.

'What the actual fuck, Hollow?'

'Just like they taught us, Fish. Trust your commanding officer like your life depended on it.'

Fish pulled the boy tighter to her body, there was blood on her neck where his fingers had gripped her. 'I swear on the Balloon Fiesta, you kill him, Hollow, and you'll have to kill me too.'

The captain sighed. 'You're already dead, soldier.'

'Fuck you!' Fish hauled her gun straight and aimed it at the captain, blood dripping slowly, relentlessly, from the unblemished barrel of the SA80 assault rifle. In the fluctuating half-light, it took the camera a few seconds to register that the blood didn't belong to the child.

Fish fell in slow motion, letting the boy slide out of her arms and away into the shadows, blood still pumping from his leg wound. And Fish, fumbling at the shrapnel in her neck like she couldn't quite figure out what it was.

Hollow fired two bullets into the child's head.

'Out!' Captain Brooks shouted, snatching up Fish's gun and

firing off half a dozen shots. She wasn't trying to hit anything; she was buying them time. 'This isn't over. All of you, OUT!'

Hollow tried to run then, but nothing happened. Her body didn't belong to her any more. She could hear Captain Brooks yelling, but it was lost in the ethereal song of a sandpiper fluttering overhead. Something was coming. She could feel it in all the negative spaces. Not a thing; an absence of thing. Vast and untamed. She knew she should be scared, but it wasn't fear that met her on the threshold of death, it was a soft kind of homecoming. Hollow closed her eyes and let it take her.

The captain bulldozed into Hollow, hurling them both out of the hut along with the sound engineer. Video was streaming via REMI. IP link to Plug Productions. Hollow's gun flipped over and over until it hit the wall of the hut opposite. The dead child. Fish's blood on the white doorway. The screaming, tearing, insane rage that was inside of Hollow. Kicking, scratching, biting at her captain. And Captain Brooks, absorbing the fury, pulling a grenade and throwing it into the hut.

The camera dropped to watch it land, too far inside the building to get out. Quiet on the patterned carpet for a few heartbeats. And a pale dust drifting a Gaussian blur on a closing scene that couldn't be rubbed out.

Hollow woke up coughing, a fly crawling over her mouth. She was propped up against the truck, covered in dust, her ears still ringing from close gunfire. The production vehicle was gone. A curling wisp of sand showed it hadn't been gone for long.

She found Captain Brooks throwing petrol over the decimated hut.

'Captain.'

'Are you fit?'

'Oh God…I thought I'd dreamt it.'

'Your brain's trying to sort it out, give it time.'

Hollow was looking around. 'Fish?'

The captain nodded towards the truck. 'We also lost one from the camera crew, if that's of any comfort.'

'Comfort?'

'The sound engineer got out fine, as fine as you can expect from arty types. I sent him back to camp for a medical check. Give me a hand here.'

Hollow rubbed at her eyes. 'So many people are dead.'

Captain Brooks doused the last of the petrol on the hut. 'I asked you to give me a hand, soldier.'

'Permission to sit in the truck.'

'Denied.'

There was nowhere to go when an officer shut you down. Hollow unclipped her helmet and threw it on the ground. It was all she had. She could have been put on a charge for less.

'Pick it up,' Captain Brooks said.

'Last week, a squadron of three hundred soldiers turned on itself.' Hollow was pulling at her uniform. 'There wasn't even any Mandolin, they just killed each other.'

'Pick your helmet up, Quinn. We have work to do.'

'The biggest threat to our survival on the whole goddamn earth.' Hollow gripped a handful of her own flesh, twisting it until she finally felt something worse than the crushing loss inside her chest. 'In the hut, I felt what it was like to die, and now all I want is to go back there.'

'What you felt was the Mandolin.' Captain Brooks pulled out a flare. 'People think the Mandolin take your mind away, but they don't. They give you what you want.'

'How the hell do we fight them, Captain?'

'We survive.' Captain Brooks struck the percussion cap on the flare and threw it into the hut. 'The best damn way I've found to fight any enemy, is to not die.'

The hut burned to a mark on the ground. Hollow and Captain Brooks didn't speak much; they just bagged the bodies and took them back to camp. Hollow volunteered to strip down Fish's locker and take her kit to the ISO shipping container reserved for the belongings of fallen soldiers. She told Sampson she wanted to do it for her friend, but it didn't take an avoidance strategist to know that Joanie's unit was due back from a call and she didn't want to be anywhere near him when he heard about what had happened.

It was hot inside the ISO, muffled like a pine forest. Each kit was a life. It was hard to find an empty place to put Fish's things.

PRODUCER:
Is there anything you'd like to say, Hollow?

HOLLOW QUINN:
Sometimes, you can be so close to the edge it doesn't seem like an edge, because all the bits that aren't edge have been taken away. And then one day, there's only edge left. I killed a child without feeling anything, Elspeth.

I would've pulled the trigger on Fish if Captain Brooks had called it.

In the end, Hollow just sat with Fish's kit, her back to the room and feet braced against the wall. When Joanie turned up, she didn't move much beyond hiding the little white feather she'd been brushing across her wrist. If anyone watching at home had been waiting on a show of grief, there was none. Salt was worth more than tears in the Afghan sun.

'Hey,' Joanie said after a while.

Hollow didn't look up. 'Don't expect anything decent from me.'

'Captain Brooks has put you up for a commendation. She said you behaved admirably.'

339

'Shit.'

'It was a trap,' Joanie said, squirming to sit next to her. 'There's nothing you could have done except survive.'

'And the army give you a commendation for that?'

'I guess they think staying alive is harder than dying out here.'

Hollow picked up her phone to scroll through saved photographs. 'I hope you're not waiting on a fridging moment, Joan. I'm not turning into Retribution Ruby just because someone I know got killed.'

'The Hubert is someone you know.' Joanie reached over and took Hollow's phone. 'Fish was your friend. It's not the same.'

Hollow shrugged. 'Why's she even called Fish anyway?'

'Right, you're actually going there?'

'Like I said, don't expect anything decent from me.'

'Did they hurt her?' Joanie asked.

'No.'

'Don't try to protect me.'

'She disobeyed her commanding officer to save an Afghan kid, Joan. Nothing else in the whole fucking world matters except that.'

Joanie leant his head against her shoulder. 'The same as Sylvie.'

'Yeah,' Hollow said, 'the same as Sylvie.'

'I've put in a request to be transferred to your unit.'

'Hubert Frank is my unit.'

'The squad lost four people in a week.' Joanie sat up straight. Steady, detached like he was working in a call centre. 'We're too thin on the ground to run all the units. The Hubert said he doesn't mind swapping out in the circumstances.'

'The Hubert said that?'

'His exact.' Joanie stood up, slow with it and handed Hollow's phone back. 'Fish and her family were refugees. When the appeal for host families came out, my parents gave up part of the house so they had somewhere to live. They thought I might be upset, but I was just stoked because I got a big sister out of it. I was always toddling around after her to play with me.'

'And you called her Fish?'

'Fish was always Fish.' Joanie shrugged. 'Sorry to disappoint you, Hollow, but some things don't have a story.'

'It's okay, I get it,' Hollow said. 'How are the others holding up?'

'Variable,' Joanie said.

'You?'

'Me? Nothing,' Joanie said. 'It's like, I want to cry. I can feel it in my eyes, all there ready to go. But nothing happens. Like I stall the engine. Maybe I left the handbrake on or something.'

'I'm serious about you not transferring to my unit,' Hollow said. 'And FYI, I already asked Sampson to refuse if you asked.'

'Yeah, she told me. It was a bit of a stalemate situation, so she agreed we could work it out over a game of D&D.'

'A roll-off?'

'Stan's playing us some atmospheric music on the accordion,' Joanie said. 'Alma has offered to join as a guest.'

'Alma is a level twenty half-orc.' Hollow laughed before she could stop it. 'Can you imagine a level twenty half-orc on a quest with Jar's disco elf?'

'Maybe she's thinking of multiclassing her character.'

'Fucking hell, I'm talking about D&D, Joan,' Hollow said, grabbing Joanie's arm and hauling herself upright. 'Now I get why they give you a medal for staying alive.'

Joanie walked back to the bunkhouse with Hollow. It didn't feel like walking with someone who'd just lost a best friend; it didn't feel like walking with anyone. 'The first time I met Fish,' he said, 'I thought she was a cartoon. Not just because of her hair or her freakishly large eyes, it was the way she moved, the way she stood, the way it felt like the story would turn out all right now she was in it. Except, she's gone now, and I'm not sure everything is gonna turn out all right any more. Not for me or you, or anyone.'

'First time I met you, it felt like indigestion.' Hollow punched Joanie's arm. 'Now you're my friend. Most first impressions are based on a series of past impressions. They don't mean much in the end.'

ITM SCENE
COMMENTARY
JOANIE MAGRATH:
It's weird, I don't feel anything. It's like I jumped to a multiverse version of my life where Fish didn't come to Afghanistan. She's still back in Bristol, watching me on TV, waiting for when I get back. She can always drink me under the table, and by then I won't have drunk any alcohol for three Balloon Fiestas. She'll have to carry me home. She always carries me home.

PRODUCER:
Have you spoken to the counsellors about this?

JOANIE MAGRATH:
I made a deal. So she must be back in Bristol waiting for me.

PRODUCER:
What sort of deal?

JOANIE MAGRATH:
With the rabbit. And I don't want help with this. I want to keep it. Because I made a deal, with the rabbit.

Jar moved his bunk to hide the gap, but there were so many losses, and more gaps than anything could hide.

'It's too soon, Jar,' Hamid said.

'Just making a bit of space for myself.'

'Give us time, will you.'

'Death is why we're here,' Jar said. 'And the army's more used to dealing with death than anything short of an undertaker should be. You're best cutting the reminders out quick. There's no help ever came from dwelling on it.'

'We've lost four of our friends inside a week,' Hamid said. 'We need time with this, Jar.'

'Fucking kids, you all have chronic FOMO for your feelings. Like you'll literally die if you don't talk about how dreadful it felt when your friends didn't include you in a group photograph. Seeing someone stub their toe needs time to process with you lot.' Jar sneered a look around the bunkhouse cameras. 'I'm not disrespecting anyone, but fucking hell, it's hard on the ear.'

'Ignore him.' Mika pushed past Hamid. 'He's just doing it for the attention.'

Jar lay back on his bunk, arms tucked behind his head. 'I lost my whole squad in the time it takes for a Taliban to say the word ambush. War ain't considerate with your feelings, it goes like this sometimes. And when it does, you drag all the screaming poison right down to the core of you, and you build a wall around it so you never have to feel it again. You don't need no synthetic brain chemicals for that, you just need bricks and mortar.' Jar squirmed his pillow straight. 'Look at me, I'm doing okay.'

'You're not doing okay,' Hamid said.

'Grow up, Hamid,' Jar said. 'The past is over with. Here and now is all we've got. Start chemically blocking out the here and now and we're no better than state-programmed machines. This is war, we've been damn lucky to get this far without losing anyone, and that's the non-synthetic truth.'

'I think we lost you,' Hamid said. 'We lost you a long time ago.'

'Is that right?'

'The biochemicals aren't there to stop us feeling anything,' Hamid said, sitting next to Jar. 'They just make the feelings easier to deal with. They might help you, if you give them a try.'

'I don't need no help.'

'Funny, that,' Mika said, and awful mean with it, 'how you walked away without a scratch, when everyone else in your squad died.'

Hamid held a hand up to check him. 'Mika, don't.'

Jar just laughed. 'I saved your life, you ungrateful little shit.'

'No,' Mika said, 'you traded it for Nell's life. And I'm nowhere near forgetting whose fault that is.'

Jar went to say something, but Joanie and Hollow were in the doorway, caught in the crossfire of grief and not knowing whose side was the side they wanted to be on.

Hollow backed away. 'I need a cigarette, Joan, catch you later.'

'I'll come with you.'

'No,' Hollow said. 'It's just odd, her bed being gone. I need to get some space for that.'

'Me too.'

'No.'

'Let her go,' Jar said.

'Wait for me, Hollow!' Joanie shot a look at Jar. 'And I swear, if you so much as try to give me a pair of Fish's boots, I'll...'

Joanie had nothing much else to say, but it burned in him enough for Jar to shrug and let him go. 'Don't eat the bad oysters, kid.'

By the time Joanie got outside, Hollow was gone.

28

A secret is like the wind

Hollow hid herself behind the water bottling plant, chain-smoking until she was sick. Then she smoked again. There were dark clouds crouched along the horizon, but there was no rain. Storm clouds were always sandstorms in the desert. She could hear Joanie calling her, but she had nothing to give him and everything to take away. And all that stood between Hollow and the monster was a single white feather.

There didn't seem to be much point in explaining things. Hollow asked Sampson for permission to go and see the company medic. Sampson didn't question her reasons; she just signed her off along with a sympathetic pat on the arm.

Caster Dupont was sat at his desk; dark circles under his eyes and no sweet smile to meet Hollow. He took a cursory look at her file. 'You might be better off talking to the studio counsellors.'

'With respect, Captain, I need a doctor, not a therapist.'

Caster took another look at Hollow's file, longer than before. 'Any headaches?'

'No.'

'Nausea?'

'It's not like that.'

Caster looked up. 'What is it like, Hollow?'

'You need to send me home, Captain.'

'Why do you need to go home?'

'It's too dangerous for me to be here,' Hollow said.

'Dangerous?'

'Yes, Captain.'

'We're still trying to understand why some psych jackings take and some don't,' Caster said. 'It's the key to this whole war if you ask me. Category three exposure to the Mandolin, on the other hand, has a set of relatively mild side effects. That's not to say there aren't any. Your first R&R is available from the end of next month. I'm going to pull it forward to tomorrow. Two weeks at home will give you a chance to recover. How does that sound?'

Hollow kept swallowing the same answer. 'Thank you, Captain.'

'Can we speak off the record?'

'Yes, Captain.'

'No captain, just me.' Caster sat back. 'You play computer games, yes?'

'I used to.'

'In computer games, there are save points, places where you can save what you've done so far and never have to repeat it.' Caster took his time, speaking slowly. 'Two weeks' R&R is a save point, Hollow. A place to stop and take a breath. A chance to say, I've made it this far and I am still alive.'

'Most games are autosave now,' Hollow said. 'Danger included.'

'As your friend, I know there's more going on here than fear,' Caster said. 'But as your doctor, I can only treat the injuries you show me. I'm signing you off sick for the rest of today. Get your kit in order. The travel papers will be with you this afternoon.'

'Thank you, Captain.' Hollow stood up, turning to leave.

Caster pushed away from the table a little. 'You know, my mother was a lifelong gambler. She gambled on lies just like she gambled on spins. Lying and gambling go hand in hand. Don't gamble with your mental health, Hollow.'

346

'I won't, Captain.'

'Any bad dreams, flashbacks, sweating, shaking, unreasonable emotions; don't keep it from the cameras. Make sure the studio knows what you're going through. And for pity's sake use the counsellors, most soldiers don't have the luxury of their services.'

'I will.'

'This is no business to deal with alone.'

ITM SCENE
COMMENTARY
HOLLOW QUINN:
Jar's right. Except he didn't say what happens to all the things you keep behind the wall. You build a prison for all the poison so you never have to feel it again, but you're the prison. And the poison keeps on being poison. Killing you from the inside…like alpha radiation.

I took the cocktail, Elspeth. Why do I still feel this way?

PRODUCER:
You've just lost your friend in the worst way imaginable. No mood-regulating biochemicals are going to fix that.

HOLLOW QUINN:
War is a place where even if you win, you still lose. I have to quit the army. There are too many monsters in Afghanistan already.

The production team were on top of the situation. Elspeth Hart called Hollow in for a meeting before she'd even made it back to the bunkhouse. No cameras, low-threat lighting, legal representation via video link.

'You haven't done anything wrong, I promise,' Elspeth said, putting her headset on the table between them. 'You've just been through a huge life experience, maybe the biggest you'll ever go through. You need time to process it all. Let's get you home, Hollow, give you some space to be around the people you love. Things can look very different after a few days back home.'

'And if they don't?'

'Then we can talk about it again.'

'Okay,' Hollow said.

Elspeth picked up the headset, holding it like it was a missing part of her body. 'I should warn you that things back home may be a little different to when you left. As a high-profile cast member of WØLF, many people will recognise you, approach you, possibly harass you. Travelling with a crew can only protect you if we've agreed an advance filming schedule.'

'No crew,' Hollow said.

'Hollow, I don't think you understand what that would mean,' Elspeth said. 'Without a crew, you're heading back as a civilian. You'll be on your own.'

'Jar did it.'

'Jar has skin as thick as a rhinoceros, and he's had more than one showdown with the paparazzi.' Elspeth sighed. 'I'm going to be straight with you, Hollow. By the time you land in London, the episode we filmed today will have aired, which means the media tabloids will know you're heading back. Losing Unit One was the mother of all stories. Then we lost Fish. WØLF is trending in every area of public life, and I would be having this same conversation with Jar if he was making that trip today. Even if we manage to keep your arrival under wraps, there will be reporters waiting at your house. Are you prepared for that?'

'They'll be at my house?'

'Yes, Hollow, they'll be at your house. They'll be outside

the door asking for interviews. They'll be filming through the window when you draw the curtains. They'll be on your phone. They'll be following your car. They'll be speaking to your neighbours. They'll be offering your friends money to wear a wire. They'll even have drones crawling through the cat flap. This is the reality of how your life has changed. If you travel with a crew, we can protect you from that.'

'If I could interject,' the legal rep said. 'I'm here to remind you of the non-disclosure agreement. You are legally forbidden to talk to anyone about WØLF, matters arising from WØLF, or your association with WØLF, including, but not confined to, on-the-spot interviews with broadcast channels, streaming services and the associated press. If you do talk to anyone about WØLF, and that includes friends and family, you are breaking the terms of that agreement and may face criminal prosecution.'

'I don't want a crew.'

Elspeth stood up, pacing the room. 'Do you know what you're asking? You would have to keep your flight secret and stay close to the other military personnel. Get yourself into a change of clothes when you get to Cyprus. Arrange to be met at the airport by someone you trust implicitly. Try your absolute best to avoid drawing any attention. But there are thousands and thousands of people between Kabul and London. Any one of them posts seeing Hollow Quinn on their social media, and the hyenas will be all over you before you've cleared the arrivals gate.'

'I just want to go home.'

'And you are going home,' Elspeth said. 'Travelling with a crew makes it easier on everyone.'

'...I don't know.'

Elspeth sat down next to Hollow. 'Let's run through a low-profile option. The studio sends up a dummy flare and keeps your arrival bouncing between airports. You stick close to the military while you travel, have your mum meet you at Heathrow.

We use a single camera, that's all. A one-person crew. You can even pick who you'd like to go with you if it makes you feel better. Plug Productions will lock down the whole area around your house as a live film set, and that includes wherever you want to go while you're there. It's just you, your family and a low-impact crew operating out of an OB van. How does that sound?'

'You'll be filming me, though?'

'I'm not going to lie to you, Hollow, this is a mutual arrangement. But from our side, travelling with a crew isn't all about screen opportunity. It might be hard for you to accept, but we do care about you. Filming is as much about keeping you safe as it is about shooting footage for *WØLF*.'

'I don't feel like I've got a choice.'

'Your story is the story of everyone who has lost someone to this war. They've seen you fall, and that means they need to see you stand up again, Hollow. They need to believe it's possible.'

'What if I can't stand up again?'

'Then they need to see that too.' Elspeth put her arm around Hollow. 'You are important to them, Hollow Quinn. For once in your life, let yourself matter.'

Hollow told the rest of the squad she had two days off duty for a bad back. She hung around, doing yoga in the gym, only heading back to the bunkhouse to pack up her travel bag when she knew there'd be no one around. She left the next morning, heading to the helicopter landing site on the pretence of going to the gym, and catching the first available flight back to Bagram air base. The CH-47 was at full capacity with wounded soldiers, and a faked bad back wasn't a legitimate reason to say goodbye.

Bagram was chaotic, a constant arrival of new troops forcing the base to bulge out into the surrounding area. From her seat inside the Chinook, it looked like an overfilled water balloon. *WØLF* created heroes and a straight-line way to be like them. Official losses were sketchy, hidden away in suicide and accidental deaths, but there were always plenty of new recruits to fill the gaps. Hollow barely had time to clear the landing site, catching the military transport to Khwaja Rawash Airport. Kabul to Cyprus, Cyprus to London Heathrow. She sat with the other returning soldiers, gawks on, head down, pretending to be asleep. Finding her would have been like finding a desert camo needle in a haystack of desert camo needles.

Gemma should have been waiting at the arrivals gate with the single-crew camera, but neither of them were there. The returning soldiers peeled away, met by their families and so much happiness it was hard to watch. Hollow bought a coffee and wandered around the terminal, keeping to the edges, keeping her head down, trying to be any other soldier on leave from the war. In Afghanistan, everyone she hung out with lived in cookie-dough camos. It was so normal she'd forgotten it wasn't. People were already looking, pointing, whispering about WØLF. The more Hollow tried to look inconspicuous, the more conspicuous she looked. Two security guards flicked her a nod and let her out of the building without checking her travel documents. The pavement of an airport terminal could hardly be considered a snapshot for London tourism, but the air was cool and fresh in her lungs, and the sunlight on her skin was achingly soft. She'd lived in England her whole life but never considered what it would be like to come home to it.

'You're her,' a guy said, pushed close by his three companions. 'You're Hollow Quinn.'

'I'm not her, okay?'

The guy was buzzing around her, shouting her name, attracting all sorts of attention. But Hollow had already disconnected. Her eyes fixed on a plane coming in to land. Trying to calculate how long it would take for their unit to reach the crash. Trying to figure out how far the firestorm would reach. How many people would die. So many people. Noise and people. Hollow pushed through and got pushed back, too hard to be kind. There were reporters now, cameras.

'Let me through,' she said. 'I have to get to the ambulance.'

'Did you quit *WØLF*, Hollow?'

'Hollow, do you feel responsible for Fish's death?'

'Hollow, will they be bringing in more new recruits now you've lost four of the squad?'

Hollow was drowning in people. 'I have to get to the ambulance.'

SMART SLATE

Whiskey-Zero-One-Foxtrot/s5e3/OB REMI IP link PP confirm: EFP single crew - *Bassie*
Producer: *Elspeth Hart*
INT/EXT. GBR. HEATHROW AIRPORT – DAY

Scene: Civilians *Gemma Quinn* and *Rey Badigar* arrive at Heathrow Airport to meet *Hollow Quinn*. Gemma and Rey are an hour late. They find Hollow in a security office. Single crew camera stays with them – continuous

Gemma turned up at the security office, all waves and handholds with a guy and a single-crew camera panning behind her. Hollow was sat on a white plastic chair with a high vis jacket wrapped around her.

'For goodness' sake, Holl, you look a right mess.'

'Sorry,' the guy said, 'traffic on the M25.'

Hollow ditched the jacket. 'They said we could use the VIP exit. There's a transport vehicle waiting to take us to the car.'

'VIP,' Gemma said.

'I'm Reyansh,' the guy said. 'Rey. It's nice to finally meet you. I don't know how much Gem's said about me, but I've heard a lot about you.'

Hollow shouldered her bag. 'Which car park are you in?'

'Did I say the sill under the bathroom window fell out?' Gemma said, as they trundled the hidden corridors of Heathrow Airport. 'It took ages getting the insurance.'

Rey thanked the driver of the transport vehicle.

Gemma sat with her hand on Rey's leg.

There was a comfortable familiarity about the two of them that suggested it wasn't a new relationship. Rey offered to sit in the back of the car. There were rig cameras on the dash. Hollow turned Rey down. Gemma didn't say anything either way.

'My grandad served in Northern Ireland,' Rey called over his shoulder, pointing Gemma towards the southbound exit lane. 'He used to say it was hard being out there, and even harder coming home.'

'Sure.'

'Did you tell Ez you're back?' Gemma said.

'No.'

'Ring now if you want.' Gemma half caught the look Rey threw at her. 'Or best wait till later, eh?'

Joining the A27. Arundel. Chichester. Havant. Cosham. Hilsea. Gosport. Portsmouth Ferries. Junction nine for Fareham and the Northern Subway. Hollow couldn't get out of the car. She just sat there, gripping the seatbelt, shaking and sweating with cold while her mum apologised to Rey and blamed it on jet lag.

ITM SCENE
COMMENTARY
HOLLOW QUINN:
I've been in the desert for five months. You're spooked if you see another vehicle out in the field. The airport traffic here is insane, like, how the hell does anyone drive in that. And then we get on the motorway, and that's triple insane. Rey kept overriding the auto-

353

navigation, trying to get Gemma onto the right M25 slip road. Gemma's hanging on the horn, ignoring him. There's so much to look at, and so much colour it made my head hurt.

I tried closing my eyes, but it made it worse. So I sit back, holding my seatbelt strap like it's an assault rifle. Not even realising I'm doing it until I can't let it go.

BASSIE, CREW:
Do you think it was panic?

HOLLOW QUINN:
No, it wasn't panic, it was relief. The relief was unbearable. I should have thought about that. I should have been prepared for that.

The front door had a fingerprint touch pad. Frosted glass inserts down either side made the hallway brighter. The coats that always hung by the stairs were gone. The shoes were gone. The starburst mirror was gone. The cream carpet was gone. The little blue bowl where Hollow left her keys was gone.

'I'll pop this up in your room, shall I?' Rey said. He was trying; it deserved more than the cold nothing he got in return.

Gemma squealed as a round object came to a standstill by her foot. It moved like a grenade. Hollow shoved her mum back, shielding her with her own body before it had even registered that the grenade was a beaten-up tennis ball and the mortal danger was two little dogs hurtling out of the kitchen. Tiny, hairy, yappy.

'Calm down, Holl, it's just the dogs.' Gemma pulled herself clear and scooped them both up. 'How are my babies, did you miss me?'

'Rey,' she yelled up the stairs, 'you didn't say hello to the girls.'

'You got dogs?' Hollow said.

'I told you.' Gemma snuggled them into her face. 'I'm sure I told you, at the parade?'

'No, you didn't tell me.'

'Oh, well, introductions are in order then.' Gemma held out two black and tan dogs. One had ears that stood up; the other had ears that flopped forward. 'Byron and Lorde, say hello to Aunty Hollow.' Lorde growled. Then she barked. Then Byron barked. Gemma backed away, juggling the two snarling animals under her arms. 'It's probably the uniform; they're so protective of me. It's adorable really.'

'They're all right when you get used to them,' Rey said, grabbing hold of Byron and steering Gemma towards the kitchen. 'I made you a promise of tea, Holl. Let's get that sorted, eh?'

'Do you have sugar?' Hollow said.

'Gem,' Rey called over the yapping dog, 'do we have sugar?'

'For what?'

'For tea?'

'We don't have sugar in tea.'

ITM SCENE
COMMENTARY
REY BADIGAR:
I'm a builder, and builders don't like to leave gaps in anything. I got Holl some sugar from the petrol station. Gem even made us a mug cake in the microwave. It was a bit chewy, but we put ice cream on it.

Poor kid, I was busy showing her around the house like she'd never been there before. It took me a few minutes before I realised what I was doing.

GEMMA QUINN:
I asked Holl if she wanted to walk the dogs with me,

but she wanted a shower and a change of clothes first. She loved her bedroom. She didn't say, but I could tell by her face. There's no way I was throwing all that stuff out, behaving like she'd died or something.

She asked if she could borrow my pink hoodie. Weirdest thing, seeing Hollow in pink. I suppose it smells like my perfume, and she misses me. I like that she misses me. I told her it's best to stay awake with jet lag.

BASSIE, CREW:
How does it feel to be home, Hollow?

HOLLOW QUINN:
England is so removed from the war. It feels like walking out of a desert that no one comes back from. The metal of the bed is cold. Everything smells wrong. There's no sand. I dressed in pink.

God, I made a huge mistake coming back here.

Hollow sat at her computer desk. Everything in the room had been put back exactly how it was before she'd packed it into boxes. Even her computer was laid out like five months in Afghanistan was just waking up from a bad dream. More out of habit than anything, Hollow fired up her computer and downloaded a game from the Cloud. She'd meant to delete it on the day she left for boot camp, but when the time came, she'd just deleted all the windows and doors instead. The virtual town had run online for months, and no way for any of the inhabitants to escape from their own houses. A handful had made it out alive; some had tried to help the others. From a population of ninety-nine, there were seventeen civilians left. Hollow built them a luxury swimming pool so they could get washed, and then deleted all the ladders.

Late in the afternoon, Gemma suggested they go to the supermarket. She was walking tall, and all the time looking around for people she knew. Hollow wore the pink hoodie pulled tight around her face and walked like she was ten years too old for the world.

Ezra turned up at the front door the next day. It wasn't as if Hollow was surprised. She was chuffed in a way, but mostly she was terrified. She knew that Ezra would arrive upstairs and see how she'd moved her bed so she was facing the door now. How she sat at the front of the bus now. How she sat at the front in the cinema now. How she got up early now so she could be outside when Rey's alarm went off. How aircraft freaked her out, how phone calls freaked her out, how fireworks freaked her out, how she kept her earbuds turned loud enough to hear from a metre away. And Ezra would know exactly what it all meant, just like Hollow knew what it all meant.

Hollow paced her way through Gemma's gushing greeting, introductions and cheerful calls to come downstairs. Punching her legs until they felt numb. By the time Ezra reached her bedroom, Hollow was as close to composed as she could be, considering it was all a complete forgery.

'Hey,' Ezra said.

'Since when did you knock?'

'Since your mum got a new front door, a new hallway, new dogs and a new man. Is she doing a midlife or something?'

'Probably,' Hollow said.

'The new man seems nice.'

'Yeah, he's okay.'

It was hard for both of them, and neither of them knowing how to let the truth of that soften into affection.

'You moved your bed,' Ezra said.

357

'Gemma moved it.'

'Oh, that's a bit…'

'You know what she's like for watching makeover shows.'

Ezra sat down on the edge of Hollow's bed. 'It feels weird this way around. Like you're ready to run.'

'Yeah? I didn't take much notice.'

'So…' Ezra said. 'I see you do D&D now.'

'Right.'

'Not that I've been on at you to try it for years. Tiefling are a great race, I had you down as Tiefling too.' Ezra grinned. 'And since you're about to ask, I'm a Druid, Wood Elf, of course.'

'I'm not talking D&D with you.'

'Give it time.' Ezra looked around the room. 'Oh, I got a GiFT at Fabian Evirate House.'

'Right,' Hollow said, 'all the care homes were full then?'

'They offered me a job there.'

'Congrats.'

'Except, I haven't decided if I'll take it yet,' Ezra said. 'What with uni and…'

'Being a dork.'

Ezra choked a laugh. 'What the actual are you doing on TV, H?'

'I'm not allowed to say anything about *WØLF*.'

'Yeah,' Ezra said. 'I got scanned for wires and had to sign three Plug Productions agreements before they let me through the filming enclosure.'

'Did you read them?'

'I actually don't miss you,' Ezra said, leaning closer but not getting a purchase. 'I mean, I got your posters, which was hard to get my head around. They don't stink of cigarettes and they're less awkward to get on with. It's an improvement, if anything.'

'That's not weird.'

'Fine.' Ezra puffed it out. 'I didn't want to get all emosh on you, but it's hard watching you go through all that stuff.

Watching what happened with Fish. Watching you talk about being a monster. Seeing it all happening like I'm right there with you, except I'm not right there with you.'

'Wow, you really didn't read the Plug agreements.'

'I'm not having a go.' Ezra shrugged. 'I just wanted to tell you that I wish I'd been a better friend.'

Sunlight cut the room in half. Wisteria curled at the corner of the window. A dragonfly was beating against the glass. Hollow stood up and closed the blind. 'Fabian Evirate House. You get free passes?'

'Yeah, sure, of course.' Ezra pulled a smile from somewhere. 'Or I can give you a guided, if you want.'

'I meant for Gemma and Rey.' Hollow looked at her phone. 'Only, I have to go out in a minute.'

'Is this us now?' Ezra said. 'Finding ways to avoid each other?'

'It's like a studio therapy thing, I'm contracted to do it.'

'Give me some credit, H. Even Joanie would spot that for a lie.'

'Joanie is on TV, Ez. Just like Mika is on TV and The Hubert is on TV, and Jar is on TV and I'm…' Hollow chewed at her lip. 'Don't act like you know him.'

'I know you, though,' Ezra said.

'It's okay, you're off the pact hook.' Hollow snatched another look at her phone. 'Shit, I have to go.'

'What if I don't want to be off the pact hook?'

Hollow shrugged. 'You're off anyway.'

'When do you go back?'

'Yeah, I'm not allowed to tell you that.'

Ezra watched Hollow scuffling around the bedroom, picking stuff up, preparing for an appointment they both knew was fake. 'I'll catch up with you before you leave, right? I can bring the complimentary tickets over tomorrow, after work, if that's okay.'

'Yeah, I'll message you.'

359

Ezra looked down, running a finger over the scar they shared. 'My mums were beyond furious when I got this. I didn't even try to lie about it. I was proud of what we'd done.'

'Good for you.'

'Don't be like this, H.'

'What do you want from me?'

Ezra glanced up then. 'I've got some stuff going on. Stuff that I really need a friend for, if you're still available in that capacity.'

'Just take the fucking job, Ez.'

'No, it's not about the job,' Ezra said. 'It's about a secret.'

'You want to tell me a secret?'

'I want to...'

'If you want to tell someone a secret,' Hollow said, 'then it's not a secret, it's a gossip.'

'Say there was this huge secret, at Fabian Evirate House. And they called it the Sebastian Incident, and everyone got changed by it. Except they wouldn't say what happened, not even Emporia, and she spills everything. How would you even keep hold of a secret like that, for example?'

'You don't keep hold of it,' Hollow said. 'A secret is like the wind.'

'Right, because it destroys things.'

Hollow sighed. 'You can't see the wind, but you can see the shape of it in all the things it touches. If you're protecting a secret, how it disturbs you is what you need to keep hold of.'

'Wow, I can actually see how that would work.'

Hollow nodded Ezra towards the door. 'Glad to be of assistance.'

'Kind of assistance. Not completely, though.' Ezra hesitated. 'Can we talk about it later?'

'I'm out later,' Hollow said.

That evening, Gemma worked herself into a screaming frenzy about whether watching *WØLF* was an infringement of the temporary contract she'd signed. Rey went to the OB van and asked if it was okay. Hollow refused to watch it.

SMART SLATE

Whiskey-Zero-One-Foxtrot/s5e12/OB REMI IP link PP confirm: EFP single crew - *Bassie*
Producer: *Elspeth Hart*
EXT. GBR. FAREHAM – DAY

Scene: *Hollow Quinn* spends her last day in the UK before she heads back to Camp Bastion. Walking with *Rey Badigar*. Hollow has offered to help him clear the garden. Single crew camera stays with them – continuous

ITM SCENE
COMMENTARY
GEMMA QUINN:
She's a bit odd, like with the tennis ball. I mean, I keep the dogs in the conservatory now, but that's just having a different person staying here. It's great to have her back, though. She looks thinner.

BASSIE, CREW:
Do you think Hollow resents you living here, Rey?

REY BADIGAR:
Yes, of course. It would be strange if she didn't. But I don't think it's just me being here. My grandad was never the same after Northern Ireland. Everything that wasn't life or death was mundane.

Hollow and Rey stood looking around the neat-as-a-pin garden, less of a family, more of a mutual association. Hollow was doing her best to be amicable; Rey was doing a grand job of containing his happiness when Hollow wanted to spend time with him.

'As you can see, I like gardening,' he said. 'Beyond a lawn trim, there's not much that needs doing out here. Building a house is great, but gardens are better for growing themselves on what you build.'

'I thought I could cut that cherry tree back,' Hollow said. 'It's grown out the top and the roots will be getting too big.'

'Good call, I've got some heavy-duty branch cutters in the shed.'

'I quite like using a hand saw,' Hollow said. 'Does Gemma still have that fire bin to burn the rubbish in?'

'We'll take it up the tip in my van.'

'A fire is better, though,' Hollow said. 'We could maybe get some marshmallows and stuff.'

'Last supper?'

Hollow shrugged. 'I guess.'

'Leave it with me,' Rey said. Off to the garden centre and back with a family-size firepit before Hollow had finished cutting back the cherry tree.

As a couple, Gemma and Rey were tolerable, likable even. They toasted marshmallows, wrote their names with sparklers, told childish ghost stories, and went inside at nine o'clock to avoid upsetting the neighbours. Hollow waved them off, claiming one last smoke for the road. When their bedroom light went out, she fetched the cushion that leaked feathers from the sofa in the lounge, cut a small hole in the seam and pulled a feather free. She took it back to the firepit and held it in the smoke for a while, before letting the warm air take it. A delicate, inconsequential thing; bound to the fire but not consumed by it. Hollow smiled, touching the tip of her finger to the feather, not enough to set it free, just enough to upset the balance and drop it into the embers below. It burned blue, bright and complete in its ending. This time, Hollow took no care with the cushion, ripping it open and throwing handful after handful of the white feathers into the fire. Watching the blue flames die away. When the cushion was empty, she burned the cover. Lighting any remnants with a match until there was only ash left behind.

ITM SCENE
COMMENTARY
HOLLOW QUINN:
It's weird. I couldn't work out why England felt so different, and I'm not talking about the little things like Rey being here, I'm talking about England. England is the same, but it feels completely different. Then I figured out that it's me. I'm what's different.

I'm possessing my old life like a demon. Every day after the day before, waiting to be exorcised back to hell.

BASSIE, CREW:
So the fire represents hell?

HOLLOW QUINN:
Shit, Bassie, I wish I'd thought of that. That would have been something profound, eh? Boringly, the fire was a necessity, not a metaphor.

I needed the fire because I had to know I could destroy it, if I wanted to.

BASSIE, CREW:
The cushion?

HOLLOW QUINN:
The only feather I didn't burn.

29

Welcome to the ant nest

In war, it didn't take long to become an old soldier. Hollow caught the next flight to Cyprus. All the other troops were straight from boot camp, talking in groups and keeping their distance out of respect for more than her celebrity status. One of them was sharing a picture of a camel spider like it was a fixed moment in every new deployment and the rest of the world just moved around it. At Bagram, she was put on a transport flight to Camp Bastion along with a dozen fresh-faced soldiers and the same transfer sergeant. They sat in stiff rows. Rifles loaded. Gawks on. Chameleon to factory mode, matt and dark against the shiny interior of the Mi-8 helicopter, and the benzidine strips changing through to indigo. As they approached Camp Bastion, the transfer sergeant stood up, steadying herself on the rigging as the helicopter banked and prepared to land.

'Each and every one of you needs to be aware that you are about to enter a white zone. Gloves and gawks to desert setting. Chameleon on. Weapons ready. Await the order to disembark.'

Hollow watched the soldiers like she was watching herself arrive in Afghanistan a few months ago. It was hard to remember the first-year uni student who'd been scared of using the tube. She knew how unprepared they were, and she knew there was nothing she could say that would prepare them. As the sand settled, she stayed inside the Mi-8 with the transfer sergeant, letting the others run to the truck, letting the heat take her like some kind of fucked-up compensation.

'Good to be home?' the transfer sergeant said.

'Apparently so, Sergeant.'

'Afghanistan. It's a bastard of a country, but there's something here that gets under your skin.'

'Camel spiders.'

The transfer sergeant slapped Hollow on the back, still roaring with laughter as she reached the DAF lorry. 'Welcome to Helmand,' she bellowed, pushing through the sweat-soaked soldiers, climbing up the iron squares to the gun perched on top of the cab. 'Minds closed. Eyes open. Weapons ready.'

SMART SLATE

Whiskey-Zero-One-Foxtrot/s5e14/REMI IP link PP confirm: EFP rig/crew
Producer: *Elspeth Hart*
EXT. AFG. CAMP BASTION – DAY

Scene: *Hollow Quinn* returns to Camp Bastion. She stops at the replica Afghan village and watches the new soldiers settle in. Fixed rig and crew cameras stay with Hollow – continuous

Hollow bought a glass of kahwa tea from one of the vendors and sat by the stall, watching the new arrivals as they opened their shipping container and arranged themselves into teams to get the tents up. The weather was already turning mild enough to figure it all out without asking for help. Hollow left her glass upturned and accepted a second tea along with a saucer of sugar lumps to hold in her mouth as she drank it.

The local vendors honour the Bastion soldiers like they honour visitors in their own homes. They refill your glass until you turn it over. It doesn't matter where you've been or what you've had to deal with, there's something about knowing you're coming back to that, it gets you through.

When the new arrivals lit their cooking stove, Hollow turned her glass over and went to the command centre to report for duty. Sampson was cold, older, curt with her instructions to get a haircut and pick up her kit. She also informed Hollow that Joanie had been transferred to Unit Three, and there was no room left for appeal.

Whatever Hollow had expected of Joanie, she wasn't prepared for the change in him. She'd almost walked past before she realised that the nondescript soldier standing outside the *WØLF* bunkhouse was her friend.

'Joan? Shit, I didn't see you there.'

'Sampson said you were back.'

'You look…different.'

'You don't,' he said.

'It was out of my control.' Hollow shrugged, trying to find the old Joanie under the plaster of cold responses. 'Captain Dupont ordered me to go home, and the next flight out was already loading. I didn't even have time to say goodbye.'

'Hubert Frank got taken.'

'Taken?'

'Three to a unit,' Joanie said. 'Except there were only two of them left to call out. Jar is really cut up.'

'What do you want me to say?'

'Nothing, there's nothing to say.'

'You know Fish would fucking tear you apart if she saw you like this.'

'Fish is gone and I'm still here.' Joanie looked at her then. 'We have a pickup. Lynx transport. Multiple casualties. Sampson's setting up the truck to give you time to get yourself into gear. Chameleon, breathers, gawks and gloves. Get what you need and meet us at dispatch.'

'It was out of my control, Joan.'

'Whatever.' Joanie turned away.

'I'm not lying,' she said. But Hollow used lies like a recreational drug, and neither of them wasted time believing it.

They arrived into a squalling mess of activity around the dispatch site. Their body mics were synced live, but the crew cameras were lost in the bustle and there was no time for them to catch up. If Camp Bastion had felt like a war fort before, it was nothing compared to this.

Sampson was waiting by the field ambulance. 'Lynx transport. Multiple casualties confirmed. P3 priority. You up to this, Quinn?'

'Yes, Lieutenant.'

'We won't get long, if I give the order, we pull out,' Sampson said. 'Anyone not in the truck gets left behind.'

Hollow turned to Joanie. 'What the hell happened while I was away?'

'The Mandolin happened,' Sampson yelled, jumping into the driver's seat and firing up the truck. Waiting on clearance from dispatch like they had sixty seconds to live.

Hollow climbed in the back next to Joanie, sitting between the stretchers as best she could. 'Since when did P3 take priority?'

'Since we can patch them up and send them back out.'

'You're kidding?'

'Welcome to the ant nest,' Joanie said.

'Shit, Joan.'

'ETA fifteen minutes,' Sampson called from the front of the truck. 'Smoke on the horizon.'

The call had come in from a lorry carrying Afghan refugees. They'd stopped when they saw the smoke and stayed to drag five soldiers and a civilian clear. Dangerously close to enemy lines and no one much to admire their courage. By the time Hollow's unit arrived, the surrounding desert was on fire.

Sampson was out of the truck before the engine faded. 'Magrath, get those Afghans out of here!'

Joanie shoved Hollow out of the way, shouting as loud as Sampson. 'All of you, back in the truck, now!'

Hollow held her rifle tight to her chest, too out of the loop to think straight.

'Quinn,' Sampson yelled, 'on me!'

There was enough twisted metal left to be a joke about a helicopter. Fire had turned it inside out, but the clues were still there. Sampson reached the first of the soldiers a full half-minute before Hollow, not stopping long enough for her to catch up. 'Pilot and co-pilot are P1. Flight engineer is near enough P2 to make the trip.' She rounded on the smoke. 'Find the civilian. If they're not mobile, leave them.'

Hollow could make out two figures in the smoke, Joanie was helping someone to stand. 'Magrath has the civilian.'

'I'll check the others. Get the stretchers from the truck.'

'Yes, Lieutenant.'

'Quick about it,' Sampson yelled. 'We don't have much time.'

The stretchers were heavy, uncontrolled and catching on the rigging. By the time Hollow was done, Sampson had dragged two of the soldiers halfway back. Behind her, Joanie was coughing, supporting the civilian. Hollow threw the stretchers down, scrabbling to help Sampson. 'We should move the others away from the smoke, Lieutenant.'

'Leave them.'

'They'll die.'

'Check your ozone strips,' Sampson said, pushing ahead of Hollow, 'if we're not gone in two minutes, we're all dead.'

Hollow's strips were flicking close enough to white to know what Sampson had said was true. 'Is this a scam!' she yelled. 'Is this a scam, Lieutenant!' But Sampson was too far away to hear her. Hollow grabbed the other soldier and hauled him to his feet. By the time she reached the ambulance, it was already moving. Joanie took the soldier from Hollow and then hauled her inside by the hand or she would've been left behind. There wasn't even time to find a steady foothold as the truck hit the desert like every nightmare in hell was behind it. The civilian had curled up close to the cab, turned away from the horror and wrapped in a cookie-dough jacket. The wounded soldiers were thrown around where they dropped. There was blood everywhere. Too much to tell who it belonged to. Hollow scrabbled to stay on her feet. 'What do you need, Joan?'

'Pressure bandages.' Joanie was leant over the nearest soldier, cutting his uniform open and throwing saline to clear the blood. 'Blunt force to chest and abdomen. Find a way to keep him immobilised. I'll check the other one.'

The soldier was awake, eyes open and death quiet. Any life left in him was concentrated on staying alive. 'You're okay now,' Hollow said, clearing the soot from his cheek. 'We're Medivac, you're gonna be okay.'

'Immobilised, Hollow.'

Whoever Joanie had once been, he was all Medivac now. Hollow grabbed a blanket and rolled it to fit behind the soldier, bracing her foot against a stretcher rail to stop herself from sliding around. Sampson had changed too. It wasn't just that she was colder; she was harder, more part of the machinery of war. And the wedding ring she'd refused to take off, even when her hand got infected, was gone.

'Grab me a morphine tube,' Joanie said, 'and where are those pressure bandages?'

Hollow stared at the medical kit bolted to the bulkhead; her hands were shaking. Joanie had said she looked the same, but she wasn't the same.

SMART SLATE

Whiskey-Zero-One-Foxtrot/s5e14/REMI IP link PP confirm: EFP crew/IGH remote
Producer: *Elspeth Hart*
EXT. AFG. CAMP BASTION – DAY

Scene: *Hollow Quinn, Joanie Magrath, 2LT Felicity Sampson* return to Camp Bastion. IGH stays with arial shots. Crew cameras commence on Sampson as she climbs out of the truck – continuous

They reached Camp Bastion behind the news that they were coming. Somewhere in the time Hollow had been away, bringing three in alive had turned into something to celebrate. Sampson rose like a superstar to the top of the field ambulance, stamping a foot on the roof, crossing her arms with the first roar, tongue out, fists slapping her legs, Māori style. And every one of the crowd a mirror to her. The collective call of the *haka*, a challenge to the enemy. Be afraid, be very afraid. They brought the paintbrush through like a trophy, the same red paint in stripes on their faces. And Sampson drawing an AT symbol on top of the cab. The address of humanity: @earth. Sampson, decent, just-out-of-the-academy Sampson, standing tall as a mountain. 'Put that in your search engine, you bastards. If you think we're going down easy, you've got another think coming.'

Hollow looked around for Joanie, but he was gone.

'*Omne trium perfectum,*' Jar said, sliding in closer than

usual. His face all cuts and bruises, left arm in a sling, plaster cast from shoulder to wrist. 'You got to admit, the army loves itself a three.'

'Shit, Jar.'

'Everyone thinks they're too good for mob mentality.' Jar took a leisurely look around the jubilant crowd. 'But mob mentality doesn't care what you think you're too good for.'

'Joan said you were cut up.'

'And you thought he meant about Hubert Frank?' Jar puffed a laugh of sorts. 'You and every armchair shrink going. You'd think he was employee of the month the way people have been talking about him. The Hubert was a dickhead. We should be celebrating his dickheadedness, not sensitively weeping like we lost us a fucking hero.'

'Sorry, for not being here.'

'We don't get to control these things, kid.' Jar nodded towards the hexagonal block of hydrogen fuel tanks. 'Fancy a smoke?'

They didn't talk much while they were walking, falling into step with each other and not much noticing it.

ITM SCENE
COMMENTARY
MIKA KAMARI:
The fuel tanks are reactive and strictly off limits unless you have the right authorisation. There aren't any signs to prohibit smoking near them because only someone with a death wish would be stupid enough to light a match around the hydrogen tanks. Jar takes the lack of a sign as a green light to smoke there. Honestly, I'm not stopping him.

JAR:
Omne trium perfectum. Everything that comes in threes is perfect. One time, I asked my old drill

sergeant why it's always three in the army. He just said three was a good number for drill patterns.

'Nineteen, eh?' Jar lit Hollow's cigarette from his. 'Sometimes, I wonder who I was when I was nineteen. A damn sight more annoying than I am now, I'd imagine. And if I could go back, you know what advice I'd give myself?'

'Don't get the dick tattoo?'

ITM SCENE
COMMENTARY
JAR:
In case she was thinking of sloping off on the pretence of needing a nap, she was smoke-screening the wrong person. Private Hollow Quinn was gonna listen to everything that happened to me and The Hubert out there, because she'll hear it anyway, and at least this way I'm telling it.

PRODUCER:
You think someone else would tell a different story?

JAR:
Different agenda, that's all. Mika wriggled a slot with the counsellors to moan about me, which left Hubert Frank to cover for him. Seems I saved Mika's life twice now, not an easy thing to wake up to every morning. I told him, the way things are going, it'll be just me and him left fighting the war.

PRODUCER:
Do you think Hollow sees herself in you?
JAR:

I see her in me, and that's reason enough for both of us to run.

Jar leant against a fuel tank, settling back into the story. 'Me and The Hubert, we're down at the gym when we get the call. Two Taliban snipers. P1. We're an officer down, but it's a standard return and no one else left to take it. Dispatch tells us to get into kit and wait on orders, what with the weather dropping and no hurry now on a P1. But you know me and the Taliban, I couldn't be thinking about them, left out there, all up close to dying and winning something over on me.'

'I grok you.'

'Yeah, no doubt,' Jar said. Cigarette ash fell on his sling as he talked, but he didn't shake it off. 'We pull up and it's all quiet. Two Taliban laid out neat and tidy like they went to sleep. And you know how The Hubert is, he goes dicking through the war like there's a fucking respawn point built into every scene. He's not bothering to follow protocol, not noticing that the whole area is a landmine zone.'

'Shit.'

'You're telling me,' Jar said. 'One wrong step and he's windscreen art.'

'That was down to him.'

'Better if he'd taken the step,' Jar said. 'Still, there was no knowing that at the time or I'd have kept my gob shut. As it was, I leap out the truck yelling for him to stand still. And The Hubert goes freezing mid-step, face all full up figuring out what he's got himself into. Meanwhile, I'm there, trying to keep a lid on my own adrenalin, trying to keep it calm, telling him to step back in his own footsteps before the wind takes them. Except, the wind doesn't take his footsteps, it opens them up, all the way back to the truck and back beyond where we came. Pressure mine on pressure mine as far as the eye could see.'

'You drove into it?'

'Never in the whole of my life have I seen anything like that minefield. Hundreds of them, all the way back to the opium fields. I stand there, stiller than the P1 pickups we came to get. And The Hubert, stepping back into each footstep, one gust of wind away from oblivion.' Jar took a long drag, tapping his cigarette into his left hand like it was an ashtray. 'Eventually, The Hubert makes it to the truck, and we're both dripping with relief, thinking we can radio it all in. Then one of the mines goes off. Just goes off. Poooof. No reason, no sense to it. Bits of shrapnel dropping around, any moment setting off a chain reaction we got no chance to run away from.'

'Crap.'

'The Hubert, he was fit to panic, and me not far behind. I shove him in the truck, slam it into reverse and take us out down the same tracks we came in on. We got close too, as close as thinking we might just make it out alive when one of the front tyres clipped a mine. Next thing, I'm waking up in a fox hole with my arm bending the wrong way and The Hubert all up in my face, screaming at me to wake up.' Jar drew his cigarette close to the filter. 'And there we are, the two of us. Looking at each other. Laughing like we just did something fucking outstanding.'

'But you were both okay?'

'Sure as the sun burns my arse. The truck was wrecked. We didn't have much of a plan beyond The Hubert walking back here, and that's still a death walk even with the heat dropping. What we needed was a miracle, and, right on cue, along comes the Pathfinders. I figured they must have seen the smoke from the explosions. A goddamn bit of luck for us they were marking a drop site that close to the opium fields.' Jar was shaking his head, stubbing the cigarette out in the palm of his hand. 'A goddamn bit of luck, that's what I figured. Luck like us driving that deep in without clipping a mine, luck like us being thrown clear right on the edge of a minefield, luck like us being dumped in a fox hole and only a busted arm to show for it. But it made sense. It all made so much sense.' Jar was staring at the red burn mark on his hand. He dropped the cigarette butt and screwed it into the sand with his boot. 'Light us another, will you.'

'So you can burn your hand again?'

Jar snatched Hollow's cigarette, twisting it in his fingers. 'I should get myself another addiction. The ones I got don't seem to be killing me quick enough.'

'You can't wish yourself into dying,' Hollow said.

'Audie Murphy slept with a loaded gun under his pillow,' Jar said. 'All that beautiful, creative life in him, and he wasn't anywhere except for war.'

'That why you took his name?'

'Jar Audie Murphy Jar,' Jar said. 'That's JAM Jar on all the forms.'

Hollow scuffed her foot through the sand. 'I didn't think the Pathfinders came this far down?'

'Right enough.' Jar drew what he could from the spent cigarette, spitting the rest towards the fuel tanks. 'The army don't go wasting what's left of the Pathfinders on Helmand. But stuck in that fox hole with my arm busted up, I'm not looking for anything more complicated than morphine and a soft bed. So there I am, trying not to blub like a relieved baby, looking sideways at The Hubert, because he's suddenly freaking out. Then this Pathfinder, he leans down into the fox hole and grabs hold of The Hubert by the straps to pull him out. And hey, The Hubert, he puts up a real good fight, punching and screaming that the ozone strips are white. Punching and screaming while I sit in the fox hole, waiting for the Pathfinder to come back for me, looking and looking at how coalmine black my strips are.' Jar stuck his thumb into the burn. 'Those strips ain't been black since we landed in this godforsaken country.'

'It was a scam?'

'I'm guessing the landmine we hit was real,' Jar said. 'The rest ain't one way or another now. Still, it don't bear thinking about, The Hubert being taken alive like that.'

'What will the Mandolin do to him?'

'We'll find him.' Jar was flexing his arm in the sling. 'Soon as I'm fit for duty, we'll find him.'

Hollow took her time, lighting two more cigarettes and letting the smoke curl between them. 'Why did you come back here, Jar?'

'Someone had to look after all the Gen-Z.'

Hollow shook her head. 'Do you wish it'd been you instead of Hubert Frank?'

'Hell, no. The Hubert's a crap soldier. If they took me, we'd all be screwed.'

'I've seen you in the shower.' Hollow dropped her cigarette, watching it glow on the sand. 'If the Mandolin took you, they'd be the ones screwed.'

Jar choked on laughter, coarse and medicinal, more than enough to get them noticed. 'I'm not disagreeing with you there, kid.'

'I'd better report in,' Hollow said. 'It's no good leaving Sampson to clean up the ambulance.'

'How was home?'

'Just what I needed. Did you see where Joanie went?'

'Last I saw, he was headed to the hospital.'

'Great, thanks.'

'Not anywhere except for war,' Jar said. 'It ain't about what gets left behind on the battlefield, it's what comes back with you, that's the problem. I've lost more friends to suicide than service, but sat in that foxhole, I got to figuring it's not the ones who go mad that need a shrink, it's the ones who don't go mad. Made me appreciate that I got the sort of mind that goes mad.'

'No one says mad any more. It's a psychological injury.'

Hollow was further away now, almost out of the conversation. 'And have your hand looked at, Jar, before it turns septic.'

'You ever hear of the Order of the White Feather?'

'Tell me next time.'

Jar leant against a fuel tank. 'First World War, Admiral Charles Penrose Fitzgerald started the White Feather Brigade. Young women walking around, pinning white feathers to any men not in uniform. A lot of those men, they were in reserved occupations, and some of them felt so ashamed they enlisted. They might have ditched the white feathers, but they carried the shame of cowardice around with them their whole lives.'

'And your point is?'

'Someone give you a white feather, Hollow?'

'Yeah, right.' Hollow shrugged, laughing it off. 'We have a chicken, Jar. My mum rescued it when it fell off the back of a slaughter lorry. Bloody thing was bald to its skin, but the feathers grew back after a few weeks. We keep it in the back garden, and every afternoon it comes strolling in the front gate. Turns out it has a walk through the whole housing estate. People leave scraps out and everything. I miss that stupid bird.'

'You want to know why I carry Audie Murphy's name around?' Jar was nodding along, tapping his heel against the fuel tank. 'I carry it because he got left behind on the battlefield, and I'm Medivac. I had to bring him home.'

'Thanks for the pep talk.' Hollow threw a mock salute and headed towards the hospital.

ITM SCENE
COMMENTARY
HOLLOW QUINN:
Jar thinks he's helping me. It's fine, if it gets him through the bad days, I'm not stopping him.

PRODUCER:
We can pin ourselves with white feathers, Hollow.

HOLLOW QUINN:
Cowardice is what I need, Elspeth. A cowardly monster stays hiding under the bed.

JAR:
She's a good kid. Some days, I remember why I came back here.

PRODUCER:
The partial mobilisation recalled all regular reservists, Jar. You were under oath to come back here.

JAR:
You're fucking telling me. I was only in it for the money.

If Hollow had expected to find more shipping containers extending the hospital, she was wrong. Nothing much had changed except for fewer injured people and more empty beds. She stopped a medic. 'I'm looking for Private Magrath. He brought in a civilian.'

'Today?'

'Yeah, like an hour ago.'

The medic shook her head. 'Joanie hasn't been in today, not that I've noticed.'

'The Lynx crash?'

'Two soldiers, no civilian. Try the morgue.'

In contrast to the hospital, the morgue had extended a dozen refrigerated units out beyond the latrine block and back on itself. Hollow tapped on the door and crept inside.

'Over there, on the left.'

'Captain, I'm looking for a civilian fatality. It would have been around an hour ago. The Lynx crash.'

'No civilians today.' The doctor didn't look up. 'Did you try the hospital?'

'They sent me here, Captain.'

'It takes time for the system to catch up.' The doctor finally looked at Hollow. 'Quinn, is it?'

'Yes, Captain.'

'I'm sorry, Quinn, there's no easy identification process for civilians. As you know, the best we can hope for is to put the right bits back together.'

'They were alive when they arrived here, Captain.' Hollow kept her eyes fixed on the doctor. 'Private Magrath gave them a jacket. They might look like a soldier.'

'No bodies without QRID in today, complete or otherwise. Most civilians are already halfway across the planet if they have any sense. By all means, check for yourself, but unless this civilian of yours has military ID, there's no point in putting yourself through it. You might try the hospital again. They could be lost in the system.'

'Thank you, Captain.'

Hollow went to leave, scooting back to hold the door for a couple of hospital personnel carrying a stretcher.

The doctor lifted the sheet. 'Yours?'

He looked sweet, young enough to be at school, but there were too many bullet holes in his chest for it to be right. 'No, Captain.'

'We'll take that as a victory, eh, Quinn,' the doctor said. 'Either of you chaps seen Private Magrath today?'

'He was in Heroes half an hour ago.'

'Thank you, Captain,' Hollow said. 'Looks like he's giving me the runaround.'

The ISO door didn't have much time to shut before the next body. Hollow pulled out another cigarette and headed towards

Heroes bar, taking the long route to avoid meeting Jar again. By the time she got there, Joanie was gone.

ITM SCENE
COMMENTARY
HOLLOW QUINN:
I don't know if he's deliberately avoiding me or winding down after the pickup. Something's off with him. It's probably to do with losing Fish, but that's not my problem to solve.

PRODUCER:
How are you handling being back here?

HOLLOW QUINN:
Okay, I think. It feels familiar. Like I grew up here.

I suppose I have grown up here when you think about it. And I was sitting in the truck watching the desert, thinking about England. England feels a million miles away, it's another planet almost. Yeah, another planet, that's it.

PRODUCER:
You said you felt relieved when you got to England. What changed?

HOLLOW QUINN:
Yeah, well, it's no secret that Gemma never loved me. Don't get me wrong, I'm not judging her for that. In a messed-up kind of way, it was fine, because after the rape, Gemma couldn't love anything. But now, there's the dogs, and there's Rey. And Gemma, who can't love anything, she loves them.

It's hard, not to take something like that personally.

PRODUCER:
Rape is a haunting word, Hollow.

HOLLOW QUINN:
He was a PTI corporal. The police said she should
have met him in a public space. He claimed consent.
The army took his side of the story to be the truth.
There's nothing much more to say. And she kept the
baby; most people wouldn't have kept the baby. That's
something, I suppose.

PRODUCER:
The baby?

HOLLOW QUINN:
And I'm nothing like Gemma, so I guess that makes
me like him, right?

Hollow got undressed, left the body mic on her bunk and
walked to the showers without taking a towel. She ran the water
hot enough to steam up the cameras, taking her time with
washing off the smoke. She even stood looking into the mirror
for a while, holding her hand against the glass, and long enough
about it to be convincing. Then she got dressed and went back to
work. An ordinary soldier cleaning up the field ambulance after
a brutal and bloody return. When she finished, she sat on the
tailgate and lit a cigarette, the doors thrown wide open to dry
the disinfectant. Ten minutes later, Joanie turned up. He didn't
even make an excuse.
    'You on mic?' Hollow said.
    'No. You?'
    'Ditched. Wanna catch me up?'

'On what?' Joanie said.

'I went looking for you at the hospital.'

'Yeah, they said.'

'And the morgue.' Hollow looked around the compound. 'And Heroes.'

'So I get a truancy letter to my mum now?'

'Hey, cut the backsnap,' Hollow said. 'I was only looking for you.'

'Because?'

'Maybe I just wanted some company.' Hollow turned the cigarette in her fingers. 'Not to mention the fact that no one remembers the civilian we brought back from the Lynx crash today.'

Joanie shrugged. 'I think they went home.'

'They went home?'

'The airfield is running flights night and day,' Joanie said. 'They probably got a last-minute seat or something.'

'Jar said you took them to the hospital.'

Joanie turned away. 'They were completely overrun at the hospital, so I took the civilian straight to dispatch. There's no big secret, Hollow, just good old boring reality.'

'Overrun?' Hollow laughed. 'You didn't go to the hospital, Joan.'

Joanie rubbed both hands into his eyes. 'How did you manage to ditch the body mic anyway?'

'I fed Elspeth something juicy,' Hollow said. 'She'll be chewing on it for a while.'

'I lost mine at the crash site. Guess I should report it before they come looking for me.'

'What's going on, Joan?'

'Nothing.'

'Nothing?'

Joanie crumpled then, all the way back to the sweet kid she'd first met. 'I took the civilian to dispatch.'

Hollow budged over so Joanie could sit on the tailgate. 'Alma told me about the rabbit skin.'

'That was confidential.'

'So you made a deal with a rabbit to protect someone you love.' Hollow offered Joanie a cigarette. 'The rest of us ate it. No one's claiming any moral high ground in that situation.'

'Correction, I *used* a rabbit to protect someone I love.' Joanie shooed the cigarette away. 'I knelt by a long barrow, I used a rabbit to make a bargain, and then I killed it. I guess even Almanac Johansson couldn't find any merit in protecting that little secret.'

'Not a bargain, a pact,' Hollow said. 'And the power of a pact lies in not breaking it.'

'I didn't break it.'

'But it got broken, right? So you're in the clear.'

Joanie paused. 'Not completely.'

'Fish is dead, how is that not completely?'

Joanie looked at Hollow, full-on intense. 'You can't tell anyone.'

'I knew it, Fish got kicked out of hell for talking!' Hollow laughed, but it didn't catch fire.

'I'm serious, you can't tell anyone.' Joanie shot a look around, leaning in, close enough to breathe Hollow's smoke. 'Promise me, or we let this drop.'

'Joan,' Hollow spoke as softly as she could without sounding like a condescending dick, 'ozone levels were spiking at the crash site. It's always a good idea to see the medic after exposure, just to make sure you're all right.'

Joanie choked. 'You think I'm hawking a psych scam?'

'Just to check out your lungs and stuff.'

'Don't mistake me for who I was before you went away.'

'Fine,' Hollow said, 'I promise I won't tell anyone.'

'You have to promise on something you care about.'

'Shit...' Hollow stared up at the metal roof of the field ambulance. 'Now you're asking something.'

'Promise on my life.'

'What?'

'That's the deal.'

'Okay,' Hollow said, 'I promise, on your life, that I won't tell anyone.'

'And again without your fingers crossed.'

Hollow held her hands up. 'Joanie Magrath, I promise on your life that I will punch you in the fucking face if you don't tell me what's going on here.'

Joanie almost grinned. 'Not now, later, when the camp's asleep. We can go then.'

'So the civilian didn't get the transport out?'

Joanie shook his head, looking down at his boots. 'I didn't know what else to do, Hollow.'

'Where did you take them?'

'The ISO where all the camel spiders hang out.'

'Jesus,' Hollow said, 'the army fumigated that a hundred times.'

Joanie jumped down from the tailgate. 'Tell that to the camel spiders.'

'Any injuries I should not know about?' Hollow jumped down next to him. 'Did they get checked out?'

'Technically...' Joanie squirmed his way through an inner judgement call. 'Superficial head injury, some deep layer bruising to the lower legs, a couple of broken ribs. Stage two dehydration. Nothing that can't be fixed with a standard medical field kit.'

'You're kidding me?' Hollow paced a circle. 'We can't just go randomly treating civilians, Joan. Especially ones being carried in a military transport. Do you know how much trouble we can get in?'

'Yep,' he said. Like he absolutely knew what it meant for him and for Hollow, and didn't care.

'I'm only agreeing to this because you're my friend.'

'I don't need a friend,' Joanie said. 'What I need is a liar.'

'Right,' Hollow said. 'That's probably easier.'

'We need to keep this shut down tight, Hollow. I'll come to your bunk around midnight. Meanwhile, we just act like it's any other normal day. Maybe we could have a full-on domestic about me hiding from you. And you're pissed off because you're transferring your guilt about Fish onto me. The crew will be all over it and not looking where we don't want them to look.'

'Guess I'm bringing the coleslaw then,' Hollow said.

SMART SLATE

Whiskey-Zero-One-Foxtrot/s5e14/ REMI IP link PP confirm: EFP rig/crew/IGH remote
Producer: *Elspeth Hart*
INT. AFG. CAMP BASTION – DAY

Scene: *Hollow Quinn* and *Joanie Magrath* are reprimanded by *2LT Felicity Sampson* after a fight over a D&D game. Fixed rig and crew cameras stay with Hollow and Joanie. IGH unlock s5se2.0 – continuous

Sampson slammed her hand on the table. 'Quinn, I almost expect this sort of conduct from you, but it's a bloody black day to see you in here, Magrath.'

'Sorry, Lieutenant.'

'And over a blasted roleplaying game, of all things.'

'Sorry, Lieutenant.'

Sampson was shaking her head. 'This sort of bullish behaviour is not acceptable. I will not tolerate fist fighting on my watch. By all rights, I should put you both on report.'

'Yes, Lieutenant.'

'However,' Sampson walked around the two of them, 'I can also appreciate that grief finds a manageable way out. Take this as a dressing-down. Whatever led you to this point, you talk it through, you make your peace. Use the studio counsellors if you must. You're in the same bloody unit now. Don't make me regret that decision.'

ITM SCENE
COMMENTARY
HOLLOW QUINN:
Me and Joan, it was a stupid fight, that's all. We both knew it wasn't about the D&D map. Lieutenant Sampson gave us a good dressing-down. It could have been a lot worse.

JOANIE MAGRATH:
I felt like I was at the headmaster's office. But Lieutenant Sampson was right, it shouldn't have got that far.

PRODUCER:
Why did it get that far, Joanie?

JOANIE MAGRATH:
It's easier to be angry than sad, I guess. And I think Hollow is transferring her guilt about what happened with Fish onto me. I understand that.

PRODUCER:
But you started the fight?

JOANIE MAGRATH:
Yeah…on some level, I must blame her too.

2LT SAMPSON:
I understand why it happened, but things like this need to be stopped before they start. God knows none of us want another Jar and Mika situation.

There were cameras in the bunkhouse, but Jar had put a flannel over the one above his bed and none of the riggers would move it. The personnel section was deserted, deathly quiet except for the humming of insects and ozone towers. Joanie took a quick look up and down the empty spaces and flicked Hollow a signal, keeping low, keeping to the shadows all the way to the infested shipping container.

'I don't think we were followed,' Joanie said, tapping his fingers along the side of the ISO like it could have been the wind brushing past.

'We've walked around this three times, just go in already,' Hollow said.

'Shhhhhh, keep your voice down.'

The sky was moon dark, clear enough to see the Milky Way. Up on the door frame, a solitary wasp crawled in the torchlight, searching for wood in a forest of metal.

Hollow went to try the handle. 'Is it locked?'

Joanie batted her hand away. 'We wait for an answer.'

'What if there's no reply?'

'Then we try again later,' Joanie said.

'Fuck that for a game of soldiers.' Hollow pushed past him and opened the door. Her torchlight spilling only as far as the first ammo container. Beyond that, there was nothing more than vague geometric shapes, the buzzing flight of a wasp and the scritch-scratch scurrying of camel spiders scrabbling into the shadows.

Joanie shoved Hollow into the dark. 'If we're caught, we came in here to make out.'

'We came to an ISO full of camel spiders to make out?'

'What's wrong with that?'

'You have to make the lies believable, Joan, and people would struggle,' Hollow said. 'On quite a few levels.'

'Okay, then we tell them it's a fetish,' Joanie said. 'One hundred per cent guaranteed they'll shut up.'

Hollow stopped right in front of him, almost tripping him up. 'We have a fetish now?'

'Sure.'

'For camel spiders?'

Joanie chanced a look around. 'What's not to have a fetish about?'

'You want me to stand up in front of Sampson and say we have a fetish for camel spiders?'

'Stop saying it like it's the truth.'

'How do you want me to say it?'

'Fine,' Joanie said. 'We came in here to make out, because of all the sexual tension between us spilling out into a fight. But then I heard something scuttling around and remembered about the camel spiders, and you said it would be okay if we didn't go into the shadows, but I freaked out, and nothing at all happened in the sex department.'

'Shit, Joanie, you really do need a liar.'

'Keep heading towards the back,' Joanie said. 'There's a stack of old office furniture from the last time we were here.'

'For our camel spider fetish?'

'The army,' Joanie said, pulling another torch out of his boot, 'but they robbed it from an older occupation.'

'I thought Bastion was trashed.'

'Only three things survive an apocalypse, Hollow. Cockroaches, viruses and Soviet office furniture.' Joanie grabbed a double-layer camo net and pulled it clear. 'And at least two of them are back here.'

In the unpredictable movement of torchlight, it was hard to see anything except a stack of grey metal boxes, higher than felt safe. Even for the army, it was ugly. Hollow almost laughed. 'You made a fort?'

'To be fair, the furniture did most of the work.'

'And the...?' Hollow kicked at the head of a dead camel spider. There were enough bits and bodies littered around the improvised fort to shame a medieval city.

'That was my idea,' Joanie said. 'To make an example of them.'

'Shit, Joan.'

'No, no, they were already dead,' he said. 'I just collected them up so it looks like they come back here to die.'

'An elephant graveyard?'

'Except for the scale.' Joanie stopped like he'd caught himself out. 'Yeah.'

'What's happening here, Joan?'

Joanie didn't answer, he just tapped on a filing cabinet and waited. This time, the answer came: soft, near enough nothing to be nothing. Joanie stuck the torch in his mouth, rummaged in his pocket and pulled out a key. The key was small, angular and rusted through the silver coating. Once upon a time, it would have been enough psychological security to keep top-secret documents out of reach. Now it was just an out-of-place thing from a different time. The filing cabinet was stacked on its side, eye level, four drawers and enough dents to make it redundant. Joanie put the key in a circular lock, turned it and pulled the drawer open.

'Please don't tell me that's a doorway?' Hollow said.

'Yep.' Joanie kept on pulling until the whole drawer was out, laying it flat on the floor to make a step.

'You're fucking kidding me.'

'Watch the edges, they're sharp.'

It was dark in the gap where the drawer had been. If there was something beyond it, there wasn't much seeing it yet. Hollow waited on Joanie as he hauled himself into the hole like he was deep cave exploring, calling her through at the end, and the gap tight enough to unnerve anyone. She took a breath, climbing one boot on the makeshift step. 'Does my arse look big in this?'

'Put your arms in first,' Joanie said. 'I'll pull you through.'

'No way.' Hollow took off her jacket, grabbing the stainless-

389

steel handles of a desk above the cabinet. 'I came into this world feet first, and that's how I intend to leave.'

'Shit, Hollow, don't you dare get stuck in here.'

'I won't get stuck.'

'I'd have to eat my way out.'

'This better be legit.' Hollow swung away, kicking her feet into the hole with enough momentum to carry her most of the distance and scrabbling the rest. She landed an untidy bundling into Joanie, her face inches from another stack of cabinets. 'Because if this is a wind-up, I'm gonna kill you. Then I'll give you CPR, so I can kill you again.'

'Welcome aboard, comrade.'

Hollow held her breath. 'Please don't be a camel spider nest.'

'You think I'd go to all this trouble to present you with a camel spider nest?'

'Yes, if you've been scammed.'

'Well, it's not a scam, *ergo* it's not a camel spider nest.'

'Is it a massive mistake?' Hollow said. 'Because it feels like a massive mistake.'

'Single file, keep your arms and legs inside the aircraft.' Joanie shoved a drawer backwards through the gap, shining the torch to where a double stack of grey blankets had slumped against the back of the container. Even without decades of sand dust, they looked indecently itchy.

'What am I supposed to be looking at?'

'Blankets, if I've done this right.'

'You brought me here to show me some old blankets?'

'Ah, not just any old blankets,' Joanie said. 'Soviet military blankets. You can use them to sandpaper roads.'

'I mentioned what would happen if this was a wind-up, right?'

'You did.' Joanie looked at her, and nothing but sweet sincerity in his face. 'And it's not a wind-up.'

'There's no shame in being excited about Soviet military

blankets, Joan, not for any of us. But dragging a person out of bed to look at them under the pretence of a lost civilian is not okay. Why don't we take a wander over to the hospital? See if Caster's around for a chat.' Hollow reached out to touch his arm. 'We can have a look at their blankets, if you want.'

'This isn't about blankets.' Joanie pulled away. 'It isn't a wind-up, it isn't a psych scam, and it isn't about blankets.'

'Just a massive mistake, then?'

'I was at the Balloon Fiesta one time and this hench was hitting on Fish. He dared me to eat a ghost chilli. The chilli was a small mistake.' Joanie ducked low and crawled to sit next to the stack of blankets, carefully catching each one as it fell away. 'The massive mistake was thinking I needed to impress a hench who thought it was funny to dare a kid to eat a ghost chilli.'

Up above Hollow's head, the solitary wasp crawled between a table and a heavy-duty notice board. Fanning its wings to clear the dust. A leg at a time over faded paper and drawing pins. Keeping true to the gaps. Slowly making its way towards the torchlight.

30

It was the eyeballs that did it

Ezra buzzed Atticus Valentine through the community gate, scrolling the options to override the exit protocol. 'See you later, guys.'

Tulip looked up from chopping coriander. 'You off out, kiddo?'

'What even constitutes out nowadays?'

'What time will you be back?' Sheila said.

Tulip nudged her. 'Only, we're obviously chained to the sofa tonight awaiting this latest bloody *WØLF* hype. We thought we might as well make a bit of an event of it. Fusion buffet. Like we do for Eurovision.'

'What *WØLF* hype?' Ezra said. 'I've been off grid.'

'According to *WØLF* sources,' Tulip grabbed a pan and swirled oil into it, 'what we see tonight will change everything. Personally, I can't imagine it's anything more than a ratings stunt.'

'I think it's a spin-off,' Sheila said. '*WØLF US* or *WØLF Afghanistan*. And they're all Navy Seals or Taliban.'

'My, how eclectic.' Tulip picked up a red onion. 'Personally, I think a lot of people will be disappointed if it's just publicity for a new spin-off.'

Sheila turned to look at Tulip, resting an elbow on the counter. 'What if it's *Celebrity WØLF*?'

'Set on the frontline of a paraspecies war?' Tulip winked at Ezra. 'I'm excited already.'

'Maybe they'll be politicians.'

'Interesting.' Tulip leant to rest next to Sheila, twirling the onion like a Christmas bauble. 'I guarantee the war would be over by the first episode.'

'I won't be long,' Ezra called, heading towards the front door.

'What if they're ending *WØLF*?' Sheila said.

'Oh, of course.' Tulip put down the onion. 'You know, I think that might be it.'

'They've lost five of their squad,' Sheila said. 'It's hard to imagine how they'll come back from that. We'd all understand if they ended it.'

Ezra made a seamless getaway, leaving Tulip and Sheila distracted by what *WØLF* had planned for the evening. And with just enough time to catch a last desperate look in the mirror by the door.

As an advocate for public transport, Ezra had never felt the slightest inclination to learn to drive. Still, a beautiful car was a beautiful car, and no one could feel unmoved by that. 'This is fancy,' Ezra said, stroking the dash like a tentative vet.

'Her name is Nikola,' Atticus said, driving a full circle around the square, and not a sound except for the roosting squabble of starlings on the petulant wind and the uneven surface of a tiled road. 'Far from original, but she insisted.'

'You look tired.'

'Tough week. It's good to get outside.'

'And before you ask, Mr Valentine,' Ezra said, chirpily, 'I have remembered your research item. I have also managed to fit a five-course picnic and two bottles of alcohol-zero wine into a rather modest backpack. And I'll tell you exactly how I did it, but we'll need to stop off at the Co-op first.'

'Do we need a picnic?'

'I guess not,' Ezra said. 'I did bring two mugs and a flask of tea, if that's of interest.'

'Are they nice mugs?'

'One of them is,' Ezra said.

Within a couple of miles, the city had dropped away and the sky opened up all the way to the sea. Ezra touched the reflection of clouds on the window. 'Have you been to Haifengate before?'

'No, I haven't.' Dappled light kissed Atticus' face. 'I've seen a few of the questions online.'

'It's the wrong time of year for that. Which is good news for us, because it gets a bit busy around question time.' Ezra paused. 'Even with the...thing.'

'There's a thing?'

'You know what social media is like,' Ezra said. 'Content creators live for the interaction a spooky story generates. And what Mesolithic site doesn't have a reputation for being a veil between realms? Yes, there's been reports of strange lights. Eerie noises. Sheep mutilations. Dogs disappearing. Dead bodies. But that's ancient landscapes for you. Half terrifying, half recompense for having to live in the twenty-first century.'

'Dead bodies?'

'Everyone wants to know until you tell them.' Ezra sighed. 'Fine. A couple of months ago, this guy got tied to the stones and left up here to die. The ravens ate his eyeballs and everything. It blew up on social media for the sacrificial aspect, but there's no historical evidence suggesting the rings were ever used in that way. In the end, the police issued a statement saying it was just made to look like a sacrifice, to cover up a gang killing.'

'The eyeballs, though? That's grim.'

'And when I say tied, it was more glued, on account of the... glue,' Ezra said. 'The truth is that most people only come here to say they've heard the stones. But Haifengate is a beautiful, unspoiled place, and if superstition and creepy stories mean people teach their kids how to fly a kite on some other hillside,

I'm not complaining. Sure, there was the murder. And Dicky's dog went missing up here. But she's the wrong side of the spaniel gene pool, and she often goes missing.'

'Any new insights into who built the stones?'

'We know they were transported to the south coast via glacier, and arranged by the marginal ancestors of a species battling its way out of yet another ice age.' Ezra traced the outline of a tree on the window as they pulled into the designated car park. 'This arrangement is unusual in the fact that at certain times of year, the wind blows through the stones at a particular angle, causing the stones to resonate with a spoken question. Often, the questions relate to sheep, but lately they've been about soil erosion, climate change and the unreasonable cost of a dental X-ray. It's not yet fully understood why these marginal hominids felt the need for a random question generator, mostly because the weathering of the stones means they've kept pace with contemporary language and dialect, and that's enough of a research project to be going on with.'

'You're awesome,' Atticus said.

'Poppycock.'

The ancient monument of Haifengate had been there before the hillfort. A ring of stones within a larger circle, flecked with flint and forced open into a scream.

'It's a bit outdoorsy.' Atticus pushed through a ruckus of stinging nettles, using Ezra's backpack as a makeshift path-clearing device.

'I don't suppose there's much outdoorsy in upper management.'

'Some of them play golf.' Atticus looked up. 'Oh, okay. Wow.'

And maybe it was the sweet song of the skylark. Maybe it was the setting sun like blood on the glacial scars and beaten copper fields. It might have been the sigh of a soft wind that curled up and fell asleep in the trees and wild grasses. Or perhaps there was a desperate temporariness to the beauty of it all. All but the standing stones of Haifengate. Unmoved, unyielding, unconquered by something as careless and deliberate as time.

'Pretty amazing, eh?' Ezra pushed ahead, striding towards the centre of the stones. 'Legend has it that five elementals came together and battled for ownership of this place. And I'm not disrespecting the physical sciences, but there's a magic to these untouched places that science can't explain. When you're alone up here, legends can make a lot more sense than geography.'

'Except...' Atticus hesitated at the stones, crouching to touch the earth with the tips of his fingers '...I'm not alone.'

'Now, I know it looks like dry glue,' Ezra said, 'but it's just moss.'

He laughed a little but he stayed where he was. 'Is it too late for golf?'

'And miss having the crap freaked out of you?'

'Guess I'm not so brave when it comes down to it.'

'I used to think I was brave,' Ezra said, 'back when life was easy.'

'Before the war?'

'Before you, mostly.'

'I do seem to have a knack for it.' Atticus looked up then. 'Could I just stay here, Ezra?'

'Sure.' Ezra leant back and embraced the panoramic sky, breathing with the universe. 'Or, you could come and sit inside a Mesolithic circle with a flask of tea and the delightful company of an historian who can look at a landscape and tell you why the final conquest of the Iron Age didn't go without a fight.'

He grinned. 'It was the eyeballs that did it.'

'Talking of.' Ezra grabbed the backpack and pulled out a blanket. 'I hear on the Emporia grapevine that you avoided the opportunity to buy one of our souvenir mugs on your whistlestop tour of the Fabian Evirate House gift shop.' Ezra laid the blanket out, sitting down neatly, rummaging through the backpack and eventually pouring tea into a sculptural mug. 'FYI, if you wink at the hologram, it sends you a sternly worded letter of reprimand.'

'And this is the nice mug?' Atticus finally stood up, dusting earth from his hands as he stepped into the ring of stones. 'I honestly can't wait to see the nasty one now.'

'It's quite narrow,' Ezra said, holding up a mug the shape of a courgette. 'And if you wink at the hologram on this one, it sends a letter to the *Gazette* with your name and address on it.'

'About winking?'

'About there not being enough bike lanes in Chichester, usually.' Ezra sighed as Atticus sat down. There was something so normal and relaxed about being in his company, but there were also a lot of emotions bouncing around and it was like trying to hold water in a sieve. 'Did you hear the skylark?'

He smiled, but it wasn't a shared kind of thing. 'The song that can't be seen in the sky.'

'I was about to say it reminded me of family picnics. Yours is way more beautiful.' Ezra leant into his shoulder. 'Is that from a poem?'

'An idea.'

'Sweet.'

For a while they sat in the resonance of the universe, no room for anything but silence, and the last drop of sunlight a ruby gemstone for the sea.

Ezra sat up. 'Is it because a skylark is so small?'

'Maybe.' Atticus drank the last of his tea. 'You said you had the pendant?'

'I left it in the car.'

'Great, thank you. We should probably head back before it gets dark.'

'Yeah.' Ezra was half watching him, pretending not to. 'Good idea.'

'The perils of reality TV.' Atticus rubbed at his temple. 'Monday is always playing catch-up for the weekend.'

'I'm sorry,' Ezra said, accidentally tipping the courgette mug over and spilling tea across the blanket. 'I'm really sorry.'

'We're good,' he said, scooting out of the way of the tea, 'it didn't get me.'

'I'm so sorry, Atticus.' Ezra stood up, backing away from him. 'I know it's totally cliché, but honestly, here I am and I just can't think of anything else to say.'

'It's fine, it's…' Atticus went to stand, but his legs had only weakness in them and he stumbled forward on to his hands '… only tea.'

'I'm sorry.' Ezra kept on backing away. 'I'm really, really sorry.'

'I don't feel so good.' He was breathing heavily now, one hand gripping hold of the earth. 'Can we just sit for a minute.'

But Atticus didn't sit for a minute. And when he looked up, Ezra saw the moment of betrayal take his eyes. And it was like ripping all the stars from the sky.

'You, you roofied the tea,' Atticus said. 'That's why you knocked yours over. Why, why would you do that?'

'I'm sorry.'

'This is what, a date rape?'

'NO!'

'What the hell?' Atticus leant forward, trying to steady himself.

'Funny you should say that,' Mac Eden said, one foot on a stone and holding a flaming torch. Battery-operated flashlights were barred from standard field kit, but natural light was a good substitute, and there was nothing like fire for cleaning up a spillage.

Ezra had expected the emotional aftershock to be brutal, but not like this, not like the world had ended in ice. 'Mac…'

'I got this from now on, poppet.' Mac wedged the torch between two stones and took a careful step towards Ezra. 'You gather up your stuff and get yourself back down to the car park. Sit in my car and wait for the others, just like we talked about.'

There were ribbons tied to the torch, eager and bright in the firelight like they were there for a festival or something. Ezra looked desperately at Mac. 'Did I do it right?'

'Mission accomplished.' Mac picked up Ezra's backpack and held it out. 'And accomplished altogether better than my first mission, I can tell you. Now collect up your things, poppet, and off you trot.'

'Ezra, wait,' Atticus tried to stand again, 'if this is about Hollow, I can—'

'Can what?' Mac sneered, shoving him back down. 'Can mistakenly assume a flaky kid wouldn't have the wherewithal to see you for what you are?'

'I *am* flaky,' Ezra said.

'Please,' Atticus leant forward on his hands, 'just tell me what you want.'

'I want for you to shut your bastard mouth!' Mac hit his head with the backpack. 'Among other...worse things.'

'I'll stay,' Ezra's voice wasn't much more than a whisper, 'I'll stay with him.'

'*Just tell me what you want.*' If Mac heard Ezra, there was no showing it. She grabbed Atticus' hair and pulled him over. 'That's almost amused me.'

'I'll stay with him,' Ezra said, louder this time. 'You can go back to the car park and meet the others.'

'Ezra Blake, I need you to go back to the car park now.' Mac glanced towards the yew wood. 'They'll be here any minute.'

'It's fine,' Ezra said, all hands on hips and chirpy like someone who'd accidentally bought the wrong version of a film and now everyone was on the sofa watching. 'It's all fine.'

'Is that right?' Mac kicked Atticus.

'No!' Ezra yelled.

'Still think you're fine?'

'No, no, I just wasn't ready.' Ezra puffed a motivational fitness stance. 'Kick him again.'

'I'll be exhausted at this rate.' Mac went to kick Atticus again, but he grabbed hold of her foot, twisting it around. She looked like she might fall, but he was too weak to do much more than knock her off balance. 'You really know how to piss a person right off,' Mac said, swinging the backpack so it hit him on the head again.

'Don't!' Ezra yelled.

Mac shoved the backpack at Ezra. 'You're not fine, poppet, you just think you are. That's what happens with shock. Pack up your stuff and get back to the car park. Wait for the others. Tell them where I am. Then stay in my car till I get back. Just like we talked about. Now GO.'

'Help me,' Atticus said.

Mac wrenched the torch free, holding it close to his face and letting the ribbons curl around him. 'If I had my way, you'd already be chopped up in jars.'

'You don't need to torment him,' Ezra said.

'It's you in torment, Ezra Blake. That's why we don't let everything you've already been through go to waste.'

Ezra took a step away from Atticus, clutching the backpack like a safety cushion. 'I have been through a lot.'

'Yes, you have,' Mac said, with a deal more sincerity than Ezra expected. 'And before you know it, I'll be back at the car and we can have a nice cup of tea. I got us cow milk and everything.'

Ezra looked down at the courgette mug. 'You brought me tea?'

'Keep your eyes on me.' Mac held her hands up, corralling Ezra's attention. 'That's it, keep looking at me.'

'I don't believe this.' Atticus rolled onto his back, turning his head away. 'I thought you were my friend.'

'It's no friend, poppet,' Mac said, all reassuring smile and stepping one foot on Atticus' chest. 'If it knew the meaning of the word, we wouldn't be here.'

'No, he's right,' Ezra said. 'I was his friend. He deserves to know why I did this.'

'Bastard thing deserves nothing.'

'Please, Mac.' Ezra put the backpack down. 'I need to tell him.'

'And then you'll go?'

'I will,' Ezra said. 'I promise.'

'Make it quick.'

Ezra knelt next to Atticus. 'You knew the questions.'

'What...' Atticus closed his eyes, breathing through a wave of nausea '...questions?'

'In Minstrels Park. I was there to get intel on you. Your family history, your backstory, your hobbies, what you like to do on a Sunday evening. That was my mission. Except you answered every question before I asked it. Even the hobbies, and I had no idea how to approach that one.' Ezra took a breath, trying to keep it together. 'You knew the questions, Atticus. You already knew the questions.'

'I don't understand.'

'I tried to give you a way out,' Ezra said, slowly backing away. 'I thought you might be in a hurry to get back to work, but you stayed for the questions. You shouldn't have stayed.'

'You asked about my family...'

'No, I didn't. I just listened to you answer every single question before I asked it. And you sounded so sad, and so lost.' Ezra hesitated, almost taking a step back towards him. 'Atticus...'

'That's enough,' Mac said, pulling Ezra clear of the stones.

'I can't leave him.' Ezra was flapping around for Mac's arm like it was a muscular lifeboat. 'Please, you have to help me, Mac.'

'Remember how we talked about this,' Mac said. 'It's not Atticus Valentine, CEO of Plug Productions, it's the Mandolin. Bastard thing had itself a nice little creep-crawl around your mind and didn't even have the decency to hide it. That's disrespectful to you, and lazy to the game. You walk away now, poppet. You treat it like it don't even matter. Because that's exactly what it did to you.'

'It's not human.' Ezra gripped Mac's arm. 'It's the Mandolin.'

'That's right.'

'Why does it feel so bad, Mac?'

'Because you've done the right thing, and that often feels like crap. Now off you trot, I got it from here.'

Ezra finally let go of Mac's arm. 'I've done the right thing.'

'You've done the right thing.'

'I have to...' Ezra picked up the backpack, looking around '...did you see the nice mug?'

'It's fine, leave it, I can sort it.'

'You can sort it...' Ezra dropped the backpack and ran. All the way back through the nettles and brambles and tangled yew trees. Atticus' car was still parked in the little asphalt pull-in, all shine and shameless beauty next to Mac's brick-built hatchback. Everything about the trap had panned out how it was supposed to, even Mac said so, and it was hard not to trust someone with such a natural frown. Ezra scrabbled into Mac's car and waited for the others to come. There was a blanket on the back seat that could have offered comfort but doubled as a straitjacket, depending on emotional requirements. Some other person might have cried themselves to sleep, but only the owls could tell.

Back in the circle, fire flickered the stones to a cage. Mac watched the woodland until she was sure Ezra had gone from sight, then she crouched down and grabbed hold of Atticus' hair again. 'Well now, looks like it's just the two of us.'

Atticus struggled away. 'Get the glue already.'

Mac laughed, sitting chummily next to him. 'You know, that day you came to the teashop, I reported you in. Straight in like a good side character. And bugger me, they didn't believe me. All that time in the field and they'd rather believe I have game fatigue than risk taking a second-hand celebrity for a ride in the questioning chair. Can you even credit it?' Mac looked back towards the woodland. 'But hark at me, you'll be telling them yourself soon enough.'

'If this is…' Atticus struggled to organise his words '…about the website.'

'Like you don't know.'

'Research,' Atticus said. 'It was research.'

'Fucking hell, give it up.'

'I tried to explain…about the tattoo.'

Mac stood up and set to pacing, waiting on the arc of fire torches that would come. 'Will you look at that. I'm almost anxious.'

'Please,' he said, distraught and dear enough to be her son, 'please…you've got this all wrong.'

Mac pulled in close to him, hard as nails. Then she grinned. 'Shit, you're good.'

'I know, right,' Atticus said.

Mac's grin widened to a natural laughter that softened her into someone she could have been. She plonked herself back down on the ground next to him. 'Wanna catch me up on a few things?'

'Wanna let me go?'

'Iron. I mean, how the fuck did you do that?'

'That's a lot of answer…for one question…' Atticus dragged the words through another wave of nausea. 'Maybe we could… block out some time next week.'

Mac laughed again. 'Here's an unexpected turnip. I almost find myself tolerating your company.'

'Back at ya.'

'Aye, well…'

'We're not so different, eh?' Atticus said. 'You and I.'

'Aside from one of us being a disgusting abomination of all that's right and decent in the world?' Mac nodded. 'Aye, maybe you're right.'

'They won't believe you.'

'And what's with making the game into a televised social experiment? After all this time, it makes no sense.'

'Hey, come on,' Atticus said, 'only the prompt…was televised.'

Mac frowned then. 'The experiment was never *WØLF*?'

Atticus waved her on. 'It was…?'

'It was all the fucking people sat at home watching.'

'It's something to do, eh?'

'You sick bastard.' Mac hadn't meant to punch him in the face, but once she'd opened the window to it, there was no containing the fury and the pain and the loss, only his blood across the bone-white chalk. 'You sick, sick bastard.'

'Mac Eden.' The old woman farted, and not downwind. 'As it was, and is!'

Mac snapped to Attention. Heels in line and touching. Knees braced. Arms straight, tight to her body. Forearms behind her hip bones. Fingers dripping blood down the side seam of her jacket. 'And always will be.'

To say Brigadier Sissy Hatter was a bit of a rockstar among the side character ranks was an understatement. As Director of the Operating System, the spindly octogenarian had been born into the grandiose estates of the upper aristocracy, and she'd made it all the way to the bottom on her own merit. The day she lost her last million to a dodgy investment portfolio was the stuff of legend. The brigadier leant around Mac to look at Atticus. 'Report.'

'I actually set this up for my cell.' Mac bobbed around, all bashful and skitty with it. 'So we could bring it to you, Brigadier Hatter. Like a united front sort of…thing. I wasn't expecting for you to act on it yet.'

'Understood.' Brigadier Hatter adjusted the floral shoulder strap of her housewife tabard. 'And which part of that united front is happening here, exactly?'

'Oh, yeah, of course,' Mac said. 'I'm still a bit blown away, if I'm honest.'

'In your own time.' The brigadier was only half paying attention, looking back to a woman wearing a pair of wellington boots that had yellow ducks on them. 'Get a medic up here, would you, Lucy.'

'I'm fine,' Mac said, looking at her hands. 'It's just a few scratches.'

'I'm still waiting on that report, Mac Eden.'

'This!' Mac threw a triumphant wave towards Atticus, but there was too much blood to support her big reveal. 'It's the Atticus Valentine. From the submitted report. I don't know what you got told, but you should probably give it a read, if you haven't.'

'I have read the report,' Brigadier Hatter said, flicking a low signal for the others to circle around behind Mac. 'There's undoubtedly something of interest in it.'

'And the report recommendations?' Mac said, kicking Atticus' arm away from the brigadier. 'Bastard thing picked up my ladle.'

'Highlighted recommendations,' Brigadier Hatter said. 'If I recall.'

'There's seasoned blacksmiths won't go near that ladle.'

'And sixteen pages of additional footnotes.'

'Yeah.' Mac shuffled slightly. 'You can credit Beverly Smith for that.'

'Thank you, Mac Eden, you are dismissed.'

'This player is a slippery one, mind,' Mac said. 'One of the top rank players, I'd say. Nearly had me fooled at one point.'

Brigadier Hatter took a slow step back, nodding like a dash ornament. 'This young man is in our custody now.'

'Young man?'

'Quick march back to the car park.'

'No,' Mac said, not quite making it to look the highest-rank side character in the droopy eye. 'With respect, Brigadier Hatter, we're not done here.'

'That's an order.'

'No!' Mac lunged forward, grabbing Atticus around the neck. 'I'll show you.'

'Don't do something you'll regret, Mac.'

Atticus groaned and struggled to pull away. 'No…'

Mac took a small glass bottle out of her pocket, holding it against Atticus' cheek. 'If I was you, I'd start talking now.'

'Please,' he whispered, 'I don't know…what you want.'

'Yeah, you do,' Mac said, flicking the bottle lid open with the tip of her thumb. 'Start with the ladle if it's too much to choose from.'

Brigadier Hatter took another step away. 'This isn't how we do things any more, Mac.'

'I honestly thought it was gonna run,' Mac said. 'You could see it trying to ground the magnetic field, but no Mandolin can tolerate the levels of infrasonic noise coming from the stones for long. And I was ready to fry the bastard thing right then.' Mac patted Atticus on the head. 'But to its credit, it stuck on through.'

'Single command function achieved.' The brigadier added a brief nod of approval. 'Mac Eden, you have done your duty in bringing this matter to our attention. Return to your post. We have it from here.'

'With respect, Brigadier, no, you don't.'

'It's imperative that we follow the correct channels with something this…' Brigadier Hatter looked Atticus up and down '…media sensitive.'

'No, no, I understand that this has to be done properly.' Mac held up the bottle. 'That's why I can give you some straight-up proof.'

'And you think an enzyme toxin will give us this proof?'

'If it's an innocent bystander, it'll be fine. For a Mandolin, guaranteed it'll be a rough ride.' Mac turned back to Atticus, stroking his hair like he was a wounded dog and untangling the barbed wire was going to hurt like hell. 'Don't take this personally. I'm not normally one for getting answers from torture, but in this particular case, I am.'

The brigadier shook her head, turning away. 'You better be right about this, Mac. You better be bloody right.'

'Sure as hell is coming.' Mac cradled Atticus' body into hers. 'And if you have any trust left in me, you'll fire up the nets, cos it'll be coming in hot.'

They set net canonns inside the ring of stones, ozone triggered and tight enough with iron powder to catch a raindrop if it came at them rabid and unexpected.

'One last chance,' Mac whispered to Atticus. 'I'd take it if I were you.'

'Please...I don't know what you want.'

'Well then, buckle up, cos this is gonna get ugly,' Mac said. 'For you mostly, and us to the extent that we have to look at it, but mostly you.'

Brigadier Hatter was pacing the stone rings with more impatience than her navy loafers were used to. 'Just get on with it, Mac, before I change my mind.'

Mac flexed her shoulders, holding the bottle against Atticus' cheek as the toxin came slipping in black ash, searching out his mouth like something alive. He struggled then, dragging his sleeve across his face to wipe it away. Mac thrust her knee into his side, tipping the rest of the liquid directly into his mouth and clamping her hand over it to stop him spitting it out. He pulled at her hand, but she held him firm as the black liquid found its own way down his throat.

Mac put the empty bottle back in her pocket. 'Now we'll see what's what.'

They all waited, a group of women as overlooked and left behind as a book on cooking with gas, while the chief executive officer of Plug Productions broke through a cold sweat that soaked his skin and twisted his hair into curls.

'How long will this take?' Brigadier Hatter said.

'It should be almost immediate,' Mac said, clearing her throat. 'Give or take.'

'Can I get some water?' Atticus said.

Mac stroked his cheek, curling a line of ash and blood to his temple. 'You know they used fire back in the day. I can see the appeal as far as a hard reboot goes, but this enzyme toxin contains synthesised helicases and a nanobot delivery system. Not quite enough to unwind the double helix of your DNA, but enough to trigger a deionisation episode.' Mac patted his cheek again. 'Plus, fire has a high carbon dioxide emission, and we're all mindful of the environment these days.'

'Anything on the monitors?' Brigadier Hatter said into her sleeve.

Mac clicked her tongue. 'Just change into a freak already.'

'I don't know...what you...want.' The words caught in Atticus' throat and he almost cried out, but instead he turned and buried his face into the earth, digging his fingers into the chalk and the blood and the wild grasses.

'Blah, blah, blah,' Mac said.

Brigadier Hatter shot Mac a look. 'This is taking too long.'

'No, no, we're still good.' Mac leant in, gently stroking the back of Atticus' head, so close it was hard to tell a space between them. 'We both know how this ends, poppet. You don't have to be needlessly heroic about it.'

Atticus closed his eyes, his voice barely loud enough for Mac to hear. 'Ørma.'

Mac twisted away, pulling another bottle out of her pocket. 'That filthy speech, you can keep to yourself.'

Brigadier Hatter snatched the bottle out of Mac's hand. 'Enough.'

'Wait! I can tell you how it tolerates iron. That's got to be worth something.'

'You have this information?'

'Give me the bottle and I will.'

'I've seen enough.' Brigadier Hatter tucked the bottle into a place that might once have sported a cleavage. 'You'll have this young man die before you admit you were wrong.'

'I'm not wrong,' Mac said. 'Look at it. It's right on the edge of a catastrophic deionisation.'

A soft breeze sprang up and spiralled around them. The torch Mac had wedged between the stones danced with it, and blew out.

'Time's up, Mac. For your sake, I hope this young man is strong enough to survive the ordeal.' The brigadier pulled the spent torch out of the stones, throwing it down next to Ezra's backpack. 'And, for both our sakes, too messed up to remember any of it.'

'At least let the lab have a look,' Mac said. 'You don't have to believe me. Just let them have a look before you release it.'

'Close this shit-show down!' Brigadier Hatter yelled into her sleeve. 'Lucy, where's that damn medic?'

'But you'll get the lab to look at it?'

'What a bloody mess.' The brigadier sighed loudly, turning to face Mac. 'I've been a side character for over sixty years. Believe me, I understand how hard it is to hide in the no-frills archetype. But if this innocent young man decides to press charges, no social stereotype on earth will be able to hide us from the consequences. And I'm not sure a return to custodial sentence would suit you, Mac. Not after all this time.'

'No, no, wait, listen to me.' Mac pushed Atticus away from her, grabbing at the brigadier. 'It tolerated iron, beyond anything I've ever seen before. Makes sense it would take a bit longer to work. But the enzyme toxin is crippling it, and no innocent young man is gonna have a reaction like that. I might not know exactly what sort of mutation protocol it initiated, but this thing is Mandolin, Brigadier Hatter. Everyone here can see that.'

'All I see is a litigation nightmare.'

'Look at it!' Mac screamed, shoving Brigadier Hatter towards Atticus.

The brigadier wrenched away, unsteady but never quite falling. 'Macadamia Eden, if the whole of your sorry arse isn't down in the car park by the time I next look in your direction, I'll have you stripped of your rank and returned to non-player character incarceration.'

Mac backed into a crouch. 'You can see it with your own eyes. What the hell is wrong with you?'

Brigadier Hatter spoke soft enough to make it feel like sympathy. 'Beverly Smith has informed us that you have been showing signs of game fatigue. This mission takes its toll on the best of us.'

'Fuck you,' Mac said.

Someone dressed in overalls called to the brigadier, her voice snatched by the wind so that Mac couldn't hear what was said. Brigadier Hatter nodded, spoke into her sleeve, and turned away like Mac wasn't much part of all the things that happened from now on. And Mac, left not knowing whether everything they thought about her was true.

'Oh, and that NPC you coerced,' Brigadier Hatter said, fumbling with the button on her tabard so she could pull her tights up. 'Make sure you clean that up before you leave.'

'No, no, Ezra doesn't know anything.' Mac scrabbled to her feet. 'I kept it to the book, I swear, it's contained. Ezra doesn't know anything.'

'It's unfortunate, but there we are.'

'I take full responsibility for this.'

'Don't make me ask you again.'

'It was a mistake!' Mac yelled, breathless with the gravity of it. 'Brigadier, I made a mistake. I think Beverly might be right about the game fatigue.'

'What a bloody mess.'

'It's my mental health what's done this. That young kid down in the car park can attest to me being as confusing as fuck.' Mac straightened her shoulders, speaking clearly, precise with each word as though delivering a mission report. 'Game fatigue is a hot topic right now. Our cell just had an emergency meeting on it. I understand that mental health isn't something any side character should ignore. Permission to report to sickbay straight away. Right after I check our policy on wrongful NPC deaths. With our lawyers. Just to be on the safe side.'

Brigadier Hatter held up her hand, listening to an incoming communication. 'Understood. Cleaning the rest up now.' She nodded to Mac. 'Looks like there's no need after all. The NPC has already been deleted.'

Whatever control Mac had left exploded. 'You evil piece of shit!'

The brigadier just sighed out another disappointment as the night faded and a low mist crawled like clouds of steam around them. She was turning away, talking into her sleeve, still trying to rebutton her tabard so it flapped in the wind like a little wave goodbye.

'The tabard camouflage is no more,' Mac said.

'Why are you still here?'

'The tabard camouflage is no more.'

Brigadier Sissy Hatter smiled. 'Tell that to your mind.'

'Enemy among us!' Mac screamed, running at her and the momentum carrying them both over the edge of the Neolithic rampart. 'On me! On me!'

'Sandbox granted,' the brigadier said.

Mac scrabbled to her feet. 'Access denied.'

'Sandbox granted,' the brigadier said again, tilting her head, bit by bit breaking and reforming, ice and water in the starlight.

'Access denied. There's no fucking open world access to this homeland, not without...' Mac choked back a cry. 'No, no, no, no, no.'

'As it was, and is, and always will be.'

Mac screamed again, diving at Brigadier Sissy Hatter, and nothing left to find.

Sometimes, the Mandolin killed you. Sometimes, it was more of a death to leave you alive.

Ezra scrabbled to unlock the driver side door. 'You were ages, is everything okay?'

'It's all fucking dandy.' Mac threw the backpack at Ezra, squinting at an ozone strip stuck along the dashboard with masking tape. 'Did this change colour?'

'I don't think so.'

'No one turned up?'

'Sorry,' Ezra said. 'I might have fallen asleep.'

'You did the right thing staying in the car.' Mac was fumbling around the ignition. 'Keys?'

Ezra pulled a bunch of keys from under the seat. 'Is he... gone?'

'Don't you even dare ask me any questions, because I have a burning need to...' Mac shoved the car into reverse, words catching in her throat like she was trying not to swallow a gobstopper '...do something not very nice.'

Ezra shrank into the passenger seat, clutching the pendant and some flicker of hope perhaps. Mac's ambiguous answer had left many possibilities alive. And considering how Mac reversed into his car several times, her answer might even indicate that Atticus Valentine hadn't been taken away to be interrogated by the Ministry of War at all. It took everything Ezra had to hide the wave of relief. Betrayal could be weird like that.

Mac screeched to a halt just inside the iron gates of Conqueror Square, grabbing Ezra by the collar. 'You don't speak about this, not to anyone.'

'What do I say if people ask about tonight?'

'Say you was out with me.'

'Okay, yeah. That makes sense. Yeah.' Ezra looked around the gated square. 'Only, the neighbourhood watch will have his numberplate on the spreadsheet.'

Mac proper growled. 'You let it pick you up?'

'I'm sorry, Mac, I didn't think.'

'Fucking hell,' Mac said.

'What should I say, though?' Ezra twisted on the words. 'In case it's in the community newsletter?'

'The community newsletter?'

'There's a pinned section on visitor regulations and permits.'

'You tell visitor regulations and permits that you're working for the war effort,' Mac said. 'Then send them over to me for a visitor regulations and permits debrief. No one is taking the blame for this except the person who deserves it.'

'Was it that bad?'

'Just keep your fucking mouth shut.' Mac shoved Ezra backwards out of the car, squealing enough on the handbrake to wake up a whole town of numberplate takers.

Ezra scrabbled to open the gates again as Mac revved a cloud of exhaust smoke, decimating a privet hedge on her way out and not even stopping to leave a note. If Atticus Valentine didn't make the community newsletter, Mac Eden certainly would.

Ezra opened the front door, editing the overwhelming relief of it into something that could pass as normal.

'Hey,' Sheila called from the lounge.

'Hey.'

'Did you have a good time?'

'It was short and sweet,' Ezra said. 'I ended up meeting a friend in town after.'

'Is that who dropped you off?' Tulip called.

'Yeah.'

'Did they hit something?'

'I don't think so,' Ezra said, coming to stand in the doorway.

'We've triumphed with the buffet supper,' Sheila said. 'It's like a wedding reception in here.'

'Any developments on the hype?' There was too much duplicity

413

to stand any closer, but *WØLF* was a part of Atticus Valentine that belonged to everyone, and Ezra couldn't commit to walking away.

'Oh, no,' Tulip said. 'They've kept us in the waiting area all day. *WØLF* certainly know how to play to an audience. Or is it play an audience? Heaven knows where we fit in the influencer loop.'

'Yet here we all are,' Sheila said, loading olives into a sprout-heavy pasta, 'still talking about *WØLF*.'

Tulip plumped a pillow and held her arm for Ezra to snuggle into. 'This programme has created a new kind of industry standard when you think about it.'

Sheila stared at Tulip. 'Girl, since when are you the man?'

'I'm not agreeing with the function.' Tulip patted the seat next to her when Ezra stayed in the doorway. 'I'm just admiring the form.'

'We love that we hate that we love it,' Sheila said. 'That's the whole key to reality TV.'

'There's been too much hype for it to be an unscripted event,' Tulip said, looking over her shoulder at Ezra. 'I thought we'd cracked it earlier. But *WØLF* has just squashed our theory with another teaser. Everything okay, kiddo?'

'Yeah, yeah,' Ezra said. 'I'll just go get changed.'

'Be quick.' Sheila passed Ezra a glass of wine over the back of the sofa. 'I don't want to explain any stuff.'

The TV babbled to the end of a quiz show that no one cared about. A woman was leaping around to a life-changing question that changed nothing except the money she had and what she did with it. Every house was waiting on something bigger; a contract for a story one hundred per cent guaranteed to entertain. If *WØLF* was teasing for viewers' approval, there was no need. If it was manipulating its audience, it was working. But none of that mattered. What mattered was that something was coming, and all over the homeland it felt like Christmas Eve.

31

They'll pop out in Moscow

Ezra poured the wine into the bathroom sink and watched it drain away like blood. Some people were bad drunks or sweet drunks, or fall-asleep drunks. Sheila was a chatterbox, and being a chatterbox meant it didn't take much more than a glass of cheap wine for her to spill even the most protected secret. Tulip could hold her tongue like she could hold her liquor, but there were no secrets between Tulip and Sheila, so the whole thing was a hopeless circle. Still, it would have been so easy to cuddle up on the sofa and tell them the whole sorry story. As easy as missing a bus.

Tulip messaged twice to say *WØLF* was starting. By the time Ezra got back downstairs, Sheila was kneeling close to the TV, hugging a naan bread tight to her chest. 'Don't ask me anything.'

'What, what is it? Did something happen to Hollow?'

'No, no, she's fine.'

'So it's not a spin-off?'

Tulip wasn't as close to the TV, but she kept her eyes fixed on it. 'It's certainly not a spin-off, that's for sure.'

Sheila waved her into silence. 'Something's happening.'

The soldiers were somewhere dark, not much more than torchlight, and the camera angle too high to see their faces. One of the soldiers hauled themself up into a hole like they were deep cave exploring or something, calling the other through at the end, and the gap tight enough to unnerve anyone. The second soldier took a breath, one boot on a makeshift step. 'Does my arse look big in this?'

'That's Hollow,' Ezra said.

'And Joanie Magrath.' Tulip grabbed a slice of beetroot, dipping it into peanut butter. 'He's taking her to see something.'

'Bless him,' Sheila said. 'He's adorable, but he's a strange lad.'

'To see what?' Ezra said.

'We don't know yet.' Tulip reached across to pick up a digestive biscuit. 'It's very exciting.'

Hollow was grabbing the stainless-steel handles of a desk above the cabinet. The camera was moving now, crawling into the next scene.

'Welcome aboard, comrade.'

Ezra knelt next to Sheila. 'Why's Hollow in a filing cabinet?'

'Apparently, the Russians left it behind after their last occupation.'

'Maybe it's a portal,' Ezra said. 'They'll pop out in Moscow.'

'Shush.'

Hollow was talking about psych jackings messing everything up. How it was no one's fault, how it all felt like a massive mistake, as Joanie ducked low and crawled to sit next to a stack of blankets, carefully catching each one as it fell away.

Sheila leant closer to the TV. 'Is that blankets?'

'It can't just be blankets, surely,' Tulip said. 'Move back a bit.'

'Not very nice blankets by the look of them.'

'Oh dear,' Tulip said. 'That's not good.'

The camera moved between a table and a heavy-duty notice board. Fanning through the mechanical workings of wings to clear the dust. A leg at a time over faded paper and drawing pins. Keeping true to the gaps. Slowly making its way towards the torchlight.

'No, there's something moving under there,' Sheila said.

Tulip grabbed another digestive biscuit. 'Perhaps it's camel spiders.'

'Too big.'

Ezra scrabbled backwards to perch on the edge of the sofa. 'What's up with the camera?'

'It's streaming live from Afghanistan.' Tulip passed Ezra a plate. 'WØLF has switched to remote intelligence filming. Apparently, these insect generation hybrids can go anywhere. They're fitted with smart-tech nano transmitters that capture sound better than the existing wireless receivers. The cast don't know they're being filmed because the IGH cameras just look like any other insect.'

'Shush.' Sheila was watching the WØLF episode like a detective examining their yoghurt for evidence of who ate it. 'Elspeth Hart said we needed to see the real war.'

'Personally, I can see it being a bit contentious,' Tulip said. 'No doubt their legal team will have everything screwed down tight.'

'I thought we were seeing the real war.' Ezra said.

On the screen, Hollow crouched next to Joanie. 'Why don't we head back to the bunkhouse, come on, I'll make you a nice cup of tea. I can even trip over Jar's bunk, if you want.'

Joanie smiled. 'I couldn't believe it, I mean, I still can't quite believe it. She's walking away from a copter crash, fire and smoke everywhere, and she's still the most beautiful thing I've ever seen.'

'Wait,' Sheila said. 'Is he talking about...?'

'It's not her,' Tulip said. 'He's just messing with Hollow. It's probably Jar under there.'

'Girl, he wouldn't joke about finding Sylvie Stevens.' Sheila leant back, grabbing her glass of wine. 'I mean, if he has really found her, that's like a whole romance spin-off by itself.'

Joanie tilted his head. 'It's okay. It's safe to come out.'

It might have been that the whole homeland held its breath then, everyone in the moment, half afraid to see what was there, half afraid that the episode would cut to sponsorship announcements before they saw it. But there were no announcements, there was just the unfolding story of *WØLF*, as bit by bit, second by second, Sylvie Stevens came back to them. It was obvious from the hesitant way she moved, from the dark circles under her eyes, from the shake in her hands as she reached out to Joanie, that she'd been changed, hurt, frightened. But nothing so meaningless could hide who she was.

'Shit,' Hollow said, clamping her hand over her mouth.

'I know,' Joanie said. 'I keep thinking I'll wake up any minute and it's all been a dream. I don't even know how I held it together at the crash site.'

Hollow slumped against the wall. 'Shit.'

'I know,' Joanie said, 'I had a lot of questions.'

'She's dead.'

'No, no, they just told us she was dead.'

'We need to get out of here,' Hollow said, grabbing Joanie's arm and dragging him away from Sylvie.

'It's safe, we can talk in here.'

'It's a scam, Joan.'

'Hollow, I'm breathing,' Sylvie said. 'Scams are like dreams. We never make dream people breathe, remember. It's okay, sweetie, it's only me.'

'W-w-what the fuck!' Hollow spluttered.

Joanie dragged his arm away from Hollow. 'Major Hyde told us that Unit One were dead, but they're not dead. The cartel didn't kill them.'

Hollow staggered backwards. 'Mattoo and Nell are in here too?'

'I had to leave them,' Sylvie said. 'They're still at Camp Leatherneck.'

'Leatherneck?' Hollow was shaking her head. 'No, that's where they take the Mandolin.'

'The International War Agency holding facility,' Joanie said, solemnly. 'It's not a nice place, Hollow.'

'Shit.' Hollow tried to steady her breath. 'Lieutenant Sampson needs to see this, Joan.'

'No.'

'This isn't an off-duty sneak-out,' Hollow said. 'This is Sylvie not being dead. We have to report this.'

'Just hear us out first.'

'You, you should be the one to wake up Lieutenant Sampson, Joan. I'll stay with Sylvie. It'll be worse for you if I report it.'

'Hollow, please,' Sylvie said. 'Just hear us out first.'

'I know you're scared, Sylvie,' Hollow was nodding, 'because I'm bloody scared, and I'm late to proceedings. The army made a mistake, they got the ID discs muddled or something, and you know what the military are like, they'll investigate every possible explanation before they admit they made a mistake. But Lieutenant Sampson will know what to do. She'll sort it out.' Hollow nodded again, breathing slowly to steady her heart. 'Trust your commanding officer like your life depends on it.'

'We're not reporting this,' Joanie said.

Hollow pushed him out of the way. 'You're injured, Sylvie. Let's get you somewhere safe.'

Joanie pushed back. 'I told you, no.'

'Back off, Joan, this isn't about you.' Hollow crouched down. 'I'm not talking about a homecoming parade, Sylvie. We don't even have to involve *WØLF*, not if you don't want to. Just the people at Bastion, people you trust.'

'You don't understand,' Sylvie said.

'I do.' Hollow flicked a look to Joanie. 'I really do understand. On one level, you're so together, and on another level, you're watching yourself fall apart. And it feels so lonely, like no one is strong enough to help you. But Bastion is strong enough, Bastion can hold it all. Let Bastion catch you, Sylvie. All you have to do is nod, and it will catch you.'

Sylvie looked up then, to where the solitary wasp crawled in torchlight. 'I'm already caught.'

'Okay, okay.' Hollow dragged her hand over her mouth. 'What about if we bring Captain Dupont here? You trust Caster, right?'

'We don't know them,' Sylvie said, 'and they've always been with us. Just like fungi and viruses have always been with us. The game between angels and men. But we've changed things, Hollow. We've melted the polar ice caps, we've polluted the skies, we've deoxygenated the oceans and we've destroyed the ancient forests. The Mandolin love the earth. They won't let us kill it.'

Tulip sat forward. 'That's it, she's been eco scammed.'

'Angels?' Sheila said. 'Like in the bible?'

'Like in her head,' Tulip said. 'Poor kid.'

'It would explain the feathers.' Sheila moved back to sit next to Ezra on the sofa. 'Let's hope Nell and Mattoo are alive too.'

'That'll be a shock for Mika.'

'Oh, Mika,' Sheila said, clutching her hands over her heart. 'He's been in absolute pieces. He'd have to tell Mattoo now, he'd have to say something.'

On the TV, Hollow spoke for the viewers. 'The enemy are angels?'

'Angels?' Sylvie said.

'A game between angels and men,' Hollow said. 'You think the Mandolin are…angels?'

'I didn't say they were angels.' Sylvie looked over to Joanie. 'They're not angels.'

Hollow sighed out her frustration. 'You're talking in circles, Sylvie.'

'The game between angels and men.' Sylvie held her hand up to Joanie like they could make a prayer between them. 'And they are the game.'

'They don't take your mind away,' Hollow said, shutting her eyes to reset the world. 'They give you what you want.'

'We call them the Mandolin,' Sylvie said, 'but it's not their name.'

Hollow spoke slowly, soft, kind. 'There's time for talking, as much as you need. But right now you're hurt, and I'm Medivac. Let us look after you, Sylvie. Just this once, let Medivac look after you.'

Joanie took Sylvie's hand, squeezing around to sit next to her. 'What Sylvie is saying is that sapiens already know the Mandolin, just by another name.'

'Fuck's sake, Joan, can't you see what's happening here?'

'Something that should have happened a long time ago.'

'Listen to me, Joanie Magrath,' Hollow said, 'I know it feels like you're helping her right now, but we've all seen how people can get secondary scammed. A victim doesn't always need to be in direct contact with the Mandolin. They can be corrupted by a scam on the primary target.'

Joanie shook his head. 'The army were right about one thing. Unit One did stray across the boundary of an active opium field.'

'The cartel dragged us out of the truck,' Sylvie said, leaning into Joanie. 'They lined us up at gunpoint. And we knew the rules, Hollow. We knew they were going to shoot us and there didn't seem much point in begging. The men, they were talking among themselves, loudly, aggressively. But when they put their guns away, it suddenly felt worse. Mattoo was so brave. He was ready to defend us if the need was there.' Sylvie sat up a little straighter. 'The cartel members don't have social media, but their group photographs were quite lovely. They made us kahwa tea and something to eat. Mattoo and Nell joined a children's football game, then we went to look at the poppies. It wasn't really the season, but it was still nice to see so much colour in the desert.'

Joanie smiled at Sylvie. 'Turns out the cartels love *WØLF* as much as we do.'

'Shit,' Hollow said.

'But they have a fierce reputation,' Sylvie said. 'And justifiably so, judging by the other photographs they showed us. It was obvious they didn't want to kill us, but the cessation of hostilities agreement is binding, on both sides. They couldn't let us go and they couldn't make a trade. We're soldiers; we understood that. When they took our ID discs and put us into the Ridgeback, we thought they were dumping us somewhere remote, leaving us to live or die according to the grace of Allah. But they didn't dump us. They took us to that awful place.'

'Leatherneck is more than a prisoner-of-war camp,' Joanie said. 'Leatherneck is the place where the broken soldiers go. The ones they can't send home. But Unit One weren't broken, Hollow, they should have come back to us. Instead, the International War Agency gave them to the Mandolin.'

'This is crazy,' Hollow said.

'Exactly.' Joanie didn't speak for a few seconds. 'As far as the IWA were concerned, Sylvie, Mattoo and Nell were officially dead. Executed by a drug cartel who were in no place to deny it. And the army had the ID discs to prove it. Which made Unit One a no-risk tradable commodity. Our friends, Hollow. Even a drug cartel had more human integrity.'

'There's no blame here,' Sylvie said. 'The IWA thought they were doing the best thing for all of us. When they handed us over, they thought they'd reached a breakthrough in peace negotiations, but it wasn't peace they got, it was the truth.'

'I am listening to you.' Hollow tried to keep a lilting tone to her voice. 'And you know how I never talk about the day Fish died, right?'

'I always understood why,' Joanie said. 'Because if you don't talk about it, it didn't happen.'

'I don't know what we were expecting to find in that hut.' Hollow paused. 'The Afghan kid, he had this massive piece of shrapnel in his leg. Captain Brooks was trying to dart him, but Fish was screaming that he was breathing. She picked up that little boy like he was her baby brother and she protected him with her own life.' Hollow bit the inside of her lip. 'God knows what the Mandolin showed that poor little kid to make him kill Fish like that, but whatever it was, it felt real to him…real enough to die for.'

'You want to know what the Mandolin told the IWA?' Joanie said.

Tulip picked up a carrot stick. 'I certainly do.'

'Is it safe to watch this?' Ezra said. 'It's getting a bit…'

'Plug Productions have cross-network control tonight. We'll get pinged if we don't watch,' Tulip said, dipping the carrot into a bowl of tahini. 'It's our civic duty.'

'Shush,' Sheila said, 'Hollow's talking.'

'I met the Mandolin that day.' Hollow spat a mouthful of blood. 'And it's the first thing I remember when I wake up, and the last thing I forget when I go to sleep.' Hollow focused on Sylvie then, taking hold of her shoulders. 'None of this is your fault, not one single part of it. We're ants to them, Sylvie, and all we ever know is the boiling water.'

'The Mandolin told them the truth, Hollow,' Joanie said. 'They told the IWA about the war, about who we are, about the game.'

'Their truth, Joan. Their twisted version of something that might have been the truth once upon a time,' Hollow said. 'Believe me, all lies are based in truth, and the bigger the lie, the more people want to believe it.'

'Exactly,' Joanie said. 'For example, this whole war is a lie. An orchestrated lie designed to perpetuate a game that no one even remembers why they're playing any more.'

'This is the fucking army, Joan.' Hollow span away from him, more frustration than anger. 'They're not set up to entertain an orchestrated lie; they wouldn't know where to fold it.'

'We walked this world alone,' Sylvie said. 'Ten thousand species of bird on this planet, and we walk alone. The last of our species. The final human.'

'Not the last,' Joanie said.

'Shit,' Hollow said, taking a step back towards the exit.

'History called them Neanderthal,' Sylvie said, 'but it's not their name. It's just another name we've given them.'

'I actually prefer Homo sapiens neanderthalensis,' Joanie said. 'People leave the sapiens bit out all the time, which is just rude, considering the technology.'

'Neanderthal?' Hollow said. 'As in…Neanderthal?'

Joanie nodded. 'As in, George Washington didn't know about dinosaurs.'

'Extinct dinosaurs.'

'The evidence of dinosaurs was there, but not the thinking,' Joanie said. 'And there must have been an adjustment period, a time when people wanted to carry on believing the fossils were the bones of giants. So, of course, there'll be an adjustment period when people find out who the Mandolin really are. Everyone will want to keep believing in a superspecies spontaneous evolution event for a while. It takes a bit of mental stepping down to admit that another human species might have used their time on earth more wisely than hating each other and inventing money.'

'Is this Neanderthal crap what the Mandolin sold the IWA?'

'Just think about it,' Joanie said. 'Another human species survived, just like the sapiens survived. Mostly by avoiding sapiens, to be fair.'

'Neanderthals went extinct thirty thousand years ago, Joan.'

'No, Hollow, we didn't.'

'Wait.' Sheila dropped her tofu sausage. 'Did he say…?'

'He doesn't mean actual Neanderthals,' Tulip said. 'He's talking about the hominoid genome. Most of us carry a proportion of Neanderthal DNA around in our genomes.'

'Up to eight per cent,' Ezra whispered.

'There you have it,' Tulip said. 'He's talking about his DNA inheritance.'

On the screen, Joanie took a deep breath, steadying himself.

'I've wanted to tell you so many times, but I couldn't tell anyone, not even Fish.'

'Stop it, Joan!' Hollow yelled. 'Just stop it. Sylvie's been through a terrible, terrible ordeal. Don't make this worse for her.'

'Joanie's telling the truth,' Sylvie said. 'And the first time I saw him, I knew he would change everything.'

'Not me, by the way,' Joanie said, sharing a conspiratorial wink. 'Wow, it's so weird, and freeing, being able to talk about it. You should ask me something. Go on, ask me something.'

'I can't even...' Hollow staggered backwards, fumbling to find the way out. 'I'm just gonna pop out and find Lieutenant Sampson. Lieutenant Sampson really needs to evaluate this... situation.'

'Like, ask how come, if I'm a super-secret, super-advanced species of human, I live in Bristol?' Joanie grinned. 'Long story short, my family are anthropologists. We've been integrated for six generations. We live exactly like sapiens, talking about the weather and having opinions about everything. Obviously, we have to be careful around iron. I mean, you saw what happened to me in the DAF lorry. Otherwise, we fit in like we belong.'

'You had a panic attack, Joan.'

'Iron disrupts the magnetic field, and we're super-sensitive to changes in the magnetic field. It's like living with a peanut allergy. Background traces are fine, but direct contact triggers an immune cascade reaction. If you hadn't pulled me off the iron grid, I would have died.' Joanie looked down at his boots. 'And I couldn't even say a proper thank you.'

'I've got to be honest, Joan, you're freaking me out now.'

'Is it the psychic thing? It's the psychic thing,' Joanie said. 'There are ways to suppress the connection. Synaptic desensitisation techniques and stuff. Or we can cut our hair before the fledging, which is a more permanent solution. And a bit of a radical lifestyle decision when you're not even a teenager yet. I thought about it, but I was never brave enough to face the noise.' Joanie reached for Sylvie's hand. 'For Mandolin, choosing the endless dialog of our own mind is an act of conviction and courage. To be alone with that level of noise. Every day. Forever. It's unbearable.'

'Right...'

'I mean, you probably think a whole flock of voices would be the noise. And, yeah, at the nesting sites it can be a bit full on. But Mandolin language is allegory and image. Words aren't so important to us.' Joanie smiled, a little shy with it. 'And the flock isn't noise, it's belonging.'

'Sure...'

'We all know what's going on, all the time. Communication is an immersive involvement of thought. Except, with sapiens, because sapiens think they really know what's going on, but mostly it's just a jumble of all the things they really want to be going on.' Joanie sat up, speaking like he'd learnt it from a children's book about sharing toys and playing together nicely. 'As a species, we have to respect that sapiens have a single-view outlook. It's not worse, it's just different. And exploiting that difference isn't communication. It's violation.'

'Huh.' Hollow shifted from one foot to the other. 'I have to say, the Mandolin I met seemed happy enough to violate my outlook. They're sadistic monsters, Joan. Evil, sadistic monsters.'

'She's right, Joanie,' Sylvie said. 'Some are, more than there should be.'

'In the game, though,' Joanie said.

'You're not getting much time to process all this, Hollow,' Sylvie said. 'I didn't want to believe it either, not in the beginning. It's hard for anyone outside the Mandolin to comprehend how important the game is.'

'It's not important...' Joanie paused, long enough to seem like hesitation. 'It's central to our existence. Kinda like humanism is central to you guys, and we have no idea how that makes any sense.'

'Sapiens don't *have* a centre of existence.' Sylvie laughed, young and adorable. 'We *are* the centre of existence.'

Joanie didn't laugh, and he was old with his words. 'Too close to see. Too simple to understand. Too familiar to remember.'

'Right...' Hollow took a step away.

'The game is us, and we are the game,' Joanie said. 'An abstract and a verb, and often an uncountable abstract noun. Like when it's raining, and that's totally the weather, and you're weathering the weather, but none of those things are the weather. And it's never...not the weather.'

'The weather?' Hollow took another step away.

'Reframe your worldview,' Joanie said. 'Just for one minute, Hollow. Imagine what it would be like if sapiens behaved in the world like they behave in video games. Would things really be that different?'

'Jar's disco elf,' Sylvie said. 'Alma's half-orc. Hubert Frank playing his lich? He's one hundred per cent evil, sadistic monster.'

'Sure...' Hollow was nodding along, stepping back and back until she bumped against the far end of the stacked cabinets. Feeling for the exit. Locking her fingers into the drawer handle. 'One hundred per cent.'

'Joanie built a bus route in GTA.'

'So people could get home safely,' Joanie said.

'Sure.' Hollow pulled the drawer out.

'I don't think you are sure,' Joanie said. 'None of us are. That's the whole trouble. The game is chaos. And the Mandolin adore the exquisite unknown of chaos. Sapiens, on the other hand, you love the feeling of being in control. We complement each other like the wings of a bird. But the game isn't chaos like it should be, and you've been chasing control for too long. The flight has lost its balance, Hollow, we're flying in circles and going nowhere.'

'Circles, right.'

'I know you want to report this,' Joanie said. 'I understand.

It's what we've been trained to do. I'd probably do the exact same thing in your place. But George Washington didn't know about dinosaurs, Hollow, and they still existed.'

Hollow didn't so much stop, as snap. Rushing at Joanie, grabbing him by the collar and slamming him backwards into a pile of blankets. 'I'm fucking sick of fucking hearing about fucking George Washington.'

'We're not outsiders,' Joanie said, taking all of Hollow's anger. 'We come from a different branch of the same tree. The same family tree. And, yes, some of the things the Mandolin do are abhorrent to you. Just like some of the things sapiens do are abhorrent to us. That's family for you.'

'The Mandolin killed Fish!' Hollow screamed into his face.

'I know...I know what that player did, but you can't understand a whole species by the actions of a single individual.'

'Don't you dare normalise what they are.' Hollow shoved him deeper into the pile of blankets, holding him under like she could drown him. 'The sooner we slaughter every single part of the genetic mistake that allowed them life, the better.'

'Including me?'

'You're not Mandolin, Joan. And the fact that you can't see it would feel epically sad, except I'm a biochemical cocktail short of feeling anything beyond the urge to smash your fucking, stupid, fucking face in.'

'Crap, I almost forgot the evidence,' Joanie said, straining to reach something hidden behind Sylvie.

Hollow dropped her hold on him. 'What?'

'Don't panic, it's just technology.' Joanie stood up, straightening his collar. 'We obviously can't show you for long because the cold plasma fractals strip oxygen for fuel, and this is a closed environment.'

'What the hell have you done!' Hollow scrabbled sideways, slamming into the nearest filing cabinet, grabbing for Sylvie's arm to drag her away, and finding only Joanie's. Strong. Sturdy. Unmovable.

Joanie pulled Hollow to her feet, sitting her down beside Sylvie. 'I said, it's JUST technology.'

Hollow was watching Joanie rummage around in the darkness. She leant in close to Sylvie. 'We need to get out of here.'

'Not until,' Sylvie said.

'When I make a move, you head for the exit,' Hollow whispered. 'Don't wait for me, just go.'

'Not until.' Sylvie tipped her head to rest on Hollow's shoulder.

'This is beyond Sampson. Get Captain Dupont, tell him we need backup.'

'Not until,' Sylvie said, again.

Hollow turned her focus on Sylvie. 'Not until what?'

'Not until I show you this.' Joanie produced a roll of striped tubes from under a pile of box files, juggling them like he was handling a set of unfamiliar bagpipes. 'The Mandolin gave this mantle to Sylvie. That's how she got onto the military transport. Chimera technology. Sensory dampening based on owl feathers, among other things. And even compatible with sapiens.' Joanie crouched down, gently curling the device around Sylvie's shoulders. It fastened with a perfect click, disappearing her as if she'd never been there.

'Shit.' Hollow froze, every sense on high alert.

'I know, right.' Joanie grinned. 'Cold plasma fractals. Military research labs can hardly understand them yet, let alone fashion them into a usable garment.'

'Shit.'

'In exchange for Unit One, the Mandolin gave the IWA the truth, Hollow. Stewardship of this planet has to factor in another human species. I mean, that's got to throw an unexpected twist into peace negotiations.'

'Why the hell would the Mandolin be interested in Unit One, Joan?'

'Duh,' Joanie said, 'because everyone loves *WØLF*.'

'The Mandolin watch *WØLF*?'

'We might be a different species, but we're still human.'

'You said Fish was your sister.' Hollow blinked through the stinging ozone. 'What would she say about all this?'

Joanie smiled slightly. 'She'd say it was bloody insane, mind.'

'She would.' Hollow kept her breath tight, one foot braced against the side of the ISO. No running or numbing out left in her. Just the unbearable fire of fight. 'And do you think she might have a point?'

'Absolutely, it's totally insane,' Joanie said.

'Good, that's good.'

'That's why some of the Mandolin, the philosophers, they bring a new worldview to us. Ørma, it's an idea, but not like someone else's idea, like something we remember...' Joanie was shaking his head '...words are too clunky. We don't use words, and you don't have access to allegory and flock memory.'

Tulip paused mid-beetroot crisp. 'The Mandolin have philosophers?'

'According to scammed Joanie,' Sheila said.

Tulip grabbed a poppadom from the table. 'Ørma? Possibly a derivative of the Middle English word *forma*. But out of context, it's just conjecture.'

'First,' Ezra said, more wobble than intended. 'The first mark.'

'Marvellously intriguing, eh?' Tulip said.

Sheila never missed a wobble, no matter how much it was covered up by an interesting debate topic. 'How you doing with all this, baby?'

'It's a lot, for reality TV.'

'In cases like this...' Tulip squirmed next to Ezra '...it's best to look at what we know for certain. And we know for certain that all reality TV is faked. Even if we believed more from *WØLF*, it's still reality TV. This whole thing will probably end up being a sponsorship ad for ancestral genome testing.'

Sheila frowned. 'You think?'

'Credit where credit's due,' Tulip said. 'For a sponsorship ad, it's a rollercoaster of metaphysical event horizons.'

On the screen, Joanie stood up slowly, respectfully, trying not to alarm Hollow. 'Ørma is an idea…a sound. The song of the lark. The song that can't be seen in the sky. You feel it, and you remember. And in that remembering is Ørma. I can't say it properly in words, but I can show you, Hollow. If you want, I can show you.'

'Stay away from me, Joan.'

'I won't hurt you.'

'My father is a man who raped my mum.' Hollow was pushing herself away from Joanie, backed right up into a corner with no exit. 'Whatever bad seed was rotting in him is rotting in me.'

Joanie kept his movements slow, respectful. 'You're not him, Hollow.'

'Sergeant Naleigh saw it.' Hollow dug her fingernails into her palms, into the scar. 'I would have killed Fish if the captain had given the order. I shot a little kid in the head and I didn't feel anything. There's something wrong in me, Joan. You need to stop this before I hurt you.'

'You're not wrong,' Joanie said. 'You're just alone.'

Hollow almost sobbed. 'Don't.'

'Our ancestors followed the birds,' Joanie said. 'Into the trees and into the open sky. They kept the nest sites secret and raised their young to stay hidden from the sapiens. But you have this hole in you, this longing. You fill it up with money and neurosis and stuff, but the longing won't stay filled up. Sapiens are a species of greed, Hollow, a symptom of their own loneliness.' Joanie took a step towards Hollow, tender enough to feel like friendship. 'Unfortunately, that symptom is also killing our planet. The thought of our only surviving relatives going extinct is horrible enough, but the thought that you might take us with you, we can't let that happen.'

Hollow gritted her teeth. 'We all saw the message, Joan. We know what it meant.'

'You just think you know.' Joanie smiled, sincere and sweet with affection. 'And we think we know. But none of us know. That's why we need the Aphelion.'

'There's been a lot of speculation about his arrival.' Sylvie unclicked the fastening and slipped out of the mantle. 'He's a bit of a *deus ex machina*.'

'For both human species,' Joanie said. 'If the foreshadowing is to be believed.'

'I've never been one for saviours,' Sylvie said. 'But then I met him. I didn't know who he was then. All I knew was that he'd changed my life. Just like he changed your life, and Joanie's life, and every single life he comes into contact with.'

Hollow ran her hand across her mouth. 'The Aphelion…'

'Remember the song of the lark.' Sylvie was looking up at the solitary wasp again, right into the lens and into the stream and into the eyes of all the non-player characters sat on their non-player sofas, eating their non-player suppers. Then Sylvie Stevens, the darling soldier who'd been lost and found again, opened her hand for the IGH camera. A symbol cut roughly into her palm. Unsteady in the torchlight and black with old blood. A few strips of flesh forged to form a crude basket shape. Basic. Simple even. Harmless. Sylvie smiled slowly, beautifully, always more butterfly than soldier. 'And don't play the game.'

MATCH CUT
PRODUCER:
WØLF has always promised you the real war. A promise that has become increasingly difficult to maintain. Our insect generation hybrid technology allows us to provide an immersive and authentic experience without intruding on the lives of our cast. It has never been our intention to deceive anyone,

quite the opposite, in fact. Perhaps we've been more honest than the world is ready for…the consequences have yet to play out.

Our only regret is that the army will be the last to know.

As a production company, we were acutely aware of the risks involved in tonight's live streaming event. The army, however, were not. I speak for everyone at Plug Productions when I say that this was not through a lack of respect for the military services, but instead to protect them from any recriminations that may follow. As you can imagine, tonight's episode will test cooperation beyond protocol. If the army are willing to continue with this experiment, we plan to recommence filming *WØLF* tomorrow. Regardless of outcome, we will continue to support the cast in everything they do.

Which brings me to all of you watching at home. As humans, we've grown used to the echo chambers of social media. Opposing views are blocked, ridiculed and ultimately turned into something powerful and terrifying. For all our mastery of communication, we've forgotten how to listen to something we don't agree with. And we've forgotten that we can change our mind. The greatest gift we possess is the one thing we deny ourselves.

Some thresholds are dark, even to those who lit the candle. What you've seen tonight may challenge your worldview. *WØLF* will not tell you how to feel about it. The camera is yours.

SNAP CUT TO BLANK SCREEN

32

I might speculate a bit

The British army Chief of the General Staff in Afghanistan was a man who'd guarded the terrible confidences of war for seventeen years. In that time, he'd learnt that weapons changed and enemies changed, but war always stayed the same. Afghanistan had been lost months ago; the remaining battle was a matter of how much time he could buy the scientists and weapon developers back home. Alone in his office, he was dictating a damning report regarding the intolerable conduct of the bally *WØLF* soldiers and their bally production company, when he received an emailed termination notification from the Mandolin. To his brief and contained astonishment, the enemy had withdrawn, and the war was over. It took a further ten minutes of checking his list of deception markers, and perhaps a momentary lapse into a smile, before the British army Chief of the General Staff in Afghanistan allowed himself to entertain the notion that this communication wasn't a scam. That there was finally some good news, some unimaginably good news, to report from the frontline. Regrettably, that was exactly what the British army Chief of the General Staff in Afghanistan did. And along with the news of an unprecedented surrender, the message delivered a logic bomb. A mycelial computer virus designed with one purpose: to terminate the Internet of Things. Every network, every server, every security system, every smart building, every educational facility, every healthcare system, every energy provider, every utility service. Every single internet-based ecosystem right down to the dying flicker of a fake candle. Mobile phones were the last to go, delivering one final message from the Mandolin before the world went dark.

AFGHANISTAN
LEVEL COMPLETE

Ezra sat in the darkness, phone in hand, waiting on Tulip to fetch the emergency lights.

'It's probably from everyone in the world turning the kettle on after *WØLF*,' Sheila said, peering out of the curtains. 'The whole square is out.'

'Yeah.'

'What an evening.'

'Yeah.'

'Did you get any signal yet?'

Ezra looked down at the phone. 'Nothing. I can't even access my home screen. There's just the message.'

'*Afghanistan Level Complete.*' Tulip surfaced from the cupboard in a pool of light, handing over a box of matches, two camping lanterns and a gas stove. 'The Mandolin certainly love a dramatic strapline.'

'And at least it's not a threat this time,' Sheila said. 'Do you think they took the electricity out as well?'

'If it's all the kettles, the power will be back fairly quickly.' Tulip made her way to the sofa, holding the torch under her chin like she was in a horror film. 'If it's another Mandolin virus, we know it takes a while for the antivirals to clear the system. Especially if the virus has mutated into the electricity mainframe. I'll drive over to work. They should have an update on what's happening.'

'The perfect plan,' Sheila said. 'Except that Conqueror Square doesn't have any electricity. No electricity, no way to open the gate.'

'Good point.' Tulip winked at Ezra, grabbing a cucumber stick and dipping it into a dhal. 'We could be trapped in here forever.'

'Do you think it was true?' Ezra said. 'About the...rape.'

'Baby,' Sheila took one last look around the square, 'you know how much Mum and I love Hollow, but that girl can lie.'

'Like that rescue chicken story she told Jar,' Tulip was nodding, 'I found myself believing it, even though I knew it wasn't true.'

'The army give them training on what to do.'

'For hostage situations,' Tulip said. 'They're trained to say whatever will diffuse a situation. And Joanie is a very sensitive lad. He reacts with compassion if someone is hurting. Hollow played the situation to her strengths and Joanie's weaknesses. They're probably sat with Caster, talking it all out by now.'

'I guess,' Ezra said.

'As for the Mandolin being Neanderthals...' Sheila closed the curtains and stumbled her way back across the room '...I was more on board with them being angels.'

'Neanderthals were obsessed with birds.' Ezra spoke neatly, all historian and matter-of-fact. 'Archaeologists think they decorated their bodies with feathers.'

'We do love the bling,' Sheila said. 'It's all that Neanderthal sloshing about.'

'And Joanie called it a mantle,' Ezra said. 'Birds of prey mantle. When they're hiding something.'

'Lots of people have been hiding something by the sound of it,' Sheila said, narrowly avoiding a collision with the coffee table. 'Once the phones are back, we can go online, see what the almighty oracle of social media has to say.'

'Ah, but Elspeth Hart said we should think for ourselves.'

Tulip grabbed a bowl of cucumber sticks before it fell. 'We must look to the old ways, now.'

'Our other senses will kick in.' Sheila snuggled between Tulip and Ezra. 'We'll know what Atticus Valentine is wearing because of a slight change in air pressure.'

Ezra choked, more of a sob than a cough.

'Sorry, baby, that was insensitive.'

'No, I'm just…I might just go to bed.'

Tulip produced a deck of cards from her pocket. 'And miss a round of power-cut poker?'

Ezra managed a smile. 'I'll give you a hand clearing up.'

'You go on to bed, sweetheart.' Sheila stretched out an unrequited hug. 'Mum and I can sort this lot out. Take one of the lanterns with you.'

'Thanks.'

'I'll head down to the petrol station,' Tulip said. 'They run on an isolated turbine supply when the power's out. I'll see if they've heard anything.'

'Count me in.' Sheila rolled a leisurely gaze over the remaining food. 'I need to walk all this off.'

'Petrol station by moonlight,' Tulip said. 'It'll be quite the romantic stroll. Bring the chargeable devices.'

'See you in the morning, then.' Ezra stood up, not looking at either of them.

'Try not to dwell on what Hollow said.' Sheila took hold of Ezra's hand. 'She knew what she was doing, baby.'

'I know.'

'Unlike me with the Atticus Valentine quip.'

'You're fine, Mum.'

'I know this is hard, kiddo.' Tulip smiled, but it was a nervous twitch short of convincing. 'It's probably best to put your phone in a drawer and forget about it until the morning. We'll get a better picture once the programme footage has been through a disinformation review.'

'I might speculate a bit, though.' Sheila nudged Tulip. 'On the walk to the petrol station.'

Another word for betrayal was treason. Treason had started it, and treason had seen it through. Ezra left Sheila and Tulip searching for the paperwork relating to opening a smart door without any smart. Taking the lantern. Climbing the stairs. Sitting on the bed. Biting a pillow to stop the emotional chaos from bursting out. History was an unreliable truth. It was only ever an archaeological dig or a document discovery away from revealing itself to be wrong. Betraying Atticus, however; that was a reliable truth. A treason that hadn't just stepped over a morality event horizon, it had built a six-lane motorway across it. Ezra had justified it all under the excuse of helping with the war effort, but now the WØLF broadcast had thrown the password symbol out across the whole world. All the lies, all the betrayal, had made no difference at all. Atticus Valentine, the same sweet, beautiful, bewildering man who'd talked about the song of the skylark like it was poetry, was the Aphelion. The *deus ex machina*. The unstoppable event dependent on everyone trying to stop it.

The bedroom was cold. Eerie in the unfamiliar light. Silent except for an owl, somewhere close, calling for company. Ezra turned off the lantern and curled up under a blanket. Frankly, it was a flask of roofied tea and a sunset betrayal short of being a car park at Haifengate.

Everyone had moaned and explicated their way through the localised losses of power and phone signal, but they'd gone to bed expecting an overnight resolution. The early-morning birdsong brought them out into the streets, rubbing their eyes, half dressed, phones still in their hands, desperately hoping someone else had social media. Each street, each town, each city, still unable to communicate, still convinced that this irritating predicament would soon be resolved. There was something of a wartime spirit in Conqueror Square, freeing people from their houses, sharing hot drinks, avocados, soda bread, chemical explosive devices made from fertiliser to blow the gate across the road and demolish a Festival Theatre signpost.

When the cars wouldn't start and the water dried up, the realisation that this was something far more catastrophic than a localised outage began to sink in. In one single attack, the world had lost everything that kept it operational.

The Mandolin had technology far beyond the limitations of the Internet of Things, and a communication system that utilised the vast mycelial networks of the earth. If this was war, they would have prevailed a thousand times over, but this was a game. And a game didn't need to destroy an opponent; it needed them to play the game. Thanks to Mac Eden, England was also Sandbox enabled: open access, no creative boundaries, no limitations on player numbers and no rule permissions. Side character Beverly Smith checked her fringe with a spirit level, tied a scarf around her head and placed a pile of handwritten agendas into the basket of her bicycle. The emergency cell meeting was scheduled for 7pm that night. Timing was tight but not impossible, thanks to strong calves, an efficient delivery route and the requisition of a whistle. The war in Afghanistan might be over, but for all the non-player characters of England, the game was just getting started.

END OF BOOK ONE

The story continues with

BOOK TWO
of the
Mandolin

Øðer

The Thirteen Signs
of Flightless Things

The Mandolin game developers took advantage of time. Not in its concept, but in its mistake. The universe existed in an infinite singularity of standalone moments. Some moments were so similar they were often mistaken for each other, and subsequently lined up in a linear progression that was called time. For most Homo sapiens, time was much easier to understand than an infinite singularity of standalone moments, because it made sense of birthdays and investment portfolios. But at the end of the day, time didn't exist. And the Mandolin spliced themselves into its non-existence so seamlessly, it was almost as if they'd always been there.

This book is printed on paper from sustainable sources managed under the Forest Stewardship Council (FSC) scheme.

It has been printed in the UK to reduce transportation miles and their impact upon the environment.

For every new title that Troubador publishes, we plant a tree to offset CO_2, partnering with the More Trees scheme.

MORE TREES
LET'S PLANT A BILLION TREES

For more about how Troubador offsets its environmental impact, see www.troubador.co.uk/sustainability-and-community